THE
IMMORTAL
CROWN

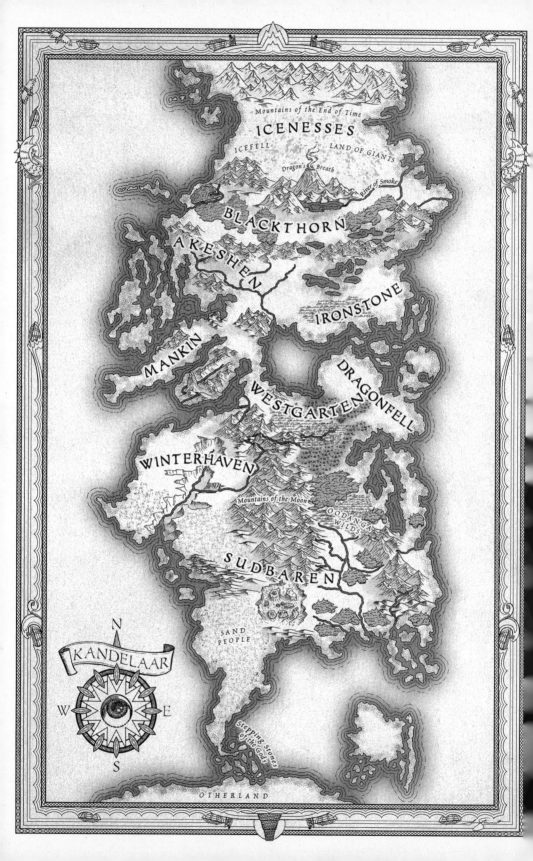

THE
IMMORTAL
CROWN

SAGA OF KINGS
• BOOK ONE •

KIETH MERRILL

SHADOW
MOUNTAIN

Maps by Isaac Stewart.

Visit us at ShadowMountain.com

Library of Congress Cataloging-in-Publication Data

Merrill, Kieth, 1940– author.
   The Immortal Crown / Kieth W. Merrill.
       pages cm — (Saga of kings ; volume 1)
   Summary: The legendary stones once touched by the hand of the god Oum'ilah will grant immortality and supreme power to whoever can gather them and place them in the rightful crown.
   ISBN 978-1-62972-025-8 (hardbound : alk. paper)
   I. Title. II. Series: Merrill, Kieth, 1940–   Saga of kings ; v. 1.
   PS3613.E7762E98 2016
   813'.6—dc23   2014040881

Printed in the United States of America
Lake Book Manufacturing, Inc., Melrose Park, IL

10   9   8   7   6   5   4   3   2   1

To my eight extraordinary children,
some of whom will actually read this book and like it.

And to Dagny
My best friend and finest fan and favorite critic
. . . *who loves everything I do.*

The seal is broken
The ancient evil is come again
The secret works of darkness rise
The Immortal Crown is blind.
And that which was lost shall be found
To be gathered in the righteous hand
By the child of pure blood
By the strength of a sword he cannot hold
Endowed with the powers of godliness
And returned to the crown of endless life
To evil or to good
In the age of chaos
And the saga of kings

—Codices of the Navigator, XXIII

PROLOGUE

Annum 1059, Age of Kandelaar

Oldbones Keep, Dominion Dragonfell

Jagged bits of bone tore flesh from Drakkor's back. The birchwood pallet pinioned his tongue and was almost bitten through.

I won't cry out! I must not scream. I will endure this agony in silence . . . or die. The grim resolve pounded through the boy's head. *I will not die. I will not die.*

The brute with the cat-o'-nine-tails lashed him again. Blood oozed from the mangled flesh and ran down the boy's legs. He was only fifteen years old but considered himself a man. He clenched his jaw tighter and closed his eyes until his mind was a blackened void where he screamed in silence. *I will not die. I will not die!*

—◆—

The sorceress watched from the shadow of the woolen cowl that covered her head.

She was encircled by the thirteen magi of the Scarlet Council, who stood beneath the graven image of she-dragon looming from the wall of the cavern.

The sorceress's bloodred robes dragged on the floor. She was old

1

and hunched, as if the lump on her back were a stone too heavy to carry. She stepped forward into the cold blue light of the winter moon that fell through the opening above. Burning faggots of yew wood smeared with suet cast a flicker of fire on her face. Her old bones and crippling pain made her limp with the awkward gate of an imp. Pallid skin stretched over a rack of twisted bones.

Talismans and dead things hung from a string of twisted grass around her neck. A dragon curled in a black tattoo from the gnarled lump of her belly to her bony shoulders where the tail wrapped around her neck and was lost in the wrinkles of her face. Her blackened, ink-stained flesh gave her the appearance of a gargoyle.

She muttered a spell and willed the boy under the lash to endure in silence, to prove himself worthy to fulfill the archaic prophecy that echoed in her head.

> *In the time of kings and the day of chaos, the seal is broken. The ancient mysteries arise. She-dragon is blind and rages from the mountains. That which was lost shall be found. The eggs of stone forged in the breath of fire, gathered in the hand of might by the child of no man—who is worthy of the blood of the dragon, being purged by death and suffering in silent darkness—and, clustered in her claws, will rise immortal by the power of the ancient secret, to rule all flesh and reign forever as god of the world.*

The cryptic meaning of the prophecy was an endless cause of contention. When the sorceress had been elevated as the Esteemed One, she had resurrected the ancient ritual and renewed the cult's long-abandoned search for the "child of no man." A generation of warlocks, witches, and a following of hapless creatures had sworn the ancient blood oath and traded their souls for the secrets of darkness.

If her desire was to be and her failing life renewed, the child must be found and the prophecy fulfilled, and soon.

Purged by death and suffering in silent darkness. Her dying heart fluttered, and a wave of faintness washed over her. *To rise immortal and reign forever as god . . . and queen?* What else could it mean? The sorceress believed because she dared not doubt. Her time was almost past.

The origin of the prophecy remained a mystery. The Scarlet Council of Dragonfell claimed it had existed since the times of creation, when Tiamat formed earth and sky and begot she-dragon of the dark world, who rose from her glimmering egg in the depths of the sea.

They believed the "eggs of stone" were the magical stones of fire, begotten in the deep and burned by the fire of she-dragon's breath to light the way from the darkness of chaos to the human world. The Scarlet Council possessed only one of the legendary stones of mystical power and had guarded it through the centuries as their most sacred duty. The rest of the stones had been lost. Some said they had been stolen from the sons of she-dragon by the one known as the Navigator, who crossed the endless deep in boats in the days of fierce winds a thousand years before.

Some claimed the prophecy was a corruption of the writings of the Navigator, twisted by interpretation and exegesis and then transcribed by a warlock to his grimoire in archaic times. The book of magic, the mythos claims, was secreted aboard a boat of the Navigator's voyaging fleet.

Others believed the prophecy originated with the shedding of first blood and the beginning of the secret oaths. The ancient alliance of evil to murder and get gain.

Ten centuries had passed away. Finding one worthy of the blood, who could gather that which was lost, had never come. The mysterious riddle of renewal, regeneration, and endless life remained unknown. None of the boys put to the trial had endured the ritual demanded by the cryptic words of the prophecy.

Purged by death and suffering in silent darkness. The sorceress mouthed the words of the prophecy, her lips a picket line of wrinkles. *Shall these things never be while I am yet alive?* The tragedy of the thought taunted her, and her heart stuttered in arrhythmic thumps. She stared at the boy with desperate hope as another slash of knotted cords was laid across his bloodied back. He did not cry out.

The sorceress ordained that the ritual of purging take place once a year and always on the shortest day of the twelve moons. Slave to superstition, she believed the long night satisfied the oracular meaning of "in silent darkness."

Suffering in silent darkness. Could this be the boy? At last?

Another lash and still no sounds of agony.

Please, the sorceress begged in silence to the confusion of gods and dragons that lived in the imaginations of her dark dreams. *Let this boy be the one to gather the thirteen stones of fire so I might become immortal and reign forever.*

Her obsession to escape death surged through her in a rush of hope. Her old frame trembled. She closed her mind lest the magi of the council divine her secret desire. They must never know the truth of her eagerness to find the child of prophecy.

Another lash. A splattering of blood. Agony in silence. Hope.

— —

The boy under the lash was of unknown blood. An ignorant, unkempt orphan from the slums of Black Flower. Like other boys the council enticed, coerced, or kidnapped and subjected to the ritual, he was an impoverished child. It didn't matter if he was born a bastard of the brothel or spawned in the rot and refuse of the harbor by the scavengers that rummaged there. He was, by the council's interpretation of the prophetic riddle, "a child of no man."

The boy had been brought to Oldbones Keep by the man who revered himself the Peddler of Souls. A lowly scum of a man who traded human misery for a jangle of coin, he had pimped and pandered over many seasons to ingratiate himself to the hooded magi.

It was not the first time he'd brought a boy to the Scarlet Council as a candidate for the chosen child, but this time was different. This time he prostrated himself and gushed, "This boy is made known to me by the dreams of night and the whisperings of she-dragon." No lie was too outrageous if it filled his palm with silver. He had seen the depth of superstition at Oldbones Keep. He had witnessed the trials and the scourging. He had learned about the legendary magic stones and witnessed the consuming power of the ancient prophecy.

When the gossipmongers in the taverns of Black Flower first spoke of the mischiefs at Oldbones Keep, the nefarious old dog of a peddler saw the opportunity to put silver in his palm.

It had been many years since he'd first arrived at Dragonfell to sow the seed. With cracked gray lips close to the old woman's ear, he'd told of desperate, barren women imbibing poisonous elixirs brewed by the hag of the woods, then giving birth to fatherless boys before dying themselves in the birthing.

"A child of no man is an *orphan*, Esteemed One," he whispered, since making it a secret seemed to make it true.

It fit the description of the prophecy, or nearly so, and in the loam of the sorceress's desperate hope, the words sprouted like noxious thistles.

The Peddler of Souls promised to find the boys born of the dark magic and bring them to her for the purging so she could find the chosen vessel. His offer was benevolent and selfless—except, of course, for the generous fee he requested for each of the children he delivered.

There were plenty of orphans in and about Black Flower, and the Peddler of Souls found it easy to entice indigent boys with the promises of all the things they'd never had.

He brought three new candidates to Dragonfell and stayed to look after them at the sorceress's request. Their first days were joyous. There were baths, hot and scented with perfume. Their bodies were massaged with precious oils, then dressed in silken robes and adorned like the prince of the North. They were given a feast with foods of such taste and abundance it was beyond imagining for the impoverished boys. And, of course, they were given all the wine they could drink.

With their bodies cleansed, their muscles massaged, their bellies full, and their shoulders draped in silk, the orphan boys from the slums of Black Flower could not help but believe they had fallen on good fortune.

It was at their height of pleasure when they learned the greatest of the Peddler's promises—"No harm will come ta' ye!"—was a lie. They were stripped of their silken garments and placed in a circular arena deep in the bowels of Oldbones Keep. The roof was a frame of arched timbers that rested on a wall of rock rising half again the height of a man.

A dragon's claw hung from a leather thong in the center of the ring. It dangled higher than a man could jump. It looked at first to be an ornament of homage to she-dragon but was in truth, a weapon of brutal death.

Candidates became contenders. They were lowered into the arena on hemp. The access portal was barred. Escape was impossible. The candidates were placed equidistant from each other with their backs against the stones. It was not until they were there, nearly naked, confused, and full of fear that the real purpose of their invitation to Dragonfell was finally explained.

The sorceress called out to them from where she and the Scarlet Council watched. She recited the words of the prophecy, explained why they had been chosen, and described the ominous events that lay before them.

"The trial of death by three is the meaning of the prophecy's cryptic 'purged by death.' There are no rules. Only one of you will be allowed to leave the arena alive," she said in a calm and level voice. "By your victory over death, you will earn the right to the second trial—the lash and suffering in silent darkness."

The sorceress had witnessed many battles, blood, and grizzly killings during her reign. She did not see the boys as impoverished children, deceived and condemned to death. Rather, they were creatures spawned to a purpose. They were less than human—otherwise such blood and torture would be too ghastly. Even for her.

The sorceress looked at the boy who had managed to hold his silence. She waited for the final lash, anxious and hopeful, but her feelings for the child troubled her.

The boy raised his bloody face and held her eyes.

She felt a nauseating wave of empathy she had never known. She could not make of him a creature less than human.

Is he the one? The thought tightened a knot in her stomach, and she forced her uncertainties away. She would not allow her rising hope to falter. Not here. Not now. *No one has come as far as this boy. None has been so close to fulfilling the prophecy.*

His intelligence, his prowess. The utter ruthlessness he had shown in the trial of death by three! Her heart beat faster as she remembered. She pursed her lips and closed her eyes and saw it all again.

— —

The only means of inflicting death in the arena were bare hands, feet, and teeth. The dragon's claw was out of reach. The ritual was more than a game of killing. It was a game of strategy. One boy could not kill the other two without a weapon. If he grappled with one, the third could seize the advantage. If two conspired against one, they could easily acquire the claw and the third would swiftly fall. What then?

The signal to begin was given. At first the sorceress thought him a weakling. His body was strong and his muscles taut, but he cowered against the wall as if he were afraid. It seemed as if he hoped to avoid the fight in some vain hope of rescue.

The other two boys raced to the center of the arena and collided in a ferocious exchange of pounding fists, slashing nails, and kicking feet. One gripped the other's neck, and they grappled to a writhing impasse of tangled limbs.

The third boy sprang from the wall and ran up their bodies like a spotted lion climbing a tree. With the momentum of his sprint, he used the thighs, hips, and arms of their tangled torsos as if they were footholds on a rotted stump. He vaulted upward and grasped the dragon's claw.

By the time the grappling duo had untangled themselves, he had landed like a cat, leaped forward, and slashed their necks. The grapplers grasped their throats in a desperate attempt to stop the blood, but their lives had ended.

The boy had stood over them, his shoulders hunched like a beast, his chest convulsing as he gasped to regain his breath. He let the bloody claw fall from his fingers. He stared at his hands, then smeared his face with his opponents' blood and raised his chin toward the sorceress. A fire of defiance danced in the black of his eyes.

———

The final lash was badly placed. One of the nine knotted cords wrapped around the boy's neck and ripped a chunk of flesh from his jaw. *Thirty and three lashes.* The mystical number was suffused with ancient power.

The scourging had ended. The second task of the ritual was finished. He had not cried out. He had suffered in silent darkness.

The brute coiled the wet cords of the whip, his breathing hard by the time he finished. He knelt in homage to the sorceress. She acknowledged him with a nod of her head, but her face remained in shadow. There was an annulus of thirteen candles between the sorceress and the bleeding boy. The candles burned with the sour odor of something dead.

"What is your name?" The question rasped up from the old woman's throat like fingernails scratching stone. The boy's knees had buckled with the twenty-ninth lash. He hung by his wrists on ropes attached to rings of rusted iron on the walls.

"Drakkor," he choked, but with such strength and defiance it cut through the silence like an executioner's ax. He stared at the sorceress with unblinking eyes.

The old woman was hidden in the shadow of her cowl, but when she turned, the flames of yew wood struck her face, and for a fleeting moment he thought she smiled. When she turned back, she cradled a chalice in her hands. The goblet was gold, inlaid with diamonds, bloodstone, and carnelian.

"Stand, Drakkor, child of no man," she said in a voice quavering with emotion.

The brute lifted the boy to his feet and untied the ropes.

Drakkor pushed the man away and stood on trembling legs in the center of the circle. He could feel the blood running down his back. He straightened his spine but could not stop the tremors of pain that rippled through him.

"We have looked for you a long time," the sorceress said as she stepped forward and raised the chalice above her head with both hands. She stared into the darkness as if speaking to a being who hovered in the pungent swirls of smoke. *"Saleem nostranu 'a mo la escornorla. Saleem nostranu 'rosnona se o vasen pusson."* The ritual words were echoed in a haunting chant by the hooded figures behind her. The sorceress lowered her hands. "Kneel and repeat the words of the oath," she said, then repeated them again in the ancient tongue. The crackle of her voice pierced the humming of the minions like a driven spike.

Drakkor knelt. His pain was buried beneath numbness and shock. His eyes moved from the black holes of the sorceress's face to the glint of candlelight on the polished brass chalice. *"Saleem nostranu 'a mo la escornorla."* He mimicked her words and her voice. When he licked his lips, he could taste his blood mixed with sweat. *"Saleem nostranu 'rosnona se o vasen pusson,"* he repeated and felt constrained to raise his eyes to the graven image of she-dragon looming over him.

Drakkor did not understand the words of the archaic language, but he had heard the rumors and assumed it was the ritual oath of she-dragon. The consecration of the soul, commitment of mind, and sacrifice of body. The beckoning.

His heart pounded. *Saleem nostranu 'a mo la escornorla. Saleem nostranu 'rosnona se o vasen pusson.* He recited the words in his mind as if speaking them in silence might somehow give them meaning.

The sorceress stepped forward, and he lowered his eyes. She offered him the chalice. Ornate rings of precious stones adorned her skeletal fingers. Her shadow scurried across the walls in the flickering light of the cavern like a frightened spider.

He took the chalice from her hands; it was warm to the touch. He recognized the biting aroma of blood.

"Drink," the sorceress said. "It is the blood of the dragon, and from henceforth and forever it is how you shall be known."

The stench of the blood made him retch. The Peddler of Souls had told him many things about the prophecy, but nothing prepared Drakkor for the emotions that collided when the bittersweet thickness slithered down his throat. Nothing had prepared him for what he saw, for what he imagined, and for the words of the mystical woman.

"You are the child of no man and have proven yourself worthy of the blood of the dragon. You are he who will gather the eggs of stone forged in the breath of fire." She could hardly control her emotions as she recited the words of the prophecy to the rhythmic cadence of the chants that echoed in the vaulted chamber as if they were living things.

Her voice was like music, and each word was spoken as if it were the only utterance in the cosmos.

Drakkor closed his eyes, and when he did, he saw the thirteen stones of fire glowing in the swirling darkness of his mind. A strange sense of destiny swept over him, and he was falling into blackness. He was seized by a suffocating presence and consumed by the darkness and a whispering voice screamed in his head. *"It is your destiny to rise immortal to an endless life and to rule all flesh and reign forever as god of the world."*

Drakkor fought to remain conscious. To grasp the reality or illusion of the voices in his head. Were they nothing more than the words of the prophecy echoing from the recess of the secret chambers in the bowels of Oldbones Keep or were they the whisperings of she-dragon?

Drakkor raised his head with fierce resolve. For a fleeting moment, he thought his feet had left the ground. Whatever the factuality or falsehood of all he had endured, from this day forward, he would never be the same.

Annum 1059, Age of Kandelaar

Village Darc, Dominion Blackthorn

At the same moment, far across the inland sea of Leviathan Deeps, beyond the thousand lakes of Pliancum, one hundred and fifty-nine leagues to the north for a raven on the wing, a wisewoman hurried through the cobbled streets of Village Darc.

The baby in the basket slung over her arm began to cry. She quickened her step, taking care not to stumble in the darkness of the moonless night. She dared not look at the newborn child lest she lose her resolve. To deny the vision would bring the wrath of the gods.

A battle of emotions raged within her soul. What a tragic thing it was to pluck a suckling infant from a breast where no heart beat. What a tragic thing that a mother so young and so alone—without husband or family—should die giving birth. And what a difficult thing the winged spirits of God had told her she must do.

It was winged spirits that had come to her in her dreams, was it not? Or had it been the wraith from the tombs of the dead who appeared when a person's time had come. No! She had seen the spirits, and they had spoken to her of the babe and why she was the one who must do what she was doing.

She reached the place she had seen so clearly in her vision. The place where she must leave the child. The place where he'd be found. She wrapped the homespun wool about the babe and put the basket on the stone steps of the cottage.

What came next still frightened her, but she knew it had to be. She stared at her trembling hand a long while before reaching into her pocket for the precious treasure hidden there. It was wrapped in soft fur. She lifted it slowly. She had not seen nor touched it since the days of her childhood. It had been a gift from her stepmother's father, a restless vagabond who was forever seeking his fortune in places others

11

dared not go. He adored the darling girl with the auburn curls from the moment they had met.

Eight years from her day of blessing, he gave her his jewel heart. "A treasure to remember me by," he had said to her. "Whenever ye hold it and look upon it, I wish that ye should think on me." Even now the old woman could remember his words. He certainly got his wish. She was most certainly thinking of him as she took the carefully wrapped stone into her hand. "'Tis a gemstone traded from a hapless fool at the black market at the waterfront," he had told her. "A pirate, I believe." He could make every act a bold adventure. And then he laughed and whispered softly, "He promised it was magic and held a mystical power."

The pirate's word had been true. As least that is what she'd believed as a child. She had touched the beautiful stone only once. It was cold, and yet it burned her fingers. The glimmering that pulsed through her being had frightened her. Her stepmother had found her curled in a corner, crying. The stone was wrapped and put away and never touched again. Until the dream! Until the winged spirits of God had come in the night and told her where it was hidden and what she must do.

Her childhood treasure was exactly where her stepmother had locked it away three score and seven years before. When the wisewoman took it from the wooden box, she was careful not to unwrap the fur. She slipped the soft lump into her pocket and hurried away into the night to find the child and his lifeless mother.

She had done what the winged spirits of her vision had required and brought both the babe and the stone to this place. She placed the bundle of soft fur against the infant's cheek. His crying ceased. The dreadful thoughts of all that might befall a helpless infant abandoned in the black of night rose up in the shadows like a dreadful living thing.

What grand purpose can there be in my errand? she wondered and pinched her eyes tight.

The child stirred, and the fur fell open.

The stone was smaller than she remembered, but her first touch had been with the hand of a child. With a courage born of living to old age, the woman pushed her childhood fears aside and touched her treasure with a single finger. It was neither hot nor cold the way she remembered, nor was there a tremor through her being. There was nothing but a gradual glow of pure white light from deep within that illuminated the pinkness of the child's cheek.

Light, and a strange sense of farewell.

"Who are you, little one?" She looked at him in awe and whispered, lest the demons she felt sure were watching could hear her. "What destiny is yours?" She wrapped her thoughts inside her heart and disappeared into the night, leaving behind the babe and the magical stone, but taking with her a secret the child could never know.

CHAPTER 1

Annum 1088, Age of Kandelaar

Temple of Oum'ilah, the Mountain of God

Ashar walked in a circle. His fingers thumped across his forehead. His eyes were closed, and his lips moved in silent recitation of the begots and begottens in the ancestry of his lineage. This was the day that Ashar had worked toward since he'd been left at the temple gates almost seven years before.

Rol's voice broke the silence. "Do you think they will show us the sacred shining stones?"

Ashar pushed the question away and tightened his eyelids.

The boys were on the tower porch of the outer courtyard of the temple of Oum'ilah, the place the pilgrims called the Mountain of God. They wore simple tunics. Nothing like the linens, embroidery, and handcrafted leathers worn by people in the village in the valley that stretched eastward from the foot of the mountain far below. Ashar and his friend, Rol, were postulants to the Holy Order of Oum'ilah, God of gods and Creator of All Things, and had been for years.

"Ashar! Do you think they will let us see them even if we're not accepted?"

Ashar opened his eyes and pinched his face into a scowl. "Shh." He raised a hand to keep Rol from breaking his concentration, then closed his eyes again and continued the recitation of his lineage from the time of First Landing. He was determined to do it perfectly when he stood before the Council of Blessed Sages.

Rol ignored Ashar's request for silence. They had been friends for more than half their lives. "If we pass the test and they ordain us, that means we're worthy? Right?"

Ashar didn't answer.

"So why wouldn't they be willing to . . . you know—"

Ashar stopped him with a gust of breath in protest and opened his eyes.

"Be quiet, Rol!" he scolded. He was about to say more when he saw the look in his friend's eyes and realized Rol was babbling to stem his fears. In spite of their preparations, neither of them knew with any certainty what the day would bring. Ashar knew the past could not be changed and the future was unknown; today was both an ending and a beginning.

"I hope they will, don't you? I think they will," Rol persisted, pausing when his voice began to tremble. "If we survive the inquisition, I mean."

Ashar had refused to dwell on the frightening stories of the inquisition, but the intriguing possibility of Rol's question fluttered in his stomach. Was it possible they would be allowed to look upon the legendary shining stones of light? The flutter became a shiver that wriggled down his spine. He pushed the boulder of anticipation aside and returned to his recitations. He furrowed his forehead and forced his mind's eye to focus on his lineage.

Shalatar was the son of Ilim. Ilim was the son of Worm. Worm was the son of Issens. Issens was the son of Syn. There was no sound, and yet he could hear his own voice in his head speaking the names as they scrolled through the darkness behind his eyes. He imagined speaking them aloud before the Council of Blessed Sages and a shudder passed through him.

"I don't think Oum'ilah would mind if they gave us a quick peek at the shining stones, do you?" Rol spoke the name of the God of gods and Creator of All Things with well-rehearsed reverence, but Ashar cut him off with a scolding voice.

"You'd do well not to be frivolous about such things!"

The sun rose slowly through a scud of clouds on the eastern horizon. A shadow crawled across the cluster of stone buildings. The ancient dwellings clung to the cliffs on the high ridge of the Mountain of God that rose from the granite as if carved there at the dawn of creation.

The Navigator had built the temple at the highest point of the plateau using the stones of an ancient city that had been abandoned and in ruins long before the mountain was discovered by the voyagers. Who the ancient people might have been and how they built a city with cut and polished stones of such massive size remained a mystery. There was evidence the ancient habitation had been used as a religious site. There were cryptic etchings on a circle of monolithic stones perfectly aligned to the stars. The stones had come from a quarry in the valley and had been carved in place. They had been lifted to the mountain and fitted so tightly together that the point of a blade could not be slipped between them.

When Ashar was eight years old, he was brought to the mountain and given to the priests of the temple. The memory of that day was blurred by the confusion of emotions. When Ashar allowed himself to remember, the anguish of it was never more than a yesterday away.

Once he had resigned himself to the service of Oum'ilah, the God of gods and Creator of All Things, and had accepted the fact he would live on the mountain until he died, his life was the substance of heart more than mind. The fear of a child was replaced by the tranquility of a young man.

He was in his sixteenth year. He was long and lanky for his age, almost five cubitums tall. He was pleased by his height, but when he looked at himself in the polished brass, he lamented what he saw. His body was an ungainly rippling of bony ribs rather than a bulge of hardened muscles. His hair was long like other initiates, but thick and tangled with a natural curl that made it seem much shorter. Unlike Rol, whose hair was dark as soot and whose skin was the color of river clay, Ashar's hair was the color of dirty straw, and his skin was pale and freckled. His large eyes were dark blue with a fringe of gray and betokened his unusual intelligence and intuition.

With his concentration broken, Ashar stepped up to the low stone wall that protected the porch from the sheer drop down the face of the granite cliff. He looped an arm around a supporting timber and leaned over the edge.

The ridge of the temple was high above the valley floor between the endless cordillera to the south and the massive monolith of rock that rose two thousand cubitums from the river on the north. The mysterious hallowed fane stood at the pinnacle of the monolith. The shrine to Oum'ilah, God of gods and Creator of All Things, was put there by the Navigator a thousand years ago to hide the dwelling place of God from human eyes, or so the legend said.

On this day of days, Ashar stared at the swirl of perpetual covering of clouds that enshrouded the top of the monolith. Master Doyan taught that this holiest of holy places was a place so sacred only the consecrated guardians of the hallowed fane and the Oracle himself were ever allowed to go there. Ashar and the postulants accepted the teachings and believed the holy site was the sanctuary of Oum'ilah on earth, the place where the Navigator had spoken face-to-face with the God of gods a second time.

The hallowed fane was so shrouded in mystery, folklore, and legend, that Ashar was uncertain what was history, what was belief, and what was myth. He was not sure that even Master Doyan knew the difference. The stories repeated for a thousand years had evolved into indisputable beliefs. Tales of the extramundane were unquenchable in the villages surrounding the mountain. Even in hamlets as far south as West River and as far north as the village of Heap's Tower, pilgrims who embraced the Way of the Navigator believed the only way to reach the hallowed fane was to fly, embraced in the arms of the winged spirits of God.

A sect of fallen priests blasphemed that the holy shrine was an idea and not a place. "Nothing on top of the mountain but the nests of falcons," they mocked. The apostate priests declared the Navigator was an allegory and not an actual person. "How did the Navigator build the shrine?" one skeptic mused when Ashar and some other postulants chanced upon the exiled priest in the marketplace. "Did the winged spirits of God haul up the stones?" the man had sneered.

Flying to the hallowed fane holding the hand of the winged spirits of God was a satisfying folktale, but not the truth, according to Master Doyan. Once each year, on the twenty-first day of Kisilmu, season Kīt S'atti, a young priest was consecrated to the highest honor as a guardian of the hallowed fane. Temple virgins escorted him to the locus of caves at the base of the monolith.

From there, the honored one was escorted by a senior priest to the Place of the Tombs, from where one could climb no higher. It was always cold and the way oftentimes frozen.

How the chosen one ascended to the hallowed fane from the Place of the Tombs was never discussed. But the unknowable was always rife with rumors, and the story passed down from the oldest of the initiates said that the guardians were lifted into the clouds in a wicker basket on silken ropes and pulleys carved from pockholz wood.

Of course, it was all speculation. No guardian had ever returned to validate or deny the telling.

As the thoughts came to his mind, Ashar's imagination rose to the top of the monolith and disappeared into the clouds. The uncertainty of what lay ahead fused with the mysteries of the hallowed fane. The warmth of the morning sun on his face made him suddenly aware that his mind had wandered. He scolded himself, knowing he should return to the recitation, but his thoughts lingered.

For as often as he had stared at the monolith and wondered, today was different. The mountain, the clouds, the temple, the grand court. They were beautiful to behold, but he was no longer one who stood on the outside looking in. He was as yet at the threshold, but for the first time, he felt he belonged to that wondrous place.

Ashar's eyes swept downward from the mountain to the narrow

trail that wound from the village to the summit of the hogback. The escarpment was steep, and the path switched back before looping around to make a final ascent. It was the only way to the ridge and the sprawling grounds of the temple. In times past, horses had hoofed their way up the rocky route. In recent times, parts of the trail had washed away and could only be traveled on foot.

Burdens were carried to and from the mountain on the backs of votaries, often with the help of a pilgrim making the ascent to pray. Sometimes the postulants were sent to the village with the priests to help carry provender and other supplies. Some of the postulants considered it a punishment, but Ashar relished the chance to go to the market even when it meant hiking back up the steep and winding trail with a heavy pack of grain or vegetables and sometimes meat.

"There's another fire!" Rol exclaimed. The angst in his voice jolted Ashar from his drifting thoughts. He looked to where Rol pointed. A plume of smoke twisted up from a village at the far end of the valley. The sun was a smudge of yellow in the smoke and the morning light an eerie glow.

Neither of the boys had been farther east than the market of the Village Candella that lay below the Mountain of God. Certainly not as far as where the smoke rose.

"Most likely farmers burning stubble in the fields," Ashar said with his usual optimism.

"Bandits, I'll wager," Rol said.

Word of the robbers creating trouble in the dominions of Kandelaar had been brought to the mountain by a wide-eyed pilgrim who had climbed to the temple to pray. Others came with similar reports. Rumors of plunder were different with each telling. Whether the bandits were as vicious as some of the villagers described, Ashar had no way of knowing, but one exploit was common to every tale. Into whatever village the bandits came, miscreants and mercenaries were conscripted into a growing army of outlaws.

Descriptions of the bandit king who led them flourished in taverns and were enlarged by the gossiping of old crones. Whatever the truth, the chief of the marauders loomed in Ashar's imagination as a ferocious giant with the head of a dragon. Few of the pilgrims had ever actually seen the robbers or their captain, but they passed the gossip along anyway: "Dangerous, savage, bloody, and barbaric." Those who had actually laid eyes on the leader of the bandits spoke different words: "Demon, incubus, and a vessel of darkness."

Had there always been such men? Ashar wondered. Had such terror and commotion started with the ancient people who had vanished? Did they destroy themselves? Petroglyphs scratched into the patina of the rock walls of the mountain left no easy clues.

Are we repeating the mistakes of the first people? Shall we also vanish without record or remembrance?

Ashar stepped from the wall and shook his head to cleanse his imagination of demons, death, and destruction.

Rol's voice brought him back. "Ashar? You never said if you wanted to see the sacred stones. Do you?"

"I don't know. Maybe, or maybe such thinking of such things is a sin of aspiration, and aspiration is ambition, and ambition is pride." The aphorism was one of hundreds he had memorized, and it came easily to his mind. Perhaps it was wrong to wish for what he could not have. "You had best stop thinking about shining stones and start thinking about reciting your bloodline to the twentieth generation."

"I know," Rol grumbled, "but it's hard, and I get confused. Who is whose son of whom and who begot who is hard for me to remember."

"Shh. I need to concentrate." Ashar closed his eyes and pressed his fingers to his temples.

"When I become the Oracle," Rol said, "I promise to sneak you into the hallowed fane, or wherever they hide the sacred stones, so you can see them for yourself."

"That is such a prideful thing to say." Ashar's eyes were scolding, but his smile gave him away.

"Sorry." Rol shrugged an apology, and Ashar chuckled.

"If *you* become the Oracle, I will know for sure there is no God of gods and Creator of All Things."

Rol punched Ashar's shoulder with affection, and the boys laughed softly.

Rol's mood was suddenly serious. "Are you so sure now?" he asked.

Ashar's face tightened. "I am a postulant of the Sodality of Priests of Oum'ilah."

"I know. So am I. It's all I've ever been, but . . . some say the story of the Navigator is only a legend, you know, an allegory like the other traditions Master Doyan taught us about. It could be that the story isn't really true but it can still be authentic because it teaches a true principle or reveals a hidden meaning."

Ashar studied his friend's worried face. Of all the days for him to have doubts about what he believed, this was the worst.

"I guess that's the reason I'd like see the stones of light." Rol whispered his confession. "I'm not sure they exist. Some say the reason no one ever sees them or the Oracle never calls upon their power is because they're only a . . ." Rol tried to find a better word but couldn't so he said it a different way. "Have you never wondered whether the story about small rocks becoming stones of light because they were touched by the finger of God is nothing but a myth?"

Ashar resisted the rote response that tumbled to his tongue. Rol's question left him uneasy. He had known Rol since they'd been given to the temple as children. He lifted his eyes to the towers of the temple soaring high above. He inhaled slowly and looked back at Rol. "It is a curious day to wonder what you believe," he said. "We've been taught to doubt our doubts before we doubt our faith. What do you believe?" Answering a question with a question was a tack of dialectics taught by Master Doyan.

Rol lifted his eyebrows, his face a glow of innocence. A quirky smile formed at the corner of his mouth. "I believe whatever the masters have spoken since my father left me here when I was eight years old," he recited. "Same as you." It was the proper and expected answer. Rol shrugged and offered a smile of resignation.

Boys abandoned and given as postulants to the Sodality of Priests of Oum'ilah were bonded in ways they couldn't explain. Ashar could see that Rol was struggling with his thoughts, but even so, he was not prepared for the question when it came.

"Do you ever wonder where we might be now, or what might have become of us if we had not . . ." Rol chewed on his lower lip. "I mean, do you ever wonder whether you and me would've picked, you know, being postulants if . . . if we'd had a choice?"

Ashar had asked himself the same question many times, but Rol asking it aloud ripped away the shroud, forcing him to face his hidden angst.

"It's not a question we should ask," Ashar said. He swallowed hard and recited the axiom that had been drummed into his young head. "We are blessed by the sacrifice our fathers . . ." He faltered on the last word and pushed the thought away. "The sacrifice they made to show their devotion to Oum'ilah, the God of gods. We are the ones who—"

"Sacrifice?" Rol cut him off. "It wasn't a sacrifice! Your father brought you here and gave you to the priests because he didn't want you!" Rol clenched his jaw. "Same way my father didn't want me and one more mouth to feed."

Ashar shook his head, rejecting the painful possibility, even knowing it was true.

I am Ashar, son of Shalatar! Shalatar was the son of Ilim. Ilim was the son of Worm. Worm was the son of . . .

With his eyes closed, Ashar saw the march of his ancestor's names as they appeared on the faded parchment of his memory. The scrap of animal skin was a private treasure. His only connection to his other life. His mother had given it to him on the day she said good-bye.

— • —

They had walked from the village to the bottom of the mountain. His father was impatient, already ascending the trail. His mother lingered, straightening his shirt and running her fingers through his curly hair.

"Hurry along now!" his father had yelled.

Ashar cried. Why did his father wish to leave him on the mountain? "Why are you sending me away? Do you not want me?" he sobbed.

His mother threw her arms around him and held him close. Her tears warmed his cheek. "I want you, dear child, and I love you with all of my heart." She crushed him to her until he could scarcely breathe.

"I know you cannot understand, but you will be safe and I cannot protect you if . . ." She stopped speaking and glanced at the man on the trail ahead who was yelling again. Ashar would never forget what happened next. She had hugged him and spoken close to Ashar's ear in a hoarse whisper. "He cannot love you as I do because . . . because he is not the father of your flesh. Do you understand?"

Ashar was not sure he did.

And then Ashar's mother had slipped a bundle beneath his shirt. She clung to him in a last, lingering embrace and whispered, "You are the son of my first love, who was lost. You are Ashar, son of Shalatar."

CHAPTER 2

Many Days Earlier

The warhorse balked at the steep bank of the river. The rocks were slick with blackened moss. The watercourse was wide, and the current ran swift. Drakkor whipped his mount across its croup. The black horse shook its head and pounded its hooves in protest. The rider sank the iron spike of his boots into its flank, and the destrier plunged into the muddy turbulence. The score and seven men who rode with him held their mounts steady along the bank and watched.

Drakkor pulled the horse's head upstream and swam him into the treacherous rapids. The horse held its head high and flared its nostrils as it thrashed its legs for the opposite shore. Drakkor calmed the charger with a hand on its neck and spoke words lost in the thunder of the river.

The men waiting on shore were a band of outcasts more than an army: bandits weary of the paltry booty from robbing travelers on the King's Road; soldiers in disgrace; unruly, restless boys; villainous men conscripted from the villages; and mercenaries willing to sell their swords for the pleasures of plunder and a place in the promised new kingdom to come.

They were clad in mismatched armor made of iron and boiled

leather. Rusted and tarnished. Scuffed and unkempt. Some wore helms. Others had leather caps. A few were bareheaded or had tied bands of cloth or leather around their foreheads.

Though no two men were dressed the same, all of them carried weapons. Long swords, short swords, scimitars, or long knives. Several had bows with quivered arrows, and others carried cleaving weapons and mauls.

The destrier found its footing on the rocks submerged along the south bank of the river. Drakkor spiked the horse again, and it erupted from the water in a single lunge. He rode the slope to a ledge of rock splayed out from a thicket of willows. He drew his sword and held it high as a signal to his men. Exuberant cheers were swallowed by the roar of the river as the men spurred their horses and charged into the water.

Drakkor was pleased by their zeal, but his smile was little more than a twitch at the corner of his mouth. They were hearty men, warriors at heart, but also a depraved lot driven by a lust for the spoils of pillage and plunder. Despite their fatigue, the men were eager for battle and blood and conquest.

These who followed Drakkor believed their objective was to conquer the temple at the Mountain of God and establish a fortress suited to the king they were certain he would become. Drakkor had planted the seeds and allowed the rumor to grow, lest he divulge his true purpose. His destiny had been set in motion when he had been a boy of fifteen—twenty-nine years before. His time had come.

His men could have their citadel and their trifling rule of kings. His purpose in assaulting the Mountain of God was of greater worth than a hundred castles.

Drakkor dismounted and pulled the sodden saddle from his horse's back. He was taller than most men. The angular bones of his face spoke of intelligence and intensity. The firm set of his jaw guarded secrets. Clean-shaven, his skin was the color of rusted iron. He had a scar on his cheek, just below his ear. It looked as if the gods had pressed a calloused thumb into the wet clay of his face before it was finished and left behind a ragged hole.

The pockmark was nearly obscured by the tattooed tail of a dragon that circled his neck before disappearing beneath the gorget where it became a fire-breathing monster enveloping his body. His raven-black hair splayed out in a fan of curls where his strong neck rose from broad shoulders. His dark green eyes were large and deeply set in the shadows of thick brows. A smudge of gold in the irises gave him the glower of a feral cat.

He narrowed his eyes and watched the men and horses struggling to cross the current. They were dangerous men that suited his purposes perfectly. He would flatter them, praise them, and pay them in spoils. He would allow them to satiate their hunger and their lust. It would be enough to ensure their loyal devotion.

How little they know. He smiled as he remembered the path that had led him to this moment.

His memory was a blessing and curse. From his earliest days, he had been able to recall images, sounds, and words after a single exposure. It was a blessing when the memory held something beautiful or worthy or important to remember. It was a curse when he remembered the tragedy and pain of his early life.

Today the sunlight on the water reminded him of the chamber of light. The killing, the claw of the dragon, the scourging and the pain. The oath and taste of blood. The feelings when the magic stone was placed into his hand. The undeniable epiphany of destiny.

He remembered the bargain he had struck with the Peddler of Souls. The memory rose like the stench of a fetid slough with a scuttle of ravenous rats hungry for his flesh. It was a long time ago and rarely came to mind except when night began to fall and wraiths of memory slipped from the shadows to haunt his dreams.

— · —

The trials, torture, and blood loss he had suffered as a boy had left him in a weakened and semiconscious state. Swallowing the rancid blood had sickened him.

You will survive. The voice rose in his mind like a hallucination. *And I've a way for ya to do it.* The night before Drakkor had entered Dragonfell, the Peddler of Souls had told him of the prophecy and described the rituals and the number of lashes he must endure without a sound. Then he had given him a birchwood stick to keep him silent, a vial of dark liquid to keep him strong, and a command. *You get through the purgin,' and they'll be givin'* you *the magic stone and sending ye off to find the others. But never mind their superstitions, you bring that stone to me, ya hear?*

Drakkor had agreed not out of loyalty or fear but out of ambition. He had survived. He had done it. *If I hold the stone, should I not be the one blessed by its power?*

Steadied on either side by men in scarlet robes, the young Drakkor had been helped up a winding stairway to a domed chamber that was open to the night sky through a circular shaft that rose from the apogee of the cupola. The men placed him on a circular dais in the center of the room. There were opposing doors at each of the cardinal directions. An annulus of glims burned on an altar. The smoke carried the pungent smell of sheep fat. Three hundred candles set in a serpentine pattern around the walls illuminated the rest of the chamber.

"Fire is the symbol of she-dragon's breath, and her breath is the symbol of creation and the force that rules the earth," the sorceress intoned in the guttural cadence of her husky voice.

Each tiny flame was reflected in the polished black stones of the walls and ceilings, until the points of light diminished to infinity, more numerous than the stars of heaven.

Drakkor narrowed his eyes and focused on the most distant point of light in the chilling universe of flickering fire. He felt suspended in an endless void, floating in a vast black sea warmed by an omnipresent breath of fire.

"The shrine of the begetter of the heavens above and earth beneath," the sorceress said with devotion.

With blood still oozing from his back, and the chanting of hooded votaries reverberating from the open dome of black stone, Drakkor felt suspended in an endless void, floating in a black sea warmed by an omnipresent breath of fire. He narrowed his eyes and focused on the most distant point of light in the chilling universe of flickering fire.

I have drunk the blood and said the words. Was I a fool? Was it a whispering of my mind or the echoing voice of the Peddler? Is there truly such a thing as a magic stone of fire? Wounded and bloodied, he wasn't sure anymore.

As an orphan, Drakkor had little exposure to religion in the slums of Black Flower. Thoughts of his future were gobbled up by survival. In the rare moments he allowed himself to ponder ideas that were incomprehensible, he favored the old gods of the ancient tower. And yet, if the stone had power, the power came from she-dragon.

If there is magic in the world, if there are powers unseen, if truth lies at the heart of myth, I can change my destiny. I will be more than a king—I will be immortal.

Men in bloodred robes surrounded him, their faces shrouded in the shadow of their hoods. Others watched from the darkness beyond.

The voice of the sorceress reciting the ancient prophecy filled the room. "In the time of kings and the day of chaos, the seal is broken. The ancient mysteries arise. She-dragon is blind and rages from the mountains. That which was lost shall be found. The eggs of stone forged in the breath of fire, gathered in the hand of might by the child of no man—who is worthy of the blood of the dragon, purged by death and suffering in silent darkness—and, clustered in her claws, will rise immortal by the power of the ancient secret, to rule all flesh and reign forever as god of the world."

Drakkor recognized the words of the prophecy. The words swirled into the void of endless stars. Drakkor closed his eyes and raised his face as if drawn to a presence that reached down to take his soul.

When the stone was placed in his hand, he was jolted back into the moment. The stone was the size of an egg but oddly shaped and strangely translucent, like crystal shimmering with a dark light. It was cold as ice but burned his hand.

Drakkor was swept up by the congregation of red-robed men and taken from the domed room. As they left, he glimpsed the scrawny Peddler standing in a fringe of shadow where he'd been allowed to watch. His eyes were wide and red with broken veins. His face was twisted in a grin of greedy anticipation, and his yellowed teeth glinted in the firelight. Drakkor answered the Peddler's hopeful look with a twitch of a smile. The skeletal scum of a man writhed with delight before a guard took him by the arm and pulled him away.

He believes I will keep our bargain. Fool! When the magic stone touched Drakkor's hand, he'd sensed a rippling wave of chilling warmth. It lingered and strangely smothered the throbbing pain in his back. With the magic stone in his hand and unimaginable thoughts pounding through his head, whatever promise Drakkor had made was gone. Broken, betrayed, and forgotten. The Peddler of Souls would never have the stone of fire.

CHAPTER 3

"So here be the young fools!" A voice cackled from behind Ashar and Rol.

The boys spun about in surprise. A bedraggled old man was standing near enough to touch—except Ashar was struck with the fleeting notion there was no one there at all.

An apparition from my mind immersed in expectation, my body starved by the cleansing fast, and my muscles fatigued from a fitful night on the hard stones.

He closed his eyes, inhaled deeply, and shook his head. When he opened his eyes again, the stranger was still there. A scornful laugh rumbled up from the man's throat.

He wore a billowing dark robe of coarse woven wool with a cowl that extended beyond his face, keeping his eyes in deep shadow. A cast-iron skull hung around his neck on a chain. Sinister and foreboding. Ashar had never seen the symbol before.

The dark arts and sorceries were forbidden by the writings in the Codices of the Navigator, but only the pilgrims of the valley and votaries of the temple kept the laws and followed the Way of the Navigator. Many people had returned to the superstition of the old gods and the conjurings of talisman and magic. In spite of the sanctions against dabbling with such things, postulants found it irresistible to frighten the younger boys by filling their heads with haunting stories about the ancient citadel on which the temple stood.

There were whisperings about the ancient caste of evil priests expelled from the brotherhood for sorcery, who called themselves the Magica. Whether it was true or not, the tale was established folklore in the village. It was an enduring mythology even among the Council of Blessed Sages.

Is this man a magus? A sorcerer? The thought sent a shudder up Ashar's spine and a snarl of hunger through his empty stomach.

"Who are you?" Ashar asked with more respect than an intruder deserved.

"Whom would you wish me to be on your day of days?"

Solving riddles was a method the masters used to teach postulants the skill of abstract thinking. The bone-chilling timbre of the stranger's voice petrified Ashar's ability to think, abstractly or otherwise.

The sorcerer, if that was what he was, had gauze wrapped across his nose and mouth. It was the color of dirty smoke and smudged yellow below his nostrils. Ashar feared the man was infected by the illness of putrid flesh and the flimsy linen was covering his oozing sores.

"Are you"—the words stuck in the back of his throat—"one of the Magica?"

"You know of us?"

Ashar's mouth was dry even with the pebble in his mouth. He had kept it there since he awoke to keep his tongue moist so he could speak clearly when he stood before the council. Cramps of hunger tightened his stomach.

From beneath the folds of his robes, the old man withdrew a loaf of bread. He held it out to Ashar. Saliva came with the sight of it. He could taste the smell of it, and the thought of sweet dough in his mouth sent a ripple of hunger through his gut.

The magus chuckled kindly. "Eat, eat," he said. "Have some." His words were cut short by a scraping cough that caused him to turn away.

When neither Ashar or Rol moved, the man shrugged and laid the bread on the stone floor between them. A streak of yellow sun turned the toasted crust to gold.

Rol reached for the loaf.

Ashar caught his wrist. "No! We are still in our period of purification. Our fasting does not end until the inquisition is through and only then if—"

"A bite or two of bread. How can it matter?" the stranger asked, sounding like a kindly parent.

Learning to control his emotions was, for Ashar, the most difficult of all the challenges of self-mastery. His anger toward the stranger started as an iron fist that gripped his gut and twisted it tight. His hunger confused the feeling, but his breathing quickened. He inhaled deeply without realizing his fingers had balled into a fist.

"We are probationers to the Sodality of Priests of Oum'ilah!" he said, straightening his shoulders. "We are in the final time of our preparation. We have looked forward to this day for more than twenty seasons. How can you be here and not know this?"

The stranger nodded. "But I do know. Of course I know. I came here *because* I know! I've seen scores of lads like you caught up in this madness. Many, many foolish boys for many, many seasons beginning before you were born."

"Then why do you entice us to break our bond? You must leave. It is almost time for the trumpets, and you have broken our meditations. Please. Go! Our time is near."

"Quite near indeed, Ashar, son of Shalatar, but it makes no difference."

"You know my name?"

"You have proven yourself worthy. You, and Rol, son of Blynes," he said, turning to other boy.

How can he know us? The thought loomed large in Ashar's mind. It frightened him.

"You are the choice ones." The stranger mocked the expression. "That is what they call you, isn't it? Choice ones?" Another guttural cluck of disdain came from the face in shadow. "You have been told you must sacrifice and suffer to show your devotion to the imaginary 'god of the mountain,' but just because they have persuaded you to believe does not make it so." He tapped Ashar on the forehead, his slender finger protruding from a woolen wrap covering most of his hand. "Suffer yourselves to endure discomfort no longer," he soothed. "They'll be none the wiser if you indulge in a bit of nourishment. You'll be better for it. The pain will go, and your minds will be more focused for the questions."

He snagged the leather flagon slung over his shoulder with his thumb and handed it to Rol.

Ashar reached out to stop him, but he was too slow, and Rol sucked gulps of water from the flask like a dying man in the desert.

The stranger watched Rol, then turned away. As he did, a bounce of light reached into the shadows of his hood. Was there a flash of disappointment in the old man's eyes? Before Ashar could be sure, the light was gone and the shadows returned.

"You ask me why I've come." He moved toward Ashar as if Rol was no longer of interest. It was unnerving, and Ashar backed into the trumeau supporting the archivolt that framed the opening above. A railing was all that kept him from falling into the chasm. He glanced down, and his belly was gripped by iron fingers. Not from the lack of food but from his dread of heights and fear of falling.

"You've yet to conquer your fear of the mountain," the magus said as he brushed past.

Ashar braced himself with one hand against the side of the opening.

"How do you know about me?" Ashar demanded. "Please go and leave us alone!"

"I know everything about you," the magus whispered, his mouth close to Ashar's ear. "I know more than what you fear. I know your doubts." His words rasped like the sound of a skinning knife dragging across dry hide. He was so close Ashar could smell the fusty, mildewed stench of his robes. "You are giving up your life and the pleasures of your body for what?"

Ashar turned to escape, but long fingers caught his arm above the wrist and pulled him back. His first impulse was to twist away, rise to anger and strike back, but the crushing pain of the grip was too much. He felt paralyzed. Under the spell of the sorcerer.

Sorcerer! Ashar tried to focus his thoughts.

"You think you follow a path appointed by the God of gods, but you are a fool." The heavy cowl kept his face in shadow except for a protrusion of dirty gauze that moved when he spoke.

"It is only a legend," he chided, the tone sardonic. "The Navigator. Shining stones of light. The finger of God. Life beyond death." His guttural laugh ridiculed the ideas. "Folktales. Myths. Stories told by old men afraid to die. And for these you are willing to sacrifice the pleasures of life?"

Ashar's paralysis of fear fled before the storm of his anger. He jerked his arm free and pulled back with doubled fists. "By the will of the God of gods, if you do not depart this place, I swear that—"

"By the God of gods?" the stranger cut him off, his voice dripping with disdain. "You really believe there is such a being as the mythical Oum'ilah, Creator of All Things?"

"I embrace our tradition with all of my being."

"Hmm." A sound rumbled from the thick robes, almost approving in tone. "Then no doubt you also treasure the mythology of the so-called stones of light?

"I trust the Codices of the Navigator, which testifies of the miracle of the shining stones of light."

"What else do you believe, Ashar, son of Shalatar?"

"That there is but one God of gods and Creator of All Things." Having affirmed the first tenant of the Way of the Navigator, Ashar recited the second canon of the brotherhood. "All that is, has always been and will forever be, and who we are and were before will continue through endless time." Reciting the dogma that had become the core of his consciousness spiked his courage. His anger flared, and he fought for restraint.

"Your face is vexed and swollen. You stand there, a young fool with your fists curled, but not the slightest skill of combat."

It was true. The dogma of the order put the well-being of others before self, thus postulants were not trained to fight. Mastery of self demanded discipline of the body as well as the mind.

But Ashar was not without physical prowess. He was remarkably strong in spite of his gangly frame, and it gave him confidence. Adrenaline gave him courage.

The only fighting he had ever done was wrestling with the other boys, but this was the day he'd worked for all his life. This stranger was not going to take that from him. Anger surged ahead of reason. He took an aggressive step toward the man hoping the threat would be enough to drive him away. He clenched his fists and prepared for a fight.

He glanced at Rol, hoping for his help, but his friend was staring at his feet. His shoulders were quaking with heaving sobs.

The magus slipped a dagger from his sash. The handle was carved from an ivory tusk and set with a ring of sapphire stones the color of a hummingbird's wing.

Ashar realized that until this moment he had never seen a weapon on the mountain before.

The rasping voice brought him back. "Have your masters prepared you to die for what you imagine to be truth?"

A reflection of sun off the blade splashed light on Ashar's face, making him think of the shining stones. He shook the thought away. "I have sworn the oath of reverence for all living things and to do no harm, but if you do not depart this place, I am prepared to break that oath." A surge of power coursed through him. He tensed every muscle and prepared for whatever was about to happen.

"And for this God of gods you would sacrifice your honor and yourself and all that you hold precious?"

"Even my life!" Ashar widened his stance without moving his eyes from the blade. "I have warned you." He had no idea what he would do if the man lunged with the dagger.

"I think, then, I might spare you from breaking your oath." The voice, still shrouded by the cowl of the man's heavy robe, was suddenly different. No longer menacing and caustic. The dagger disappeared as quickly as it had appeared. The man pushed back the hood and loosened the gauze from his face.

Ashar shied away, not wanting to see oozing wounds of putrid flesh, but there was nothing like that. The face of the man glowed in a streak of the early sunlight pouring in from the east.

"Master Doyan?" Ashar gasped.

Rol groaned in agony and sagged to his knees in despair. The intruder was not a magus or a sorcerer or an enemy of Oum'ilah. Master Doyan was their favorite teacher, their mentor and spiritual guide.

"Well done, Ashar, son of Shalatar," he said and bowed his head in a show of respect. "The inquisition is over. Your test of faith is ended," he announced with obvious satisfaction. "It will now be my great honor to present you to the synod. The Council of Blessed Sages is eager to meet you."

Ended? The inquisition? Ashar could not speak. His mind cascaded backward, trying to untangle reality from perception. "But I thought that . . . Isn't the inquisition . . . ? You have prepared us over all the years to stand before the learned masters of the blessed council."

"You need not be so disappointed. You will yet experience humility before the Council of Blessed Sages." Master Doyan grinned. His teeth were straight in spite of being alive for ninety years. "They expect the recitation of the genealogies, though I confess they do find strange pleasure in intimidating postulants. A bit of a game, I suppose, or perhaps because they are old and impatient, but you go before them having endured the trial that matters most."

"It is always like this?"

"Always, since the time of First Landing in accordance with the writings of the Navigator. An answer prepared in anticipation of a question already known can never reveal the heart like the choice a person makes when no question has been asked."

Rol sagged into a corner and put his hands over his face. In giving in to the appetites of his body, he had bungled the most fundamental test of sacrifice and devotion. He had failed.

Master Doyan lifted him up. "You must not punish yourself. Your foot has been placed on a new path. Your life shall be different, but it need not be less. Take all you have learned and use it well. Your path is known to Oum'ilah, and your destiny shall not be less."

Ashar threw his arms around his friend. They held each other a long time before Rol turned away and ran down the twisting stairs. Ashar watched until his friend disappeared from his sight.

Will I ever see him again?

Ashar left the thought on the south porch of the tower and followed Master Doyan across the hanging causeway to the grand plaza of the temple, his eyes raised to the magnificent edifice beyond.

CHAPTER 4

The shadow of the obelisk touched the vertex of the calendar stone on which it stood. The instrument rose from the center of the outer court where it had marked the flow of time since the ancient city was discovered by the Navigator in annum 7, Age of Kandelaar.

Ashar stood beside Master Doyan and stared at the portal that opened to a long arched hallway. The end of it disappeared in darkness. The time had come. He heard the escorts before he saw them. Their rhythmic chanting echoed from the tunnel in monotonous repetitions and rolled across the courtyard. Four temple virgins adorned in ceremonial vestments emerged from the shadows of the hallway carrying the ensigns of the temple furled on long poles. Their faces covered.

It was hard for Ashar to suppress the flutter of feelings when the escorts beckoned them forward. He was anxious about standing before the Council of Blessed Sages, but that was not the reason a hundred butterflies took wing in his stomach. It was the fleeting glance of eyes the color of a summer sky and the flutter of long lashes above the gossamer veil. Their eyes connected for less than a moment, but for Ashar it was a delightfully long and lovely conversation.

The girl was fourteen. *Celestine.* He whispered her name in his mind, and a flush of guilt was added to the flutters. It was only by chance that Ashar knew her by her true name.

———

Celestine had been given to the temple in the first season of her fifth year. All the temple virgins came as children and served until they were of age to be married. Most returned to their villages, but some remained and continued serving in the ceremonies and other duties at the temple. The most blessed became matrons and stayed until the twilight of their lives, finding their final rest in the tombs on the holy mountain.

The matrons who looked after the temple virgins were like mothers. Worrying about them. Protecting their purity. Keeping the girls away from the postulants when the boys entered the second season of their thirteenth year. That's when it had happened: the unexpected encounter between the temple virgin and the postulant.

———

Celestine had gone to fetch water from the fountain flowing from a grotto known as the Tears of God on the east side of the mountain. A stairway of stone, mortared in pulverized rock with lime and sand, descended from the flattened ridge of the main temple compound. It climbed down the twelve terraced steps of the vineyards to where footholds had been hand cut in the face of the rock by someone lost to history.

The grotto was filled by a deep pool that prevented easy access to the fountain that gushed from a natural cleft in the back wall. No one knew where the water came from or how it drained from the pool. Most assumed the rain and melting snow that sometimes fell at the top of the monolith seeped through fractures in the rock to find its way to the labyrinth of caverns and underground lakes the old legends said existed inside the mountains. Some caverns had been discovered. A few explored. Most remained unknown. The most intriguing of the legends spoke of a vast treasure hidden in the caverns by King Garnlot the Mighty in annum 685. The story was well-known to the postulants and the source of endless speculation and wild dreams.

Celestine filled her skin-bag buckets and attached them to both ends of the yoke. She crouched and slipped the yoke across her shoulder, adjusting the pad lest the birchwood cut into her skin. She stood slowly, adjusted the position of the yoke to equalize the weight, and started up the trail.

The stone steps climbed from the cave to the bottom of a high rock wall that formed the lowest of the terraces. A dirt path beside the wall connected the hewn steps with the mortared stone steps that ascended to the temple courtyard. As Celestine stepped onto the path, a hummingbird swept in and slipped its long bill into the red blossom of a wild trumpet vine.

Celestine loved beauty and was fascinated by the miracle of living things. She stopped to watch. In the bright sunshine, the tiny hummingbird was a dazzling display of shimmering green and iridescent blue.

The miraculous little bird moved from blossoms of red to orange to yellow. She longed to stay and watch, but she knew she needed to start the difficult climb back to the temple mount. Being late made the old matrons suspicious. She stepped to the outside edge of the trail to pass the hummingbird without disturbing its sweet nectar feast.

When she stepped on the sodden grass of the outside shoulder, the ground broke away. She fell to one knee and tried to catch herself, but the weight of the water pulled the yoke downward and dragged her into the chasm.

— —

Ashar heard the girl's cry. It was his day to fetch water for the kitchen, and he was on his way to the Tears of God. At first he thought it was the screech of a falcon, but when it came again, he realized it was a human cry, desperate for help.

The stone steps were old, worn, and irregular. Running down was dangerous, but the terror in the voice compelled him to take them three at a time. At the bottom of the lowest terrace, he saw a yoke and skin-bag bucket caught in the foliage at the edge of the trail. From somewhere over the edge the cry came again.

"Help! Help me!"

Ashar scrambled forward and peered into the chasm. A girl had fallen into a tangle of picea trees growing from a ledge of rock. When he saw her face clearly, his heart almost stopped. She was a temple virgin. It was the daughter of the temple at whom he'd stolen glances whenever he could since the first time he saw her more than a year before.

Ashar secured his foot in a tangle of roots, reached over the edge, and grabbed the end of the yoke.

"Take hold. You'll be all right," he called to her. "Hold on! Hold tight."

The girl gripped the end of the yoke with both hands as he pulled her up. When she was close enough, he reached out his hand.

Among the stringent rules imposed upon the postulants, rule seventeen stated that postulants must avoid all unnecessary interaction with the temple virgins and never make physical contact. Despite the rule, Ashar reached for her hand without a twinge of guilt. Certainly none of the disobedience he felt when he stared at her in the courtyard.

She held his eyes and blushed. After what seemed like a long time, she put her hand in his.

It was the first time Ashar had ever touched a girl. A shiver rippled through his body in a fluttering of feelings more marvelous than anything he'd ever felt before. Her hand was soft and warm. His heart was thumping so loudly he was certain she could hear it.

He gripped her hand tightly. She had not taken her eyes from him. She blushed again, but this time with a smile, then looked down to place her feet. Ashar set the yoke aside and offered his other hand. She took it without hesitation. The quiver of delight came again. Holding firmly to both her hands, he guided her carefully from the tangle of green across the sodden grass to safety on the far side of the path. The hummingbird had flown away.

"Are you hurt?" he asked and looked for cuts or signs of blood. He caught himself thinking about her perfectly smooth skin, the azure blue of her eyes, and the way her tangled hair framed her face in a soft swirl of gold. He realized for the first time that she was nearly as tall as he was and while equally as thin, her body was graced with gentle curves—unlike his gangly awkwardness.

"I don't think so," she said, but she touched a rip in her gown and winced. When her delicate fingers came back, Ashar could see a trace of blood.

"You're bleeding. Let me see." She raised her arm and Ashar could see the tear in her gown and the bright red abrasion across her pale and perfect skin. Their eyes met, and Ashar was oblivious to everything in the universe except for the girl looking back at him.

"It's not too deep," he assured her. He wet a piece of linen in the puddle from the spilled bucket and reached for the wound on her side then stopped in a sudden rush of awkward embarrassment. His face flushed, and he offered the wetted cloth to her. "Here, you should hold this tight until it stops bleeding."

Ashar retrieved the skin bags and headed down the trail to refill her buckets. He made a second trip to fill his own. When he returned, the girl was sitting against the wall. She was crying.

"Is the pain great?" he asked.

"No. I'll be all right, but the matrons will be angry with me for what I've done."

"You've done nothing wrong. The trail is narrow and the edges soft. Any of us might have fallen just as easily."

"I don't mean falling. I mean . . ." She looked at her hands.

Ashar understood. She worried she had violated the edict of her appointment. That her status had somehow changed by touching a boy.

"You've done no wrong. Nothing has changed for you," he said firmly. "The piety of the matrons is mostly of their own making." His own words startled him. "In my opinion," he added hastily. "I will

42

speak of this to no one. You need not worry." He reached in his pocket for the apple he'd brought and offered it to her. "My name is Ashar."

She took the apple, her fingertips brushing the palm of his hand. She swiped a tear from her cheek and smiled as she took a dainty bite.

"Thank you," she said. "I am grateful for your help."

Ashar wanted to ask her name, the one given her on the day of blessing, but knew he shouldn't. In the village, such a simple question would be natural and even expected between new friends, but for a postulant, such intimacy was forbidden. The name conferred upon girls on the day of their blessing as infants was never used again once they were given as temple virgins. The vestal virgins were all called by their designation. They were simply "daughters of the temple."

Ashar sat down beside the girl and leaned against the wall. He was content to sit in silence as she ate. When she finished the apple, he stood and offered his hand.

"Come on," he said. "I will help you to the top." She hesitated, then took his hand and used his strength to stand.

Ashar climbed the stairs with four skin-bag buckets of water hanging from a single yoke. The other yoke he carried in his hand. It was arduous by any measure, but he felt none of the strain. He walked slowly on purpose to make the climb last as long as he could. The girl didn't seem to mind the slow pace.

As they ascended the steps, Ashar paused to point out flowers and recite the names of the plants. Appreciating the beauty of the natural world was part of Doyan's teachings. The girl was impressed and delighted by his knowledge. It was evident to Ashar that she loved the splendor of nature and the fragrance of flowers.

When she told him why she had fallen, he teased that she needed to come up with a better story than that a hummingbird had frightened her off the trail. "A dragon would be better, or at least a lion." Her laugh was as musical as the chimes at the temple gates.

By the time they reached the top, she was laughing with abandon and any blush of guilt was gone. When Ashar returned the yoke back to her soft shoulders, their eyes met again in that timeless way.

"Celestine," she whispered. "My name from the day of blessing is Celestine." With a flash of her eyes and a quivering smile, she turned and left him standing on the path.

"Celestine," he repeated with a smile that made his cheeks hurt.

In the three seasons between their meeting on the mountain and the joyous coincidence of Celestine being assigned as one of Ashar's escorts, their secret friendship had grown. They stole shy glances across the courtyard, and during prayers Ashar did his best to kneel directly behind her, close enough to catch the scent of the flowers she wore in her hair. When they passed each other in the narrow corridors, there was the inevitable brush of shoulders and sometimes their fingers touched.

And now she was here. Ashar would not face this important day completely alone. She would not stand beside him before the Council of Blessed Sages, but he knew her thoughts and perhaps her prayers would be with him. He sent a small prayer of gratitude to Oum'ilah for this small and wondrous gift.

CHAPTER 5

A gust of wind pelted Drakkor's face with the first drops of rain and blew away his memories. He closed his eyes and lifted his face to the sky. It had been a long time since he had allowed such reminiscence of Dragonfell to linger.

He huddled beneath his cloak beside a fire some distance from the camp. His men roasted rabbits and prepared shelters for the night. None were troubled by the rain.

Drakkor's eyes moved from one man to the next. All but one had crossed the river without incident. The man gone missing had made the mistake of dismounting when his horse panicked in the strongest current and both were swept downstream. No one searched for him.

Those of his men on the far side of the fires were easily seen. Others were silhouettes crossing a blaze of yellow. Sounds of their camaraderie melded with the nickering of horses and floated to him on the swirling wind.

How would they fair in the battle ahead? "Hardly a battle," he mused aloud as if the fire could hear. It would not be the kind of battle any of them expected. Killing an armed man determined to take your life was very different than killing a monk unwilling to fight.

Do any of my men have some measure of compassion secreted away be-neath their ragged beards and boiled leather?

He doubted it. They were bound to him by more than treasure, or pleasures, or a promise of a place in his kingdom to come. Each of his men had sworn an oath, though the ultimate consequence of their vow was beyond anything they truly understood.

There were no punishments nor flagellation in the rites of avowal, but those who joined themselves with Drakkor sealed their oath by repeating the words he had chanted as a boy in the chamber of fire at Oldbones Keep—*"Saleem nostranu 'rosnona se o vasen pusson."* And then they drank his blood. He gripped their hearts and controlled their minds and bound their souls to his. Not because he put riches in their hands and allowed them to satiate their lust, but by some power of darkness they dared not whisper.

Drakkor took the stone of fire from its place beneath his heart and turned it slowly in his fingers. It caught the flame and ignited a thousand tiny fires within. A thousand points of light on a polished wall of black stone. *The walls of Oldbones Keep.* It was hard to imagine it had been so many years since the sorceress of Dragonfell had put the mystical stone into his hand.

His destrier snorted and pawed the rock with the iron on its hooves. The sound stirred a memory that crept up like a creature of the night emerging from its hole to greet the moon.

Age of Kandelaar
Annum 1059
Dominion Dragonfell

The iron shoes of the short-legged horse were a hollow echo on the wooden bridge. The first streaks of yellow light glistened across the inlet of the eastern sea as Drakkor rode through the gates of Oldbones Keep. He was in company with five scarlet-robed votaries of the cult of she-dragon and the man-at-arms who rode with them.

The day of the prophecy had come.

46

The child of no man rides forth to gather that which was lost. And they believe it is I!

His thoughts were sluggish after five days and nights of the "celebration of the chosen": the veneration, the ritual of consecration, the invocation of ancient spells, the feasting, drinking and intoxicating fumes, and, toward the end of it, the tattooing of his body. Drakkor had been in a semiconscious stupor for much of it from exhaustion, exotic herbs, the juice of the poppy, and loss of blood. Through it all, he made certain the stone of fire never left his hand.

He had been awakened the day before by the grating of rusted hinges and the thump of a wooden door. He was sprawled on a hodge-podge of pillows in an upper chamber graced by tall windows. He rolled over and tried to make sense of the noise through the fog in his mind.

A person entered the room, closed the door, and slid the locking timber into place. By the time Drakkor's bleary eyes could focus, the person was standing beside the couch.

It was the sorceress. She was alone. Her manner had changed. She showed little of the fawning adoration of previous days. Instead, she spoke with an urgency that confessed her fears. "You must be swift in finding the missing stones of fire," she said and pointed to the fur-wrapped stone Drakkor held close to his chest. "You must let this one stone speak your mind and guide you to the rest." She balled her fists. "By the will of she-dragon, you are the chosen one. Yours is the hand of might, and you must gather them all, and quickly."

She wrung her hands, then turned and walked to the window. The hooded cowl fell to her shoulders. Drakkor had never seen the full of her face before. *There was a time when she might have been beautiful.* It was a fleeting thought before she spoke again.

"Return swiftly and bring the stones of fire to me, and I will make you prince of Dragonfell." What little mystique remained of her vanished as she bargained like a crone selling trinkets in the market. But her words sank deep inside him like a seed. "Give them to none but me." Her voice was wet with phlegm. She coughed, deep in her throat.

An awful rasping, gurgling hack. "Promise me! My hand alone! I am the one who . . ." She threw a furtive glance across her shoulder as if someone listened in the shadows. "I am the one who is to be—" She stopped and held his eyes a long time.

He saw distrust and fear, and when she spoke again, her voice trembled. "When you place the stones of fire in my hand, I will reward you beyond imagining."

I am the one who is to be . . . The sorceress's unfinished words had teased his imagination all morning. What was it that she had almost revealed? Drakkor knew that which went unsaid was always closer to the truth than words spoken aloud.

The sound of the horses' hooves changed as Drakkor and his cortège left the bridge and turned west on the road that would take them to Black Flower. The warmth of the sun on his back soothed the persistent pain of his wounds.

"Ho," the man-at-arms shouted.

An overturned farm cart blocked the road with its cargo of wooden crates spilled out. The horse and driver were gone. The narrow road cut into the slope that rose steeply on the south; the other side fell away to the water on the north. There was no place to pass.

They had hardly reined their horses in before the bandits fell upon them. They sprang from the rocks on the uphill side of the road. Six of them held swords and cudgels. The hooded monks were the first to fall. The wool of their crimson robes soaked up the blood without a stain.

The man-at-arms reached for his sword, but his weapon did not clear its scabbard before he was also lying in the road with his life gurgling to an end from the slash across his throat. There was no grace nor skill to the killings, just wild bludgeoning with clubs and knives and slashing swords.

The attack happened so swiftly that by the time Drakkor turned his short-legged pony, the monks and man-at-arms were dead or dying and their riderless horses were racing back the way they'd come.

Drakkor dragged his horse's head around, prepared to flee if he could or fight if he could not. To his astonishment, none of the bandits seemed interested in him. *They have no intent to kill me.* The thought came in a puzzling rush of relief, and then misgiving.

The assailants finished their grisly deeds and stood over the murdered men. Blood dripped from their hands and weapons. They made no effort to lift the purses nor take the boots or satchels. They were not bandits. The startling reality hung in the deathly silence.

When the killing was done, all of the men turned to look at Drakkor. Two of the men strode forward. He had seen the smaller man before at Black Flower wharf. He was one of the lowborn sots who scrounged for odd jobs on the waterfront and lived on cheap wine and garbage.

"Well done!" The Peddler's unmistakable voice cracked the stillness. He emerged from hiding like a snake slithering from under a rock. "Load 'em quick now and be done." He scowled at the thugs.

Two of the six hurried to upright the cart while the others dragged the bodies of the dead to where they could be loaded in. The still-hot blood steamed in the cool of the morning.

The Peddler of Souls strode to where Drakkor sat on his horse, wide-eyed and disbelieving. He waved for him to dismount.

"I thought you was never coming out," he said. "Even wondered if maybe they killed you or that old hag twisted your head and got you to thinkin' about breaking our agreement." His guffaw did not hide the venom of his suspicions. The Peddler held out his hand. "I'll be takin' what's mine now." He grinned. Even standing at arm's-length, his breath fouled the air.

Drakkor gripped the leather bag slung around his neck and glanced to his left. The ruffians had finished their vile task and shuffled into an irregular formation behind the Peddler. The man from Black Flower had strolled to the short-legged horse and stood behind Drakkor. He held a club.

"Give it to me!" Peddler of Souls demanded in a frenzied voice.

The smallest of the hooligans wiped his nose with the back of his hand and left a smear of blood across his face. "Do it, boy," he said and raised the blade of the short sword that moments before had sliced through the heart of a man in a scarlet robe.

The Peddler's bony fingers fluttered with impatience, but he chortled softly and was once again his smarmy self. "'Twas our agreement, lad, but you'll get what you deserve, sure enough."

Drakkor slipped the bag from his shoulder and let it dangle by the strap. The Peddler snatched it like a ravenous bird plucking a mouse from a stubble of wheat. His fingers squeezed the leather sack like talons crushing the rodent. He closed his eyes in a gasp of ecstasy, unwound the leather stay, and opened the flap. He reached inside with a trembling hand. He paused, flicked a glance at the boy, then withdrew the bundle from the sack with his fingertips.

His bloodshot eyes were wide with expectation. His lips quivered with unspoken greed. He uncovered the stone and held it in an open palm. The crystal caught the morning sun and cast a dappling of light onto his face. He wrapped his fingers into a fist and clutched his treasure to his heart. He nodded to the man behind Drakkor, who leaped forward as his club came up.

Drakkor saw the Peddler's nod and sensed the movement behind him, but it happened too quickly. He whirled as the cudgel thudded into the side of his head. The blinding flash of white became a sparkle of stars that disappeared into blackness.

———

Drakkor awakened cold and wet on a coil of dirty rope that stank of fish and salt and rot. He was rocking side to side and struggled to open his eyes, but one of them was crusted shut with a scab of blood. The wound on his head was a prickling of needles. He scrubbed the dried blood away with the heel of his hand and looked about.

He was on a ship. A fishing boat from Black Flower by the looks of her. He struggled to his feet against the violent rolling of the deck and gripped the railing. The sky was overcast and gray. There was an awful ache in his belly—hunger, seasickness, or some combination of the two. He'd heard sailors in the taverns at the wharf talk about the heaves. He felt a desperate thirst and wondered how long he had been on board.

There was nothing on the right side of the ship but endless sea. The clouds were the same gray color as the water and merged in the distance without a horizon. Land was visible off the left side, so Drakkor reasoned they were sailing north.

There were a few bearded crewmen at the far end of the deck, but no other passengers that he could see.

"Huh!" The grunt startled him, and he turned around. "I thought ye was a dead one for sure." There was nothing pleasant-looking about the man who spoke to him. He stood steady in spite of the pitching deck. Obviously a seaman. The captain perhaps. "Good of ye not to expire so's I get paid the rest of what's owed. " Whatever he said next was lost in a howling blast of wet wind across the deck that slapped them both. Drakkor fell. The captain hardly moved.

"How did I get here?" Drakkor asked as he struggled to his feet. "And who are you?" he demanded, but the captain turned about and shouted to a sailor wrestling a line.

"Loosen the foresail 'fore it rips away and takes ye with it!"

"Where are you taking me?"

"Ha! Always the innocent! As if ye don't know!"

"I *don't* know." Drakkor's puzzled face was pinched tight.

"Same place as where all them what's begotten the wrath of the Scarlet Council get sent. The dungeons of Falconhead." His scoff turned to a chortle, and he raised his eyebrows. "Less'en of course ye can pay this ole captain a peck more gold than the monks that put ye aboard."

"Monks?"

The seaman nodded. "Hooded brothers of the poor defenseless buggers they say ye slaughtered." The seaman shrugged, unconcerned. "I'll have the boys bring ye a bit of bread and ale," he said as he strode away on the rolling deck as if it were standing still.

The reality of what had happened appeared in Drakkor's head with sudden clarity. The Peddler of Souls and his ruffians had put on the robes of the monks, lied to the captain, and paid him to deliver him as a fugitive to the dungeon at Falconhead.

Drakkor gripped the railing and turned his face to the buffeting winds and blowing spray. The taste of salt increased his ache of hunger. *Why,* he wondered, *did the Peddler pay to lock me away in the dungeons of Falconhead rather than murder me with the monks of Dragonfell?*

He could only conclude that for all his blasphemies and blathering, the Peddler of Souls was an ignorant and superstitious man who dared not kill him on the off chance there was more to the prophecy than he supposed and the boy he betrayed was indeed some child of destiny.

The thought brought a strange surge of hope. He pushed his hand to the wrap of rabbit skin against his hip and laughed out loud. Whatever the myth, whatever the history, whatever the source of the magic and power of the stone of fire, it was his! His fingers fumbled through the soft fur and embraced the stone of fire. He jutted his chin into the wind and inhaled deeply.

The Peddler had betrayed him. Drakkor had assumed he would and laid his plan accordingly. He smiled at how right he had been and how perfect the action he'd taken. He wondered if the greedy fool had discovered yet that he had been outsmarted by a boy. The crystal stone in the leather bag handed to the Peddler had been filched from a statue of she-dragon in the great hall of Oldbones Keep. There was nothing mystical or magical about it.

Drakkor withdrew the stone and held it in his hand. He gripped it tightly and felt the strange fire-and-ice sensation of its power. The words of the prophecy came into his mind as if the sorceress was whispering inside his head. *To rise immortal and reign forever as god and king.*

He had no idea what it meant. He was an uneducated child. What lay behind him was a blur of memory stained with blood. If the prophecy were more than myth and he was somehow a part of it, then what lay before him was a destiny he could not control. And if he was not . . .

He gripped the stone more tightly as the thoughts found a place in his mind. The wind raged and the sea reached up to swallow the ship, but Drakkor felt no fear, and in that moment, he vowed that by the will of she-dragon or the old gods of the tower or by his own strength and cleverness and blood if that is what it took and not the gods at all, he would learn to use the magic of the stone. The words echoed in his head with the howling of the wind: *To reign as king, to rise immortal, to be a god.*

On the morning of the ninth day at sea, as shrouds of mist whirled away to reveal the cliffs of Falconhead, Drakkor slipped over the railing of the foredeck and dropped into the frigid water. He took but one possession: the stone of fire.

———

Drakkor dropped a bundle of sage on the fire. It erupted in a shower of sparks that carried his memories into the night.

It was many years before he had learned what happened to the Peddler of Souls. He had delivered the cart of dead men to the gates of Oldbones Keep and reported to the sorceress that the child of no man had been killed with the monks, the stone of fire stolen from his hand, and his body thrown into the inlet of the eastward sea called Eye of the Skull.

In the days that slowly piled into years, Drakkor liked to imagine the Peddler of Souls fondling his worthless crystal and cursing all gods old and new for his most undeserved misfortune.

CHAPTER 6

The chanting of the temple virgins stopped. Scarfs woven from black silk were draped across Ashar's shoulders and wrapped around his upper arms. Celestine's eyes twinkled as their faces drew close. Her fingers touched his neck.

The daughters of the temple took an end of the silk and, holding it over their heads with both hands, lead Ashar through the portal and into the darkened hallway. As they went under the arch, the melodic chant began again. Master Doyan matched his pace to the cadence and followed seven steps behind.

As a postulant, Ashar had passed the portal every day but had never been allowed beyond. He wondered what marvelous sights and mysterious rituals were hidden in the complex of buildings beyond. The warren of passageways and clutter of structures had been built one upon the other since the time of First Landing, a thousand years before.

The temple itself was the crowning structure of a massive ziggurat. The stepped tower spanned the entire breadth of the ridge. The lowest rampart continued along the sheer face of the granite cliff as if the foundation of the temple was part of the mountain rather than put there by human hands.

It was fashioned after Etemenanki, the temple of the foundation of heaven and earth in the old world that was destroyed in the season of fierce winds. "A reminder," Master Doyan had taught, "lest we forget the foolishness of mortal beings."

Looking north from the center of the outer court, the temple was perfectly framed by the monolithic tower of rock that jutted into the sky. A perpetual mist swirled about the top where the hallowed fane was placed. When the first rays of morning light struck the tower of the temple, it glowed against the purple shadows of the monolith and seemed to be suspended in the air. For those who embraced the tradition of Oum'ilah, God of gods and Creator of All Things, the temple was above the earth.

The virgins of the temple moved to the rhythm of the haunting recitative. The sound rebounded from the sides of the chamber as if the walls themselves were singing with a hundred throbbing voices.

Immersed in the hypnotic sounds and isolated in the darkness, the reality of what was about to happen suddenly fell upon Ashar like a massive stone crushing the breath from his body. He gasped for air and turned in desperation for Master Doyan to save him.

Bonded as they were—master and pupil—the old master reached into Ashar's mind and saw the cloud of darkness that invaded Ashar's soul. A spirit of destruction from the realms of Ahriman sent to prevent him from swearing an oath of devotion to Oum'ilah. Or was it from the realms of she-dragon and the rising chaos of the dark world?

The greatest victory of all is mastery over self, Master Doyan spoke to Ashar's mind.

Ashar knew it was possible for kindred minds to communicate by the power of thought, but he had never experienced it until now. Master Doyan's voice speaking to his mind gave him courage. He recited a maxim from the Codices of the Navigator: "Fear and faith cannot abide. Embrace the one and the other flees." He closed his eyes and focused on a bluish presence surging gently in the center of his head.

He opened the portals of his inner being and passed through the gateway to a place of safety. The darkness gave way to light. Ashar could breathe again.

The temple virgins led him and Master Doyan to the end of the passage. The imposing iron gate blocking the entrance to the inner court swung open, and they stepped into sunlight.

Nothing in Ashar's imagination had prepared him for the wonder of the place. The virgins unraveled the silken ties, bowed reverently, and backed into the shadows of the ornate portico that surrounded the inner court. He knew he shouldn't look at the retreating daughters of the temple, but he couldn't resist. Celestine's hair flowed softly like a river of golden light. At the last moment before she disappeared into shadow, she turned and locked her eyes with his.

Do well, dear friend. Her thought spoke gently in his mind.

Every waking hour of every day for twenty-four seasons had been centered on this day. The lessons, the learning, the teaching and training. The rules, rites, and rituals. Meditation. Removing the barriers between physical reality and the intuitive, mental realms of the supernatural. The discipline of body, mind, and spirit.

"Mastery of self," Master Doyan called it. Demanded it. He taught that self-mastery did not end with acceptance into the order but was an endless pursuit and challenge of life. Today was the day of passage. The cleansing. The anointing. The oath bound by blood. The hope of ultimate investiture. The end of probation. The beginning of being.

Anticipation of the infamous inquisition known to all the postulants had filled Ashar's walking hours and turned his dreams to nightmares. He could hardly believe he had passed and it was behind him. There was still the prolonged and intensive questioning before the Council of Blessed Sages, but he was well prepared. And best of all, Celestine had been selected as a participant in his day of days. At the thought of her, he shivered with delight from the crown of his head to the ends of his toes.

A large robed man who Ashar had never seen before suddenly

appeared. His face was darkened by the shadow of the hooded cowl. The man bowed slightly and beckoned them to follow.

Ashar's imagination of what was hidden behind the walls of the temple was replaced at every turn by the reality of this place. The complexity and beauty was truly wondrous. Whatever he thought he had understood about the ritual of ordination to the brotherhood of priests and Holy Order of Oum'ilah, the reality unfolding surpassed his loftiest expectations.

Master Doyan followed the hooded man, and Ashar followed Master Doyan. Silence was required. Ashar kept his chin down in a well-practiced posture of humility, but his eyes could not be stayed. They flitted up and down and to and fro. He didn't want to miss a nuance of the grandeur. The trio passed through a vaulted chamber. Master Doyan glanced over his shoulder and cast his eyes upward with the hint of a smile. Ashar took the gesture as permission to look up.

What he saw was so stunning that he stopped and turned in a full circle. The legend of the Navigator and the crossing of the great deep was presented in a massive mosaic created from tiny bits of colored glass. The strange vessels. The winds. The waves. The monsters of the deep. And, not to be forgotten, thirteen shining stones lighting the way. He felt light-headed and realized he was holding his breath.

They ascended the one hundred forty-four steps on the outside of each of the first two levels of the ziggurat. They followed their guide along the top of the second level on a terrace made narrow by the wall of the third layer that rose a few feet from the edge. There was no balustrade.

When they reached the face of the east side, the outer wall fell away into the chasm. The width of the terrace was the same, but being a step from death made the walkway seem only half as wide. The fear of falling twisted Ashar's gut like hands wringing water from a cloth.

Fear and faith cannot abide. Fear and faith cannot abide. He chanted the mantra in his mind and added, *Don't look down.* A fundamental discipline. *You are master of your mind where perception is reality.* Master Doyan's voice. So easy to say, so difficult to do. Ashar's eyes were frozen on the river at the bottom of the chasm. It was so far away that the whitecaps of the rapids appeared to be standing still.

His eyes caught a glint of reflected sunlight and movement below a canopy of trees near the river far below. As he stared to see what it was, he was overwhelmed by a rush of vertigo and threw himself against the wall.

He lifted his face to the sun and breathed deeply. *If I do poorly before the council, an impatient Sage might choose to throw me from the tower.* The humor chased his dizziness away. Faith returned, along with the courage to walk the precarious path.

Master Doyan turned left through a cleft in the wall. Ashar stepped forward and followed. Pools of dusty sunlight fell through tall shafts open to the sky. The passage was intermittently blinding white or obscured by black shadow. His eyes could hardly adjust.

"Because I've never had a pupil who memorized the Codices of the Navigator the way you have or known many who understood them better," he said in a whisper, "I believe you deserve to see the chancery."

Ashar had heard that the records of all time were kept in the library of the temple. He had often wondered where it was and whether he might ever be allowed to go there someday.

"You must keep our little detour a secret," Master Doyan said. It was precisely this kind of camaraderie that made him the favorite of all.

Not far in front of them, a passage opened to the right. The man in the hooded vestment was waiting, so Ashar assumed the detour had his blessing.

They entered the passage and descended broad stone steps beneath an arched ceiling that ended at a brighter opening below. The chamber was lit by the amber glow of thirteen windows equally spaced on the walls of an oval room and placed slightly higher than Ashar's head. Stone buttresses supported the high dome of the ceiling. There was a circle of amber glass at the apex with the ensign of the temple.

The room was a hive of priests engaged in a variety of tasks. They were mostly young and of the first order. Conversation was soft. For the number of people moving about the room, the stillness was haunting.

They wore the habiliments of the brotherhood of priests with the sash and emblem designating their order as keepers of the history.

The chamber had the distinctive smell of parchments made of skins. It was strong but not unpleasant. A dozen scribes in isolated cubicles of finely carved wood were writing on thin layers of calfskin vellum. Some had ancient codices propped up on willow stands wrapped in leather for easier transcription. One old man was bent over a thin sheet of hammered copper, etching a copy of an ancient codex using a stylus with a pointed end.

Below the windows was a warren of compartments. Some were empty, but most contained bound codices, scrolls, or histories written on tablets of clay. Two young priests, not much older than Ashar, moved from cavity to cavity methodically removing, cleaning, and replacing the precious records.

"The history of the dominions of Kandelaar," Master Doyan whispered.

"Do the original writings of the Navigator still exist?"

The old master put a silencing finger to his lips, but his eyes sparkled *Yes.*

It was as if Oum'ilah Himself had thrust a hand into Ashar's chest and gripped his heart. *The legend of the Navigator is not an allegory. It really happened! It is not just a story, it is history, and the history is here, and I am about to become part of those privileged to know. To really* know.

Ashar slowly scanned the room, his eyes stopping here and there in wonder. The stories he had heard a hundred times came to life in his imagination. His gaze fell upon a stack of thick shelves accessible only by ladder. They were filled with ranks of clay tablets engraved with cuneiform inscriptions, wedge-shaped impressions dried in the sun. Some tablets appeared to be copper or brass. It was hard to see from where he stood.

Directly below the shelves was a box constructed from thick planks of black hardwood. It was half the height of a man, an arm-span wide, and wrapped with chains. There were several locks of different sizes, each sealed with hardened wax.

The stones of light! The thought pounded in his head. What else could be of such importance? They were *more* than a metaphor, then. *More* than symbols in a tile mosaic.

In his excitement, the words tumbled out before he could stop them. "Is that were they keep the shining stones?" He intended to whisper, but his voice was loud and exuberant. The instant the words crossed his lips, he regretted it. The nearest of the scribes scowled at him.

Master Doyan apologized with a gracious nod and escorted Ashar from the chamber as swiftly as he could.

"I'm sorry," Ashar said. "It just looked like a place where . . . I'm sorry."

The old master quickened his pace. "Not everything is ours to know." Doyan's tone was brusque and unforgiving. "Move quickly. We must reach the circle before the sages arrive."

They crossed an open court and ascended the final level of the ziggurat. The circular staircase was built of hewn stones and was self-supporting. Ashar knew it had been there since the Navigator built the temple almost a thousand years before. He was not sure how he knew. His mind was illuminated in ways he'd never experienced. The higher they climbed, the more refined and curious the workmanship and more elegant the appointments.

They reached the grand chamber of the Council of Blessed Sages. The vestments worn by the men who stood on either side of the double doors identified them as high priests of the highest order. Their faces were covered by substantial beards, grizzled but mostly white. Their expressions were hidden, but their eyes were soft.

"This is where I leave you, Ashar, son of Shalatar."

Ashar had felt such comfort in his teacher's presence it had not occurred to him he would have to take the last few steps of his journey alone.

Doyan smiled softly. "I should not tell you this, but there has not been one like you among us for a long time. You have been blessed with many gifts." He pressed his hand to Ashar's heart and drew him near.

"Fear and faith cannot abide," he whispered. "Remember." He bowed his head slightly and backed away, the gesticulation of respect.

Ashar bowed in a reciprocal show of his affections. Master Doyan had been like a father to him. He rushed forward and threw his arms around his teacher. Though it was a violation of every protocol, Ashar didn't care, and as Master Doyan's arms encircled Ashar's shoulders, he knew that neither did his master.

CHAPTER 7

"Lower! No, no, lower!" the king rasped in a voice that crackled with impatience.

Maharí slid the wad of shredded wood fibers to the small of the king's back and scrubbed in a circular motion. The concubine knew how to pleasure the aged king of Kandelaar.

Orsis-Kublan had lost his appetite for the succulent fat of wild pig in recent times. His obese body had diminished, but the stretch of his skin had not. It drooped in flaccid wrinkles the color of stale milk. His belly protruded, but his body was otherwise thin. With the slightest twist of his torso or the reach of an arm, the bones of his ribs bulged skeletal against his pallid skin.

The king's bath was a sunken pool made of polished marble and accessed by broad steps on two sides. Water spewed from the beak of an enormous peacock carved from marble and clutching a cluster of bloody arrows in its claw. The bottom of the bath was a mosaic of inlaid tile that included the sigil of House Kublan.

The pool was in the center of an opulent oval chamber. The ornate ceiling was supported by twenty columns connected by arches. Each column was carved with thorns winding from the floor to where flowers blossomed in bas-relief to celebrate the accomplishments and exploits of the king. Seven of the pillars were untouched. In spite of his eighty-eight years, Orsis-Kublan refused to accept an end to his reign, his conquests, his greatness, or, as the mists of fear swirled in his head, his mortal life.

The old king lifted a bejeweled chalice. A harem girl hurried to him with a flagon of wine. His hand trembled as she refilled his cup. His thin skin had shriveled from the long soak in hot water. Sunlight streaming through the tall windows struck the chalice and reflected a pattern of golden light onto his face.

A grizzled beard covered his square jaw, and his hair was a tangle of wet curls that covered his head like a blanket of lumpy cotton. His deep-set eyes were the color of charcoal with a hint of brown that glinted in the sunlight. His thick brows had retained much of their original color, but the hair on his body was white with streaks of gray and as prickly as a thistle. The sour droop of his wrinkled mouth spoke of more than the number of years he had lived.

The king savored the aroma of the sweet wine and took a long draught. He closed his eyes and let the soothing sensation of the bath reassure him of his significance. Obscure his fears.

Maharí was an exotic woman with skin the color of mahogany and long black hair. Like all the girls who attended the daily ritual of the king's bath, she wore only a swirl of thin fabric. She glistened with sweat from the steaming heat of the natural spring. A tiny eight-pointed star was tattooed around the dimple of her navel. "The star of morning," she had cooed the first time he touched it. "The star of Venice and emblem of Ianna, the goddess of war and sensual love."

Maharí was the second cousin of Ormmen of House Romagónian. She had come to the harem at Kingsgate eight seasons ago as a token of the delicate alliance with the Peacock Throne. She'd arrived in a grand cortège and was presented to the king in the primitive ritual of the goddess Ianna. She danced for him to the rhythmic chanting of twelve virgins, the symbolic giving of herself to his desires.

The king was in constant attendance by a number of wives and concubines, but he was certain that Maharí alone understood the great burden he carried as king. Where the other women complained, Maharí listened. More than once she had spent a long night with the king in conversation. Only she was allowed such intimacies. Where the other girls were innocent and unskilled, Maharí understood he was a man before he was a king. She alone truly cared for him.

Kublan knew the harem of Kingsgate was more politics than pleasure. Even the women given as his wives had been acquired by negotiations to strengthen alliances rather than any illusion of affection or love.

But there would be no queen ruling beside him on the Peacock Throne. Not even his cherished Maharí. His willingness to share the throne died when the gods of the underworld had swallowed the girl he had loved and wedded in his youth. She was the only queen he would ever acknowledge, the flower of his love and mother of his only son.

There was only one woman in the chamber who was neither wife nor concubine: Tonguelessone, was chosen as the king's nursewoman because of her mutilations. Her tongue had been cut out and her ears punctured. Her ability to share the King's secrets was gone, and her loyalty was never questioned. She often stood in wait where only the most trusted were allowed.

As far as anyone knew, she could neither read nor write, speak nor hear. But the absence of speech and hearing merely sharpened her other senses. What her eyes saw and her fingers touched was etched in memory. She watched and listened and remembered.

"Does that suit you, m'lord?" Maharí cooed close to the king's ear, using both hands to caress his back and belly.

The king squirmed against the pressure of her hand and the touch of her lips on his ear. A king as great and important as he was desired much and deserved everything.

"Ahh," the king sighed as Maharí worked her magic. His breath swirled into the dense steam that hung in the air. He breathed deeply in spite of the discomfort.

The spa at Kingsgate had been built over one of several natural springs. The hot water was filled with salts and minerals. The taste of it was bitter on his tongue, the smell brackish and stinging in his nostrils.

The court physician told Kublan a daily soak in the bitter water and inhaling the briny air insured good health and long life.

Kublan was increasingly preoccupied with both. He was obsessed by the injustice of his own mortality. Did he not reign by the will of the gods? Why would the gods wish to end the reign of their choice vessel? The king's claim to divine appointment had been spoken by so many and so often it had become as true to him as the rising of the sun.

Good health and long life? It was not enough.

He remembered the first time the Raven to the King had whispered in his ear. *Surely a king so great is destined to reign forever. Is it not written in the stars? Do the heavens not speak the mind of the gods? Do they not speak to you in dreams?*

No one knew the name or lineage of the astrologer who had become the Raven to the King. They knew only that he was a stargazer who could see a vision of the king's future manifested in the heavens. Remarkably that vision was always magnificent, filled with wondrous expectations of good things ahead and the affirmation of adoring subjects who blessed the king's name in worshipful tones.

Thus it was that the Raven to the King was increasingly responsible for the troubling problems Kublan wished to ignore, whether petty or profound. In recent days, the rumors of bandits raiding villages had come again, and Kublan could no longer push them aside. He called for his Raven. "By the gods, how dare these dogs defy the Peacock Throne? What do the stars say I must do?" he asked.

"You have a magnificent march of kingsriders for such unpleasant tasks, m'lord," the Raven had said.

"Of course." And with little more than a grunt, Kublan granted the Raven the authority to use his army of kingsriders to crush the bandits and end their petty defiance of the throne.

Those who harbored suspicions of the Raven whispered that he was a charlatan who seduced the aging king with honey-tongued flattery. To them it was not miraculous the Raven always found whatever the king needed to hear when he gazed into the night sky.

Kublan, though, held no such suspicions. "My Raven is the only one who truly understands my greatness. The only one who is truly loyal," he would often say to his other counselors. "It is he and he alone who flies to the heavens and speaks to the stars. My Raven communes with the gods."

Kublan's eyes roamed over his frail and aged body. *Then tell me, Raven, why do the gods wait to spare me?* He closed his eyes. His mind ascended beyond the briny steam, and the vision of the night dream came again.

A messenger from the gods with hair and robes of flowing white, riding on the back of an enormous bird and holding a scroll in his right hand, which chronicled the glorious reign of His Greatness, Orsis-Kublan, Omnipotent Sovereign and King, through endless time . . .

Rough fiber scrubbed across shoulders and scratched beneath his chin. He opened his eyes. *Was it truly a vision?* Kublan knew his enemies scoffed when they heard the rumor circulating through the halls of Kingsgate, hissing their contempt.

He had overheard their whisperings that he was mad. That his dream was a vacuous illusion, nothing more than a stupor of cannabis, wine, and juice of the poppy. Their criticism incited him to anger. The loathing behind their expressions of adoration was a wound in his heart he could not heal and a burden he had to carry. In private moments of despair, he tried to push away the fear that they might be right, but it remained.

Was it not providence that he reign as an immortal king? Yes, yes, the gods agreed! Desperation clogged his thoughts. If it was the will of the gods he be immortal, why must he search for the secrets of endless life? It would come from the gods, would it not? According to legend, Tishpiin had been granted immortality by Ea for saving mankind from destruction in the great deluge.

I have been a savior to my people. Why do the gods wait? Why?

Many years had passed since Kublan had seen the messenger on the white bird. Kublan's body was old and his memory punctured by vacant holes of swirling gray.

He could wait on the gods no longer.

CHAPTER 8

After escaping from the ship at Falconhead, Drakkor wandered alone among the hamlets and villages of the lands northward, from the River of Smoke and Land of Giants.

He was a thief and a vagabond and did whatever was required to survive. He was not afraid to fight, but he knew he must be trained. In a small village north of the volcanic mountain called Dragon's Breath, he befriended a soldier who had once been a member of the king's private guard. He persuaded the old warrior to train him in exchange for his service as the man's squire.

In the years that followed, Drakkor hired out as a mercenary. His dreams were haunted by the prophecy. Every night, he held the stone and sensed the strangeness of it. Every day, he struggled to awaken the magic. Was there truly a power greater than the incessant sense of self that burned with cold heat at his core?

He mastered dialects and language. He traveled as far north as the frozen hamlets of Icenesses. He scoured parchments and queried the soothsayers. He sought knowledge wherever he could find it.

At the Inn of the White Bear in Village Icefell, he met Aáug, son of Stembus, one of the Learned Ones, keepers of stories and purveyors of precepts written in the Book of Wisdom.

Aáug claimed to have a thousand stories stuffed away in his head, and his tellings every night most often lasted into the early hours of morning.

Drakkor thought it impossible for a man to remain upright with more ale than blood in his veins. As dawn approached, following a particularly long night of tellings, Drakkor was about to find a teacher less besotted, but before the words could cross his lips, Aáug started a story about a mighty man and his people who fled the great tower in the time of fierce winds.

Drakkor had never heard of the great tower or the time of fierce winds. He settled in his seat again.

"A thousand years ago," Aáug began. "First People is what they's called by some." He took another draught of ale and used his hands to animate the story of how the First People crossed the vast and endless waters in great boats and battled monsters of the sea, and somehow escaped the jaws of Leviathan. By the time the flagon of ale was empty, Drakkor wondered if Aáug's tales had grown to a great exaggeration. Or if they might be true.

By tradition, every story was a hero's journey of mythical men capable of mighty deeds. Mighty men of whom songs were sung. Massive men who were larger than life. The hero in the story of the perilous voyage of boats was no different. He was known as the Navigator.

"He had thirteen sacred shining stones," Aáug laughed and swirled the last bit of ale at the bottom of his tankard. "Some call 'em stones of fire."

Drakkor's pulse quickened. He narrowed his eyes and inhaled deeply. "Tell me about these stones of fire."

Aáug drank the tankard dry, then wiped his beard with the back of his hand. "Ah, that's what them who don't know the truth might call them, but that's not what they were. They had nothing to do with fire. They were stones that glowed with light and were put into the boats to illuminate the darkness."

Drakkor's own stone shimmered with a strange dark light from time to time, but hardly bright enough to illuminate a vessel. He scoffed in spite of the tingling in his gut. "How does a stone give light?"

Aáug steepled his fingers. "'Cause the stones were touched by the finger of God and glowed with pure white light." He smiled as he leaned toward Drakkor and spoke in a furtive whisper. "Each of them shone like the sun and was endowed with a power unique to itself."

"Each stone had a power different from the others?"

"Yes and no. All the same and each unique." Aáug's words sounded like a riddle.

"What powers did these stones possess? Besides shining with light?"

"No one knows." Aáug's pinched face was a puzzle of wrinkles. "The unique endowment of each stone is long lost and left now to superstition. Some said they could open a portal through time. Others stones was said to have the power to penetrate the minds of men. The oldest of the stories I heard claimed one stone could change a man into a bird and let him soar into the clouds."

"By what sorcery did the ancients access the powers of the stones?"

The wrinkles softened. "Ah. You're not the first to wonder." Aáug scrunched his brows and closed his eyes. "It is said the powers of the stones were wrought by heart and mind. As one believed and thought it to be, so it was." The cadence of his words changed as he recited the stories handed down for generations. "The oldest of the tellings say that when the stones are gathered and returned to the crown from which they were taken, they'll possess the power of life over death. Of regeneration and endless life."

Drakkor gripped the hard lump of his hidden stone. The promise of the prophecy whirled through his head like the fierce winds of the story. For Drakkor, the ancient prophecy was a matrix by which he measured each discovery, myth, or possibility. Or—the thought gave him pause—the *truth* of the stones.

On that day years before at Dragonfell, the sorceress had told him that the stones of fire, forged in the heat of the she-dragon's breath, had gone missing but were never truly lost. A man she called the Voyager had stolen them from the sons of she-dragon when they had risen from the darkness. Surely the Voyager of she-dragon lore was the same as this Navigator in Aáug's story. A shiver scurried through Drakkor's body as the truth washed over him.

The mythos of the voyage of the Navigator and the creation myth of she-dragon were different in all ways but one. They both spoke of mystical stones with the power of regeneration, immortality, and endless life. Stones of fire and stones of light. Was it possible the stories were the same?

However corrupted the legends had become over a thousand years, however dissimilar the stories, Drakkor felt certain the source of them was the same. *Where there is myth, there is history. Where there is history, there is myth.* The thought pounded in his head. *The tellings of two affirms the truth of the one.* The adage was old but always correct.

The stone in the inner pocket of his shirt burned like a hot coal against his chest and sent a shivering wave of cold through his body.

———

The resolve Drakkor made that night at the Inn of the White Bear returned to his mind whenever he held the stone in his hand. He tightened his fingers around its cold fire. The campfire flared in a gust of wind, and his eyes followed the whirl of sparks into the night. He thought of Dragon's Breath and his return from the lands northward. After so many years of wandering and waiting, the plan had come. His path was finally clear. The destiny that had hovered at the edge of darkness for so many years was suddenly a beam of light.

"That which was lost shall be found . . . Gathered in the hand of might . . . Clustered in her claws . . . Rise immortal to rule all flesh and reign forever as god of the world."

The meaning of the prophecy had come like a vision in the night. He would search for the lost stones of fire—each of them endowed with an unique power—and gather them "in the hand of might." Here was his epiphany. *He* must become the "hand of might." He must become king.

As king, he would rule the dominions of Kandelaar. As king, no one could prevent him from finding the missing stones. And as the Blood of the Dragon sitting on the Peacock Throne, the stones of fire would be "clustered in her claws" and then—Drakkor felt a surge of wondrous warmth whenever he allowed the thought—*I will rule all flesh and reign forever as god of the world.*

In the seasons since that night, Drakkor had raided villages, conscripting rogues and miscreants for his army. The peasants' contempt for Kublan made it easy, and Drakkor allowed his men to pillage and plunder as much as they liked. When the time was right, Drakkor would march against the king, but for now the chaos would suffice.

Drakkor needed to redouble his search for the other stones. Each one of them would put him one step closer to the Peacock Throne, one step closer to becoming the "hand of might." And then . . .

He stopped the thought. Fragments of the Navigator's story sounded like a corruption of the prophecy: *That which was lost shall be gathered in the righteous hand by the child of pure blood.*

History is recorded by the victors. Drakkor knew the maxim well. Truth evolved and reality changed from generation to generation. In stealing the stones of fire from she-dragon, "The Navigator" perverted the history, rewrote the story, and corrupted the prophecy to hide the truth of the thievery. Drakkor was certain of it.

He remembered something about an Immortal Crown and the kingdom of light, but they were surely simply details added to the myth when the prophecy was corrupted by the Navigator. He pushed the thought aside.

Drakkor now believed the missing stones—perhaps all of them—were hidden by the priests who lived in the temple atop the Mountain of God. He would know soon enough. He and his army of outlaws were on their way there. His men would surely make the assault more brutal than required, but the punishment for the thieves who stole the stones of fire was more than justified. It was long overdue.

The clanking of a warrior clambering up the hill pulled Drakkor from his reverie.

"By your leave, m'lord," the warrior said as he entered the glow of the fire and genuflected to one knee. It was an honor reserved for kings, not captains.

They think me no more than a king. Drakkor smiled at the man's naiveté and waved him to his feet.

"The outriders have returned. The chatter of the taverns is more than idle rumor. King Kublan has sent a march of kingsriders to find us. A warning has been posted to any who quarter us or refuse to give us up."

Drakkor raised his eyebrows and chuckled softly. "Is that all?" He could see there was more, but the man hesitated.

"His Greatness . . ." The brigand caught himself and spit to cover his slip of tongue. "The swine of a king is offering a poke of gold to any man among us who'll betray you, and he's promised to rid the King's Road of every 'damnable rogue' and"—the man swallowed hard—"by the words of the posting not mine, 'put the head of the bastard of a bandit king on a spike!'"

Drakkor gave an amused scoff. "And to do that the king has finally sent an entire march of his elite kingsriders?"

"Yes, m'lord."

"Finally." Drakkor smiled. "The demented old fool. How many villages have we had to ravage to get the old man's attention?" He smiled and poked the fire with a stick. The flame ignited the feral yellow in his eyes. "Select three of our best to straggle behind. Make sure they leave sufficient signs for the kingsriders to follow." He breathed deeply to savor the plans that pulsed through his head.

His fingers closed around the burning stone hidden beneath his furs. The time had come.

CHAPTER 9

The woman was beautiful and clearly highborn. Her blouse had been ripped away, leaving her shoulders bare. She clutched the tattered silk across her bosom the best she could. A tear in her skirt exposed her bare legs. Her bare feet were torn and bleeding.

She might have been killed by an arrow had Captain Borklore not raised a fist and stayed his archers. Their deadly shafts had been nocked and at full pull moments after the woman had stumbled from a copse of willows and dropped to her knees in the middle of the road.

Captain Borklore shouted for the halt of the kingsriders. His command was echoed to the end of the march. More than a hundred of the king's elite warriors, riding two abreast. Most were mounted on coursers. A few rode destriers. Twenty archers. Forty swordsmen. Twenty warriors with pikes and poles. Another score of men with axes, maces, truncheons, and flails. At the rear, a dozen wranglers with extra horses. At the front, the captain, his officers and bannermen with the coiled viper sigil of kingsriders, House Kublan, and the dominions of Kandelaar.

Kingsriders were intimidating in their appearance and feared in their reputation. Some were sons of nobles or highborns, serving to honor the family name. Some were troubled young men abandoned by their families or caught in crimes and given a choice of prison or service. Whatever a man's past or purpose, it was an honor to ride with the kingsriders and to wield a sword of layered steel in defense of the king, even if it was his Raven who called them to this action.

Borklore dismounted and strode to the woman. He wore a boiled leather breastplate and the iron armor of the kingsriders. An officer's cape of black wool hung from brass couplings and the plume of his helm was feathers of peacock. The lines of his face were hard, but his eyes were kind. His chin had a double cleft from the blow of an ax that left him scarred but had failed to take his life.

The woman reached out to him, and the silk fell away. Her bare skin was the color of fresh cream. Her face glowed in the golden half-light of the setting sun.

A flush of desire surged through the captain at the sight of her. Chivalry pushed the thought away. As he drew closer, he could see bruises on her face and a trickle of blood on her swollen lips. He swirled the black cape from his shoulders and draped it around her. With a look of gratitude, she gathered the thick wool and covered herself.

"What has happened to you, m'lady?" Borklore asked.

"Bandits!" she whispered. "They fell upon us and our company as we traveled the King's Road from Rokclaw."

"What is your name?"

"I am Lady Rordak of House Nógard."

Borklore narrowed his eyes. "House Nógard? I've not heard of it."

"Of the far south, m'lord. A minor house but loyal to His Greatness, Orsis-Kublan, Omnipotent Sovereign and King."

The captain nodded respectfully. "And what of your companions?"

"The bandits killed the men, then put the children and women into wagons and took them to their camp." She sniffled and put fingers to her lips. "The men . . . They . . ." She looked away and began to cry.

Borklore could see the terror of the tragedy on her face.

"I escaped," she continued, swiping at her tears, "but not before . . ." She looked at the captain, then blushed and turned her eyes away again.

Though chivalry was largely lost in the dominions of Kandelaar, men like Borklore still lived by the old code of honor. He tightened his resolve to punish the vile men who had done such a thing.

"Their encampment? Is it bivouac for a night or a place of hiding?"

"There were shelters among the rocks and pens for their horses."

"How far?"

She shrugged and shook her head. "I escaped in the night and ran until I could not go on."

He looked to her bloody, bare feet. "Can you lead us to them?"

She nodded slowly, a veiled look in her eye that might have been fear—or a knowing smile.

His eyes rose from her feet to where her arms crushed the black wool to her bosom. Again, he felt desire, and again, he pushed it aside. He helped the woman to her feet and signaled for an officer to bring a skin of water. Borklore was a decorated captain of kingsriders. He resolved to avenge this woman's honor and rescue her company. He would deliver the heads of these bandits to the king as the Raven had demanded.

He felt euphoric in his sense of duty. He was flush with desire for the woman who trembled in his arms. A soothing voice whispered in his mind. He felt her power over him and felt himself relinquishing his will.

"Horse forward!" he said softly, and a sergeant repeated the order with a barking command, "Horse forward!"

— ▬ —

"Are we getting close?" Borklore scanned the tumult of boulders and walls of stone rising on both sides of the narrow gorge where the woman had led them. The woman rode beside him on a gray courser flecked with brown. It had been more than an hour since they'd found her beaten in the road.

"I ran in the dark until I had no breath and could take the pain of my feet no more," she said. "I hid in the woods and waited for the dawn." She looked at him and held his eyes. "Praise the gods you found me. I hope I may find a way to show you my gratitude."

Borklore flushed, wishing more into her meaning than she intended. "Clearly it is the gods who guided us to gather these brigand bastards." He touched his forehead. "Pray, forgive me, m'lady, for assaulting your gracious ears with such language."

"Wait!" She reined in her horse. Borklore stopped the column. "There!" She pointed to a sizable boulder that had been split open. The break looked like the profile of a human face. "I think . . ." she began, then, listening to something no one else could hear, she raised a silencing finger to her lips. It was impossible for a hundred men and horses to be silent, but the hum of chatter and the rattling of equipment quieted. The sound of hooves from restless horses on rock was all that was left.

The woman slipped from her saddle and walked forward. She motioned for the captain to follow. An officer started to dismount as well, but Borklore stopped him and followed the woman alone.

The canyon narrowed and turned sharply right. A small stream ran against the wall. They waded in knee-deep water for a hundred steps before she stopped and pointed to an opening half a stone's throw ahead.

"Where did they leave the wagons?" Borklore whispered.

"There were no wagons," the woman said.

Borklore furrowed his brow. "You said they put the woman and children in wagons and—"

"Did I?" She laughed and took a few steps forward.

A shiver of inexplicable dread sliced through the captain like a blade of ice. He turned at the rattling behind him.

Four men blocked the passage. They wore rusted iron and scuffed leather. Their helms were mismatched and plumeless. Each stood with an arrow nocked and ready. At such close range the sharpened shafts of steel would pierce Borklore's breastplate, but the arrows were pointed at his face.

One of the bowmen sniggered.

Borklore whirled around. The woman had her hand beneath the black wool cape. Lightning struck, or so it seemed. There was an explosion of light, but it was somehow dark. The eruption of the air racked his body and clouded his mind as if something had siphoned away his very essence. He fell on the rocks and splashed backward through the water on his hands and feet. He stared in terror as the strange dark light retreated into the woman's hand, sucked into the small black stone she held.

Borklore kept an eye on the archers as he scrambled to his feet. They stood motionless, as if nothing had happened. He kept his hand away from the hilt of his sword. He knew the archers would fire at the first sign of aggression. He looked back at the woman in time to see her transformation in the glimmer of dark light. The woman in distress was suddenly a man with skin the color of rusted iron. His face was shaven and scarred by a ragged hollow.

Drakkor closed his fist around the translucent black crystal and slipped it back to its secret pocket. The stone of fire possessed an even greater magic than he'd been told. *Forged in the dragon's breath of fire?* He laughed to himself. So many tales and superstitions, but only one seemed to be the truth. *A working wrought by heart and mind. As one believes and thinks it to be, so it is.*

The source of the power no longer mattered. He held the magic in his hand, and his foot was on the path to a destiny of endless life.

CHAPTER 10

"Shh," Maharí's fingers rubbed the king's temples, then gently covered his eyes and brushed them closed. "Clear your mind, precious one," she murmured. "Let the burdens of your heart and the troubles of your mind rise with the steam and vanish." The pressure of her fingers on his head rose and fell in a soothing massage. "Breathe," she whispered. "Breathe."

The king inhaled slowly. He could feel the heat of her breath on his neck, and he strove to immerse himself in the pleasures of the moment. He was desperate to escape the wretched memories that troubled his waking thoughts and stalked him in dark dreams. He should be full of joy, but the stain of blood would not wash away nor rise with the steam.

━━━

It had been fifty-six years since Orsis-Kublan and his rebel army had dragged King Omnnús-Kahn the Unconquered of House Romagónian from the Peacock Throne and executed him in the village square, ending the six-hundred-year reign of Romagónian kings.

Kublan had killed the king with his own hands, and before the sun had set, he was no longer Orsis the Rebel. He was Orsis-Kublan, His Greatness, Omnipotent Sovereign and King of Kandelaar. He claimed his place on the Peacock Throne with blood still on his hands.

His first decree as king was to order a gathering in the court-yard of Rockmire Keep, the immense castle and stronghold of House Romagónian. All came. His loyal officers and allies. His valiant army of rebels. Dissenters who rallied to his banner of freedom from tyr-anny. Survivors of the royal court of House Romagónian. Soldiers of the dead king who were willing to submit to the sovereignty of House Kublan and the new king of Kandelaar.

To the rebel king's great delight, commoners, peasants, and low-borns also gathered to adore him. Some traveled from great distances. It was an assembly of such numbers and diversity there was nothing that compared in the annals of the dominions of Kandelaar. So great was the assembly that criers were sent among the throng to relay and recite the oration. His speech to the vast assembly was raw and unpol-ished, but the people cheered.

Even with his eyes closed and his mind floating on soothing waves of pleasure, Kublan could still hear their cheering voices.

Kublan had punished the monarch with death for centuries of tyranny under the rule of Romagónian kings. He promised hope and change. An end of cruelty and oppression. A new reign of compassion. Concern for the common man.

The great throng cheered again. Barrels of the best of the aged vin-tage from the cellars of Rockmire Keep were tapped, and wine flowed freely. Bread and fruits were carried in baskets among the throng.

"Gifts of your benevolent king," the couriers cried, and the cheers of the people became a chant that continued into the night. "Orsis! Orsis! Orsis! Savior of the people!"

It was when those words reached his ears that Orsis-Kublan knew he had become more than a man and more than a king.

For a time Orsis-Kublan kept his promises, but over the years, things changed. Including the king. He struggled to unite the great houses and minor dominions, but he could not overcome the hostilities of House Romagónian nor quell the ambitions of those who plotted for the throne.

Four short years later, in annum 1037, Age of Kandelaar, the earth ruptured in a calamitous upheaval, killing thousands of his subjects—and his wife.

The death of his beloved Edoora was a bitter seed that quickly blossomed into resentment, disillusionment, self-pity, and unhappiness. Charity was swallowed by greed, and kindness by callousness. Suspicion replaced compassion, and his faith in the present succumbed to his fear of the future. His mind became soaked in wine and his soul drowned by the pleasure of carnal appetites.

Kublan's decline following Edoora's death also created conflict with his only son.

Tolak grew up the son of a hero. He was raised in the brightness of the idealism that put his father on the Peacock Throne. But when he grew old enough to truly understand, he could see the creeping darkness in his father's disposition.

Tolak pleaded with his father to change. When Kublan did not, Tolak began criticizing his broken promises and his drift toward tyranny. He condemned him for turning a blind eye to both the debaucheries of the highborn and to the suffering of the peasants. Even within the walls of the castle such outspoken criticism was unthinkable, but Tolak went beyond. He was outspoken in his criticisms in the taverns and soon enough in open court.

"Treachery!" Kublan's counselors shouted. "Your son speaks treason. He aspires to the Peacock Throne. He will take your place and cast you into prison. He will burn a pauper upon a pyre and tell the people you have died. And then he will take your life!"

Kublan's great fear of a rebellion came from a simple fact. He was himself a rebel who sat on the throne by treachery.

The rift between Kublan and Tolak became a chasm that neither man seemed able or willing to cross.

In the summer, annum 1066, Age of Kandelaar, a parchment bearing the seal of the king and purportedly written by his hand—though more likely dictated by the Raven to the king—was posted in the markets and copies were sent across the land.

"Witness an extreme act of magnanimity and benevolence by Orsis-Kublan, His Greatness, Omnipotent Sovereign and King.

"Were Tolak not blood of my blood, his body would be torn asunder and his head put on a spike, and when the fowls had finished eating the flesh from his skull, it would be left as a warning to any who agreed with his condemnations or dare revile the great sovereign appointed by the gods to rule over them.

"By royal decree, Tolak, son of Orsis-Kublan, His Greatness, Omnipotent Sovereign and King, is hereby renounced and shall no longer be recognized as the son of the king, neither a prince nor heir to the Peacock Throne. He shall henceforth be banished to the prison at Stókenhold Fortress, where he shall be in exile from the royal house until his death.

"Hereafter, Kadesh-Cor, son of Tolak and grandson of Orsis-Kublan, His Greatness, Omnipotent Sovereign and King, shall be named Baron Magnus of Blackthorn, prince of the North, and heir to the Peacock Throne."

———

"I've not spoken to him since that day," the king mumbled aloud.

"M'lord?" Maharí asked. Her long dark fingers kneaded the knotted muscles of his neck.

"Nor shall I!" The old man coughed at the bitterness caught in his throat. "He is dead to me! Kadesh-Cor is my child. It is my grandson whom I love and trust."

"And he loves you with a loyal heart," Maharí said, leaning down until her lips lay lightly against his ear. "As do I," she whispered.

CHAPTER 11

The woman Borklore had desired only moments before had become a frightful warrior clad in a breastplate and a cloak the color of blood.

Fierce men wearing iron helms and armor appeared from the rocks and stood beside Drakkor. Each of them held a two-handed sword.

In the years following his encounter with the storyteller Aáug, Drakkor gradually unraveled the secrets of the stone he possessed. Quite by accident, he discovered it had the power to blind men's eyes and twist their minds. It demanded an intense concentration of mental prowess, always to the point of pain. It took him a long time to master the mystical power of the stone, but with it gripped tightly in his hand and with an intense focus, he learned to project his mind into the mind of another. Once inside, his thoughts became their thoughts. Over time, he discovered he could also control the visual perception of anyone who looked at him, forcing them to see only what he wished them to see. The price of such power was pain, but for Drakkor, it was a price willingly paid.

Captain Borklore swayed on his feet. Drakkor held the man's eyes, his smile cold. He knew about the captain, his strengths and his weaknesses. One of Drakkor's outlaws had once been Borklore's soldier and told Drakkor the captain was a man of such pious chivalry that he would do anything to avenge a woman violated by villainous rogues.

His strength is also his weakness. The thought amused him.

"By the gods, what manner of evil is this?" the captain gasped from exertion and shock.

"What is evil to one is a blessing to another," Drakkor replied.

Borklore stiffened. "I command you in the name of the king to retreat and stand aside."

A whisper of amusement rippled among Drakkor's men. He laughed aloud.

"So the tavern gossip is true?" Drakkor raised an eyebrow and recited the disparaging adage. "The courage of a kingsrider is only surpassed by his arrogance, and his arrogance only by his ignorance."

"You are a fool! Do you imagine these few can withstand a hundred of the king's finest warriors? I have but to cry out and there will not be enough left of you or your loathsome band for the birds to fill their bellies."

"Perhaps an arrow will puncture your throat before such a cry can be made."

"Give me leave to do it now, Raja," the smallest of the archers said, his bow drawn, an arrow aimed at the captain's throat.

The captain jutted his chin forward as if daring the archer to release. "Raja? He calls you a king. Ha! You are a rogue and a thief!"

"He is Drakkor, Blood of the Dragon," the archer hissed and pushed the point of the arrow into Borklore's neck. It punctured the skin, drawing a rivulet of blood.

"Blood of the Dragon!" Borklore spat. "A scum who aspires to greatness by adorning himself with a meaningless title." His words dripped with contempt. "More likely the blood of the pig!" He was about to say more, but another jab of the arrow forced him to swallow his words.

"He is the future king," the archer chided. "Say, 'Hail, lord prince and future king.'" The archer tightened his grip on the bow and gouged the arrow deeper into the captain's neck.

Borklore choked and dropped to his knees to keep the arrow from puncturing his neck any deeper. He spat again, defiant. "Do as you will to me. You are all dead men!"

Becoming a commander in the king's elite army of kingsriders required courage. Death rode with them on every campaign. It was not *if* they would die in battle, it was *when* and *where* and *by what circumstance.* Being killed by an arrow at point-blank range with a hundred armed kingsriders a shout away was not a death that inspired songs to be written and tales to be told. Courage challenged death. It didn't die on its knees.

Drakkor signaled the archers, and they lowered their bows. He picked up Borklore's black wool cape and laid it across the captain's shoulders. "Have you no curiosity, Captain? Do you not wonder why you are yet alive?"

———

Drakkor stood on a ledge of rock the height of a horse's head above the floor of the narrow canyon. The kingsriders were assembled below him.

An archer had shot an arrow into the midst of the waiting march with a parchment and feathers from the plume of Borklore's helm. The message promised no harm if they would leave their horses and come afoot into the canyon to parlay with the bandits. If they did not comply, their captain would be killed at sundown.

Borklore knelt on the rocks at Drakkor's feet. His face was close to Drakkor's boots. He was stripped to the waist with his hands tied behind his back and tethered to his feet. The archers stood in a semicircle behind him with their arrows pointed at his head, heart, and groin. Warriors were on either side with double-handed swords.

"Again!" the little archer said. "Go on! Do it again!"

The captain dragged his tongue across the dusty leather of Drakkor's boot.

The air hung heavy with hate. Murmurs of outrage from the

kingsriders over the humiliating treatment of their commander rever-berated from the walls. The sun was going down. A streak of golden light slipped below the scud of clouds that hovered over the mountains of Oum'ilah and fell on Drakkor's back. The flowing red of his cloak rippled in the breeze like a flame.

"I am Drakkor, Blood of the Dragon," he said, his voice forceful but quiet. "Hear me well, noble riders of the king. You have come to kill me and these good men whom I have sworn to protect. I have been cursed by your king, but he is the one the gods should damn!"

A rattling protest of anger and contempt erupted. The kingsriders had kept their weapons, and despite Drakkor's warning, some drew their blades.

The archers tightened their pull and moved closer to the captain.

"Stand easy!" Borklore shouted. "Stand easy." His voice trembled. His tongue flicked across his lower lip, still smudged with the dirt of Drakkor's boot. Courage toasted by a tankard of ale in the tavern was very different from the courage it took to kneel in front of your men and lick the boots of your enemy.

"You think me your enemy, but you are wrong. The king is your enemy!" Drakkor bellowed. "He entices you with flattering words, but he cares nothing for you. He knows nothing about you—who you are or where you came from or what matters in your lives. Each of you is a man equal to your king, but you lack the courage to believe. You are persuaded that what you do here is noble and honorable, but think on this! You who chose to die this night in this desolate place will not be remembered by your king or your captain or any man. The birds will eat your flesh, and the dogs will find your bones, and there will be no songs of valor or poems of bravery. It will be as though you never lived."

The threat of death settled over them like darkness stumbling into the edge of night.

"I am not your enemy," Drakkor repeated. "You believe only what you have been told. I do not wish to take your lives. I wish you to live as free men, as I am free. As my men are free. I wish for you a new world, patterned after the world of ancient days."

A buzz of contention erupted like a hive of black wasps as reluctant voices collided with hard-line loyalists.

"The time of changing has come," Drakkor continued. His hand rested on the hidden stone of fire. "The time of the prophecy is here, when the wrath of the old gods shall sweep the earth and the time of kings will be done away with. We shall take their royal bread and leave them crusts. We shall restore the ancient ways, and men such as you shall take your rightful place, not as servants or soldiers, but as princes of glory in the splendors of the earth and the pleasures of the flesh."

Drakkor allowed the words to hang in the darkening gloom. He reached down to where the captain knelt. He gripped him by a fistful of dark hair and pulled his chin up. The rattle and commotion fell silent. The only sound was the faint shuffling of the horses below and the eerie screech of blood bats emerging at the trailing edge of twilight.

Drakkor spoke to Borklore in a hoarse whisper. "I do not wish to spill your blood. I wish for you and your kingsriders to join me and wield your swords in the coming kingdom of promise, the kingdom of prophecy, where there is no wrong, and men like these shall never die." Then, turning to the men, he raised his voice. "You who vow to stand with us and swear the ancient blood oath shall be given our great secret, the fruits of the sacred tree, and the power to be as the gods."

The murmuring stopped. The rattling of arms quieted, and all but a few kingsriders stood spellbound by the promise and the strange power the man held over them.

Drakkor tightened his grip on the captain's hair until the man winced. "Let it begin with you, noble captain," he said, then shouted again to the men. "Is your captain a man of honor and courage? A man of intelligence and wisdom?"

The answers tumbled out in a cacophony of praise and adulation. The captain's eyes were hopeful as Drakkor twisted his head and forced him to face his men.

"And will you spare your blood and follow him into the kingdom we must make anew?"

"No!" the captain screamed before any of his men could respond.

"Do not listen! He is a liar, a sorcerer, the seed of evil. Kill him. I command you in the name of the king—kill them all!"

The sound of swords sliding from their scabbards, mauls taken up, and pikes swiveling forward sounded like the pelting of ice driven into iron by the fierceness of the wind. Loud as it was, the sound of it was swallowed by the bawling rage of men who began yelling to bolster their courage. Then it stopped.

A hundred shocking gasps of disbelief were as a single breath. Every man saw it at the same time.

Drakkor seized a great sword and in a single slash severed the captain's head from his body. It thumped to the dirt and wobbled to the feet of a kingsrider about to charge. The man stepped back in shock. As if the thump of the captain's head was a signal, a rain of flaming arrows ignited the darkening sky. Drakkor's archers aimed for any unprotected part of the kingsriders' bodies—legs, arms, necks, and faces.

Flaming arrows left a trail of burning oil. Wounded men were set on fire. Men collided in confusion, dropped their weapons, and floundered to escape the deadly pikes and the hail of fire.

Taking out the archers was the kingsriders' only hope, but they dared not stand in one place long enough to take aim. Those of the king's archers who stood steady to draw a bead were struck by arrows from the heights. Drakkor's bowmen were concealed in the cracks and crags of the cliffs and hidden by the looming darkness.

Drakkor's swordsmen killed those few who escaped the fusillade of arrows and tried to climb the rocks.

Drakkor returned to his ledge above the fray, raising a flaming arrow high in his hand. He shouted with a voice of thunder. "I can spare your lives!" The flame illuminated half his face; the other half merged with the darkness. The remnant of his torture at the hand of the sorceress so many years before was now a black hole of shadow on his face.

"Stand with us and live," he said, raising his voice above the sounds of battle. "Cross that line and be free." He pointed to an open area below.

The first kingsrider to surrender was a badly burned swordsman with the broken shaft of an arrow in his arm. He dragged his sword with his wounded arm. When he reached Drakkor, he looked up and pounded a fist across his heart. The salute of loyalty.

"I am Lliam Rejeff. My sword is yours." The kingsrider bowed his head and took his place as a conscript in the army of the Blood of the Dragon.

The battle turned as others surrendered. A few paused on their knees beside their wounded comrades, but more of them simply stepped over the smoking bodies of the dead and laid down their swords. An officer grabbed a man to stop him from such treachery, but another kingsrider killed him with a short sword and joined those turning traitor to the king.

Drakkor called for his archers to climb down and sent a runner for the horses. Of the entire march of kingsriders, more than half were dead or would be dead by morning from their wounds. Thirty-one pledged their swords to Drakkor.

Five refused to surrender. They were dragged forward one by one, forced to their knees by the archers and beheaded by Drakkor. As the fourth of the loyal kingsriders was dragged forward and pushed to his knees, the horses arrived. In the commotion, the last of the kingsriders, an archer named Ablon, sprang to the back of a horse and whirled its head about. The courser lunged forward with the archer low on its neck.

He was little more than a dark shape racing in the failing light, but as he was about to disappear behind the canyon wall, an arrow slammed into his neck.

Drakkor looked to see which of his men had made the remarkable shot. None of them had. The commander of the king's archer had already drawn his bow with his second arrow nocked when the horse and its fatally wounded rider disappeared from view.

"Meshum Tirbodh, m'lord," the archer said and pounded a fist across his heart.

Drakkor smiled. His army had doubled in size in the space of an hour.

He swept his gaze from one man to the next, locking eyes with each one. The air was thick with the smell of death. Satisfied at last, he slipped a short knife from its scabbard and dragged the blade across his hand. Blood filled the wound. "Those who would follow me, step forward and swear an oath by taking my blood into your bodies."

"And they who will not swear the oath?" his swordsman asked.

Drakkor answered by rolling Borklore's head face up with the toe of his boot.

CHAPTER 12

The high priest opened the doors. The man standing under the arch was the largest human being Ashar had ever seen. As a child, in the days before he was left at the temple, his mother told him stories about the giants who lived in the north and rode on the backs of monsters.

I never imagined giants were real. Are giants even human? Stop! Concentrate!

The giant gestured, and Ashar followed the enormous man into the room. It took a moment for his eyes to adjust from the brightness of the open court to the gloomy darkness of the chamber, and he stumbled on the steps. The giant gripped his arm to steady him. His fingers went all the way around Ashar's bicep. The width of his hand covered all of Ashar's upper arm.

If there are giants, what then of monsters?

The doors closed behind him. Ashar stood at the edge of a new life.

There were no windows. The chamber was illuminated by thirteen candelabras fastened to the walls. Each was a pyramid of double-wicked candles. He was ushered to the center of the room. The floor was concave to ensure that the head of the person appearing before the Council of Blessed Sages was lower than the shortest among them.

Ashar knew that some of them were very short. He had never met Blessed Sage Kurgaan but had seen him about the grounds and knew he was a Mankin.

The Mankins were an indigenous tribe that occupied an isolated finger of land that stretched into the sea between the fjord of Akeshen and the waters of Dragon Deep. They weren't dwarfs like the indigenous clans of Summercross or the legendary imps who inhabited the boroughs of Wug. They were just little people, with the exception of their heads, which seemed disproportionately large. Mankins stayed mostly to themselves except when they crossed the fjord of Dragon Deep to mine bluestone in the pits of desolation.

Ashar stood in the shallow pit and closed his eyes. He tried to assure himself the inquisition had ended, but standing there he wasn't so sure. Was Master Doyan certain there was nothing left but the recitation of his genealogies to the time of First Landing? He searched for the bluish essence at the center of his soul and breathed deeply to find calm.

He understood that any one of the sages could "excuse" a candidate at any time without explanation. Ashar was amused that such a gentle word actually meant "expelled." He thought of all the more appropriate words they might have used—*dismissed, thrown out, humiliated.* If any of the sages arose and left the chamber, the ritual was ended and the candidate was rejected. How he wished Master Doyan was still at his side.

Ashar had memorized his genealogy perfectly. For the first time since beginning his cleansing fast two days before, he allowed himself to think beyond this moment. If he did not expire from the sheer gravitas of the ordeal, he would be taken to the high priests where he would be given the ritual bath and anointed with oil of the sacred blackthorn, then dressed in white and taken to the Oracle for the oath in the holy sanctum.

And perhaps see the shining stones of light? Ashar pushed the thought away as his eyes adjusted to the dimness. Surrounding the circle were thirteen wooden chairs, large and carved with elaborate designs. The arms were thickly padded, and the broad seats were piled with cushions adorned with silk embroidery. The high backs were made of thirteen spindles that narrowed at the top and were crowned by a wide rail that curved side to side like a scroll. The chairs were empty.

Like thrones of ancient kings, Ashar thought. His notion of kings' thrones came from the legendary tales of the Navigator, of tales of kings and captivity. The fall of the great tower. Escape into the wilderness. The prophecy. For a long period there had been no kings in the dominions of Kandelaar. No kings. No thrones. No tyranny. That changed with the rise of darkness.

At first glance the magnificent chairs all seemed to be the same, but as Ashar looked closer, he could see the ornate carvings on each was unique—with one exception. A symbol carved into the scroll across the top rail was the same on every chair: a strange vessel in the midst of a tumultuous sea within a circle of radiating light.

The Council of Blessed Sages was a remnant of the original order of governance established by the Navigator. In the generations following the First Landing, the dominions of Kandelaar were ruled by wise and learned men who were chosen by the voice of the people to represent each province. They sat in council, upholding a sacred pledge to look after the interests of the common good. The council looked to the Oracle for guidance. The Oracle was the keeper of the Way of the Navigator, protector of the hallowed fane, and guardian of the shining stones of light.

The ages without kings had been a time of peace and equality. People had all things in common, and there were no poor among them. It was a time of enlightenment. Some said it had been called the kingdom of light.

Then evil came, and chaos swept over the land like a whirlwind of fire. The people abandoned the Way of the Navigator, men proclaiming themselves kings arose, and the dominions were divided one against the other. The governance of the council shrank to the village of Candella and the peninsula of the holy mountain. During the years of chaos, it became the last bastion of believers and a refuge for pilgrims.

The Sodality of Priests of Oum'ilah clung to the traditions of the Way of the Navigator and preserving the ancient writings lest the history be forgotten.

The sound of heavy doors opening wrenched Ashar's attention back to the present. A shiver scurried down his spine like a spider caught in his tunic. Sages entered the chamber through doors behind the chairs. Ashar turned in a slow circle as the aged quorum shuffled forward and settled into their places. To his surprise, there were only eight of them. Five of the chairs remained empty. A glimmer of what must have been.

All but one of the sages was old, and Ashar wondered if any of them had come there as boys with the highest of all high priests known only as the Oracle. The Oracle was said to have lived four hundred and sixteen seasons.

If there really is such a person. Ashar had never seen the Oracle but immediately regretted the speculation. *Why do such prickles of doubt trouble me?* he wondered. *Why here and now?*

The years of the sages were not known, but the length of their lives was written in the wrinkles, scars, and blemishes of age on their cheeks. Wisdom glimmered in their dark eyes, sunken in shadow and rimmed with drooping skin. The dominion of their birth was evident in the color of their skin, which, for most of them, had long since turned to leather.

Sage Kurgaan, the Mankin, had a hoary head too big for his body and a face the color of old ivory.

Sage Ahmose was a Plucian whose ancestor had made the great crossing. His swarthy face seemed even darker surrounded by his white hair and beard.

Ashar was so accustomed to the monotony of priestly habiliments, he was surprised to see that each Sage wore some semblance of the traditional costumes of his province.

Sage Batukhan was the most elegant. He wore a long coat made of red silk and trimmed in a border embroidered with black and shades of gray. The collar was open in front but stood straight and encircled his neck to the bottom of his ears.

Sage FarzAn wore layers of elaborate robes. The outer layer was wool adorned with appliqué. The emblems reminded Ashar of the curious symbols etched on the stone wall south of the temple court. His turban was a braid of linen and white leather and was wrapped about his hoary head. His chin was covered by an enormous charcoal-colored beard with streaks of silver. His face was long and narrow, as if the earth had pulled him closer over the many seasons of his life.

Looking into their eyes was like gazing into a tunnel of eternity. Ashar could not look away. He hoped to see a champion. An ally. A glimmer of hope. A hint of a smile. He saw none. It wasn't entirely unexpected, and yet, as he stared into the austere faces gazing down at him, he felt deep affection: he for them whose lives were given to a higher consciousness; they for him in ways he could not describe. It was a joyous, liberating feeling. A wave of confidence. *Fear and faith cannot abide.* He took a deep breath, and the trembling in his knees stopped.

"Who is it that comes before us?" A voice came from behind. Formal. Demanding. "Speak."

Ashar turned to face Sage Hakheem, who had spoken. His headpiece was disheveled. His thick eyebrows were the color of lava, and though they obscured his dark eyes, there was a spark of light visible in the blacks of them.

Ashar extended his hands and bowed from the waist. He had practiced it a thousand times. He stretched his spine to perfect posture. "I am Ashar, son of Shalatar," he said, his voice filling the chamber.

As the recitation of his lineage began, he pivoted in a slow circle, facing each Sage in turn. He returned each penetrating stare with unblinking eyes. He smiled to manifest confidence, but carefully lest he appear immodest. He drew strength from the affection he could feel from the sages.

He inhaled deeply and began.

"Shalatar was the son of Ilim. Ilim was the son of Worm. Worm was the son of Issens. Issens was the son of Syn. Syn was the son of Corus. Corus was the son of Kotar. Kotar was the son of Qaqos. Qaqos was the son of Tsak."

As he spoke the names of his ancestors, he felt a curious welling of emotion in his heart, a sense of peace he'd never quite experienced before. As he pronounced each name, he felt as if those whose blood he bore were present in the room, whispering their names to him. The voices were so real that, when he glanced about, he fully expected to see them standing near. But he saw no one, and a shudder passed through him. He felt outside of himself, as if other forces were governing his movements, his memory, his speech. He was filled with a calm and confident humility. He abandoned himself to the sensations.

"Tsak was the son of Izek. Izek was the son of Ashar, whose name I bear . . ."

A disagreeable murmur rippled its way around the circle. The cadence of the recitation was an important part of the tradition. A lapse of memory, a break in cadence, a cough, or crack of the voice were thought to bring shame and disrespect to one's ancestors.

" . . . but the lineage of Ashar as preserved by our oral tradition is not true, and I . . ."

What is happening? Ashar was overwhelmed by a sudden sense of dread. How had such a thought entered his head? How had it spilled from his tongue? He shook the feeling away and tried to resume, but a power beyond himself compelled him to speak the words flooding into his mind.

"By your patience, gracious masters. The tradition of my lineage is not correct. I cannot speak it." Ashar heard the words coming from his mouth, and though it sounded like his voice, he had no idea what he was saying or why. The words had certainly not been part of his carefully memorized genealogy.

The powerful feelings surging within him were putting words into his mind with clarity. He gasped for breath and struggled to regain control. He scanned the circle of old faces, nearly all of which were now twisted in shock and incredulity. Only Sage Kurgaan seemed amused.

Sage Hakheem floundered to his feet on rickety legs. Displeasure turned his face into a spiderweb of cracks. *"Lano reli' ono muanoese,"* the old man barked at the boy in the ancient tongue and wagged a scolding finger.

Ashar stopped breathing. *What madness is this? I have failed.* He inhaled deeply to thwart the dizziness that suddenly rushed over him. *Fear and faith cannot abide.* The story of his ancient ancestors appeared in his mind as if it had always been there, hidden by a gossamer veil that was now being lifted away. The telling of it came with a trembling, but it could not be constrained. "Izek was the son of Ashar—but Ashar was abandoned. He was found and raised by Krolin, and thus the bloodline was broken and the lineage askew."

Most of the old men rose from their chairs. They contended both in disapproval and curiosity. Sage Ahmose started for the doors. "You are excused, Ashar, son of Shalatar," he said over his shoulder. The tone of his voice made it clear that *excused* meant *rejected*.

The fire ignited in Ashar's chest. The light in his mind grew brighter. Foreboding pounded in his head. He raised his voice above the commotion.

"Ashar was *not* the son of Krolin! He was the son of Nanesh."

Sage Ahmose turned in astonishment.

"Nanesh was the son of Faron. Faron was the son of Palan. Palan was the son of Joram!" The final name pierced the clamor like the bell of the temple. In the silence, the air seemed to thicken. The sages stared at Ashar, transfixed.

"And Joram was the son of—"

"Stop!" Sage Hakheem cried.

The giant stepped forward and lifted Ashar from the center of the circle with one hand and started for the door.

Some of the sages were yelling, and their words jabbed like sticks.

"The attestation of one's lineage is a sacred trust!"

"To lie to the council about your blood is to blaspheme!"

"There are worse punishments than being expelled!"

"Please," Ashar said as he squirmed in the giant's grip. The massive hand let him go, and he fell to his knees. "Would that I had never spoken the words, gracious masters, but we are taught to listen to the voices that come with light into our minds. I dare not forswear the truth of these sayings." He kept his eyes on the floor. His body trembled, but his mind was clear and his resolve certain.

The murmuring began again.

"We demand that you renounce your claim to the lineage of Joram." Sage Hakheem leaned down and gathered a fistful of Ashar's robe. The deep furrows between his eyes were so pinched his thick brows quivered.

Ashar raised his voice above the tumult. "Enlightenment of heart is greater than knowledge of mind." It was a familiar tenet of Master Doyan.

"What evil has enticed you to say such things?" Sage Hakheem demanded, pushing Ashar away.

"My heart is contrite, but I speak the words pounding there." He touched his chest. "You may do with me as you like, but I beg you to bring Master Doyan to help me explain—"

"Do you not understand what you claim?" Sage Hakheem demanded.

Ashar did not. He searched their faces for an answer but found nothing.

"I am Ashar, son of Shalatar. Shalatar is a distant son of Joram." In that moment of calm, clarity came. He rose slowly from the floor as the truth settled in his mind, astounding him even more than the sages who gasped for breath.

He swallowed hard. "Joram is son of the Navigator—and I am of his blood!"

CHAPTER 13

The castle of Kingsgate came into view. The peasant whipped the rump of his scraggy horse with a willow, and the two-wheeled cart lurched forward as the weary beast hurried to a trot. The road sloped down the ring fault of an extinct volcano, which rose from the spit of land where the fjord of Akeshen divided the bay into long, narrow fingers. Only a few had ever sailed the entire length of the fjord; tradition claimed it led to the great deep that ran westward to the edge of the world.

The walls on the seaward side of the crater had eroded away, leaving a horseshoe-shaped bowl. Landward, the valley was surrounded by ragged mountains with peaks so high they held snow into early summer. In recent times, the fierce winters had crowned the mountains with ice as late as Frog Moon of Aru in season Res S'atti.

Seven hundred years ago, the fortress of Akeshen had been erected on a dome of hardened lava. Named for the ancient fjord, Akeshen now lay in crumbled ruins around the base of the glimmering new Kingsgate castle. The edifice was not yet finished, but rose from the broken ruins like a magnificent bird emerging from the broken shell of a stone egg.

In annum 1025, the rebel king, as he was known back then, began the construction of a new castle that would not only be the home of the Peacock Throne but also the grandest citadel ever built, a monument to His Greatness, Orsis-Kublan.

The castle at Kingsgate was where Kublan would live and rule. Upon his death, it would become a mausoleum where he would remain in glorious remembrance forever.

The taverns along the King's Road were rife with rumors about the king's obsession with death. "A sickness in his mind and growing madness," some dared whisper when deep into their cups. "Kublan's tomb," some called the monolithic castle endlessly under construction.

That was before the vision. Before the gods told the king he was destined for immortality.

It had been sixty-three years since construction had begun, and Kingsgate was still unfinished. Even so, it was an imposing fortress of startling beauty. The foundations were the colossal stones of the old fortress of Akeshen. The walls and towers were made of white granite brought by boats from the quarry on the Isle of Windshore.

The outer walls were twice the height of any other castle. The inner walls were covered with a mixture of crushed quartz, bluestone, glass, and plaster that caused the walls to glimmer when touched by sun or flame. Their faces were decorated by fluted pilasters crowned with ornate entablatures with the sigil of House Kublan in bold relief: an angry peacock clutching arrows that dripped blood.

Twelve slender towers soared above the battlement. Each was a different height and crowned by a diminishing number of pinnacles until the upmost held only one. It pierced the clouds. Viewed as a whole, the spires looked like a stairway ascending into the heavens.

—-—

The grating of the iron rims on gravel heightened the farmer's angst. He twisted on the seat and looked over his shoulder. It was hardly the first time. He had glanced back with dread a dozen times since his ordeal began.

The kingsrider lay in a pool of his own blood on the flatbed of the cart, the broken shaft of an arrow protruding from the back of his neck. Whether his movement was caused by the jostling of the cart or from the glimmer of life left in his body, the farmer could not be sure.

The farmer and his grown son had found the wounded kingsrider lying in a swale beside the road west of Village Nellaf. The warrior's destrier was standing over him, a thick stain of blood running from its saddle, across its shoulders, and down its legs. Sweat from what must have been a desperate ride was lathered to a sticky froth.

"The king," the injured kingsrider had gasped. "Take me to . . ." His words gargled in the blood of his throat.

"Leave him be," the son advised his father in a low voice. "No good'll come of anything to do with the madman on the king's chair."

"Help me!" the kingsrider begged.

The farmer leaned down. The warrior gripped his shirt with a weak fist. His words came in short bursts. "The king . . . you must . . . warn . . . so many dead . . . recompense."

Recompense was the only word the farmer heard. The thought of coin filled his head.

"Don't you go being no fool for the king!" his son said.

"Are we fools not to accept this good providence?" the farmer asked. "One fellow's bad luck 'tis another fellow's fortune." It was an old saying, oft quoted to salve a conscience when snatching an advantage. "Are we not deservin'? And what if he's right and they'd thank us with recompense?"

They argued briefly before the father persuaded his son to seize what the gods had given, "Lest we offend them," he said. They struggled to lift the fallen kingsrider and roll him into the cart. He lost consciousness, which was just as well.

"Fetch his horse and tie it behind," the farmer said.

"I say we keep the horse."

"Now *you* are thinkin' like a fool."

"The man was fallen. His horse must'a surely ran away," the son said and raised his eyebrows. "Wouldn't want to offend the gods now."

Before his father could speak, the son gathered the horse and started for the village. The farmer watched him go, his face twisted with conflict. *But then . . . 'tis a fine horse, and my own is near its end.* He turned the cart around and headed toward the fork that lead to Kingsgate.

The dread of what might befall him was overpowered by a single word: *recompense*. He said it again in his mind. He wasn't being greedy. It wasn't his idea. The king's warrior was the one who had said it.

But what if he's dead, and I deliver a corpse to the king? Shall I be blamed? The farmer shuddered at the thought and urged his horse forward with a willow across its croup.

The edifice of His Greatness, Orsis-Kublan, Omnipotent Sovereign and King of Kandelaar, loomed before him. The monolithic stones flanking the outer gate were being carved with his image. *Shrine to a mad king,* the farmer thought, and his son's warning was a chill at the nape of his neck in spite of the sun on his neck. The closer he got to the castle, the greater his fear. No recompense or praise was worth the king's wrath. *What good is coin in the hand of a dead man?* Some of the folks in village Nellaf had learned that lesson often enough.

He suddenly came to his senses and looked for a wide spot in the narrow road to turn the cart around. In that very moment, three kings-riders rode into view from around the bend in the road and galloped toward him.

"Hold your place in the name of the king!" one shouted as they drew near.

The farmer pulled up hard and stopped the cart. The pounding of the heavy iron hooves approaching matched the pounding in the peasant's chest, and he knew he had made a terrible mistake.

CHAPTER 14

The Oracle sat on a wooden bench in the archway of the temple porch that looked eastward over the precipice. It offered a breathtaking view across the plains of Mordan north of the Narrows to the inland sea of Leviathan Deeps.

The porch was an octagon and open on all sides. Thirteen posts supported its graceful archways. The roof cantilevered five cubitums over the posts. The floor was white and black, inlaid marble, and extended under the arches to a spacious patio.

Colossal squares of silk were suspended as shade against the sun. The harsh light of midday was a shadowless glow. Numerous plants, trees, and flowers in clay pots transformed the patio into a garden. The air hummed with bees that buzzed from blossom to bloom and flower to floret before returning their sweet treasure to man-made hives.

The humming filled Ashar's head, and his thoughts wandered. He had been taught that bees were sacred creatures because they had been brought across the great sea by the Navigator. The emblem of the bee adorned the robes of the blessed sages and was graven on the walls of the temple.

Ashar blinked the thoughts away and forced himself to focus on the moment. He stood at the center of the patio with the giant, Rorekk Breakstone. The sages stood in a half circle behind him. The Oracle studied the boy with a kindly curiosity.

If what Ashar learned as a postulant was true, the man sitting in the shade was the oldest human being in Kandelaar. Everything about him was old, yet in a curious way he seemed young. Unlike the masters of the council with their woolly heads and beards of fleece, the Oracle's hair was short and he was clean-shaven.

The Oracle shifted on the bench as if to rise. Two temple virgins appeared and moved quickly to help him to his feet. Ashar had not seen the girls in waiting. When they appeared, his heart beat faster, but neither girl was Celestine. One of the daughters of the temple handed the Oracle his staff, a twisted length of wood with carvings along the length of it.

The old man fluttered his fingers, and the second girl handed Ashar a brass goblet filled with peach nectar. He bowed his head to the Oracle and held the cup aloft in ritual gratitude to Oum'ilah, God of gods and Creator of All Things.

The nectar was thick and sweet, and it renewed his vigor. It ended the cleansing fast but hardly in the way he had imagined. He savored the last drops and wished they'd bring him more. Why such unworthy thoughts continued to invade his head was a persistent plague.

The Oracle hobbled forward with his imposing staff. His eyes never moved from Ashar's face. Ashar wanted to look away, but he was gripped by the peculiar sensation that the old man could penetrate his mind and hear his thoughts.

The Oracle smiled as if he held a secret of such enormous importance that Ashar's very life was in the balance. Perhaps he did. Perhaps it was.

"Tell me again," the Oracle said, drawing so close that Ashar could smell the distinctive fragrance of the santalum wood of his staff and see the detailed carvings, hewn at different times by different hands, that depicted events of significance in the Oracle's long life.

Again his thoughts wandered. The voice of the Oracle brought him back.

"Your lineage," he said. "Recite it for me."

Ashar inhaled deeply. "I am Ashar, son of Shalatar. Shalatar was the son of Ilim. Ilim was the son of Worm. Worm was the son of Issens. Issens was the son of Syn. Syn was the son of Corus. Corus was the son of Kotar. Kotar was the son of Qaqos. Qaqos was the son of Tsak. Tsak was the son of Izek. Izek was the son of Ashar."

The Oracle's eyes narrowed. His pursed lips twitched into a grimace of challenge and doubt.

"Go on," he urged.

"I was taught by our oral tradition that Ashar was the son of Krolin, but now I know that he was not."

"And how do you know that, Ashar, son of Shalatar?"

Ashar had no answer that made good sense. Not even for him. He and the Oracle looked at each other for a long time. Ashar had the strange feeling that they were the only two people on earth. And then the answer came.

"Master Doyan taught us that the veil between what we can see with our eyes and what cannot be seen is as delicate as gossamer. The veil was not transparent to my eyes, but a voice from the light spoke to my heart." Ashar's fingers rested lightly on the leather strap that crossed his heart.

"I understand," the Oracle said.

"Ashar was *not* the son of Krolin. Ashar was the son of Nanesh. Nanesh was the son of Faron. Faron was the son of Palan. Palan was the son of Joram."

"And Joram is the son of the Navigator," the Oracle finished, speaking the name with reverence, his voice fragile. Ashar knew the legend, but the Navigator, whoever he might have been, was never real to him. Until now.

"Follow me," the Oracle said and, with the help of the daughters of the temple, he started for the steps to the holy sanctum. "Wait for us here," he said to the sages without turning his head. "What we are about may take some time."

———

The holy sanctum had been built with the stones of a lost civilization and lay at the heart of the temple. The ancient builders had aligned the altar of the temple to the vortex where the lines of the earth crossed. The pendulum swung in a perfect circle of perpetual motion.

The daughters of the temple assisted the Oracle as far as the ornate gates outside the entrance to the stairway in the outer hall. They were not allowed beyond. Even priests of the highest order were only allowed inside the sanctum during certain festivals and the performance of traditional rituals. No one but the Oracle had unrestricted access.

The Oracle clung to the crook of Ashar's elbow, and together they climbed to the top of the stairs. Random thoughts darted through Ashar's head like a swarm of dragonflies. He felt unworthy. Stories about how wicked men who presumed to walk in holy places suffered instant death flooded his mind.

Am I among the wicked? What voice is it that asks? Am I a liar? Are the beguiling wraiths of Ahriman, the spirit of destruction, inside my mind?

The litany of reasons Oum'ilah should strike him dead grew longer. He had not received the ritual bath. He had not been anointed with the oil of the sacred blackthorn. He was not dressed in the proper habiliment. He was entering the holy of holy sanctum with the Oracle of the temple because of a voice in his head!

I am doomed.

The entrance to the sanctum was a silk curtain covered with symbols. The Oracle lifted the curtain with a trembling hand. Ashar hesitated, fearful his next step might be the end of him.

The Oracle searched his face. "If you are who the whisperings have told you that you are, you have nothing to fear." He stepped past the curtain and let it fall. It furled into place, stirred softly by the movement of the air.

Ashar was alone. He closed his eyes and slowly filled his lungs. He longed to hear the voice again, but nothing echoed in the bluish swirl of his thoughts. He pushed the curtain aside, closed his eyes, and took the step he felt sure would be his last. When nothing happened, he opened his eyes and breathed again.

Ashar expected the room to be a mysterious and foreboding place. Instead, it was illuminated by a vertical shaft of sunlight, captured at the apex of the vaulted chamber by a disc of polished copper and reflected downward. The warm glow of amber light fell on a coffer of black marble, covered by a shroud of white silk. The box rested on a plinth of hardwood. The sides were covered with carvings, including a vessel caught in a tumultuous sea and surrounded by a tiny sun emitting thirteen rays of light. Ashar had seen the symbol before.

Without the slightest sense of ceremony, the Oracle crossed to the coffer and lifted the silk. He gestured for Ashar to remove the fitted lid.

The pungent smell reminded him of Master Doyan's workshop where the postulants worked leather. The sides, top, and bottom of the box were lined with black fur. *The hide of an ursine beast?*

Ashar had heard harrowing tales of the fearsome black beasts of the northern forests. He had watched men in the marketplace barter bluestone or even gold for their rare pelts. Whatever the box contained, it was hidden by a perfect cut of black fur.

The Oracle placed his hand on Ashar's shoulder. His skin was as thin as fine papyrus. Protruding veins bulged blue, seemingly eager to escape. The Oracle closed his eyes.

Ashar could feel the tremors of the old man's hand intensify and ripple through his being. They stood in silence. Ashar sought the bluish essence the way his masters had taught him. He strained to hear the old man's mind, but a barrier of light kept him out. A confusion of thoughts collided in his mind. He was unsure how long it was before the tremors ceased, but he felt a sense of loss when the Oracle took his hand away.

The Oracle turned the fur aside, revealing three white stones. They were smooth on the surface, clear and pellucid as crystal. In spite of an even surface, their translucence revealed a thousand tiny facets. Each stone was similar to the other, but no two were exactly alike. Ashar knew what he was looking at without being told. He stopped breathing. *The stones of light, touched by the finger of God.* In that moment, the stones of light were no longer a legend. They were a *confirmation* of the legend. An affirmation of an ancient truth. But there were only three. In some strange way, Ashar felt responsible for the ten that were missing.

The Oracle grasped Ashar's hand and held it in his own. "Do not fear," he said and picked up a small dagger encrusted with bluestone. In a swift but gentle movement, the Oracle drew the blade across Ashar's open palm.

Ashar jerked back. He balled his bleeding hand into a fist and cupped it in the other. He searched the Oracle's face, his eyes wide and uncertain.

The Oracle picked up a stone and offered it to Ashar, who instinctively reached for it with his uninjured hand. "The other one," the Oracle said, and Ashar opened his bleeding fist.

The Oracle closed his eyes.

A prayer? A ritual? A petition of hope? Before Ashar could settle on the meaning of it, the Oracle laid the stone on his outstretched palm. It felt cold but it also burned in his hand.

The instant his blood touched the stone, a euphoric tremor of pure joy surged through him. His devotion to Oum'ilah. His love for the Oracle. The affection of the sages. Celestine's eyes. The touch of her hand. A quiver of delight. A welling of emotion. A blissful peace and calm. Confidence and hope. Humility and gratitude. Every emotion compounded into a single wondrous warmth.

Ashar's lacerated palm was bleeding, but there was no blood. Instead, a translucent substance shimmering with a thousand points of light oozed from the wound. There was a tiny sun rising at the core of each sparkle. Wonder and terror collided in his chest. The shining stone grew brighter with a cold white light until it was a glowing sun unto itself. It was so bright that Ashar was forced to look away.

"It is he," the Oracle whispered to someone Ashar could not see.

When the white light was absorbed back into the stone, the Oracle took it from his hand, returned it to the fur, and closed the lid. He bowed his head to Ashar. "I have longed for this day."

Ashar stared at his hand in disbelief. The laceration had vanished. There was no blemish nor blood.

"The blood of the Navigator flows in your veins," the Oracle said. "We have much to talk about. So very, very much. From this day, your life can never be the same."

CHAPTER 15

The king stood in his marble bath. Sunlight warmed the room in the colors of the stained glass windows, but Kublan felt aged and aggrieved and shrouded in darkness. Memories swirled in his head like wraiths rising with the steam from the brackish waters. Wine could sometimes keep the pain of the past locked away in an iron box of regrets, but today the wine betrayed him and the box fell open and his past loomed up to punish him.

Who could he trust? No one.

Tolak, his own firstborn, had repudiated his divine right to rule as king and continued to rail against his reign. In a rage over the betrayal, Kublan had disavowed, disowned, and exiled his only son and rightful heir to the Peacock Throne. Tolak had good cause to disfavor him.

As the thought came, the king pushed the truth of his mistake away, but not before feeling a rush of regret. His wrath against one had fallen on many. He hadn't intended to punish the children—the grandchildren. He thought of Meesha, his granddaughter, the child he cherished most in all the world.

Is she well? he wondered. *Or has she also grown to loathe me?*

He was too proud to undo his foolishness or even try. He hoped the tokens sent and gifts bestowed in the years she and her family had been in exile had earned the child's affection. He longed to see her but could not. In exiling his son, he had foolishly exiled a tiny, tender piece of his heart.

Delusions of persecution rushed through him. He was alone and the feeling frightened him. *No. That was a long time ago.* For a moment he couldn't remember where he was. His eyes fluttered as they swept the room. He glimpsed a woman holding out a robe.

She was young and fair and familiar but . . . he felt dizzy. The girl smiled and held out the garment for the king to slip over his arms. Her oval face held large eyes and was framed by flaxen hair. She was very young.

Kublan narrowed his eyes to pierce the swirling fog. *Do I know her?* He tried to remember her name. His breathing quickened. He clutched his face as a tremor of pain shot through his head. He turned at the touch on his shoulder.

Tonguelessone held a small stoup of dark liquid to his lips. He sipped it, then grasped it with both hands and gulped the bitter potion. He squinted his eyes to help his memory. He knew this woman as well but couldn't remember who . . .

Has she poisoned me? Where is my grandson? He will know. Kadesh-Cor is loyal.

The thought shuddered through him as the concoction of herbs and spirits thinned the fog in his mind.

He looked up at his nursewoman. "Where is my grandson?" He demanded.

Tonguelessone answered with a twirl of fingers, a gesture that floated gracefully toward the window.

"She cannot hear nor speak, gracious lord," the woman with the robe whispered loudly.

"Yes, of course," he flushed, not remembering if his nursewoman could read lips. He was troubled by his sporadic lapses of memory. They were happening more often than before, but he was determined none should know. *Does Mahari know?* His eyes moved until they found her.

She was watching and smiling as she always did. "Maharí? Where is my beloved grandson, Kadesh-Cor?"

"I do not know, m'lord," she said and lowered her head. "Neither my heart nor mind has place to think of any but you."

The king put his arms into the sleeves of the robe. "I want my grandson."

A loud knock spared the young girl from answering. She traded an uneasy look with Tonguelessone, and the two of them retreated to the shadows.

"What fool disturbs me in my bath?" the king growled loudly as if wanting to make sure whoever was on the far side of the heavy door could hear him.

"I'll see who it is, gracious one," Maharí said and crossed to the door. She opened the small gate that covered a grated window. She listened, then turned from the window.

"It is the Raven to the King, your greatness." She raised her voice slightly. "He intrudes with his deepest apologies, but he says it is most urgent."

The king groused but waved his hand. Maharí unlatched the door and pulled it open. Several of the kingswatch were gathered in the corridor beyond the open door. The Raven to the King entered.

"By your leave, m'lord," Maharí said and slipped quietly into the parlor where vessels of oil and vials of perfumes were kept. She left the door ajar, but her eavesdropping was noted by Tonguelessone, who watched her from the shadow of the alcove on the other side.

Kublan wrapped himself in his robe and took a seat on the marble bench. He sat upright and jutted his chin at the counselor striding toward him.

The Raven was less than half his age and taller by a hand. His hair and brows were thick and dark, but his slight beard was tightly trimmed. He held the king's eyes with his own. They were the color of moss flecked with gold. Catlike. His lips were perpetually set in a wry smile that hinted of untold secrets. As always, he was fashionable and elegantly dressed in clothes he had designed and which had been created from costly fabrics and hand-tooled leathers. He wore a cap that sported feathers as black as the bird after which he was named.

Orsis-Kublan both admired and envied the man who strode toward him. He admired the man's confident deportment. It reminded him of himself—the man he had once been. A man with the hubris, arrogance, and courage to challenge a king. *The courage to kill a king who needed to be killed.* The thought rarely came without a shiver of guilt. He envied his counselor's youth, and though the Raven was hardly a young man, he had his health. Death was not on his heels.

"What great sign of the sky is more important than my bath?" Kublan bellowed as the Raven crossed the room. There was a curious affection in his blustering in spite of the scolding sharpness of the question.

Though the Raven's position of influence had increased greatly from his early years as the king's personal astrologer, the Raven continued to read the king's horoscope almost daily.

"The signs continue to speak to your good fortune, m'lord king," the Raven said, lowering his head in respect. "You are Leo, sign of the sun." He narrowed his eyes as if gazing into the night sky in search of signs. "You have absorbed its light and brilliance and are imbued with its strength, supremacy, and glory."

A murmur of adulation rippled among the girls.

The king smiled, allowing the flattery to soak deeply into his consciousness.

After a moment, the Raven added, "There is a matter of such urgency I am compelled to violate the seclusion of your chambers. I beg your wisdom and guidance on this grave matter."

Grave matter? The perpetual knot in the king's stomach tightened.

"You may judge me harshly if you must, but hear me first, gracious lord."

The king was pleased by the formalities, though both he and the Raven understood the game they played. "Speak to me as my friend, Raven! By the gods, I know you too well to be charmed by such sycophancy."

"As you will, Orsis." Both men briefly smiled, then the Raven's expression grew grim. "A march of kingsriders has been attacked. Many have been slaughtered."

"Slaughtered? There is no force that can stand against my elite warriors. Punish the fool who told you such a lie!"

"It is from the lips of one of our own. The news he bears must be spoken for your ears. We have brought him, but he is near death and will not last the hour."

"Would you have me parade thus through the halls of Kingsgate?" The king opened his robe without a blush. His body was surprisingly firm for his years in spite of the droop of pallid skin.

"No, m'lord," the Raven said, averting his eyes. "The wounded kingsrider is at the door, and upon your nod he shall be carried in."

Orsis dismissed the girls of the spa. Tonguelessone lingered in the shadows, her eyes fixed on the king's favorite concubine in the adjacent parlor. Mahari rubbed oil on her long legs and feigned disinterest, but her ears were tuned to the voices echoing from the spa.

The king closed his robe to cover himself and nodded to the one man he trusted. "Bring him in."

The Raven crossed to the door and opened it. Four men of the kingswatch shuffled into the room with the wounded kingsrider on a litter. His armor had been removed, but the broken shaft of the arrow remained in his neck. None had dared take it out. Pushing the spike through to cut the point away might slice an artery or cut his windpipe. Pulling the point against the notched ears would tear a gaping hole in his flesh. He would bleed out what little blood he had left.

The warrior's eyes were open. His knees rose and fell on the litter in a vain effort to kick away the pain. Juice of the poppy had not yet dulled his senses.

"Speak to your king," the Raven said as the wounded man was laid on the marble slab at the edge of the pool. Blood soaked into the thick fold of linen. The king scowled. The cloth would have to be burned to ensure he not be tainted by common blood.

The kingsrider's voice was weak, his words choked by the blood in his throat. "Mighty lord. . . . We have failed. . . . The bandit . . . our march. . . . Men slaughtered. Every man . . . put to the ax unless . . ."

The king looked to the Raven, his brow pinched with the question.

"Unless what?" the Raven asked.

"Who are you?" Kublan demanded. Without armor or shield, the man bore no mark of his rank.

"Ablon, m'lord. . . . Archer." The warrior choked and his body stiffened. His voice faded.

"He is a kingsrider from the march of Captain Borklore, your grace," a man of the kingswatch said.

"Borklore?"

"The march I sent to apprehend the roving bands of robbers and to protect travelers on the King's Road," the Raven said.

"He enticed us. . . . Tricked us. . . ." The wounded man became more lucid as the opium floated him above his pain. "Ambushed."

"What manner of rogue can beguile a seasoned captain of kingsriders into such folly?"

"Drakkor. . . . Blood of the Dragon," the man slurred.

"He told you his name?" Kublan's face twisted with the snarl of an animal backed into a corner. He scowled at the Raven. He had heard the rumors of a ruthless bandit, but the name Drakkor meant nothing to him. It was the other name that caused him to shudder with fear. "Blood of the Dragon! Was killing every man of your march so easy he had time to introduce himself?"

The kingsrider's words were lost in a gargle of blood. He shook his head.

"Then how can you be sure it was him?"

"He forced the captain speak his name before . . ." He arched suddenly as if a knife had been thrust up through the stretcher from below.

"Before what?" The Raven gripped the man's hand, his knuckles white.

"Before he cut off his head," the wounded archer managed to say.

"What of the others?" the Raven asked.

"All were slaughtered or—"

"Or what?" Kublan demanded, stepping closer.

You need not fear, lad," the Raven said in a soothing voice. "Your loyalty is proven well."

"Slaughtered or . . . surrendered."

"Surrendered?" The king gasped. "You lie! My kingsriders are sworn to fight to the death. How could this bandit and his drudge of thieves massacre a march of the king's finest warriors or force them to surrender?"

"He was merciless, great king. More savage beast than man."

"But you were armored and armed and . . ." The king's face went dark at the thought of such betrayal, and his frail frame began to quake. "How many cowards ran from the battle like you?" He gripped the man's tunic and half lifted him before the Raven intervened by laying a gentle hand on the man's chest.

"He promised us a world . . . like the world of ancient days and to make us . . . free men!"

"Free men!" Kublan's scoff was full of scorn. "Free from what?"

The archer was almost beyond conversation. The blood on his neck was clotted black. "A sorcerer . . . the seed of evil," he muttered, reaching for the last of his strength and failing. He lay still, his eyes open and staring.

The blood drained from Kublan's face.

—--—

"Ablon! Ablon!" The Raven shook him, then placed his ear against the warrior's chest. "He is dead." As he lifted his head, he saw the markings on the broken shaft. It was stained by blood and fouled with dirt, but there was no mistaking the sigil of Kublan. The arrow had come from the bow of a kingsrider. The dead man on the slab of the king's bath had been killed by one of his own.

"By the gods!" Kublan shouted. "This cannot be so. My elite captain beguiled and ambushed, and now his own men fight against me? I shall hang the traitors by their ankles and keep them alive until birds pluck out their eyes out and their flesh rots from their bones." He whirled and pointed a trembling finger at the men of the kingswatch. "Are there traitors among the kingswatch as well? Schemers who conspire with my enemies behind my back?"

"These men are not traitors, your grace." The Raven calmed him with a hand to his shoulder. "If there are traitors among the men of the march, they are few. Impotent fools with egos bigger than their brains. Fewer than five. Of that you can be certain!"

Even as he spoke his soothing words, the Raven's eyes returned to the markings of the arrow. Lying to the king was increasingly necessary. The line between what was best for the king and what was expeditious for the Raven was increasingly blurred.

By what persuasion had the man who claimed the blood of the dragon been able to twist the minds of men? By what power did this bandit turn brother against brother until they were willing to murder their own?

A cheap magician's trick? Or was he more than a rogue and a bandit?

Seed of evil and *sorcerer* were the words slurred out in the man's dying breath.

The Raven knew little of the dark arts of thaumaturgy, but icy claws dragged uneasiness from the bottom of his spine to the top of his head. He must never trouble the king with the possibility that the bandit, Drakkor, was an enemy with powers of the unseen world.

CHAPTER 16

Ereon Qhuin covered his nose and mouth with a wrap of coarse linen to keep the dust from choking him.

Beyond the Narrows southward, the red dirt of the King's Road was ground into a fine powder that billowed up from hooves and wheels in a dirty cloud that filtered the sun to a glowing smudge. Qhuin felt imprisoned by the thick, dark air, but at the same time, he experienced a strange sense of freedom.

He turned his head and squinted into the plume of dust. The rearward guard of kingsriders could not be seen, which also meant that they could not see him.

Qhuin drove one of five chariots at the end of a procession of horses, riders, wagons, wains, and coaches. It was the hunting expedition of Kadesh-Cor, Baron Magnus and prince of Blackthorn, grandson of His Greatness, Orsis-Kublan, Omnipotent Sovereign and King of Kandelaar.

The cortège was traveling south to the Tallgrass Prairie, the vast grassland west of the Ophidian Swamps and north of the mysterious Oodanga Wilds. They were hunting wild tarpan, the legendary horses that sometimes came north and crossed the Swamps of Dead Men to graze in the lush meadows.

Qhuin drove a chariot, drawn by three coursers abreast. The horses were the color of sour milk. In the red dust they were more pink than white. It was uncommon for coursers to be trained to draught, but the chariot was lightweight, made for hunting and designed for speed. Unusual as it was to see coursers pulling a chariot, it was far more uncommon for a man of Qhuin's caste to be at the reins.

— —

A'quilum Ereon Qhuin was a slave. As a bondsman in the Blackthorn stables, he trained the milk-whites to harness. The expedition to the Tallgrass Prairie was the first time he had ever been beyond the gates of Blackthorn for more than a day.

A'quilum was a designation, not a name. It meant "a man of unknown blood"—a curse worse than being lowborn. Qhuin knew nothing about who he was or where he'd come from. He was still wet from birth when he had been abandoned in a wrap of homespun wool in a basket left on the stone steps of a blacksmith's cottage in Village Darc more than twenty years before.

Qhuin was taller than most men with wide shoulders and narrow hips. His body had been hardened by the rigors of servitude and the life of a slave. His hair was black as a moonless night. His nose was broad and straight between the prominent bones of his cheeks. His skin was the color of weathered bronze, but his eyes were blue. Ethnic origins and a mingling of blood? A connection to the indigenous peoples of the ancient past? He didn't know and never would, so he left such speculation to those for whom lineage and the color of one's skin mattered so dearly.

Leo Rusthammer, the blacksmith of Blackthorn, had found the abandoned baby boy. Having no wife nor female kin and without the slightest notion of how to care for a child, Rusthammer took the baby to the Baron Magnus of Blackthorn, who those many years before had been Tolak, firstborn son of His Greatness, Orsis-Kublan.

Rusthammer delivered the basket and the baby still wrapped in the homespun wool. He described the strange circumstance by which he'd found the tiny child but told no one about the curious stone he discovered nestled against the child's cheek. Nor did he say anything about the strange premonition he'd experienced when he'd lifted the boy from the basket.

Lord Tolak's new wife, Katasha, was pregnant with her own first child and insisted the abandoned infant be taken in and given to the care of a kitchen maid. The woman's own child had died at birth only days before, and her breasts were swollen with milk. She nursed the babe, loved him, and raised him as her own in the servants' quarters of Blackthorn.

It was only in vague dreams that Qhuin remembered her. How warm and safe he felt when cuddled in her soft, plump arms. The smell of her—a blend of sweet and sharp. Hot baked bread and steaming broth. Blackberries, herbs, and onions. Her breath was sweet as if she'd nipped a bit of honey from the combs before they had dripped dry.

Qhuin was seven years old when Tolak was exiled by his father, and Kadesh-Cor was made Baron Magnus and prince of Blackthorn. And everything changed.

His adoptive mother seemed to know what was going to happen, and in the days that followed the king's decree, she held him longer and kept him closer and slept beside him through the night. Singing softly. Talking. Crying.

"Do you know how much I love you?" she asked. His answer was to snuggle in her arms. "Whatever happens, you must never forget you are loved and that love can make you strong." She drew him closer still. "You must be brave and patient. The winged spirits of the God of gods are watching over you." She held his face between her hands. "Sometimes the bad things that happen to us turn out to be good things, and sometimes we must pass through the dark before we can come into the light."

It was only years later that Qhuin understood what she had meant.

The morning following Tolak's departure, two large men dressed in black came to the kitchen. One wore a long cape. The other had a molded leather breastplate with a scabbard and short sword strapped to his hip. They looked like the men who came to Blackthorn when Master Tolak went away.

Qhuin had seen them gathered in the courtyard from the window of his sleeping loft above the pantry, but he had never seen a soldier so close. He was excited by their presence in his sheltered world. His excitement turned to terror when the larger of the men put a heavy hand on his shoulder. Qhuin twisted away, ran to his mother, and clung to her legs. She shuffled him into the pantry. The loud voices of the men were demanding and angry. His mother blocked the pantry doorway with her body and cried. The man with the leather breastplate struck her in the face, then pushed her, and she fell. The man in the cape gripped Qhuin's arm with a crushing fist. As much as it hurt, it was the pain in his heart and sight of his mother on the stones of the kitchen floor that he remembered most.

Though he was not yet seven years old, Qhuin was given to keeper of the stables as a slave. He saw the woman who'd been his mother only once after that. She came to the barns and peeked at him through the wooden slats of the outer wall. When he saw her, his heart leaped with joy and he ran to where she was hiding. Before he reached her, she turned and hurried away. He remembered the sound of her sobs being swallowed by the noise of the stables. Like smoke from a blacksmith's fire swirling into nothingness, the memory of her was faint and far away, except for the dark dreams when the two men in black came again to haunt and frighten him.

Rusthammer had seen the orphan boy from time to time before Lord Tolak was exiled. When the child was given to keeper of the stables, he offered to look after him. "Toughen him to the labor demanded of a bondsman," he offered. On that day, the blacksmith of Blackthorn became Qhuin's mentor, teacher, friend, and, in the years that followed, the closest man to a father Qhuin would ever have.

It was Rusthammer who named the boy *Qhuin,* which meant "wise" in the old language. He sheltered the child under his wing and tutored him in secret. In truth, what Rusthammer offered was much more than a wing. It was an enormous, protective shelter arching over the blacksmith's curious world of fanciful ideas, creations, and contraptions. Rusthammer opened the boy's mind to ideas and wonders he had never imagined. Qhuin huddled beneath the blacksmith's sheltering wing as often as he could.

The cluttered shanty adjoining the blacksmith shop became a magical place for Qhuin. He learned to read and found endless fascination in Rusthammer's collection of books and parchments, kept in secret in the massive trunk of oak and iron. His education at the feet of the blacksmith was so personal and of such depth it likely exceeded that of a princeling.

Beneath Rusthammer's wing, Qhuin was free in spite of the sigil of Kublan branded onto the inside of his thigh when he was a child and in spite of the iron ring that was put around his neck when he became a man.

CHAPTER 17

"Where is my son?" The king interrupted the Raven, who was speaking before the great chair in the chamber of counselors. The Raven held his tongue with a patient smile. He knew the king, and he knew his place, but most of all, he knew how to hold the king's favor.

"Where is my son?" the king asked again, his eyes bleary and confused. He turned to the eunuch who sat in council. "Why did my son not come as I commanded?"

"Your son?" the eunuch said. His eyes blinked rapidly, and he looked to Tonguelessone, who stood by the wall. She grimaced and stared back, unblinking.

"Your son remains in exile, m'lord," the eunuch said.

Kublan's face wrinkled in confusion and his cheeks reddened.

The Raven watched the king carefully. The blackouts, as they were called by the court physician, were becoming more frequent.

Kublan mumbled a curse under his breath and jutted his chin as if the eunuch was the one who'd misunderstood. "I have no son in exile," he said, his tone condescending. "Tolak is no longer my son. He is a traitor to me, to House Kublan, and to the sanctity of the Peacock Throne. In asking after my son, I meant, of course, the son of my heart and blood of my blood. It is my grandson, Kadesh-Cor, I ask after. Why have I not been given word of his arrival?"

The eunuch's smile quivered. His eyes darted to the Raven.

"He has gone to the south on a hunting expedition to the Tallgrass Prairie," the Raven said to rescue the eunuch, speaking as if it was the first and not the third time he had answered the same question. "To catch the wild tarpan for your stable," he added, hoping to spark the king's memory.

Kublan disapproved with a wrinkling of his brows. The same expression as twice before. "Why would he leave to hunt horses when I sent for him?" He scowled at the eunuch with suspicious eyes and spoke in a tone that made the poor fellow responsible. "No one is allowed passage to hunt the Tallgrass Prairie without my permission."

Raven intervened again. "You requested that he go on your behalf, your greatness, and gave him leave ten days ago. You may remember that you sent him with a march of kingsriders to ensure safe passage."

"I've no lapse of memory. I remember. Of course I remember."

But clearly he did not.

"Your greatness has too many important matters consuming your attention to allow your mind to be cluttered with things of insignificance." The Raven spoke with a soft laugh that sounded sincere. "It is the burden of a great king, m'lord. Matters of consequence can only be judged by you. No other has the intelligence to grasp what must be done nor the ability to weigh the options and maintain the focus required."

Kublan acknowledged the Raven's flattering assessment with a gracious nod. "What is it you have for your king?" he asked.

Raven, eager to bring the king's attention back to matters at hand, spoke quickly. "Your greatness, tales of this bandit who calls himself the Blood of the Dragon blow through the realm like yellow leaves in the winds of the black calf moon. My faithful minions move freely among the towns and taverns to learn what is spoken about Drakkor from the gossipmongers in the taverns and what is discussed among nobility within the great houses of the dominant dominions."

Kublan's fear of discontent, disaffection, and open rebellion was deeply rooted in his own violent past. Among the crucial duties the Raven had assumed for himself was the responsibility to be the eyes and ears of the king. The Raven's network of spies was known only to him. Perfidiousness came cheap among the lowest caste of men who prowled the taverns and moved easily among the despairing and deprived. Treachery among the nobles cost much more. Finding eyes and ears in the great houses was the most challenging of all. Contacting and enticing men or women who were truly in a position to see and hear, and who were willing to report, was risky business. Betrayal of royals could only be purchased with a promise of power or fear. The Raven wore the two-fingered sigil of the king and House Kublan.

"What does he intend? Is he no more than a bandit or does he stir rebellion against me?"

"You need not fear, m'lord." The Raven answered the question with what he knew the King needed to hear. In truth, he did not know Drakkor's plans.

The questions the Raven's spying eyes and ears had not answered swirled in his head. How had the bandit ambushed an experienced kingsrider captain? How was it possible a band of brigands could massacre a march of the king's finest warriors? What power had persuaded kingsriders to strip the sigil of House Kublan from their chests and become enemies of the king? Which of the kingsriders had put an arrow in his brother's neck to keep him from escaping?

Much of what the Raven had to report was hearsay and rumor. Inevitable folktales that sprung up in taverns like weeds watered with ale. The Raven took care to avoid the words he knew would feed the King's paranoia: *Ruthless. Ambitious. Warlord. Sorcerer. The powers of darkness.* But all of them were on his mind.

"Your greatness!" The Raven rarely raised his voice to the king, but the old man was nodding off, and the Raven awakened him to protect his dignity.

"Hmm!" Kublan growled as his eyes fluttered open. "Is there more?"

"Regarding the farmer who brought the wounded kingsrider to the gate—"

"I put him in prison."

"So I was told, but by your leave, great one, it seems to many that the farmer who brought the wounded kingsrider is a loyal citizen and a courageous man. Putting him in prison has caused a disturbance in Village Nellaf."

"I will hear no more of it!" The king strode from the room with the eunuch and Tonguelessone following behind.

The Raven wasn't sure why he felt sympathy for the farmer and tucked the feeling away. He knew his counsel held little sway when Kublan's judgment was tangled by his psychosis of mistrust and outbursts of paranoia.

A kingsrider had been killed. A farmer who had tried to save him was blamed for his death and thrown into the dungeons of Kingsgate. This latest tale of the king's madness had already reached as far south as Inn of the Fatted Goose.

— – —

An hour later, the king met alone with the Raven on the patio of his private chamber. Shafts of sunlight sliced between pillars and bathed the men in golden light. They sat on cushions on either side of a low table spread with fresh fruit, bread, cheese, and wine.

"The captain was an idiot if he could be ambushed so easily," Kublan began. "I shall send the entire army of kingsriders to crush this villain."

"Your greatness should think carefully before sending him another march of kingsriders to beguile and subvert, lest you play into his hands. A man with the power to beat a kingsrider captain"—*and coerce half the men of his march to defect and follow him*, he thought to himself—"may not be an easy man to kill. He does not disrupt the dominions of Kandelaar for pillage and plunder like a petty bandit, but to provoke you into putting your armies within his power."

"Why?"

"I can only conjecture."

"I will send only the best."

"Many of the best are gone."

The sound of agony that emerged from the king's throat was a retching death rattle.

"This man is unlike any of the enemies you have faced before, m'lord. You must be cautious not to misinterpret his motives or underestimate his cleverness. You must not misjudge his access to dark powers, if indeed the man is a sorcerer, as the archer said."

"I will rip the sword from his hand and cut him into pieces."

"It would seem that his tongue is far more dangerous than his sword."

"The vultures will eat his tongue when his head is on a spike."

Raven allowed a moment for the king's anger to fade. A cloud scudded across the sun, and a shadow swept over the patio. "If by some dark magic, this man can enchant your captain and seduce men sworn to you by an oath of blood, then who among the disgruntled rulers of the great houses might be persuaded to join with him in an alliance against you?"

Kublan lifted his goblet, and the Raven refilled it with wine. The king stared into the cup for a moment. When he finally looked up, he locked eyes with his trusted counselor and friend. "What shall I do?"

"Rally the rulers of the great houses and unite the seven dominions against him."

Kublan's laugh was cold, a rare gust of self-depreciation. No castle wall was high enough to isolate him from the discontent and disaffection that fermented like rotted fruit in the castles, manses, and taverns throughout the dominions of Kandelaar.

"I am not loved," he confessed with a clog of phlegm in his throat. "Even hated by some." He said it with a sadness the Raven rarely saw. "The kingdom remains a kingdom only because of my elite kings-riders who enforce my commands. Kandelaar has not been united in many years. Not since . . ." He shook his head. "I have sought to be a benevolent and worthy sovereign. I have tried to—" The lie stuck in his throat and he couldn't talk.

The Raven cherished his influence over the king, but he did not aspire to take his place. At least not in the same way as others who yearned to sit the throne and who waited, like vultures above a wounded dog, for the king to die. The thought brought a twitch of a smile. He knew the king's secret. *He believes the idea I put into his head. He believes he is destined to live forever!*

The Raven knew that controlling the person others perceived to be in command was the ultimate power.

"You must call a grand council," the Raven declared as if he had just thought of it. In truth, the plan had been brewed over many long and thoughtful nights. He stood and paced a few steps and stroked his chin thoughtfully. Measuring his actions for the full effect, he finally turned and faced the king. "You must assemble the rulers of the great and minor houses, the baron magnums of the five dominions, overlords of the outer provinces, chieftains of the indigenous clans, and even the giants of the north and the sand people of desolation, if we can find a way to reach them. You must bring them into a grand council, all together with their firstborn heirs.

"There is nothing more potent than survival to rally a people to a common cause. Drakkor has given you a great advantage. The fear of his ruthlessness is sweeping the nine dominions. Fear shall be reason enough for the squabbling rulers of the great houses to set hostilities aside and unite beneath a single banner. This Blood of the Dragon can be described as the ruination of all we hold precious and the end of Kandelaar as we know it."

The king pressed his lips into a thin line and raised his eyebrows. "What madness is this you suggest? The rulers of the great houses despise the throne and distrust each other. Few, if any, would heed such a call to a council without a dire threat or force of arms, without the loss of blood. What hope can there be for an alliance among men compelled to gather at the point of a sword?"

"They will not be brought at the point of a sword."

"Then why will they come?"

"They will come, and they will listen and they will unite if you promise to give them something they never imagined and entice them with what they want."

"What they want is my body on the pyre."

The Raven held his expression to hide his thoughts and waited for the king to continue.

"I cannot give them all the Peacock Throne. Nor can I promise to die, as all of them pray to the gods for day and night." With that, he smiled and choked out a laugh.

In spite of the tribulation of the king's reign, his age, the disorder of his mind, and even an occasional lapse into madness, the Raven was pleased to see there remained a spark of humanity in the old man.

"You reign in humility by the will of the gods," the Raven said, already verbally drafting the proclamation for the king. "Hostilities divide the kingdom and distract us from the evil rising in the land. Drakkor possesses the powers of darkness. He claims the blood of dragons and pillages our villages. His men rape our wives and carry our daughters into bondage. He enchants our sons to his awful service, and, with his sorcery and elixirs of red death, he turns their hearts against kin and kind."

King Kublan was spellbound by the Raven's words.

"The story of the slaughter of kingsriders must be heralded to the farthest corner of the realm. No one must escape the horror of what awaits them if they fail to come to council and unite with their king."

Kublan's face wrinkled in disapproval, and the Raven spoke as if the king had voiced his concerns aloud.

"We need not speak of betrayal or defection," the Raven said. "Only death and execution. We will speak only of the obscene atrocities committed by this pitiless man. We will sound a trumpet of warning that Drakkor will not be satisfied until the ruler of every principality and great house lies in a pool of blood along with their firstborn and family. We shall tell them the bandit will not stop until he sits the

Peacock Throne and reigns in blood and horror, ravaging the kingdom in the name of she-dragon."

"Is that true? He would drag me from the throne and—"

"No, no, m'lord. You are safe—he is but a petty thief—but you must use fear to compel your enemies to gather at First Landing."

"What must I promise them?" the king asked after a long silence.

"You were once hailed as savior of your people," the Raven said. "That time has come again, but not without some sacrifice."

Kublan narrowed his eyes.

The Raven breathed deeply. "To a king who is immortal, sacrifice is the shortest of the seasons, and the future of all things rests in his hands."

"You must help me," Kublan said. His lip trembled.

"Of course, gracious lord," he said. "There is power in humility."

The king tilted his head as if the Raven was speaking in a foreign tongue.

"Present your best nature, m'lord. Present your greatness as a benevolent sovereign and humble king. Entice men to your grand council with sweeping reforms. Promise that, forthwith and forever, the nine dominions shall be sovereign kingdoms unto themselves. The Peacock Throne will be governed by a council of lords representing all the great houses. Governance will be by common consent. A legacy of honor and chivalry will return. The borders of bloodshed will be brought to peace under a common banner. You will be Orsis, savior of the people, once again."

Kublan raised a hand, and the Raven helped him to his feet. He shuffled to the balustrade from where he could look through the gleaming towers to the fjord of Akeshen. The scud of clouds had disappeared, and the sun hung low in the western sky. The rippling surface of the water was a shimmer of gold.

"Dare I open the portcullis of Kingsgate? They will not come without their guardsmen and a show of arms." He spoke without turning around.

"Ah! As always, you are wise. It should not be held at Kingsgate.

It must be in a place of common tradition, but of supreme importance, suitable to your greatness."

Kublan nodded as he turned. Sunlight ignited his hoary head with a halo of gold. "Where will I find it most suitable, in your opinion?"

"On the outer isle of Akeshen? The place of First Landing?" The Raven shrugged his suggestion and let the questions hang.

Kublan nodded slowly. "Precisely my thoughts," he lied.

First Landing was the traditional landing site of the Navigator, the place he supposedly arrived with his boats of refugees. The teachings of the Navigator were lost save for the remnant cult of pilgrims, but the coming of the boats was a part of the history and generally embraced. Remnants of the ancient boats were esteemed by some as a historical site; for the pilgrims of Oum'ilah, it was a shrine.

"Call for the scribe," Kublan said. "I will write the proclamation while it is yet fresh in my mind." He looked at the Raven, who nodded to affirm who would actually write it. "These things tend to slip away," he muttered mostly to himself.

Kublan looked up suddenly. "Where is my grandson, Kadesh-Cor?"

The Raven hesitated.

"Yes, yes. I know, he is on his way to the Tallgrass Prairie for the wild horse. My memory serves me well enough. I mean where might he be this hour? He has been ten days on the King's Road, you said?"

"Yes, your greatness."

"Could a courier reach him with a copy of what we write if he departs before sunrise on the morrow? I wish for my grandson's advice in this matter of a grand council." Then, after a short silence, "He is the only honorable son of my blood and, by decree, my only heir."

"A good rider with extra mounts could travel by night as well as day and catch the expedition before they stop at Stókenhold Fortress."

"He will not stop there. It is forbidden!"

"By the time they cross the Isthmus, they will need to resupply provender and refresh or replace their horses," the Raven said gently. "There is no place else."

"But, I have forbidden anyone to visit Stókenhold Fortress—even my grandson. His father is a traitor banished for sedition. I grant him no solace. I would put him to the blade and his head on a spike if he were not the seed of my loin."

"Seeing his son again will hardly be solace, m'lord. Was it not by the word of Kadesh-Cor that you exiled your son?"

"He is not my son!"

"If discomforting Tolak remains your intent, your grandson's visit serves you well. A reunion with his son is punishment, not cheer or consolation."

The Raven poured himself a chalice of wine, but slowly to allow the monarch time to muse. Time to embrace the Raven's suggestion and make it his own, as he so often did. After a time he said, "M'lord, there is one thing you must consider in planning your grand council. Perhaps the visit of Kadesh-Cor to Stókenhold may serve a larger purpose."

Kublan folded his arms defensively and raised his chin slightly.

"You cannot unite the kingdom without your son's allegiance. Without reconciliation. He must be a part of our grand council of the king."

"He is in exile!"

"True enough, but he is not a prisoner and travels freely in the dominion of Westgarten, which I am told flourishes because of his influence and presence. He is loved by the common folk, not only because they see him as one of them, but also because they agree with his outspoken disdain of the rule of kings. I know these are hard words for you to hear, your greatness, but my loyalty will not allow me to lie to you."

"You vex me, Raven!"

"With apologies, m'lord."

"How can a king reconcile with a traitor who denies I reign by the will of the gods?"

"Exoneration? A royal pardon? Reconciliation between a father and a son?"

"How can a father reconcile with a son who loathes him?"

"Forgiveness?"

"You are a fool."

"Perhaps, but your promise of a different future will change him."

"Or embolden him to open the gate of his treachery to rebellion and force me to send him to the gallows!"

The Raven quietly rejoiced to see the zealotry in Kublan's eyes, knowing that his fear of rebellion would make him far easier to influence. He held the king's eyes, then, leaning close so none could hear, he whispered, "What would an immortal king do?"

Kublan's face darkened in deep thought. "Tell the master of the stables to ready the swiftest horses and prepare his finest rider to leave at first light. He must catch my grandson with word of this gathering before he reaches Stókenhold Fortress. Kadesh-Cor will know how to deal with his father, my traitorous son."

CHAPTER 18

The pungent scent of horses kissed Qhuin's nose as the breeze blew past. He loved horses and the smell was a fragrance as fine as flowers. The weather was warm, and except for an afternoon thunderstorm on the second day, the sky was clear. The only clouds were the plumes of red dust billowing up from the King's Road, and yet for Qhuin, there was nothing but beauty. The sights and scenery flowed past his chariot on either side. Each new vision delighted his eyes and teased his imagination.

In truth, the days of the journey from Blackthorn to the Tallgrass Prairie were the finest Qhuin had ever known. There was a steady succession of travelers moving north on the road between Knight's Tower and the historic hamlet of Mordan with its ancient canals and crumbled ruins.

They passed many hostelries, alehouses, and taverns, and though the procession rarely stopped at the inns, the curious names of them made Qhuin smile. There was precious little merriment in his life, and he committed the whimsical names to memory: Inn of the Fatted Goose, Inn of the Stone Hag, Inn of the One-Legged Jester, and, his favorite, Inn of the Yelling Horseman. He imagined the proprietors who poured the ale looking quite like the names they'd chosen.

Beyond Mordan, the expedition of Prince Kadesh-Cor had the King's Road largely to themselves. When gusty winds blew the dust away, Qhuin could see the royal road of kings winding ahead of them until it was nothing but a squiggle of brown swallowed by the shimmering haze of the horizon.

Days into the journey they had camped north of the Isthmus, a narrow bridge of land connecting north and south. It was where the waters of Dragon Deep filled a hole dug by the hand of a giant—or so the story was told.

Qhuin arose before first light to care for his team and prepare for another day on the road. The rays of the rising sun broke over the horizon and ignited a mist of clouds that swirled around a monolith of stone far to the west. The morning light crawled slowly down the ragged face of rock. It was unlike anything Qhuin had ever imagined. Rusthammer had spoken of this place many times, but no picture painted with words had prepared him for the splendor his eyes beheld.

"There is a temple there." Rusthammer had spoken about the mountain with reverence, as if there was more to the place than mere beauty. "From the time the temple was built in the years following the time of First Landing, it has been the place the pilgrims call the Mountain of God."

As Qhuin gazed upon the monolith of stone he thought he could see the cluster of buildings on the ridge. He wondered what it would be like to live in such a place. He closed his eyes and, as he often did, allowed his mind to drift away and for a moment be somewhere else . . . be someone else.

He wondered if at that very moment the man he might have been was standing on the mountain to watch the sunrise. The thought had scarcely formed when he felt a quivering of warmth that frightened him. The pulsing waves of heat seemed to emanate from the center of his being, but Qhuin quickly realized they came from the mysterious treasure Rusthammer had given him a few days earlier—a small, white stone of clear crystal—which Qhuin had hidden in a secret pocket sewn inside his leathers.

Glancing in all directions to make sure no one was near, he took out the stone and held it in his hand. It felt both cold and hot. It shimmered softly, then brightened and, for a moment, seemed bright as daylight. Qhuin closed his fist around the stone and carefully tucked it away again.

— — —

In the weeks before the expedition of Kadesh-Cor left Blackthorn for the Tallgrass Prairie, Qhuin had worked side by side with Rusthammer to prepare for the journey. They toiled through endless days and sleepless nights. New iron for the horses. Soaping leather, oiling saddles, mending harnesses and tack. Building new wagons and repairing the old. Ensuring that the royal coaches were serviced and prepared to endure the arduous journey. Of greatest interest to Qhuin was finishing the special chariots designed by Rusthammer for use on the hunt.

Qhuin had gone to the blacksmith shop to repair the buckling of a broken harness. On his way back to the tack room, he heard an angry voice coming from the portal where the chariots were stored.

"A slave? Are you really so stupid to believe I would disgrace myself?"

The high, shrieking voice was unfamiliar to Qhuin. He knew he shouldn't listen, but the voice grew louder and angrier. He could not stave off his curiosity, so he slipped into the narrow space between buildings. He crept closer and peered through a crack between the blackened boards.

Horsemaster Raahud stood face-to-face with Princeling Sargon, youngest son of Kadesh-Cor. Rusthammer stood nearby with one hand on the cowling of the chariot.

Qhuin had seen Sargon many times but had never spoken to him. The princeling was younger than Qhuin by only five seasons, but by any standard of manhood he remained an immature boy. He was spoiled by the pampering of royal blood and known for his churlish behavior and harsh treatment of those who served him. The whispering of slaves was rife with rumors of his blatant cruelty. Qhuin had wondered if the stories were true. The royal tantrum unfolding before him left little doubt.

Sargon was of average height and slight of build, though he was rarely seen without his sculpted chest plate and shoulder caps. The boiled leather gave him the appearance of a muscular body and widened his narrow frame. He was not unattractive, but his face was soured by a scowl, and his brows were pinched in a perpetual expression of disapproval and self-importance.

"You presume to give *me* a reinsman who is lower than a lowborn!" He gasped for air. "I am a princeling of Blackthorn!" The veins on his forehead bulged. "A slave!" he screamed again. "By the gods, I shall have you put in irons before I will be driven on the hunt by a slave bastard with the stink of the stables on his breath and a brain the size of a withered pea!"

Qhuin was stunned by the princeling's pathetic behavior. Horsemaster Raahud was highborn, skilled in his trade, and highly reputed among his peers. He was also nearly twice the age of the arrogant prince who was throwing a tantrum like a spoiled adolescent.

"The chariot was made for the hunt. It is of special design and easily overturned. It will demand the finest of reinsman." Rusthammer's voice was calm.

The princeling whirled and pointed his finger as if it were a lance intended to run the old man through. "You will speak when spoken to!"

"It is our finest chariot. It was made for your father, but he suggested it was best suited to a younger man of great skill and agility." Rusthammer was a man of impeccable integrity, but Qhuin knew him well enough to know that what he said was a diplomatic shade of gray.

Sargon's finger quivered with uncertainty, then slowly withdrew.

"A'quilum Ereon Qhuin is our finest horseman," Master Raahud said. "The chariot will be drawn by the horses he has trained. As master of horses, I can tell you there is none more capable than he. In his hands and in this chariot, you will be the champion of the hunt."

The war between the princeling's contempt and vainglorious ego was being fought by the muscles of his face in a fusillade of indecisive twitches.

"Sargon!" Kadesh-Cor stepped from the darkness of the passage that led to the stables and motioned for the boy to come to him. There was a disapproving scowl in his voice.

Sargon's indecision ended quickly when he realized his father had been watching. "Well enough, but he shall be last in the procession where he can breathe our dust." He whirled and strode after his father, who had already started down the passage. Sargon turned just before he disappeared into the darkness beyond the arch. "And he shall be chained!"

"M'lord, for a driver to be chained to the chariot does not give him—"

Sargon cut him off. "And nothing can happen to your 'finest horseman,' eh? If he allows the chariot to falter and is dragged to death by his neck, it will be his fault, not mine."

Rusthammer watched the princeling disappear, then stepped forward and put a hand on Horsemaster Raahud's shoulder. All that needed to be said, or could be said, was evident in the exchange of their expressions.

"Qhuin is a gifted horseman because of you," Raahud said, allowing a smile at last. Rusthammer shrugged the compliment away. Then Raahud, leaning closer to the blacksmith and glancing about as if wanting to make certain they were alone, continued in a whisper, "If this boy's blood were known, I wonder if we'd be surprised. He is no ordinary man."

Rusthammer bobbed his head slowly and smiled. "I've known that since the day I found him on the steps," he said and tapped his fingers to the grizzled shag of hair at his temple.

Found on the steps? By Rusthammer? Qhuin had never been told the story. A whirlwind of questions filled his head. Rusthammer's voice brought him back.

"Not sure why I've felt the way I do," the blacksmith said. "Might'a been the winged spirits of the God of gods whispering in my head all these years, though I confess they've little cause to speak to me." There was a flash of lightning in his eyes, the smile widened at the corner of his mouth, and Qhuin could see there was much more to be told.

Rusthammer returned to the blacksmith shop. The pounding of his hammer covered the sound of Qhuin's footsteps. The blacksmith was fashioning a rib of iron, and when he laid it to the fire again, Qhuin gripped the handle of the billows and began to fan the flame. The blacksmith glanced up and thanked him with a smile.

"You were the one who found me and brought me to Blackthorn." It was not a question.

Few things could discomfit Rusthammer, but Qhuin's words clearly had. Rusthammer held his eyes until the silence was uncomfortable, then nodded and glanced at the portal. "You were listening?"

Qhuin nodded. "Behind the wall." They stood in silence for a moment, then he spoke again. "Tell me."

Rusthammer set the hammer aside and let the rib of iron lie. The hot white cooled to yellow, then orange, then gradually went dark. "There's little to tell. You were left on the stone step of my cottage in the middle of the night. I was awakened by . . . Well, it was not your crying—you didn't cry at all—it was something else. Something that I . . ." He shrugged away whatever else was in his head and took a deep breath. "I felt a strange urge to walk into the night, and when I left the cottage I found you in a basket on the steps."

"That's all? That's all you know of who I am, or was, and where I came from? Why have you never told me?"

Rusthammer narrowed his eyes. "Because that is *not* all. Because until now, until Horsemaster Raahud made his decision to send you to the Tallgrass Prairie with the Baron Magnus, I have never felt the time was right to . . . I was not sure if . . ." He shrugged the thought away and looked at Qhuin a long time. "From the day I found you on my steps to, well, until this very moment, I've endured a nagging premonition that you are different. Special, somehow."

Qhuin's face tightened with unspoken questions.

Rusthammer turned abruptly and, pulling the thick leather gloves from his hand, disappeared into the cluttered chamber behind the stone furnace. Qhuin heard the rattle of things being moved and the squeaking of hinges. There was a thud of a lid closing. Rusthammer emerged with a small bundle in his hand and offered it to Qhuin. "This was with you in the basket when I found you."

Qhuin's face twisted in confusion as Rusthammer placed the bundle in his hand. He lifted away the folds of fur to expose a stone of unusual beauty. It was smooth and white, opaque and yet translucent in a curious way. Whether by the sensation of the strange stone in his hand, the fatigue of long, laborious days, or the whirl of expectations spawned by Horsemaster Raahud's pronouncement, Qhuin could not be sure, but in that moment a shudder of warmth he'd never felt before rushed through him.

A slave was not allowed to own a single personal possession. As he held the strange stone, he could hear Rusthammer's graveled whisper. "'Tis a treasure that belongs to you. You must never divulge it nor be without it. It holds the secret to who you are and a window on your past. More than that, it is an emblem of your life beyond the dominance of your masters. A promise from your past that you are not what they have made of you. It is a symbol of the freedom that no man can take from you. The freedom that is here and here." Rusthammer touched Qhuin's head and heart.

The last thing Rusthammer said was, "Someday this stone—whatever it is and wherever it came from—will lead you to who you really are." And then he mumbled under his breath, "And what the winged spirits of the God of gods were sent to help you become."

Winged spirits of the God of gods. Qhuin was struck by a memory. The voice of his kitchen-maid mother who had said nearly the same thing to him so many years before: *"The winged spirits of the God of gods are watching."*

Qhuin slept that night with the stone clutched in his hand and his hand curled beneath his arm. His dreams were a vivid profusion of impressions with no basis in anything he'd known.

He rode on the back of a magnificent horse in a place of exquisite beauty, with endless meadows and a sea of flowers and trees that reached clear to the stars, and the great horse could fly and it carried him to the columns of clouds that became a temple of white filled with luminous beings.

The next day, as they prepared to depart Blackthorn, Horsemaster Raahud petitioned Kadesh-Cor to allow Qhuin to drive free of restraint. "Like the other reinsman," he argued. "If the horses spook and the chariot topples, he will be unable to escape the chain and collar and will be dragged to death."

Prince Kadesh-Cor had listened, then nodded and walked away.

Presently, someone came and unlocked the clasp and took the iron collar from Qhuin's neck. He was so accustomed to the weight of the iron that he felt a strange rush of freedom when it was lifted away, but it was more than relief from the iron. It was the feeling of the secret stone hidden next to his hip.

The sense of freedom was short-lived as the attendant who removed his collar attached it to the chariot instead. "By order of Sargon," he said quietly.

—-—

The billow of powdered red dirt on the King's Road worsened. A choking cloud swirled up in a gust of wind; the wheelhorse shied and jolted Qhuin back to the moment.

Qhuin looked for the rear guard of kingsriders, but they had turned their horses from the road to avoid the strangling dust, and he could not see them through the murky pall.

And they cannot see me, he mused. The thought made his heart pound faster. He slowed the milk-whites and allowed himself to fall behind the other chariots. In the dust and rising wind, no one seemed to notice. As the procession pulled away, the billow of dust went with it.

Qhuin pulled the wrap from his face and took a deep breath, inhaling the scent of the horses.

He swept his eyes to the open country east of the road, then back to the way they had come. The road wound northward to the Narrows. It was still empty. No sign of the rear guard.

Until that moment, all of Qhuin's thoughts had been forward. By day, he'd been enraptured by the unexpected beauty of the journey. At night, his thoughts were consumed by a vision of chasing wild horses in the Tallgrass Prairie.

Looking to his future with a sense of excitement, rather than routine and certainty was an unfamiliar experience. But then, almost everything during the fourteen days of traveling was new and unexpected. But, for all the joy Qhuin felt and in spite of his eagerness to go after the wild horses, he could not quell the temptation to run away.

A dust devil swirled away to the north, daring him to follow.

This was his chance to turn the chariot and race for freedom.

What then? He pushed the thought away. He reminded himself that slaves lived in the shadow of punishment, or death, for the smallest misdeed on an impulsive whim of a master. The iron collar was more than a restraint. It was a reminder.

Rusthammer had given him the curious stone only days before, yet it had already given Qhuin a strange sense of destiny, the unreasonable sensation that someday he would be free. Irrational and unjustified as it was, there was a part of Qhuin that would not accept his circumstance as the final reality of his life. Thanks to Rusthammer, he had long since refused to see himself as nothing more than the property of another man. Today, in some small way, that belief was evolving into certainty.

Is it my destiny to flee? Is that how freedom is to come? Is that the reason this object of my past has come into my hands? The temptation flitted through his head, enticing him, making him promises.

It would be so easy to turn around. *With the speed and agility of the milk-whites, I might make it over High Pass before the dust clears. Before*

I am missed. I could leave the King's Road and head east to the Plains of Loonish, then—

Clank! The iron collar hammered against the cowling at the end of the swinging chain and jolted him from his intoxicating flight of fantasy. *Clank!* The sound drove a fist into his stomach, reminding him who he was. What he was. The clanking was deafening. Iron striking iron stabbed his ears and rattled his being. The grievous weight of bondage settled on his shoulders, ending his escape.

His future was forward. There was nothing for him on the road behind but fear and flight and, ultimately, death.

The dreadful thought came as the red dust settled, revealing a long stretch of ugliness that violated the beauty of the King's Road. Qhuin had heard of such things, but never seen it for himself. He hardly believed such atrocious punishment could be true. The sight of it was a vivid image he could never expunged.

The King's Road was lined with the heads of men condemned for treachery impaled on a row of wooden spikes. He recognized one of the hapless souls. There was no mistaking the shag of red hair. It was a slave from the stables of Blackthorn who had run away.

Qhuin stared ahead, and the cool stone of crystal grew hot against his skin.

CHAPTER 19

Meesha stood at the mirror. She turned her head until the dusty light from the window fell across her dark red birthmark. She had never seen her face without it, but it had been years since she had stood and stared at it as she did today.

Today was different. They were coming. How long had it been since the boys of Blackthorn had seen her? The sons of Prince Kadesh-Cor were no longer boys. Chor and Sargon—would they remember her? The fragile smile that came with the memory trembled as she stared at the dark side of her face.

When she was younger she had stood at this same mirror with her eyes closed tight and her fingers crossed and recited the wishing rhyme taught to her by her governess. The woman was wise and kind—and compassionately blind to Meesha's blemish.

Meesha had not thought of the rhyme in many years, but standing before the mirror it floated into her mind. She closed her eyes.

> *With fingers crossed*
> *And eyes shut tight*
> *I ask the fairies of the night*

To hear my wish
And come to stay
And make my wish come true today

No matter how many times she had repeated the whimsical words as a child, and no matter how many times the little girl had lain in her bed in the darkness and listened for the fluttering of fairy wings, and no matter how many times they had not come, she never lost hope that someday when she stood before the mirror and opened her eyes, the blemish would be gone. That someday she would open her eyes and her face would be shining white.

She felt the familiar warmth of hope flickering deep inside. She opened her eyes slowly, then touched her face with her fingertips, moving them slowly across the redness of her ruined skin.

Today was not the day the miracle was to be. A little flush of anger pushed her hope away.

Moved by an impulse more than reason, she stepped to where she kept a long sword hidden behind a fold of curtain. She drew the weapon from the leather sheath in a swift and graceful motion and whirled to face an invisible opponent. To wreak vengeance on them that betrayed her with the curse. Who was it and what had she done to deserve their wrath? She lunged and slashed at her enemy with her blade, then whirled and slashed again from the opposite side. She parried their frail efforts to strike, then thrust the sword all the way through their heart, spinning about to smash the iron pommel into the mirror. A spiderweb of jagged cracks raced away from the point of impact.

Meesha recovered her breath as she stared at herself in the broken mirror. It had been more than twenty years since her day of blessing, and it was not a little girl looking back from the fractured glass.

Had Meesha been born a peasant she would have been demonized as a witchchild, marked by Ahriman, the spirit of destruction, with a splay of darkness on her face. The old crone of the village would have taken her to the woods and abandoned her to the wolves. Had she escaped the old hag, her childhood would have been a painful experience of rude curiosities, teasing, and open ridicule. She would have been shunned by other children and pitied by adults. Had she survived to adulthood, she would have been driven to the fringes of society to suffer the pains of self-loathing.

But Meesha was not a peasant; she was the daughter of Tolak, son of Orsis-Kublan, and thus granddaughter to the King of Kandelaar. When Tolak had been exiled to Stókenhold Fortress, she had been three years old, and her birthright as a princess had been nullified by an edict of the King. Ironically, he was the only one who still thought of her as royalty.

Lovely gifts arrived from Kingsgate from time to time. They were never personal, at least not in the way a grandfather might show his affections for a granddaughter. The presents were lovely. A shawl of delicate lace. A feathered hat. A porcelain cup or figurine. The gifts were always accompanied by a parchment sealed by wax and impressed with the sigil of the king. The message inside was always the same: *For Lady Meesha, a royal gift from His Greatness, Orsis-Kublan, Omnipotent Sovereign and King.*

Only once had there been a personal note. It was the only clue Meesha ever received to understanding her grandfather's obvious affections for her, despite his disdain for her father and the whole of his household. The words were written by an unsteady hand and said simply: "I have been told by one who serves at Stókenhold Fortress that you are the incarnation of my beloved Edoora."

It was true. Meesha's exquisite face tapered in a gentle curve from the high bones of her cheeks to her perfect chin. Her eyes were dark brown, softened with a flare the color of honey that matched the highlights of her long hair.

Meesha had never met her grandmother, but she liked to imagine she resembled her in more ways than simply appearance. She certainly didn't feel that she took after her mother.

Katasha, of House Dressor, was Tolak's second wife. She was younger than Tolak by a few years and considered by some to be too old for marriage or children. She was almost thirty-five when her brother, Romonik, proposed the marriage. Because she married so late in life, Katasha's superstitions ran deep. Katasha never spoke of it, but Meesha knew her mother blamed herself for her daughter's disfigurement.

The winter she had been in her mother's womb had been harsh. The sleeping chambers in the old fortress were so cold that water left standing for the night was covered by a layer of ice come morning. Even when the weather was temperate, Katasha was chilled, and she spent long hours by the fire. She heeded the old superstition that said if a pregnant woman stared into the flames, the child would be born with skin badly burned.

Katasha took great care not to gaze into the fire, but when her baby was born and she touched the wine-red stain on her face, she knew she had failed. She had been the one to bring the curse upon her daughter.

As a result, Katasha felt a deep responsibility to nurture her daughter in a way that would compensate for her failings before Meesha was born. From the earliest days, she reassured Meesha that "True beauty lay within and not without." She taught her feminine graces and the social codes and manners of House Kublan. She praised her intelligence and reminded her that it was character that mattered most.

Katasha's diligent mothering endowed Meesha with a curious sense of confidence, but she had no illusions. She learned quickly that men had little interest in character and inner beauty. She knew she was not like other girls and, with a face like hers, could never be. If she was never going to be pretty or sought after or flirted with by handsome boys, then she would make no effort to be like other girls. Since she knew there was not a man in the dominions of Kandelaar who could see past her face, she accepted the truth that she would never marry.

Meesha had shunned the ways of women and focused her life on books, music, and art. She resisted laces and linens, pampering and powders. She did not follow fashions and stopped dressing in the elaborate silks worn by the fine ladies of the great houses. She did not adorn herself with bracelets, bangles, and bijoux. She remained feminine, but in her own way, and preferred a fashion of her own creation that included the coarse cloth and leather of the villages. She was more a woman of the woods than a lady of a great house.

In her teenaged years, Meesha's disdain for feminine ways was discounted by her mother as the rebellious nature of growing up. "The strong independence of her nature is a passing fancy," her mother was heard to say. In truth, it was a conflict between the lady tradition expected Meesha to be and the woman she truly was.

Because she did not aspire to be like her mother—or her stunningly beautiful sister-in-law, Sarina, with her perfect red hair, eyes the green and gold of soft moss, and the delicate smattering of freckles on her pale skin—Meesha grew up preferring the company of her brother, Valnor, to the ladies of Stókenhold Fortress.

Meesha was a little girl when Valnor left to be trained by their uncle Romonik. When he returned, she was a young woman and demanded he teach her everything he had learned about fighting and weapons and combat.

"These are not good things for a lady to know." He laughed.

She knocked him to the ground and playfully pounded him with her fist until he agreed.

An abandoned part of the old fortress became their secret place to practice and train. They went there as often as Valnor was willing. Besides her fine mind, wit, and confidence, Meesha had surprising physical strength and adeptness, and over time, she became remarkably proficient with a sword.

"You are better than many with whom I have trained," her brother often told her. There were few words that brought her greater delight.

CHAPTER 20

Qhuin reined the milk-whites to a stand. He wrapped the reins around the iron hook and stepped from the chariot. He stretched his arms above his head and twisted to relieve an ache in his back. He squatted to a count of fifty to stretch the muscles in his thighs. The wheelhorse nickered and nudged him, hoping for a scratch.

Qhuin heard the sound of hooves on the road behind him. He gripped the bridle of the wheelhorse lest the team bolt. *Bandits on the King's Road!*

"Hail, traveler!" the approaching man shouted, out of breath. "Hail . . . hail, good friend." He led a chestnut horse, lathered in sweat. The horse's nostrils were bleeding.

Qhuin frowned at the exhausted state of the animal. Such a fine horse deserved better treatment. "Steady girl," he whispered to his wheelhorse, his hand tight on the bridle. *Does a bandit hail a traveler as a friend?* He breathed more easily.

The man leaned over with a hand on each knee and took a long, slow breath. "Forgive me, m'lord," he said, his fingers fluttering an apology. "Are you, by some good fortune, with the expedition of Prince Kadesh-Cor?"

Qhuin was taken aback by the deference of the man's salutation. It struck him in a rush of delight. *He doesn't know I'm a slave.*

"I am," Qhuin said, graciously lowering his head and biting his lip to keep from adding "master" or "m'lord." He was amused by his rather good impersonation of highborn gentry.

"The gods be praised," the man gasped. "I am Nagor, son of Romnolof, royal horseman of the stables of Kingsgate and courier to His Greatness, Orsis-Kublan, Omnipotent Sovereign and King. I ride with an urgent message for Prince Kadesh-Cor. Is the good prince here, m'lord?"

"He is some distance ahead," Qhuin said as he knelt beside the courier's horse. There was a gash on her left front leg. The cannon was bloody to the hoof, and the feather of hair soaked through. The animal trembled.

"How did this happen?" Qhuin scowled at the man. "You have ridden her too long and hard and given her no water!"

"I have ridden night and day by command of the king, m'lord!" He glanced at the horse's ruined leg. "The poor beast lost its footing and fell in the rocks."

If the bone was cracked, the horse would not survive, but Qhuin had no heart to put it down. He wrapped the wound with a linen cloth. The bleeding stopped. If they reached Stókenhold Fortress in time, perhaps the horse could still be saved.

"Please, m'lord. Take me to the prince." He lifted a parchment from his leather satchel as if it were a scepter endowed with magical powers.

Qhuin stood, looking from the courier to the wounded animal. What message was so urgent it justified riding a horse nearly to death?

———

By the time Qhuin and the courier caught up with the end of the procession, the red dirt of the road had turned to hardened clay. It was evident the courier had never ridden in a chariot because he stood be-hind Qhuin and clung to the railing with both hands.

The chariot driven by Qhuin was the one Rusthammer designed for the prince. He had replaced the iron parts with wood, which made the chariot smaller and lighter but still retained its strength and bal-ance. Rusthammer had also designed a modified harness and saddle pad for the horses. On the bridle, he had placed a bronze rosette en-graved with stylized foliage and the symbol of a bleeding rose with thorns. "Your sigil," he had said to Qhuin in private, adding one more treasure to the cache of secrets between them.

Qhuin's iron collar clanked against the cowling. The courier made no comment but stared at the redness on Qhuin's neck with suspicion.

Qhuin was not thinking about his passenger. A single question pounded through his head. *How will the prince react to a slave taking it upon himself to leave his place in the rank?*

Rusthammer's voice whispered in Qhuin's head. *"To do, not to think, is the burden of bondage. Masters and highborn dare not consider that the mind of a man in bondage might be brighter and better than their own. You must never forget that the burden of bondage does not keep you from being free!"*

Qhuin closed the distance to the end of the procession. He waved a casual salute to Jehu, who drove Prince Kadesh-Cor's chariot. It was the largest of the cortège and heavier than the other chariots. The iron cowling was decorated with the Blackthorn sigil in bronze relief. The four horses were black and perfectly matched, each with ragged stockings of red dust. It was a chariot made for riding in parades, not hunting.

Jehu cocked his head and raised his eyebrows in an unasked ques-tion. Qhuin jerked his head toward the courier. Qhuin liked to think of Jehu as a friend in spite of the unbridgeable chasm between a slave and freeman.

There were four chariots on the expedition. Qhuin and Jehu drove two of them. The third was driven by a freeman named Jewuul, reinsman to Horsemaster Raahud, and the fourth by a reinsman Qhuin did not know.

Qhuin understood Princeling Sargon had demanded he ride last in the procession, but he thought it curious Raahud put the other chariots to the rear as well. The other drivers were freemen. Raahud was a hard master in many ways, but his respect for Qhuin's skill as a horseman showed itself from time to time in obvious ways. Qhuin decided putting all of the chariots together was Master Raahud's way of acknowledging him as a peer among the drivers in spite of his caste.

The wranglers and extra horses were next. By the time Qhuin saw Raahud in the procession, the horsemaster was already riding toward him, his face in a scowl.

"By the gods, Qhuin, what are you doing?" he yelled as he caught up to the chariot.

"He's a courier of the king with a message for the prince, Master Raahud," Qhuin said with appropriate deference, indicating the man behind him. "His horse is injured." He nodded to the chestnut tied to the back of the chariot.

Raahud untied the horse and frowned at the animal's injuries. "I'll see to her; drive on."

Qhuin nodded and rolled the leather reins across the croups of his horses with a snap.

The narrow road forced Qhuin to stay in the weeds as he passed the wagons loaded with foodstuffs, supplies, and equipment for the camp. Camp gillies rode in the last of the wagons or walked behind, while the crew of stewards and cooks found places to ride among the bundles in the wagons. Six kingsriders guarded the wagon train, which was a tempting target for robbers or bandits.

Qhuin passed six horseman of the Order of Huszárs, a fraternity of cousins and kin of House Kublan, however thinned the blood. These men were guests invited by the prince to join him on his hunt for wild tarpan.

The youngest of them twisted in his saddle to look at the chariot as it passed and waved at Qhuin. He smiled broadly, bright-eyed and exuberant. He was no older than seventeen, Qhuin guessed. Young for an expedition of such prominence. The young man showed none of the disdain Qhuin saw so often on the faces of the highborn. He smiled and returned the salute.

Ahead of the Huszárs, three kingsriders rode abreast, and ahead of them there was a small, brightly painted coach the color of plum and trimmed with burnished brass. The windows were covered by yellow silk curtains. As Qhuin drove past, the curtain was pushed aside, and he looked in time to see a girl smiling at him. He looked away quickly. Everyone knew the prince's courtesans rode in the plum-colored coach.

The coach of the princelings was next, and as Qhuin passed it, Princeling Sargon looked up at him from the window of the carriage. His body stiffened, his eyes widened, and his nostrils flared.

A fist of iron gripped Qhuin's gut.

Qhuin knew he should look away. Eye contact with the royals was forbidden, and failure to look away from one as arrogant as Sargon would surely bring severe punishment.

Sargon growled something to his older brother, who sat across from him. Chor glanced up but showed no interest.

Qhuin hurried his horses past the carriage, but the iron fist of fear held its grip, and he could feel the princeling's eyes burning on the back of his neck.

Prince Kadesh-Cor's coach was still some distance ahead and flanked by three kingsriders abreast, two in back and one in front, who wore the rank insignia of captain. Ahead of him, and leading the procession itself, were the bannermen who bore the sigils of Blackthorn—a standing bear—and House Kublan—a peacock on a field of black with arrows dripping blood clutched in its claw.

As Qhuin's chariot pulled even with the prince's coach, his heart thumped with anticipation. He had seen the prince a few times in the stables, but a slave was taught to keep his eyes down and speak only when spoken to. He drew slightly forward of the coach's window and looked inside. There was no prince.

The face smiling up at him through the rippled glass was Prince

Kadesh-Cor's squire, Nimra. He was young. Almost more a boy than a man.

Nimra caught Qhuin's eyes and nodded. He had a bright countenance about him and a face incapable of a frown. *A squire so esteemed he rides in the royal coach?* Qhuin's thought was whisked away by the sudden movement of the kingsriders spurring their horses forward.

"Halt!" One of them shouted. The kingsrider riding guard in front whirled his horse around and galloped into the weeds to stop the chariot.

Qhuin reined in as the captain seized the horse by the bridle. The other kingsriders flanked the chariot, their long swords drawn. The rider on the lead courser stopped, and the procession stuttered to a stop.

"What is this?" the largest of the men demanded.

This close, Qhuin could see the captain's face was badly scarred, ruined by fire.

The courier withdrew the parchment from his leather satchel. "I am the courier to the king. I've a message for the prince."

The captain was about to speak when the sound of iron hooves on the hardened clay of the road drew his attention.

Prince Kadesh-Cor rode into view. He was mounted on a long-legged horse bred from the wild tarpans. It was black with a blaze of white on its forehead and a muzzle the color of cherry blossoms. His two large Alaunt hunting dogs ran just behind.

Qhuin saw at once that Kadesh-Cor was a fine horseman. The way he sat the saddle, the gait of his horse, and his cape rippling in the wind created the illusion he was floating. At the sight of him, a shudder traveled up Qhuin's spine.

The bannermen turned their horses aside, and Kadesh-Cor rode to where the kingsriders held the chariot.

The courier began again. "I am Nagor, son of Romnolof, royal horseman of the stables of Kingsgate and courier to His Greatness, Orsis-Kublan, Omnipotent Sovereign and King. I bear a message for Prince Kadesh-Cor, the noble Baron Magnus and gracious prince of the North." He bowed and held up the parchment.

Kadesh-Cor dismounted and walked to the chariot.

Qhuin was relieved the prince did not appear disturbed that a bondsman had taken it upon himself to bring the courier forward. Had he even noticed who it was that drove the chariot? No. He remained invisible to the man who owned him. Qhuin had saddled the prince's horse at the stable many times. Each time he had hoped to be noticed or hear a word of acknowledgment, but in all the years, the prince had never spoken to him or even looked at him.

The prince reached for the parchment.

Eyes to the ground. Speak only when spoken to. Qhuin knew the dictum well and was about to lower his gaze when he was taken by a sudden impulse that would not be denied. He looked directly at the face of the prince as if it was his right as a nobleman of highest birth. The act was bold and brazen and dangerous, but it came with a rush of emotion Qhuin had never felt. He was seeing—*truly seeing*—the man who owned him.

Qhuin was taller than Prince Kadesh-Cor, and if measured the same way they measured horses in the stable, the prince was eighteen hands. From a distance the Baron Magnus of Blackthorn and prince of the North looked younger than his forty-nine years. He was lean without being thin and carried himself upright.

There was a ridge of furrows between his brows and weathered cracks in the skin around his gray-green eyes. His beard was the color of burnt bread and looked like a gnarled hand holding his chin. His hands and arms were bare and tanned by the sun. His only jewelry was the heraldic ring on the index finger of his right hand.

Unlike many among the regal classes who sought to define their position by an ostentatious display of costly raiment, Kadesh-Cor preferred the sturdy polished leathers of the kingsriders and a bloodred cape slung from one shoulder. Even then he was less imposing in his dress than most knights. Dressing down created a sense of accessibility among the common class that made him beloved among many of the villagers.

Qhuin noticed a strange symbol inked into the skin on the inside of the prince's arm as he reached for the parchment.

The courier bowed his head as he handed over the king's message.

Qhuin likewise bowed, but as his head came up, words tumbled from his mouth as if put there by another power. "I brought him quickly as I was able, m'lord prince." He stood straight and looked at the prince, unblinking. What prompted such madness? He felt the presence of the stone close by and for an instant felt a strange sensation that he was watching the events unfold as if they were happening to someone else. His muscles tightened. He had stopped breathing.

Kadesh-Cor glanced up and locked eyes with his slave for a fluttering beat of Qhuin's heart. Qhuin thought he saw the slightest twitch of a smile at the corner of the royal mouth before Prince Kadesh-Cor broke the wax seal on the parchment and walked toward his carriage.

"*Of awful fears, both great and small, the things that never happen are the greatest of them all.*" Rusthammer's whimsical platitude danced through Qhuin's head.

I made a decision to leave the procession and drive the courier forward by my own free will. I have broken the rules and taken action. "To do, not to think, is the burden of bondage," but I cast it aside and made a choice to disobey. I met the prince of Blackthorn and did not look away. I gazed into his royal eyes and spoke to him without being spoken to. A thousand tiny prickles danced at the nape of Qhuin's neck as a sense of joy shivered through him along with a wave of terror.

Rusthammer had taught Qhuin that a man was the accumulation of his experiences. Each event changed him in some small way for good or for ill. A'quilum Ereon Qhuin of unknown blood could not undo what he had done, nor did he wish to, for in that moment Qhuin knew that he was changed and would never be the same again.

Of all your awful fears . . . The words were almost a song in his head until a loud squawk behind him shattered the tranquility of his hopeful illusion.

"Put the slave back in his chain!" Sargon snarled and slammed his ebony walking stick against the iron of the chariot to punctuate his scorn.

The strong hands of a kingsrider gripped Qhuin by the shoulder. Iron clanked on iron as the collar was lifted and put around his neck.

"Put the bastard of a dog back in our dust and see that he stays there until we get to Stókenhold Fortress."

CHAPTER 21

Maharí's thumbs massaged the pallid skin on the bottom of the king's bare foot. She added pressure as she slid her thumbs slowly upward from his heel to the softness below the padded ball. It was calloused where it rubbed on his boot, and the largest of his toes bent inward. His nails were cracked and stained an ugly yellow. A guttural groan of pleasure gurgled up from his throat.

"Too much pressure, m'lord?" the concubine cooed.

"Hmm," was all Kublan could manage. He sprawled on a couch in his private chamber with his feet propped up on a low seat that was heavily padded and covered with embroidery. Maharí sat cross-legged on a cushion, rocking forward with each crush of her thumbs. She increased the pressure until she felt him flinch. Giving him pain satisfied her for reasons that never entered the sovereign's mind.

"Oh, ouch, ouch," he complained, and she smiled.

Maharí lifted the stopper from a small vial of perfumed oil and poured a few drops on her hands. She rubbed them together and worked the sides of his feet with the palms of her hand. The tips of her fingers pressed into the bony ridges on the top of his foot.

Kublan groaned again in a mixture of pleasure and pain.

A drape of sheer silk lay across Maharí's shoulders and twined about each arm. Another layer of silk was wrapped around her body and hung to her feet in graceful folds. The pearls and shells woven into her top shone bright against the deep copper of her skin. She wore bracelets around her upper arms, and a tiara with dangling pearls was snuggled into her raven-black hair.

The knock on the thick wood was not the timid knocking one would expect of a person invading the privacy of the king. Kublan rolled his head toward the door, and Maharí braced herself for his wrath. There was none.

With Maharí's help, Kublan swung his legs from the low seat and put his feet on the bearskin rug on the floor. "Enter the presence of your king," he bellowed with a delightful laugh.

The heavy door swung open, and Kingsrider Captain Ilióss Machous entered the room. "Your greatness," he said, pounding his hand across his heart. He dropped to one knee, the iron shanks of his leather boots clanking against the stone. He was clad in the formal armor of the kingsriders with a massive helm beneath one arm and the coiled viper of the kingsriders emblazoned in relief on his chest piece of boiled leather.

"Arise, arise," Kublan said. "Come forward."

Captain Machous strode across the stones until he was standing next to the king. Machous was half a head taller than Kublan and half again his weight without a pinch of fat on his battle-hardened body. His skin was dark, and his hair and beard were the color of red river mud. His orbital arch was thick, the brows thrust up from a furrow between dark eyes. His nose was large and broken, like the knuckle on a giant's hand. A double-handed long blade had left a lumpy scar from the bridge of his nose to his jaw, his skin raw where it passed through his beard.

"You called for me, great one," Captain Machous said. His voice was deep like a pattern-maker's rasp on iron. His eyes flitted to Maharí.

A spark of fire caused her neck to flush, and she looked to see if the king had noticed, but his gaze was on his captain.

"How may I serve you, mighty king?"

"Bring me the head of the bandit Drakkor," Kublan said. "You must exact vengeance for the murdered Captain Borklore, the poor fool, and put those traitorous kingsriders who betrayed me to the sword."

"Traitorous kingsriders, m'lord king?" Machous asked, puzzled.

The king caught the slip of tongue and flushed. The few who knew of the humiliating betrayal were sworn to secrecy, lest the shame of their defection be known.

"You must never speak of it," he said, "but some few of Borklore's men were seduced by their fear, or threat of death, or"—the words trembled across his lips—"by some dark magic to betray their oath of blood and join with this son of a whore who calls himself Blood of the Dragon."

"I do not believe in magic, your greatness. I believe in this!" The captain gripped the handle of his sword. "I will savor the stench of his blood when it flows from his neck and soaks into the dirt."

Kublan smiled. "Take a double march of kingsriders, more if you like, and officers of your choice, but hear me now and listen well." He stepped closer to the captain and put both hands around the fist holding the hilt of the sword. "It *must* be done before we leave for the great council at First Landing—before the first day of the Moon of Falling Leaves in season Mis'il S'atti. You and your march shall go with me to the place of First Landing, and there I shall present the head of this bandit as a symbol of my power and the invincibility of the Peacock Throne."

"And the prowess of your most remarkable captain," Maharí whispered in his ear.

"Yes, yes, of course," he said, "my most trusted Captain Machous, the mightiest of the kingsriders."

CHAPTER 22

Meesha was in the great hall when the rider wearing kingsrider's armor arrived with the unwelcome news that the hunting expedition of Prince Kadesh-Cor would reach Stókenhold Fortress by nightfall, the day after next. He'd been sent in advance, as was the custom.

Meesha was startled by the news.

Though born of different mothers and many years apart, Kadesh-Cor was Meesha's half brother. He was the son of Tolak's first wife, Arina, daughter of Remos-Kahn of House Romagónian. She had been taken by the black death in the plagues of annum 1059. Tolak rarely spoke of her.

Meesha was three years old when Tolak was exiled from Blackthorn and the dominions of the north were given to Kadesh-Cor by their grandfather, the king. She had only seen Kadesh-Cor once in the many years since then and hardly remembered him from her life at Blackthorn as a little girl. She remembered being afraid of his badly behaved boys, and those childhood fears had turned to disdain once she was old enough to understand what happened to her father.

She had been too young to remember any of it. Valnor had been the one who told her that it was Kadesh-Cor who betrayed their father and brought about his exile. Tolak never spoke of his son's betrayal or the conflict with his own father, but to this day, Meesha felt a flush of anger at the mention of his name or the names of his awful sons.

Little as she knew of the schism that had divided her family, she understood the reunion would be fraught with apprehension and distrust. *What dire events resulted in a father exiling his only son? Could such disloyalty ever be forgiven by either a father or a son?*

Meesha knew the kingsrider had not come as a courtesy to announce the arrival. Rather it was a warning for Tolak and his household to prepare to host his son, not as family, but as the esteemed Baron Magnus of Blackthorn and prince of the North together with his princeling sons, Sargon and Chor.

Princeling sons! Must I truly stand before that prig again?

She took a deep breath and closed her eyes. It had been thirteen years since the last time she'd been face-to-face with Sargon, but surely he had not forgotten what happened. He was not a person who would ever forget or forgive such humiliation.

The moment the kingsrider departed, Meesha retreated to her room, closing and locking the door. She stood at the broken mirror and stared at the dark stain of her face, angry with herself for obsessing over a blemish she could otherwise easily ignore. But now the day was almost upon her. That loathsome boy was coming. Boy? No longer. He was now a grown man.

The light from the window fell away as a cloud moved across the sun. In shadow, the crimson stain of her face turned purple, almost black. A flutter of moon moths erupted in Meesha's stomach.

Her memory of Sargon as the bully child of Blackthorn, pointing at her wine-red face with mocking chants, should have faded by now, but his meanness toward her lived in a dark corner where shame was not easily forgotten.

She was certain Sargon had only seen her once after she'd left Blackthorn as a child. She was fourteen, and he had come with his father to Stókenhold Fortress. The memory was as crisp as yesterday.

———

It was the first time Kadesh-Cor had seen his father since Tolak had been exiled ten years before. A palpable tension filled the halls of Stókenhold Fortress. The antagonism separating her father and his oldest son was far greater than the seventy leagues between Blackthorn and Stókenhold Fortress.

Meesha's governess had been all aflutter about the visit of Kadesh-Cor and his "handsome young sons." She reminded Meesha that the younger boy was about her age. The woman enjoyed a well-earned reputation as a matchmaker.

"The king may mandate such a marriage," the governess had encouraged with hopeful eyes.

The thought of seeing Sargon was dreadful enough. The thought of marrying him made her sick to her stomach. She took solace in her confidence that no princeling could ever want a girl with such a face.

Meesha saw the teenaged sons of Kadesh-Cor before the boys saw her. She planned it that way. In spite of her resolve, she needed that advantage to bolster her courage.

Remember the impression that came in the light, she reminded herself. *Trust your feelings.*

She watched from her hiding spot on the balcony above the great hall as her father greeted his son and grandsons. It was strange to have a nephew only a year older.

Half nephew, she thought to distance herself.

Sargon was fifteen. It was shocking to see him as a young man. The puffy face in Meesha's memory was that of an ugly little boy. He was not as tall as his brother but handsome in a soft and coddled sort of way.

Nothing like Valnor, Meesha thought proudly. Then her stomach fluttered, and she fought the misgivings that flew into her head. *Will he say something rude about my face?* The discomforting thought challenged her resolve.

She tugged up on the bodice of her dress and flushed with the recognition at how much she had changed in the past year. She wanted to fill her lungs, hold her breath, and calm her nerves, but it was impossible. Her breathing was constricted by the corset cinched tight and laced up on either side. If her governess's goal had been to give her figure a swelling of softness at the neckline, she was more than successful. Meesha tugged at the bodice again.

"Your father wishes to make peace with his son," Meesha's mother had said when she appealed to her and Valnor to be civil and well-mannered. Meesha would do anything for her father—including wearing a dress.

Meesha watched as Sargon crossed the hall with his father and took his place at the large table directly below the balcony on which she stood. She had heard him described as "affected by the arrogance of Blackthorn." *Affected or infected?* She had giggled out loud at the thought. She hadn't understood what was meant by it until now. Watching Sargon fuss with the ruffles of his blouse as he was escorted to his padded chair made it very clear.

"Meesha?" Her mother had come to escort her to the great hall to meet the guests. On their way down, her mother reminded her that her nephew should be addressed as "Princeling Sargon."

Half nephew, Meesha reminded herself again, grateful it put distance between them. Grateful their blood was not the same.

Kadesh-Cor nodded to Meesha. "You remember Sargon, my son and princeling of House Kublan?" He emphasized the bloodline and punished Tolak with a disdainful glance. "You were children together at Blackthorn."

Meesha caught her half brother's eyes flitting to the blemished side of her face. She struggled to hold an expression of ambivalence.

Kadesh-Cor turned to his son. "Do you remember Meesha?"

"How could I forget *Auntie* Meesha," Sargon oozed with a condescending smirk.

Meesha dipped slightly in a curtsey and held out her hand, taking care to keep the dark side of her face turned away. The rules of etiquette for greeting kith and kin of common blood mandated a kiss upon the hand and then upon each cheek.

The courtesy of the kiss had been tainted, however, when the rebel Orsis-Kublan kissed the conquered queen of Omnnús-Kahn. As warriors of his rebel army shouted, hooted, and looked on, he had kissed her on the hand, on her arm, and then on her lips before dragging her husband from the Peacock Throne and cutting off his head. Whether fact or folklore, the thought of it sickened Meesha, but she held her resolve.

Sargon took Meesha's hand. She turned her face to him and smiled. His gaze turned to stone. He could not rip his eyes from the blemish on her face. By his expression, one might have thought he was looking at an evil spirit painted there in a crust of dried blood.

She could feel his hand trembling in hers. What social grace or chosen word was proper? What etiquette could possibly allow him to escape? There was none. He opened his mouth to speak, but no words came. His face betrayed his thoughts more loudly than his voice ever could, and Meesha could almost hear them.

How could I be expected to touch that face? How can I touch my lips to that crimson skin? How can I not be infected? His face twisted into an odd expression, and still she divined his thoughts. *If I fail to follow etiquette, what will my father think of me? What will these others think of me? What will this pitiful girl think of me?*

Meesha smiled as Princeling Sargon's marvelous manners were swallowed in his gauche, self-conscious stupor. "It's a birthmark, m'lord half nephew," she said. "It is nothing but the pigment of my skin. It is not the mark of evil as the ignorant believe. You think me a witchchild, dear lovely Sargon?" Her tone was mocking.

A tremor of humiliation cause the boy's face to twitch. He closed his mouth and looked to his father for rescue. There was none.

Meesha brought him back. "Would you like to touch it, m'lord?" Without waiting for an answer, she lifted his hand to her face and placed his palm against her cheek. "It's nothing you can catch," she said, "not like the black death or the plague." Without releasing his trembling hand, she kissed him on both his cheeks. "But, then, I can't be sure."

The boy of fancy manners became a stupid oaf. He stumbled backward, rubbing his face as if the blemish was contagious and had set his skin on fire. He tripped on a bench and fell hard on his buttocks. There was a hearty bellow of laughter from almost everyone.

Meesha covered her mouth with her fingers to hide her broad grin. Her eyes flitted to her father. Tolak was smiling at the boy's comeuppance but was too much of a gentleman to laugh out loud with the others.

Kadesh-Cor flushed and clenched his jaw. His eyes heaved javelins at those who laughed. Not for the boy's sake, Meesha could see, but from his own mortification.

She glanced at the blushing Princeling Sargon, who fumbled to regain his feet before falling again. It was now his face that glowed bright crimson—both sides—and his neck and ears.

Kadesh-Cor and his boys left Stókenhold Fortress the next day.

Some few days after that, Meesha and Valnor stole away to their secret place. Meesha was only half teasing when she said that after being around Sargon she needed to spend time with a sword in her hand.

The abandoned hall was glorious by morning light. "You were as brave as you were charming yesterday." Valnor smiled and kissed her on the dark side of her face. "You are remarkable! Where did you find such courage?"

"It wasn't courage," she said. "This is courage." With an exuberant burst of energy, she whirled her blade in a mock thrust. He parried, but just barely.

They laughed, then Meesha became reflective. Valnor knew his sister well and set his sword aside. He sat cross-legged on the window shelf, where he often listened to her.

"It didn't come from courage. It came from calm acceptance," she said. Without intending it, her fingers touched her face. She recited the archaic platitude she learned as a little girl from her governess. "Of awful fears, both great and small, the things that never happen are the greatest of them all." She didn't know where such tidbits of wisdom came from. Like so many precious things in life, the things that mattered most seemed always to have been there.

"When I was five, I stood in front of my mirror and cried." She pulled her hair back to reveal the birthmark as if Valnor had never noticed it before. She wore her hair long in a way that shrouded some of the discolored blotch. "It is embarrassing. It is ugly."

"You have never been ugly," Valnor protested, but she shook her head and waved his words away.

"And when people see me for the first time, it is always the same. They just stand there with their eyes wide and their mouths open with no idea what they should say or do. I have wished a hundred times for a hole to open beneath my feet and swallow me up."

"You don't mean that," Valnor said, but Meesha only smiled.

"Knowing I had to face that awful boy again kept me awake the night before. I climbed to the abandoned bower of the west parapet. The light of a half moon shimmered across the black waters of the fjord of Dragon Deep. I kept thinking about how much I didn't want to meet the bully of Blackthorn again. And then . . ." She raised her fingers to the dark side of her face.

"You were on the west parapet all night?" Valnor asked.

She nodded. "I had a curious impression. It was as if a sunbeam came right through the top of my head and left an idea there in a flash of light. I felt more confidence than I've ever felt before."

"An epiphany from the gods."

"The gods have no interest in me." She smiled. "I don't know what it was, and I can't explain it, but . . ." Meesha let her hair fall back, but her fingers lingered on the side of her face. "I realized my fear and humiliation are not here." The tips of her fingers moved lightly over her discolored skin. "They are here." She touched her forehead.

"All of my dark feelings have come from my fear of what others would think of me, but the inkling in the light was that others are not thinking about me at all. Oh, they are shocked by what they see, but their first thought is not about me or the birthmark or even a flicker of sympathy. They are not thinking about me; they are thinking about themselves. They do not know what they should say or do. They feel awkward and uncomfortable. The moment a stranger is face-to-face with me, they are in greater turmoil than I am ever in. When I saw the look on poor Sargon's face, I knew that it was true."

Valnor leaped from the windowsill and hugged his sister.

"Seeing the reaction of that arrogant bully of Blackthorn affirmed what the flash of inspiration said to me. I need not fear the pity of those troubled by my face. I've decided to make a game of it," she said. "I've seen enough reactions that I can put them into three categories. They are, first, 'Completely Blind,' and second, 'Oh, Look, There's a Bird,' and third, the 'Flycatchers.'"

Valnor knew Meesha's wit and waited with expectation.

"'Completely Blind' are people who act as if my face is normal," she explained. "Sometimes they are so convincing in their expressions I have to look in the mirror to see if the fairies came after all." She laughed, and Valnor joined in.

"'Oh, Look, There's a Bird' are people whose eyes get this big." She used the fingers of both hands to make a circle the size of a grapefruit. "Then they catch themselves staring and quickly look away as if a royal peacock had suddenly flown into a tree just over my head."

"Let me guess," Valnor said with a grin, "'Flycatchers' are the ones who just stare at you with their mouths hanging open." He mimed the description, and Meesha laughed with delight.

"And stand there with a gaping mouth so long a fly lays eggs on their tongue."

"And what of those who make rude comments?" Valnor asked.

"Oh, Father puts them in prison." Meesha laughed until she cried.

— ⋅ —

Years had passed since "The Hilarious Humiliation of the Pompous Princeling Sargon," which was how Valnor referred to it.

And now he was coming again. Meesha rarely greeted visitors who came to Stókenhold Fortress. She still found strangers fascinating and enjoyed watching them from a distance, but she had little interest in meeting them. Since her epiphany on the west parapet so many years ago, she felt it a courtesy to spare them the awkward moment of seeing her face.

Tomorrow would be different. Meesha knew her father would never allow her to escape a formal greeting of the visitors arriving at Stókenhold Fortress. He would expect her to welcome them with gracious hospitality.

The Princeling Sargon would surely remember his humiliation. Meesha crossed her fingers and hoped her father's oldest son might change his mind about visiting. *Or drown with his sons in the Isthmus River.* She should feel a barb of self-reproach with such an evil thought, but it was lost in the flutter of moon moths in her stomach.

Meesha moved the mirror slightly and turned her head to the dark side of her face. A glint of sun on burnished brass danced on her face like the memories dancing in her head. Meesha suddenly longed to be with Valnor and wondered if he would return from hunting in time to stand beside her.

The knock at the door was gentle. She knew the sound of her governess well. "Yes?" she said.

The woman's voice was muffled by the heavy oak door of the chamber. "Your father wishes your company, dear one. He awaits your presence in the solarium."

"Kindly tell him I will come to him shortly," she said and took a last look in the mirror.

The cloud had passed, and the sun had come again.

CHAPTER 23

"You think me a fool?" the king shouted at the men who sat in the semicircle of stools before the Peacock Throne.

The throne was a symbol of splendor and terror. The seat was cut from a single block of granite and decorated with elaborate carvings of birds. The king was nestled in a crush of cushions at the breast of a colossal peacock, which was made of iron and whose head arched over the throne on a long neck encrusted with glistening bluestone. The head was huge and its eyes fierce.

There was an old wives' tale in Village Darc that the eyes of the peacock had been put there by a sorcerer and cursed by dark magic. Some said the look of the peacock's eyes could kill a man. Others claimed the glimmering was an evil fairy trapped inside and trying to escape.

The beak of the giant peacock was a threatening spike of curved iron, more the jaw of a raptor than the beak of a peacock. It loomed over the head of whoever stood before the throne.

Enormous iron claws gripped the thick arms of the chair and protected the king on either side. A fan of feathers made of burnished brass splayed out in a circle of full plumage behind the sovereign ruler.

The rigid plume was taller than one man standing on the shoulders of another and etched in meticulous detail. Every barb, barbulles, plumule, and flue was painstakingly engraved until they appeared to have the softness of real feathers. Two hundred eyes were created with a profusion of inlaid gems from the pits of desolation. Topaz, sapphire, and emeralds, dug by Mankins and bought by blood.

Kublan wagged an accusing finger that, but for the wrap of thin skin and bulging blue veins, might have been a broken stick with a gnarled fingernail. "I can tell by your shuffling and your loathing to look me in the eye that you think me mad!"

He sagged into the pile of cushions, brooding and mumbling under his breath. "I will admit it is hard for common men to fathom the will of the gods, but I have heard of late that you . . ." He let whatever he was about to say drift away and scowled disapprovingly at the men huddled before him.

The circle of men seated before the king was a clandestine cult of mystics and practitioners of magic and dark arts: the Wizard of Maynard, Magus Zuwor; Sorcerer Vorrold, one of the priests expelled from the brotherhood of Oum'ilah for sorcery; Bawork, Necromancer of Oldwoods; and the Dwarf of Summercross, bewitched some said, by the sorceress of Dragonfell. Chief among the king's secret order was Than-lun, the alchemist and transformer of elements.

Was he not, of all, the most important? Few knew or understood the nature of their dark arts and inscrutable works. Even those gathered did not know the fullness of the king's purpose.

Also present was the high pontiff. The king had given him the task to search the nine dominions for those who did wondrous works by the powers of darkness and to entice them to bring their supernatural powers to Kingsgate. To swear an oath of secrecy.

The Raven thought the high pontiff an odd choice to gather a sodality of sorcerers, supposing his religious convictions would condemn the dark doings of Wiccans and witches. He was right.

"Blasphemy!" the high pontiff had blurted in pious indignation when the Raven had told him of the king's assignment. "It is a mad, unholy quest."

The Raven replied that voicing such opinions of the king's command would likely cost the high pontiff his royal appointment. "Or even," the Raven added, "your tongue or your pious head."

After their tête-à-tête, the high pontiff found enlightenment. "A miraculous epiphany," was the way he described his change of heart with tears welling up in his reddened eyes.

The high pontiff's religion demanded nothing. Life was a journey of fate, determined by the gods without recourse or appeal. Life was a haphazard and helpless existence, and then you died.

He mocked the cult of pilgrims who lived on the Mountain of God who spoke of prayer and purpose and the notion of life beyond death.

Beneath the shroud of ceremony, elaborate vestments, and feigned religious piety, the high pontiff embraced a single truth: *The king is the only god with whom I have to deal.*

And so he had gathered the cult of mystics, and now he stood as one of the king's most secret circle.

The king pierced each member of the circle with a glare.

"You speak in forgotten tongues and baffle the wise with your riddles. Why are you so impotent in this divine appointment? It *is* the will of the gods. It is for you to make it so!"

He glanced at the Raven, who stood beside the throne and nodded affirmation as he always did. Kublan raised a chalice, and Tonguelessone hurried forward to fill it with wine. He savored a swallow, then swirled the cup and stared into the tiny whirlpool of wine.

"You think me mad, but you are the fools," he croaked. "Tell them. Tell them," he said, turning to the plump man with rounded shoulders standing near the treacherous claws of the giant bird that gripped the arm of the throne. "They need to hear it."

"As you wish, m'lord," he said. His face sagged, and his bleary eyes bespoke a life of books and candlelight. His name was Quohorn Milner, of House Milner, an obscure family and minor house. He was the keeper of the codices, scrivener, and the loremaster of Kingsgate. He held a battered codex and quires of papyrus in his hands.

Quohorn cleared his throat and waited until each man had given his attention. He took a step forward and began. He recited the epic poem with scarcely a glance at the parchment. His voice echoed in the vaulted hollows of the throne room.

"Hear ye now, all present, the epic of Tishpiin, hero of the great deluge and poem of Melgeshrabin, king of Uruk, from the tablets of Sha naqba īmuru."

Sha naqba imuru. Kublan knew the meaning of the ancient tongue. *He who sees the unknown. He who was immortal.* He closed his eyes and immersed himself in the images that always came. He knew the epic of Tishpiin nearly word for word. He was Tishpiin, favored of the gods. Whether by the words of the loremaster or by the voice of his memory it mattered not, the epic of Tishpiin wrapped its warm arms around him with a whispering assurance of his immortal destiny.

"The gods were troubled by the noise created by mankind so they held a council and agreed humanity should be destroyed by drowning in a great flood that the gods would send—"

"No, no, go ahead. Past the rain and the flood to where the animals are all gone and Tishpiin plants the garden and is blessed by the gods." Kublan fluttered his fingers impatiently.

Loremaster Quohorn turned the page, found the new place in the text, and began again. "The gods were pleased by Tishpiin's sacrifice. Ea persuaded Enlil to bless Tishpiin and his wife, and the gods granted them immortality in a beautiful garden beyond the rivers.

"Many years later, a man named Melgeshrabin arrived at the garden and asked Tishpiin to grant him immortality. Tishpiin agreed to the request, but only if Melgeshrabin could remain awake for seven days and seven nights. As soon as Tishpiin finished speaking, Melgeshrabin fell asleep. Tishpiin instructed his wife to bake a loaf of bread for every day he slept so Melgeshrabin could not deny his failure.

"Tishpiin prepared to send Melgeshrabin away, but in secret, his wife revealed to Melgeshrabin the location of a magical plant that grew at the bottom of the ocean. It was the plant of endless life and would make him young again and bring him power over death—immortality.

"Melgeshrabin followed her directions and tied heavy stones to his feet so he could walk on the bottom of the sea. He found the plant of endless life and brought it from up the depths. He began the journey home to Uruk. Before eating the plant himself, however, Melgeshrabin stopped to bathe and fell asleep. It was then that the plant of endless life was stolen and eaten by a serpent. When Melgeshrabin woke, the serpent had shed its skin and was reborn!"

"Reborn . . . reborn . . . reborn . . ." The echo of the promise lingered in the silence before it was swallowed by the shadows of the vaulted arch.

"You must bring me the plant of endless life," the king commanded.

The assembly of magi flitted their eyes to each other lest they alone be skeptical and find themselves abandoned. Their fears were ill-founded. Rigid posture, pursed lips, and raised eyebrows showed little change of heart. The soothsayer fiddled with the talisman around his neck.

The Wizard of Maynard swallowed hard and wet his lips. He stepped down from his stool and bowed to the king. "With humility for my ignorance, your greatness, but there are some who say this plant is only a myth."

The king squinted and rubbed the back of his neck but did not speak. His silence was taken as a willingness to listen, and others found the courage to speak. The comments that followed were insightful. Each was crafted to lead the king to his own conclusions. None dared a declaration of their doubts.

The wizard spoke again. "There are many tellings of the great deluge, m'lord."

"Is it not written in the oldest versions of the story that the serpent became the guardian of the sea and no one but Tishpiin was ever able to obtain the plant of endless life?" Sorcerer Vorrold offered.

The king looked to the loremaster, who averted his eyes but then bobbed his head in slow affirmation.

"Even the mighty Melgeshrabin lived out his life in Uruk and abandoned hope of regenerated youth and immortality," the Dwarf added.

"He wished to overcome death, but he could not even conquer sleep," Bawork said softly, but his words fell like heavy stones.

The king sagged back into the pillows. If any present continued to breathe it could not be heard. At last the king looked at Than-lun. "You, transformer of the elements, shall help me do what Melgeshrabin could not. You will prepare an elixir that will make me tireless, hold my eyes open, and keep me awake for seven days."

Every head turned toward the alchemist as if they were connected, and the man grimaced.

"And when this dreadful ordeal of sleeplessness is over, you will bring the plant from the bottom of the sea for me to eat."

The alchemist took a few steps forward. "I can prepare a potion of insomnia, m'lord king, and do so immediately, but finding the plant . . ." He looked to his brothers for help. The wizard came to his rescue.

"For you, your greatness, we are willing to search the isles of Otherland and go beyond the Mountains at the End of Time, but the sea that runs to the edge of the world is vast, m'lord, and the bottom is endless."

"Are you nothing but charlatans? If it was no more than a search for a thimble in a silly child's game, I would have no need of you. You must summon the spirits who travel the earth and know all things and conjure demons with the power to destroy the guardian serpent."

"By your leave, great king." The loremaster stepped forward. He steadied his trembling frame with a hand on the iron claw. "I am the least among you. In the shadow of your wisdom, my insights are but shucks in the wind." His tone returned to that of the storyteller. "Melgeshrabin returned to Uruk, and as he drew nigh, he saw the splendor of the massive walls, fine buildings, and graceful gardens. The sight of them inspired him to praise the enduring works of mortal men. You, omnipotent and mighty king, have created enduring works. You have left your mark forever on the world. The magnificent castle of Kingsgate will stand as a monument to your greatness until the end of time. Perhaps the true meaning of the epic of Melgeshrabin is that immortality is not regenerated youth or endless life, but the lasting works of civilization that forever change the world."

A hum of wonder escaped the magi like a swarm of bees in a field of clover.

Kublan huddled in his cushions and stared into the swirl of wine in his goblet. The oppressive pall of silence made the chamber feel small. At last, the king turned to the high pontiff, who stood with his head bowed and his fingers steepled under his nose. His brows were scrunched, as if he strained to hear the whispering of the gods.

"What is the truth, holy man? Is it my destiny to build this castle and die or rule forever as the gods intend?"

The high pontiff looked to the vaulted ceiling as if his words were written in the air. In truth, they were well rehearsed and written in his head. "As the voice of the heavens and as your humble holy servant, I tell you truly that the sons of Anu can grant immortality to a man of earth. You are vicegerent of the gods upon the earth, and thus if you declare these things true, so shall it be, for you can do no wrong."

"And the stars, faithful Raven?" the king asked. "What do the stars speak?"

"Aligned in favor of your greatness, and the moon also. In the very hour the vision of your destiny distills upon our minds, the moon turns to the color of blood."

The king stood slowly. By the time he got to his feet, the mystics of the order were off their stools and bowing.

"Go and do this thing the gods ordain," he said, then descended the steps from the throne and stood among them on the floor of the chamber. "Surely your wisdom and the powers of your incantations taken together can bring this about. It will be the magnum opus of your lives. Songs will be sung of you and your mighty works as long as the earth shall be." He raised his eyebrows, his face beaming the answer to his own question. "Will I not be here in endless time to insure that the songs of praise to you shall never fade? The immortality of your king must be your life's work."

With a modest and unusual nod to show respect, the king left them. As he was about to exit the chamber, he turned back. "This must be done before the council of First Landing. Who of my enemies can withstand a kingdom united by the will of an immortal sovereign?"

The fierce eyes of the peacock glared down upon those charged to bring the mad king the secret of immortality, its beak poised to pluck their heads from their bodies should they fail.

CHAPTER 24

"It troubles me greatly!" The door to the chamber at the far end of the hall was open, and Meesha could hear the sound of her mother's voice. Meesha had obeyed her father's request to come to the solarium, but etiquette required she not interrupt what was surely intended as a private conversation.

"I understand you must open the gates to receive them in accord with the custom of the King's Road, but nothing more is required than water and provender for their company and beasts!"

The anger in her mother's voice was evident. Meesha was rarely privy to conversations between her parents, and it was even more unusual for Katasha to challenge her husband. Meesha knew eavesdropping ranked higher on the scale of bad etiquette than interrupting a conversation. Still . . .

Rather than retreating a respectable distance, Meesha hurried into the alcove of a mural chamber near the door to listen. She ignored the flush of guilt she felt.

"I've been down to the kitchen," her mother continued. "I must say in all our years at this dismal place, I do not recall a more elaborate

177

feast. The steward is overwrought by the preparations you have requested. It is quite chaotic, and he came to me for my help."

"And are you helping him, sweet flower?" Meesha heard the smile in her father's voice. She knew her father so well. She loved him as an adult, even more than she had when she was as a little girl.

"You prepare for this congregation of highborns as if it were the gods themselves coming day after tomorrow rather than—"

"My son?" Tolak interrupted.

"Your son! How can you persist in calling him that after . . ." Meesha could hear the exasperation in her mother's voice. "When he is the one who—" Her voice broke.

"He is flesh of my flesh and blood of my blood."

"But he is not *my* flesh or *my* blood!" Her voice was as cold as the wind from the frozen wasteland of Icenesses.

"I understand."

"Do you? This son of your other life does *not* honor you as the good and compassionate man that you are. This son does *not* bring distinction to your name. It is not your traitor of a son who stands with you in the disgrace of exile. Valnor and Meesha and I do. And yet you call upon us to receive him and his sons as guests—as *honored* guests."

"I know it is a burden that I ask you to bear. But I hope that . . ."

There was a long silence. Meesha held her breath lest her spying be discovered.

The voice of her mother came again. It was quiet and resolute. "You call him your son, but he does not call you father. How many times have you sent a missive in the spirit of reconciliation, and yet he has refused? In all these years, he's never sought to correct the evil brought upon us by the king. You utter no curse nor wish either of them ill."

"Uttering a curse is the foolishness of village hags."

Meesha heard a stiffness enter her mother's voice. "You are a prisoner of exile by their hands, and together they have robbed you of your right to the throne."

"Dear flower of my heart, you know I have no wish to be king or sit upon the throne. Not then, not now. How often must we speak of it before you understand? I loathe the rule of kings. What they call their 'divine right to rule' by the will of the gods is a spurious creation to sanction their vain imaginations. It is a heresy of reason and blasphemy against the true cause of the universe." He paused, then added quietly, "Whatever that great cause may be."

Tolak's outspoken rejection of the gods of the tower worried Meesha. She wasn't sure why. She gave such things little thought, but the gods were woven into the fabric of existence. They were blamed or blessed for almost everything, by almost everyone.

Meesha had adopted her father's belief in a cause, in some power greater than humankind from whence all things came and to which all things returned. It was a grand departure from the worship of the old gods of the tower. Still, she couldn't help but wonder when her father spoke this way, as he often did, whether it was wise to spit in the eye of the old gods . . . just in case.

"The one great truth affirmed in every age is this." Tolak's voice floated from the chamber and into the hall where Meesha was hiding. "The rule of kings ultimately leads to tyranny, and tyranny to captivity, and captivity to destruction."

"Then why humiliate us by honoring this pretender to the throne as if he were already a king?"

"A man cannot un-plant the seed of his loins. From the first sprig to the blossoms of the endless vine that winds through time, the fruits of it, whether good or evil, are forever a part of him." The silence that followed seemed an eternity to Meesha. "As long as there is life in this body, I will not abandon hope that we may right the wrongs between us. I hope I may embrace him again."

"As you will," her mother said, her voice contrite.

"Katasha, please, sweet flower, do not . . ."

"Though you are exiled from your rightful place and made a prisoner by evil men whom you now wish to honor, I will obey. You are my sovereign lord and my first love, and I will honor you until I am no more." Given the tremor in her mother's voice, Meesha could imagine the tears on her cheeks.

"Katasha. Please. Dear Katasha."

"But you must know that I cannot abide doing this thing you ask of me without numbing a part of my heart."

Katasha stepped from the chamber into the hall.

Meesha flattened her back against the wall of the alcove and wished she were somewhere else. Tolak followed his wife into the passage.

Katasha turned and held his eyes. Sunlight from the high windows encircled her in a pool of light. From where Meesha watched, it was as if her mother glowed. Her eyes were dark gray tending toward blue. She remained slender in spite of the softness that came with bearing children.

She is beautiful, Meesha thought, a catch in her heart.

Katasha graciously bowed her head in a slight nod and left her husband with a guarded smile. Her footsteps were light on the stone floor, the echo of them soft in the vaulted passage, then lost in the swishing of her brocaded skirt.

Tolak stood by the door and watched her walk away. He took a deep breath, then tilted his head back and slowly released the air. He stood as if the silence held him captive—which, Meesha realized—he was. Though free to roam from Stókenhold Fortress as he would, he was an outcast of the kingdom and a prisoner of exile.

Meesha wondered what her father must be thinking. Unhappy as she and her mother were about Kadesh-Cor's arrival, it was surely worse for him.

Tolak turned and looked at Meesha who stood as still as a hanging tapestry. She blushed and shrugged and smiled all at the same time. "You called for me," she said, "and I . . ." She finished her excuse for eavesdropping with a weak shrug of her hands.

Tolak breathed a gentle laugh and shook his head.

Meesha knew her disregard for decorum no longer surprised him. When she was twelve, she had put on her brother's clothes, stolen a horse, and disappeared for a day. She'd returned after dark and wondered why everyone was so upset. There was scolding and laughing at the same time. That was the day she realized her father loved her no matter what. The day she knew the stain on her face was invisible to him.

"Will Mor be all right?" Meesha asked.

Tolak looked to where Katasha had disappeared. "She will be her gracious self in spite of her true feelings," he said. "There are few in all the dominions of Kandelaar who are as fine a woman as your mother." He kissed Meesha on the forehead, and she followed him into his private chamber.

CHAPTER 25

The scream came again—a cry of agony from the edge of death. Orsis-Kublan was hardened to suffering, but the pain of that cry pierced his conscience like a rusty spike. It was the scream of a woman. *Surely not . . .* A dreadful thought shuddered through him.

He was on his way to the interrogation of a traitor. Kublan was increasingly suspect of those masquerading as loyal members of his household in the light of day while trading traitorous secrets in the dark of night.

He stopped on the landing of the north parapet to catch his breath. With a wave of his fingers he assured the valet helping him that he was fine. He raised his face to where the scream came from and inhaled deeply to prepare for the final ascent.

Triangular stones were stacked in a spiral staircase that rose seven levels from the main hall to the north tower. His heart thudded so loudly he feared it might crack through his frail ribs.

Kublan needed to retch. Whether from the climb or the nasty green elixir he'd been drinking for two days, he wasn't sure. A "preparatory potion," the alchemist had called it, to enable him to endure the seven days and seven nights without sleep and to prepare him to ingest the pulp of the plant of endless life.

As the king's breathing slowed, the boy offered his arm for the rest of the climb. He gripped the lad's arm, the crumpled vellum still in his hand. It said simply:

Omnipotent king who rules by the will of the gods,

> *I urge you to come at once to the Tower of the Dead. The traitor is found out.*

Raven to the King

When they reached the highest landing, the king left the valet and passed through the iron gate secured by guardsmen of the kingswatch.

The Tower of the Dead was an ominous black pinnacle rising from the top of the cliffs on the western-most side of the fortress. The blackness came from the lava rock used to build it. It had earned its name from a grizzly history as the place where traitors were tortured, tried, and put to death. It was more feared than the dungeons that lay in the catacombs of the old Akeshen fortress in the cliffs below the castle.

The condemned who entered the tower were kept alive as long as a skilled punisher could manage it. Torture and sleep deprivation were the means of getting information, names of accomplices, and most importantly, ensuring a confession, lest any be put to death without just cause. Some were tortured many days before they finally confessed and were thrown to their death.

The torture chamber was a circular room in the uppermost level of the tower. The girders of the peaked roof were exposed and tangled with a hang of ropes and chains. Besides the brazier and irons, there was a clutter of devices accumulated over time by the fraternity of men who found pleasure in plying their sadistic arts with the blessing of the king.

A portal opened to a sizable porch, from where a narrow wooden bridge was suspended by chains and rusted iron rings. It was seven strides long and extended over the edge of the cliff with nothing below but the waves of Akeshen fjord pounding onto the rocks.

Men of the kingswatch who worked the tower joked that the distance from the end of the bridge to the rocks was hardly a stone's throw. "Nothin' but a gentle toss for even the weakest of arms," the quip went. The pull of the earth did not require a stone, or a person, to be thrown.

"No! Please, no!" The woman screamed again. The air was pungent with the stench of burning flesh.

As the king entered the chamber, his worst fear was realized. The woman crying out in agony was Maharí, his cherished concubine.

"Stop! Stop! What madness is this?" Kublan cried as he threw himself in front of a thick man holding a searing iron rod. The man was taller than the king and twice his girth, but he immediately backed away. He laid the rod in the flame of the brazier and gave the Raven a worried look.

"We had hoped to obtain a full confession, and thus be done with this unseemly exercise, before you arrived, your greatness," the Raven said. "She persists in her innocence, but—"

"Who ordered this? You?" he shouted at the Raven.

Maharí was stretched across a heavy wooden bench, her hands and feet tied. Kublan hovered over her, confused and helpless.

"Save me," she gasped. "You know I could never betray you. I love you."

Kublan removed his cloak and swirled it over her to protect her. He turned and glared at the Raven. His eyes were black pools of contempt. He pointed a trembling finger. "It is you who will fall from the tower this day!"

The Raven blanched, his face pale and uncertain. The king had never raised his voice to his beloved counselor before, but what was happening here was unforgivable.

The Raven motioned to Tonguelessone, who stood in the shadows. The king looked up and, for the first time, was aware of the others present in the chamber.

Tonguelessone stepped forward with a folded parchment in her hand. Kublan could see the humped shoulders of the loremaster behind her. *Why has Raven allowed them in this forbidden place?*

He glanced about. The punisher turned the poker in the flame and watched the king. The commander of the kingsriders stood in rigid military stance. The master steward was partially hidden behind the Raven.

The steward is here? The commander? Have they held court without the presence of their king? There can be no other purpose for such an assembly, but how dare they accuse this *woman?*

Kublan had been in this chamber and seen the devices of torture before, but with Maharí on the planks, he suddenly saw the manacles, screw presses, and spiked collars as the instruments of horror they were. He was pierced with dread. He ached for any who had suffered here. He had a wretched pain in his stomach, and choked as the bile came again.

Tonguelessone handed him the folded parchment.

Maharí cried out, "It is not my doing, m'lord. I beg you to believe me."

The king unfolded the parchment and narrowed his eyes at what was scribbled there. His old eyes failed him. Even at the end of his arm, the petite markings remained a blur. "What is this?" he demanded and handed the parchment to the Raven.

"It is the evidence the concubine is a spy and traitor, m'lord."

"She confesses to this accusation?" He directed the question to the punisher.

"Not yet," the punisher said. "But she will soon enough."

"No! It can't be so! You are wrong! You are fools."

"Aye, m'lord greatness, it is true I was a fool to ignore the servant woman's suspicions," the Raven said. "Tonguelessone tried to warn me before the tragic slaughter of the kingsriders, but I could not believe that—"

The king cut him off. "Warn you? The woman has no tongue nor ears nor wit to write or read her own name." Kublan's fingers fluttered to his tongue and ears and ended by tapping his head.

"She and I communicate in our own way, m'lord. Her loyalty is without reproach." He gave Tonguelessone a fleeting glance and smiled. "We believe it was Mahari who alerted the bandits who fell upon the march of kingsriders."

"Preposterous!"

"How else can we explain the slaughter of Borklore's march, your greatness?" the chief commander of the kingsriders asked.

By his tone Kublan knew the man's powerful influence was at play in the destruction of the woman. *Is he the one responsible for this torture?*

"How could a slave of the harem know about such things?" Even before the words tumbled from his lips, memories of the intimacies he shared with the concubine flooded his head. Inconsequential chattering. Adoring flattery. Fawning. So many questions. But she listened so well . . . His stomach burned.

The Raven's voice brought the king back. "She sent secret messages from Kingsgate via itinerant merchants whom she enticed." The parchment bobbed in the Raven's hand.

"Seduced," the commander of kingsriders growled.

"Merchants who were likely rewarded by the bandit," the Raven hastily added when he saw the king's neck reddening at the accusation of his concubine's infidelity.

"Not true, m'lord." Mahari wept in spite of the punisher's hand above her face.

"She was sent here as a spy," the Raven said. "With the help of those who stand in secret places as your eyes and ears, I have discovered the truth of her. Her name is Yeeshundu Quan. She is not the gracious princess of Romagónian kings as you were told, nor do her veins contain one drop of Romagónian blood. She is most certainly not the second cousin of Ormmen of House Romagónian. She is a whore from the brothel of Ashendorf."

King Kublan's eyes locked on the Raven's face. The man's words were cold and precise, like needles pushing into the king's head. At that moment, he felt less like a king and more like an old man whose only frail thread of human connection had just been torn away.

"We deeply regret this discovery, m'lord." The Raven shook his head. "We suspect she is working with Drakkor, the bandit who calls himself Blood of the Dragon."

"There can be no other explanation," the commander of the kings-riders said. "They move with boldness and are often seen on the roads and in the taverns, but vanish like smoke in the wind the moment the kingsriders move. They are warned, and this whore is the one who has murdered a hundred of your finest men."

Kublan stepped between the commander and the concubine. This was the woman who washed his body and shared his bed and made him believe she truly cared about and even loved him.

Maharí looked up and caught his eye and begged for mercy. "Save me, gracious lord!"

CHAPTER 26

Meesha curled her legs beneath her and settled into the cushions on the broad sill of the solarium's windows. The room was used for sleeping, but her father favored it as a sitting chamber because of the tall, stained-glass windows that caught the morning sun. She loved the room as well.

"Are you well?" Tolak asked.

"I am," she said. "I am hoping Valnor returns tomorrow before . . ." She stopped, not wanting to speak Kadesh-Cor's name. In the shadow of the conversation she'd overheard, she was reluctant to talk about her half brother, her displeasure in his coming, or what was to happen when he and his sons arrived.

"It is unlikely," Tolak said. "When Valnor takes his eagle to hunt, no one can guess when he might return. I hope he is here to greet your brother, but I fear he may not be."

Brother? The word jabbed her stomach like a dull blade. *He is* not *my brother.* But even as her thoughts rebelled, she confessed it was partly true. *Half-truth.* Her smile wavered.

"I've asked the steward to bring us a basket of pomegranates," he said and glanced at Meesha with a knowing twinkle. She loved the sweet seeds and arils of the rare, exotic fruit, but a whole basket of pomegranates meant their conversation would be serious. She nibbled on her lower lip and studied his face in search of a clue.

Tolak was three score and four as far as Meesha knew. He was no longer the robust man he'd once been. He was softer now and slowed by a persistent pain in his back that kept him slightly stooped. Old wounds required him to limp. Time had stolen stature from his body but added to the sturdiness of mind.

The seasons of his life had wrinkled his skin, but the lines of his face had gotten stronger. His jaw was square, and the cleft of his chin was hidden by his grizzled beard. Except for the white at his temples, his hair was the color of dirty steel. Dark brown eyes peered from beneath thick brows, pinched in a perpetual scowl that belied his gentle nature and benevolence. Even at rest, his face seemed disapproving, but Meesha knew it was not so.

"I am told you and Valnor share your mother's disapproval of my intent to welcome Kadesh-Cor and my grandsons."

Grandsons? Meesha had not thought of her half brother's boys as her father's grandchildren. The intrusion of the prince of the North into their lives was forcing her to reconsider feelings she had pushed into dark corners.

"We care about you," she said.

"You do not think we should welcome them as honored guests?"

Meesha wet her lips and swallowed hard. "It is difficult for us to understand why you would want to honor the man who . . ." She was picking her words carefully when the steward entered with the basket of pomegranates.

"Ah, good, good," Tolak said. "Please set them there. Thank you." The steward did as he was told.

"Knives and napkins, and a bowl for the outer peel and pulp." The steward smiled with a bow of his head.

"Thank you." Meesha was already slicing through the reddish husk and pulling the succulent seeds from their cradles in the pulp before the steward could spread the napkins or lift the bowl from the basket. Tolak smiled.

The steward's arrival was a timely interruption. Meesha knew she had started in the wrong direction with the same lament her father had heard from Katasha. She rolled the peel back and plucked the seeds out, one by one. She raised the fruit to her mouth and scraped a dozen seeds in with her teeth. Neither her mother nor her governess were there to worry about her manners, and she knew her father would not care. Meesha relished the bittersweetness of the fruit, took a deep breath, and began again. Her words were punctuated by the crunch of the crisp seeds in her mouth.

"You are kind to consider my opinion, but what I think should be of no consequence. You always know what is best. It is easy for us to prefer to turn them away with no more than water for their horses and provender for their men and beasts." She heard the echo of her mother's words and glanced up. Tolak's brows went up and his forehead wrinkled. *He knows.*

"You might have come in and been comfortable while you eaves-dropped," he scolded, but Meesha could see it was not sincere.

"I'm sorry. I thought that . . ." She took a breath. "For Valnor and me—and Mother—these men are not our family. They are more like strangers." She expected Tolak to comment, but he simply listened. "Even though we share your blood with them, they are foreign to us and . . ." She wondered if she should say it and decided she must. "And from what I know of these matters, they are considered by some to be . . . our enemies."

"And what do you think you know of these matters?" Tolak asked.

A wash of pink flushed the clear side of her face. She knew only what little she had heard, and overheard, on the few occasions she was present and her father spoke of it. Otherwise it was hearsay and rumor and Valnor, who was the major source of what Meesha knew about most things.

She had asked her father about his past more than once, but he kept the early years of his life locked away like a book in a trunk, with pages he did not wish to see again.

Tolak raised his thick brows in a question as he waited for her answer.

The question was still in her head. "I know almost nothing except what you have inferred from time to time and from the idle prattling of the kitchen and hallways of Stókenhold Fortress and gossip in the village." She knew the contempt her father held for the rumors that scurried from pub to pub, growing bigger with each telling like a drunken man's nose with each slosh of ale. She laughed softly and said, "I would likely know everything about you, m'lord father, if you didn't frown so on my going to taverns with Valnor."

Tolak laughed. "The tales of the taverns about me are delicious, I have no doubt, but you can be sure they are nothing but fairy tales."

"Tell me," she implored. "I long to know all there is to know about your life before I was born and the few short years at Blackthorn. The years Sargon tortured me," she added with a playful scowl. "I would really like to know all the bad things . . . and the truth from which you have protected me."

"You have always been two strides ahead of me, sweet Meesha," Tolak smiled, though it was tinged with sadness. "You are not an easy one to protect or beguile, but it is time for you to understand what I have done to impose this life on you and Valnor instead of the one you might have had. With Kadesh and his sons coming, it is important for you to understand what brought us to this place." He glanced about the room, but Meesha knew he spoke of their life in exile and not the crumbling walls of Stókenhold Fortress.

"I could wish for no other childhood than the one you have given me," she said. "And Valnor would say the same. I know he would."

"Only because there was never a child as indomitable as you." A smile softened the gravity of his expression. "I believe there is more purpose in Kadesh-Cor coming to Stókenhold Fortress than water and provender and the custom of hospitality on the King's Road. He would not be allowed but by the authority of the king. You may know little of my past, but you know the core of my convictions, as I've expressed them many times.

"The rule of kings is not the natural order. It exists nowhere in nature except among humankind. Man is the only creature of creation given to greed, envy, ego, and the passion to rule over other men. The rule of kings is tyranny, and tyranny is a thief that robs a man of free will, dignity, and self-determined destiny. Who and what we might be is crushed beneath the boots of oppression." His grave expression returned. "In giving you the history of our past, it is my hope that you will understand the present and who it is that comes on the morrow. What is done cannot be undone, and what happens tomorrow will surely determine your future."

An ominous pall of responsibility settled over Meesha, both dark and hopeful.

"I trust you have sufficient pomegranates to endure such a long telling?"

"I would be willing to never eat another pomegranate if you will truly trust me with the things you've kept at a distance all these years."

Tolak smiled with unusual tenderness.

"How old were you when your father killed the king?" she asked.

His smile faded, and he shook his head. He walked to the door and closed it.

"I am sorry," Meesha said. "I am too blunt, and—"

"I was five years old when my father led the rebellion against the king."

"Omnnús-Kahn the Unconquered," Meesha said, grateful that her apology had been accepted.

Tolak nodded. "My father dragged him from Rockmire Keep and executed him with his own hand in the public square." He pinched the bridge of his nose and closed his eyes. "As I grew from boy to man, my father described the execution of Omnnús-Kahn to me in such detail that I wondered sometimes if I had been there to see it." He opened his eyes and looked at Meesha. "My father called it 'my proud legacy.'"

Meesha knew of the incident, but to hear her father speak of it caused a chill to pass through her.

"I was prepared from my earliest days to perpetuate the legacy and legend of my father, Orsis-Kublan. I was tutored in language, arithmetic, history, protocol, art, astrology, and the skills of the hunt. Of all my lessons, the most impressionable and persistent were the exhortations of my father. He filled my head with tales of his courage, his benevolence, his honor, and his greatness."

"Did you believe him?"

"I was his son. I was required to memorize a recitation of my father's accomplishment in ending the tyranny of the Romagónian kings. I was raised with an inflated expectation of who I was and what I was to become." Tolak paused, and Meesha could almost see the memories swirling in her father's head.

"He told me I was ordained by the gods to follow him as king. When I was seven years old, my father took me to the Peacock Throne and put me in the ancient ceremonial chair. That ominous bird loomed over me with its piercing eyes and long fierce beak and frightening claws." Tolak shook his head and laughed softly. "A prince is not supposed to cry, but I cried myself to sleep for a week. And then my father sat with me one night and explained that a prince was not supposed to cry."

"You were just a boy," Meesha said.

"To my father, I was a prince, destined to be a king. I was reminded every day that I was heir to the throne. I was trained in weapons and the art of war by the finest and fiercest kingsriders. When I was eighteen, I was commissioned as a captain and sent with a march of kingsriders against Ormmen, son of Remos-Kahan, ruler of House Romagónian." He inhaled slowly, then looked at Meesha, his eyes filled with sorrow. "Ormmen was the grandson of Omnnús-Kahn—the king my father killed." He turned away and began to pace. "There was a rumor of a rebellion in the south. A ragtag band of renegades called the Army of Orphans."

"Uncle Romonik!"

"You know this story?"

She shrugged. "Only a tiny bit. Valnor told me some of it after he came back from his training in Rokclaw."

"Had I known what would become of us, Romonik and me, I might have ridden north to Icenesses and become a hunter for the white bear."

Meesha laughed. "Then I'd have never been."

"And that would be a loss of unimaginable proportions."

"The Army of Orphans?" she reminded him.

"It was reported that the insurgents sought revenge for the death of their parents at the hands of the rebel forces of Orsis-Kublan fourteen years before. I and my march of kingsriders faced Romonik at a place called Passage."

Meesha hung on every word.

"Both of us came with the intent to kill the other. Who could have imagined how our fortunes would be changed?

"It was annum 1037. The ninth day of the Thunder Moon in season Mis'il S'atti. The summer was hot. It was my first campaign as a commander of kingsriders. My first battle, though why it is remembered as such, I've no idea. The infamous battle of Passage never took place. An earthquake ended the conflict before it began. Some believed it was caused by the sorceress of Dragonfell and the spirits of the underworld who take pleasure in the misery of humankind. Some said it was a sign the old gods were angry."

Meesha sensed the melancholy that gripped her father's heart.

Tolak walked to the window and stood in silence. He gazed west across the fjord of Dragon Deep to the sea that flowed to the edge of the world. From where Meesha sat, he was a dark shape against the brightness beyond the arch of stone.

"It was the day my mother died," he said at last. "She was killed in the earthquake. I did not know until I returned to Kingsgate. By then she was five days dead. 'Swallowed by the earth' was the way my father described it. Her body was never found." Tolak spoke in a whisper as if even after all these years the bizarre circumstances of her death could not be real. "My father would not be reconciled. He said to me, 'What treachery of the gods should ordain she be swallowed up by the earth in the blossom of her life?' He wept and wailed long after the days of mourning were gone. He would not be comforted. The girl he had cherished from the day they met as children—the woman he had married—was gone. He loved her with passion and fidelity."

Meesha was captured by the story and consumed by the emotions of her father. She listened with wide, unblinking eyes. She felt young, naive, and ignorant. There was so much she didn't know, and questions flooded her mind. When her father turned back from the window, his face was in shadow.

"I see much of my mother in you." He smiled. "You would have loved Edoora as I did, and, oh, how she would have adored you."

"I wish I could have known her," Meesha gushed, joyful that her father connected her to the woman he loved so much.

"It was her strength and her voice that kept Kublan from losing his way in the early years."

Meesha noted that beyond a point in the history, Tolak no longer spoke of his father, but rather of "the king" or "Orsis-Kublan" or just "Kublan."

"The king never recovered from the calamity of her death," Tolak said after a long pause. "He soothed his sorrows with wine and deadened the anguish with juice of the poppy. The void left by her absence was filled with men who whispered flattering words and lies. In the days and months that followed her death, I watched him abandon the hope and promise of his coup d'état. He retreated into a world ruled by suspicion, jealousy, and fear. He demanded absolute loyalty from everyone around him.

"Those who obeyed were lavishly rewarded with titles, honors, gems, and feasts. Those who did not—those who refused the debauchery and perversions that had crept into the palace—were suspect and lost the king's trust. Those who challenged him were treated harshly, imprisoned, or put to death." Tolak's anger surged like a wave thrown up by a slab of stone falling from the cliffs of Stókenhold Fortress.

"He added rituals of homage to the Peacock Throne and adorned himself in opulent apparel. He declared himself 'divine ruler by order of the gods.' Worse, he began to believe it."

Meesha squeezed her eyes shut and took a deep breath.

"Had Kublan remarried following the year of mourning, he might have overcome his grief. There were many from the great and minor houses who offered their daughters and sisters to take my mother's place as first wife and queen. There was no honest affection, of course, only a vying for power. Kublan was crippled by a stupor of thought, and I am not sure whether he understood their conniving . . . or cared."

Meesha realized how protective her father had been of her and how sheltered she was from the intrigues and conspiracies in the saga of kings. She was surprised at how little she knew of her family's past and the emotional toll it had taken on her father.

"Kublan refused to remarry. He escaped the memory of my mother in the feigned affection of women for whom he had no feelings. It was said by some that the death of the queen unleashed an evil lurking in his dark nature."

Meesha tried to listen without allowing her feelings to show on her face, but she failed.

Tolak said, "I'm sorry. These are hard tellings. I shouldn't have—"

"No, no." Meesha's mouth was wide, and her fingers touched her lips. "Spare me none of it. I want to know. I need to understand."

"Let us hope the darkness of the past can be forgotten and your future will be bright."

"It shall be! I am sure of it."

Tolak smiled at her optimism and continued, picking his way with caution. "You must remember that I was a child when he became the hero of the people. I heard them shouting his name. Like every boy, I knew the stories of the legendary heroes, but my hero was my father. How could it be otherwise? I saw none of the carnage or horror of the revolution, only the throngs of people cheering and shouting my father's name wherever we went. Commoners lined the roadways and chanted, 'Orsis! Orsis! Savior of the people!'" Tolak mimed the voices of the throngs making them sound distant. His voice broke, and he flushed at the unexpected emotions. "Ah," he excused, "I fear my throat is dry."

Meesha filled a chalice from the water vase and took it to her father. He nodded his appreciation and drank.

"Because I was a boy and understood only what I could see, they were happy years. Sometimes I rode double with my father through the village on his white, long-legged horse. I rode in the king's carriage when he traveled to Mordan or Kingsgate. When I was fourteen, he took me north to the dominion of Blackthorn. I shall never forget it. We rode beneath those marvelous gates, and I beheld the graceful architecture of the old castle, the beauty of the grand manse, and the glorious gardens. We rode through orchards and endless hills of grass that flowed all the way to the giant trees at the far west edge. We sat astride our horses in the western hills as the sun was going down. All that I had seen was aglow in golden light. My father turned to me and said, 'On the day you marry, Blackthorn shall be yours, and from that day you shall be prince of the North.'" He smiled. "Intoxicating for a boy of fourteen."

"And eventually you married Arina. Tell me about her," Meesha said, then almost as an afterthought, "about the mother of . . . my half brother." Her throat tightened and her voice squeaked.

Tolak tipped his head to the side, and, after a moment of thought, said, "From the day he seized the Peacock Throne, Orsis-Kublan struggled to unite the great houses, dominions, and minor kingdoms. The nobles of House Romagónian gave homage in public, but in the shadows they despised and hated him. Even in the years of his virtue, my father could not contain hostilities nor lessen hatred. He spoke of equality, but those who believe themselves superior by birth or blood define equality very differently than a common peasant who lives outside the walls."

Meesha suspected he was evading her question, but every answer held a thread of thought in the tangle of intrigue.

"I was forced to marry Arina by commandment of the King."

"Forced? The King was your father."

He nodded. "It was not the request of a father who had the slightest concern for the happiness of his son. It was the command of a tyrant who controlled my life. He was my father, but as he changed, I became more his property than his son."

"And Arina?"

"My marriage to Arina began at the battle of Passage. Because of the earthquake, the rebels of the Army of Orphans of Rokclaw were not put to the sword, nor did they drink the king's blood in an oath of allegiance as the king demanded."

Meesha gagged at the thought but remained quiet.

"The rebellion of Rokclaw twisted Kublan's judgment. He trusted no one and was consumed by jealousy. His suspicions evolved into a crippling delusion.

"So why did he make you marry a girl you didn't even know?" Meesha persisted.

Tolak raised a finger in a promise that he would soon arrive at the part of the story Meesha was eager to hear. "In the days following my mother's death, Kublan sent his army of kingsriders across the Narrows with the command to kill every man, woman, and child of House Romagónian. From there they were to march to Rokclaw, kill the rebel leader, Romonik, draw his body in the public square, and put his head on a spike. The headless bodies of the rebel Army of Orphans were to be hung by their heels on the road from Rokclaw to West River."

Meesha's mouth gaped open, her breathing shallow.

"Before the great slaughter could take place, Ormmen, son of Remos-Kahan and ruler of House Romagónian, offered an alliance to be sealed by marriage—his sister, Arina, to me, the son of the king."

"His sister?"

Tolak nodded.

It was troubling enough to marry a girl I knew nothing about, but I was being wed to the sister of the man I had faced at Passage with every intention to kill."

Meesha leaned forward to catch every word.

"Kublan's threat of extermination was an extravagant boast, so an alliance, however fragile, was better than spilling the blood of his elite kingsriders.

"You were a grown man, a captain of kingsriders, but your father never asked you or discussed it?"

"By the time I learned of it, the arrangements had been made and oaths taken. My objections were met with a threat of violence."

"And you had never even seen her?"

"I saw her for the first time on the day of our marriage in annum 1038. She was seventeen. It was the opening day of the Tournament of Harvest, on the fifteenth day of Samna, Moon of the Flying Duck.

"The king presented us. I say 'king' as by then I rarely thought of him as my father. Arina was led to the rostrum and given to me by her brother, Ormmen, whom I had not seen since the battle of Passage.

"Was she pretty?"

Meesha's question stopped him, and he laughed out loud. "Ah, I fear I am giving you too many facts and not the tale of romance a woman might prefer."

Meesha blushed.

"I confess she was a comely girl, to my great relief, and though I deeply resented the imposition of my father, I made an effort to act kindly toward her. The poor girl was trembling like a cornered rabbit.

"Kublan's oration was a pompous soliloquy on the significance of the historic alliance and friendship between Houses Kublan and Romagónian. He said nothing about Arina. Nothing of her beauty, her virtue, or even the traditional invocation that the gods would grant her a fruitful womb."

"And what of you? Did he say nothing of your valor or your strength? Your remarkable intelligence and breathtaking handsomeness?" Meesha teased, with obvious affection.

Tolak smiled at her humor, but Meesha could see in his eyes that the king had said nothing to honor his son.

"No one believed a marriage could cure the rage and hatred between our two houses. Arina was the granddaughter of the murdered king, and her husband was the son of the man who had cut off his head." Inhaling deeply and letting his breath slip away in a deep sigh, he slumped back into his chair with the weary look of a man returning from an arduous journey. He shook his head as if the madness of what had happened so long ago still baffled him. He looked at Meesha. "Our marriage was a yoke of glass on the neck of oxen," he said. "How could it be more?"

Meesha set aside her half-eaten pomegranate. She wanted to put her arms around her father and hug him the way she had so many times when she was a little girl. "I can hardly imagine what it would be like to marry someone I didn't know."

"You've not finished your pomegranate," Tolak said, deflecting her comment with a smile.

She picked up a few of the seeds that remained on the napkin. They were tart, and her lips puckered. The question she wanted to ask her father was not a question she should ask, but she could not restrain her curiosity.

"You said she was comely. Was she pretty? Beautiful?"

Tolak's face relaxed, and a twinkle came to his eyes. "Not as beautiful as you or your mother, but lovely in her own way. She was very young, but then so was I, though I thought myself a man of maturity and extraordinary wisdom."

They laughed together, and Meesha asked her burning question as delicately as she knew how.

"Did you ever . . . come to love her?"

"Love?" Tolak stood and walked to the window again. "The longer I live, sweet Meesha, the less I understand about the mysterious emotion we call love. Is romance the same as love?" He asked the question softly. "I confess there was a curious excitement in meeting the girl I was to marry on the day of our wedding, but was that feeling romance or love?" He shook his head. "I was so filled with the bitterness of being told whom I was to marry that romance had no chance, and certainly not love."

"Were you friends at least? Mother told me friendship is more important in marriage than love."

"Arina and I were never friends. Our marriage was a delicate truce that kept her family and my family from killing one another for thirteen years. But she was a good woman, a fine lady. She was kind. Patient. Being fond of her was not difficult, and my expressions of affections were not unpleasant—but love?"

"But you lived together, and you must have . . ." Meesha changed her mind. She could not ask *that* question. She blushed when Tolak turned from the window with raised eyebrows.

"Yes, Arina gave me a son," he said in answer, "but Kadesh-Cor was the only child she bore." He turned again to the window. "If there was a time I finally and fully loved the woman given to me as wife, it was in the dark days before she died. You cannot imagine the horrors wrought by the plague of black death. I stayed at her side day and night until the end. I held her in my arms to quell her chills and cool her fever the best I could. I fed her broth and bathed her feet, and when her skin turned black and her toes began to rot away I rubbed her with oil. I cried to all the gods, past and present, including those I'd disavowed, and pleaded with the great cause of the universe to spare her life."

Meesha had always loved her father, but she had never felt such deep affection and empathy as she did at that moment.

"I was a fool to wait so long," Tolak said after a long pause. "The discord and aloofness that spoiled our years together were swallowed into nothingness by my grave concern for her in those final days and hours. It was not until I abandoned myself to taking care of her, with no consideration of myself, that I realized I loved her. When she died, my deepest regret was that I had not loved her so for all our lives."

Meesha blinked, hoping to stop the tears, but they escaped and wet her cheeks. She was grateful her father was still looking out the window. When he turned back to her, the smile on his face left Meesha certain the goodness and joy of his life with Katasha had more than filled the void of that past sorrow and regret.

CHAPTER 27

Kublan pointed to the parchment in the Raven's fist. "And this is the proof of it?"

"Taken from her hand as she was about to enter the bazaar and liaise with a merchant of Wilde Crossing, a swindler who trades in bluestone from the pits of desolation."

"From her very hand?"

"By Tonguelessone, who followed her."

Kublan glanced at Tonguelessone. She nodded, and he shuddered with a wave a nausea, without wondering how she followed such conversations.

"Was it intended for the bandit, Drakkor?" Kublan narrowed his eyes until they were tiny black holes beneath his grizzled brows.

"We suspect the message was intended for the bandit, but we are not sure," the Raven said. "For whomever it was intended, it is treachery."

"By the wrath of Anu, could you not extract a confession from the merchant and leave this woman be?" Kublan glared at the punisher, who trembled at the king's anger in spite of his brawn.

"He died on the wheel 'afore I could loosen his tongue, m'lord. I had hardly—"

The king cut him off. "Then you are to blame for this!" He looked at Maharí and struggled to contain his rage. "Read it to me. Read it! What does it say?" he bellowed.

"We can't read it, m'lord," the Raven said and nudged the loremaster.

"It is written in a hieroglyph unknown to us, m'lord king." The loremaster shuffled forward and took the parchment from the Raven. He stepped to the archway that opened to the bridge and held it up to catch daylight. "Fragments of the archaic language tangled into a scribbled code of sorts, I'd say. I've deciphered a few of the characters and guessed at others." His bony finger traced a certain group of characters from right to left. "Here, for example, the meaning is 'to disembark' or 'landfall,' and this is a designation of time."

"First Landing?" the Raven suggested.

"Yes, yes, that could be it."

"Meaning perhaps the king's council at First Landing?"

The loremaster studied the text for a moment, then his face brightened with a smile that failed to raise his sagging cheeks. "The archaic word is 'gathering,' but yes, 'a gathering at early landfall' could mean the same."

"I want to know what it says and who it was intended for!" the king barked.

"That is why we have arrested the woman and brought her for confession," the Raven said.

"There are single words and inferences but sparse context," the loremaster offered. "'War' is repeated in several places, the literal meaning is 'place of killing,' but . . . And here it speaks of 'furious ones,' which might be 'warrior' or 'one who fights.' The symbol for moon, here"—he tapped the parchment—"appears several places and always with . . ." He narrowed his eyes, then shook his head. "High place' or 'tall place.'" He shrugged. "This symbol is most curious. It is the character for 'beast,' or 'dragon,' perhaps, but with the added curl, you see here—" He held up the paper, though it was too far away to be seen by the king. "The mark could mean 'of ancient times.'"

"'Beast or dragon of ancient times'?" the Raven mused. "I fear your imagination has twisted your head. Might it simply mean 'horses'?"

The loremaster stroked his cheeks as he puzzled over the cryptic text. "No, no. Can't be 'horses,' not with that." He pointed to an obscure marking on the parchment. "Most likely means 'beast,' but the way its written it could be any wild creature of ancient times, a hump-bear or smilodon or even the mythical dragonwolff."

The king chortled with disdain. "You think this concubine is capable of such complexities? The betrayer is lurking in the shadows of Kingsgate, laughing at your stupidity. Or is the traitor standing among us? Is it you, or you?" He swept his finger across the room, then looked at the Raven and lowered his hand. The knot in his stomach tightened.

The old king leaned down until he was near Maharí's face. Her eyes were wide and pleading. She turned from his sour breath, but he gripped her face and turned it back.

"Who gave you this message? Who? Please, sweet flower, tell me." His voice grew cold. "Who gave it to you? Who is it for?"

The loremaster spoke suddenly. "This mark is a declaration. 'Behold' or 'attention.' And this means 'revenge,' quite literally—'eye for eye and head for head.' And this . . ." He rambled on as if they had gathered for a translation of the document rather than the execution of a traitor. He narrowed his eyes and rippled the skin of his face once again. "This is a royal title of some sort. No comparable words, really, most likely 'prince of revenge' or . . ." He mumbled to himself in low whispers. "Lord of . . . of . . . hmm. Vengeance." He cleared his throat. "'Behold Lord of Vengeance' is what I think is here written."

"Lord of Vengeance?" the king's face twisted into a fist of wrinkles.

The loremaster nodded.

The king leaned close to the concubine again. His face softened as memories of her swirled behind his eyes, but his words were hard and bitter. "Who is the Lord of Vengeance? Is it Drakkor? Is it the bandit who slaughters my kingsriders?"

Maharí clenched her jaw and rolled her head away. Her cheeks were smudged with the soot of the brazier and streaked with tears. Crusted scabs of blood clung to her skin.

Not even the savage circumstance could rob Maharí of her exotic beauty. The sweat of her body and smoke of the fire could not smother the scent of her. Kublan took her face in his hands and slapped her hard across the cheek.

"Tell me, or by the gods I shall leave them to their task. Please, please don't force me to step aside. . . . Tell me what you know of this bandit Drakkor, this Lord of Vengeance." The king's shoulders sagged, and his hands slipped from her face. He was no longer a king condemning a traitor. He was an old man with a wounded heart. "Why have you betrayed me? Speak to me! Let me save you!"

"If I tell you do you promise to spare my life?" The words came in a short gasp of breath. She wet her lips and coughed. "Will you believe me if I speak? I am dead to those who have beguiled me." She held his eyes. "Am I also dead to you?"

The king rubbed at the pain in his palm from slapping her, the sting of it deeper than the skin.

She choked on the bile in her throat. "They will torture me until I say whatever they want to hear. It is not the truth they seek. It is only the salving of their shame for murdering a woman the king loves more than them."

The king swept his eyes around the chamber in search of a sanctioning nod to violate the rules of the tower. Some ascension to his need to show the woman mercy. Every face was resolute and grim, save one.

His anger was a voice crying in his head. *May you who disapprove and dare to question me be cast into the pits of fire! I am king. I rule by the will of the gods, and I will soon have endless life and stand on your graves long after the stink of your decaying flesh is gone and the last trace of you is devoured by worms.*

The thought pounded through his head, but courage came from the gentle nod of the silent nursewoman. The look on her face was one of understanding if not forgiveness. He gave no thought to the irony that the woman who brought Maharí to justice was the only one willing to extend her mercy.

"If I refuse to confess," Maharí said, "they will torture me until I'm dead, and even if I live, they will throw me from the tower unless you prevent it."

The king jutted his chin and straightened his frame. His voice was defiant. "Betray this rogue who has beguiled you. There is no shame. He beguiled my great captain, Borklore. Tell me all you know of this Drakkor and promise loyalty to me and you will live."

"Will you swear it?"

"Yes."

"Will you swear it on your honor as King and he who rules by the will of the gods?" Maharí moaned.

"You mock me with the snarl of a witch-woman."

Kublan screamed and lifted her head with a fistful of her raven hair. He pulled a dagger from an ornate scabbard of encrusted brass and held it against her throat. "By the gods, I shall cut your throat and throw you from the tower myself if you show no humility or gratitude for granting you your life."

"Swear it," she said, her voice trembling and pinched to hoarseness.

"Curse you!" He yelled and slammed the dagger into the wood so close to her head the knuckles of his fingers touched her face. His shoulders sagged as he yielded to the strange power she held over him. "I swear it on my honor as king. Now tell me where I shall find this Lord of Vengeance, this Drakkor." He wrenched the dagger and held it up. "I will personally cut his heart from his chest while he is yet alive."

The chamber went as silent as black stone. A blister of sap popped in the fire. A crow cawed over the bridge. No one breathed. Maharí's head thumped on the wood as the king pulled his hand away.

"Gracious lord," she said and bid his eyes follow hers to the leather thong binding her bleeding wrist. The king waved his hand, and the punisher untied Maharí's bindings. She stood slowly, drawing the king's cloak around her. Every movement registered as pain on her face. Fluid oozed from the deep burns and mingled with her blood. She retreated to the open portal where she stood with her back to the wall. She scanned the faces in the room, stopping at each. Her black eyes gleamed with defiance and hate.

Every eye was on the traitor. Every ear was eager to hear her confession. Maharí stood tall and elegant.

She raised her chin and brushed aside her fallen locks, revealing her face.

"The Lord of Vengeance is *not* the bandit Drakkor. I have never heard that name before today."

The Raven was drawn forward by the shock of the woman's confession. "If not Drakkor, then who is the Lord of Vengeance?"

"I swore to tell you all I know of the bandit Drakkor in exchange for my life. I know nothing of the man. I have kept my word." Maharí sought the king's eyes, but they were wide and fierce and staring at the Raven.

"What trickery is this?" the Raven demanded.

"There is no trickery, m'lord Raven to the King. I have answered truly as I was asked."

"Who is he?" the king demanded. "Not one of House Romagónian? Ormmen would not dare. Such treachery is too easily uncovered."

"She did not come from House Romagónian," the Raven reminded him.

Not Drakkor? Is he an unknown rogue or—Kublan shuddered at the dreadful thought—*Someone I trust, hiding in plain sight, shrouded by familiar robes of respectability?*

Maharí held the king's eyes and said nothing.

The Raven came closer to the concubine. "But the Lord of Vengeance is not unknown to you. Earn the unworthy life granted to you by this gracious sovereign and reveal this enemy to us."

A mocking smile quivered at the corner of Maharí's mouth. "'Tell me all you know of this Drakkor and promise your loyalty to me and you will live.'" She recited the words of Kublan. "These are the words of your gracious sovereign." She locked eyes with Kublan. "I have told you all that I know of the bandit—nothing. And now I call upon your honor as king to grant me my life."

"I shall grant you death!" Kublan shouted, pushing past the Raven and gripping Maharí's perfect face in the bony claw of his hand. "You will speak the name of this enemy who dares to plot against me. I am the king!"

"You are no king!" Maharí scorned. "You are a pathetic old man who will soon be dragged into the street and put to death by the Lord of Vengeance."

The king's lips quivered, but he was too stunned to speak. The madness in him was rising. His eyes were wide, his nostrils flared. He crushed her face with one hand and grabbed a fistful of her hair with the other, twisting her neck.

"How I loathe the touch of your hand and the stink of your breath. Death will be a sweet escape," she said.

"Kill her!" he screamed.

The punisher started forward, but in an explosion of violence, Maharí ripped the king's fingers away from her face. The cloak fell away. She slammed her bare knee into the old man's crotch. He crumpled with a horrible groan and released his grip on her. She whirled through the portal and ran to the end of the bridge. The punisher and the kingsrider started after her.

"No! No!" Kublan groaned. He was crumpled in a heap. "I will kill the whore of a traitor myself!"

The men stopped where the narrow wooden bridge met the open porch. The Raven helped the king to his feet.

"The ax. Give me the ax." Kublan staggered to the portal with the Raven's help. The punisher handed him a bloodstained ax and stepped aside. The king approached the bridge, but the commander of kingsriders blocked the way.

"It is too dangerous, m'lord."

"He speaks truly. It is for him to finish it." the Raven said.

"Move aside!" The king pulled free of the Raven's steadying arm and gripped the handle of the ax with both hands.

The commander grimaced but stepped aside as Kublan started across the bridge.

Maharí faced him from the end of the wooden walkway. She stood perfectly still, tall, and defiant. A shaft of sunlight pierced the clouds as if the gods were watching. When the light struck her hair, it glistened with a sheen of burnished gold. The sun was low and cast her in a haunting glow as if she were an incarnation of Inanna, goddess of war and sensual love.

Reason smothered his rage. The king was gripped by fear. He stopped a few strides away and looked into the abyss. The crashing waves were faint and far away, but the sound of them rose in the swirling mist and pounded in his ears.

He was suddenly enveloped in a white haze. He wobbled to one knee, blinded, light-headed, and lost. When he was able to see again, Maharí was no longer on the bridge. She was floating downward on a shaft of light that pierced the swirling mist, a shimmering glow of silver on black wings that caught her up and carried her aloft to clouds that glistened amber in the last light of day.

He couldn't breathe, and all that was light became darkness.

—— ——

The king jolted awake with fire in his nose. The Raven knelt over him with the salts of hartshorn crystal pressed to his nostrils.

As the biting scent awakened his senses, his mind was knotted around a single question: *How soon before the Lord of Vengeance emerges from his secret place and comes to murder me?*

As he stared at the circle of faces huddled over him, he felt an urgency to convene the council at First Landing. He must form an alliance with all the houses, great and small, to quell the forces of darkness rising on a tide of sorcery beyond his ken.

CHAPTER 28

Tolak looked at his beloved daughter, who was hastily wiping tears from her cheeks. How he loved this child. Meesha had listened to the hard tale of her family's history and borne it with grace and understanding. *So like her mother,* he thought with pride.

The light from the window behind him illuminated Meesha in a halo of gold, reminding him of the night she had been born.

Katasha had been terribly distraught by the crimson stain on her infant daughter's face. Tolak did what he could to comfort his wife, but his own reaction to the blemish was unexpected. At first, he wondered if the birthmark was a punishment by the gods he disavowed. But then, like a flower opening its petals to the rays of the sun, the strange words came into his mind: "The kingdom of light will come again." It was more than a mere thought; it was the whispering of a quiet voice. The impression was accompanied by a wave of calm reassurance that there was purpose and meaning in all things—even the mark on his daughter's face.

That same sense of reassurance returned to Tolak as he watched his daughter dry her tears. He felt certain she was known by the great cause of the universe, whatever it might be.

The kingdom of light will come again, he thought. *How odd that those words have found me again after so many years.*

— —

Tolak had heard the expression the first time nearly thirty years before. The line came from a fragment of a very old parchment that had fallen into his hands, reportedly uncovered from earthen jars found in the ruins near Village Candella. The tattered scraps of calfskin were badly damaged, but certain of the curious markings could still be seen and, he hoped, deciphered. As a young man, Tolak had developed a fascination for the lost peoples who inhabited the land before the coming of the early voyagers and those mistakenly called "First People."

He sent for Rooshléembish Onlottle, the Mankin scholar of Harven, known for his adeptness at pictographs and archaic languages. Some said he even had a magic stone that allowed him to interpret ancient writings.

Tolak brought the diminutive scholar to Blackthorn to study the fragments of parchment and use his "magic stone"—if the rumors were true—to interpret the symbols. The scholar was a persnickety fusspot and insisted on complete privacy to study the old manuscripts. The Mankin was fastidious in his labors and peered at the manuscripts day after day through his stone of translucent white crystal, often from first light to dark, and then by candlelight.

Tolak was the only one allowed in the solarium when the scholar was working. As a condition of their arrangement, Tolak took a vow of secrecy and agreed not to stand too close to the scholar or pester him with questions. From what he could observe about the "magic stone," the facets of the crystal refracted the light and enlarged the markings in a way that made them legible. *Or did the light change them?*

On the ninth day of Making Fat Moon in season Res S'atti, the Mankin scholar sent for Tolak. It was midsummer and the days were long, but by the time Tolak arrived at the cottage where the Mankin worked, the sun was setting behind the forest of giant redwoods to the west.

The Mankin lighted a double-wicked candle as daylight turned to the blue of night. "It's a riddle of sorts," the little scholar said and pulled the flame closer. He puzzled over the scribbling of characters and symbols and the alternate translations he had made with his quill on leafs of calfskin vellum.

"What kind of riddle?" Tolak asked, settling beside him on the bench.

"If I knew," the Mankin chortled with a demeaning scowl, "it wouldn't be a riddle, now would it?" He leaned over the parchment until his large head was almost on the table and put his eye to his stone. He hovered over the parchment for a long time, reading aloud, but with such muted mumbling that Tolak understood none of it.

Though his view of the parchment was mostly hidden, he was able to catch a fleeting glimpse of the white crystal. At times it looked to be opaque. At other times it was clearly translucent and seemed to pulse with a soft glow. Not the yellow light of candles but a clear light of perfect white. From where he stood and what little he saw, Tolak had no idea what it was. He found the mystery of it unnerving.

The Mankin straightened at last.

"What does it say? Tolak asked.

The Mankin shook his head as he slipped the stone into the bag around his neck. By the look on the scholar's face, Tolak had the feeling he had discovered something he was reluctant to share.

"It seems to be a prophecy or . . ." The Mankin paused to scratch out some of what he'd written on the vellum.

"Can you interpret it?"

"You've paid me well, and I cherish my reputation, but I am not sure I've got it right."

"Can you make out the essence of it?"

"The manuscript is damaged, and we have no words in our language that can be directly translated from much of what is written."

"But you must try."

Rooshléembish Onlottle scratched the stubble on his right cheek with his little fingers. Against a face too large for his body, his hand looked even smaller than it was. "I cannot attest to the accuracy," he warned again.

"Well enough," Tolak agreed with growing impatience.

"And you must not speak of it!"

"Never with your name attached," he promised. "Even if I could pronounce it, remember it, or write it in the ancient tongue." Both men laughed.

"If I fill the holes with the closest words we have, it might mean something like, the kingdom of light will come again and the stones of the sun . . ." He paused and looked at his notes, shook his head to indicate there were no words to fill the gap, then continued. "The stones of shining—perhaps, the stones of light—be gathered in thy hand and returned to . . ." He paused again as if trying to decide which of the three words he had written should be used. "Returned to the Immortal Crown on the sacred mountain of him—" He tapped the symbol he had carefully copied. "This symbol was also used for the name of the god of the pilgrims, Oum'ilah," he commented and then continued, "of him who touched them for renewal, regeneration, and the promise of eternal life."

"What does it mean?" Tolak asked.

The Mankin shook his head. "I have heard something similar before, but I do not know what it means."

CHAPTER 29

Meesha respected her father's long silence but hoped he would continue the story. When he finally walked back from the window, she asked, "Did the alliance between the great houses continue?"

He shrugged. "My marriage to Arina spared the spilling of blood, but there was never a genuine reconciliation."

Meesha's voice was quiet. "What was the real reason the king exiled us to this place? I've been told several different stories."

"As Kublan promised, upon my marriage to Arina, I was proclaimed prince of the North and became Baron Magnus of Blackthorn, and we moved to the castle there. I was happy to be isolated from my father by the distance between Kingsgate and Blackthorn. When Kadesh-Cor was born, my joy made it easy to ignore the foolishness of my father."

Meesha saw the glimmer of happy memories in her father's eyes. She had never thought of Kadesh-Cor as an innocent baby and a source of joy to a young mother and father. She felt a flush of guilt, but it was Valnor who teasingly called their half brother "The Evil Prince." *Half brother!* There it was again.

"Eight years slipped by with only brief confrontations with my father. I confess I turned a mostly blind eye to the rumors of his repression and cruelty. Hunters on their way to Icenesses often stopped and brought us word. I wrote to him from time to time, urging him to remember who he had been and the righteous cause of his rebellion. All but the last of the missives went unanswered. The last one was a letter delivered by the king's courier announcing that the king was sending a march of kingsriders to Blackthorn to collect his grandson."

"Kadesh-Cor?"

"He was eight. Kublan insisted his only grandson needed to be raised at Kingsgate under his influence. I refused. It was not a disagreement between a father and his son. It was a collision between a tyrant king who used lethal force to get his way and his heir to the throne with whom there was a growing disaffection.

"Taking our son shocked me, but it was Arina who forced me to realize what he was capable of doing, even to those whom he professed to love. Arina never truly recovered from the theft of our son by the king. Even so, she manifested a strength and courage I had never imagined was in her. It was because of her that I could no longer keep my eyes or my mouth shut. I condemned my father's tyranny and openly challenged his claim of divine right to rule." Tolak took a deep breath. "I told him he was king because he had murdered a man and stolen his throne, not because the gods willed it." Tolak paused. His emotions were palpable, and Meesha felt as if she had been there to witness the confrontation.

"He told me it was my destiny to follow him on the throne. He even threatened me, but standing before him as he sat on the Peacock Throne, with the entire court there to hear, I told him I would rather die than sit on a throne that had turned a good man into a tyrant and dragged a once-wise man to the edge of madness."

"You said that to your father? In front of his entire court?"

Tolak nodded. "And that was before he was beset by his illusion of immortality."

"And for that you were never forgiven." It wasn't a question.

He smiled ruefully. "Expressing my views in the presence of others added to the disaffection."

Meesha could hardly imagine such courage or foolishness. "It is remarkable you lived to tell the tale," she mused. "And Kadesh-Cor sided with your father?"

"He was raised by my father at Kingsgate. We saw him only twice before his mother was taken by the black death. He came home to Blackthorn for the funeral. He was twelve. I was pleased he was given a break from his training and allowed to stay for a short while. In a small way, we reconnected as father and son. At least, I like to believe we did."

"Was it on that trip to Blackthorn that Kadesh-Cor betrayed you to the king?"

"You know more of the story than you confessed," he said with a scowl that fell just short of serious.

"Valnor." She shrugged an explanation.

"The trouble with Kadesh-Cor began when he returned to Blackthorn in the season of the changing leaves in annum 1059. He came with Lyra, the girl he had married at Kingsgate with the blessing of the king. We received no news of it until the day they arrived quite unexpectedly at the Blackthrone gates.

"The conflict between my son and I was not as most supposed. It was not something I did or said that turned his heart and started his vicious reports to the king. It was his contempt for your mother. Katasha and I married a few months after the death of Arina in the winter of the Strong Frost Moon in season Kit S'atti. Kadesh had grievous disaffection for Katasha from the moment they met. In truth I've never known why."

"Lyra perhaps?" Meesha offered.

Tolak narrowed his eyes. "Perhaps," he said and continued. "With Arina's death, the fragile alliance between House Kublan and House Romagónian vanished. But Katasha was the sister of Romonik of House Dressor, who was an ally and friend of Ormmen, ruler of House Romagónian."

Meesha knew her father met her mother, Katasha, when he took Arina's body to her homeland for burial, but she had not understood why Katasha was present at the burial until her father connected Arina's brother, Ormmen, with Katasha's brother, Romonik.

"I married your mother without the king's permission. There was a grave disaffection between us by then. Kadesh-Cor was indignant over the new marriage, and he persuaded the king that the blood of House Kublan would be polluted by my union with a commoner of House Dressor. 'Treachery against the Peacock Throne,' he called it."

Meesha had never understood how Kadesh-Cor had persuaded the king to disavow his own son, strip him of his title, and march him under guard to the dreary, crumbling prison at Stókenhold Fortress. Now she did.

"You were exiled because you married Mor? That is the cause of the gulf between you and your father? Of our exile?"

"Marrying your mother was the stone that brought the camel to its knees, as the adage goes, and you must never speak of it to her."

"Mor doesn't know?"

"Promise me."

"I promise," Meesha said. Her loathing for Kadesh-Cor deepened, knowing the truth of what he had done and of his contempt for her mother. And he was coming here, to her home, to her family. She did not know how she could face him.

CHAPTER 30

Stókenhold Fortress was the oldest and largest of the northern castles. It was also the least habitable. Large sections were abandoned. The inner walls and turrets were cracked, and many had crumbled over several centuries. The thickness of the outer wall was compromised as shortsighted builders had stolen stones for other construction projects.

As a home, it was an uncomfortable place to live, but as a fortress it remained formidable. Its walls and imposing towers rose from a precipice that jutted like a broken nose from the face of the sheer cliff at the eastern end of the fjord of Dragon Deep.

It had been built upon ruins of ancient fortifications whose beginnings were lost in history. No one knew when the first of the citadels was raised, but whenever it was, it had been built to protect the land from the legendary Norskers, wild men of the far north, who invaded from the sea.

The fortress evolved over centuries as a parade of tyrants, renegades, and sovereign kings attempted to mark the timeless edifice with an endless cycle of destruction and construction. The complex of pinnacles and parapets, battlements and bartizans belonged to no one. Stókenhold Fortress was conquered, claimed, and dominated for a season by whoever wielded the most violent sword, but it was never truly possessed by any man.

Unlike mortal men, Stókenhold Fortress would never die.

In annum 716, Age of Kandelaar, the catacombs were used as dungeons, but abandoned when the fortress fell to the Norskers for a season. In recent years, parts of those catacombs were revived as a prison for the king's enemies. Even more recently, a force of kingsmen had been assigned as keepers of the prison and occupied the old barracks adjacent to the stable under Kublan's orders.

Tolak, his family, and the staff occupied the newer chambers on the north and east. Meesha loved to climb to the northeast tower. The chamber at the top was abandoned. The roof was partly collapsed, and a section of the wall had crumbled, but the remains of wooden hoardings were still in place along the battlement.

Meesha had climbed the tower many times. As a child, she and Valnor would race up the flat stone steps and drop whatever they could find from the battlement into the brackish black water of the moat—broken chunks of mortar, scraps of rotted wood, and sometimes a large stone that had crumbled from the wall. They counted to see how long it took before their curious collection of missiles splashed into the depths below. *One old dragon, two old dragons, three old dragons . . .*

They often got to eight old dragons and sometimes nine, but never ten. Well, once she counted fast and got all the way to eleven old dragons before the stone hit the water, but Valnor said she cheated.

That morning, a gardener beyond the gate spotted a dust cloud where the road to Stókenhold Fortress wound its way westward from the King's Road. News that the expedition of Prince Kadesh-Cor would reach the gates of Stókenhold Fortress before the sun had set scampered through the halls like a white mouse chased by a black cat.

When Meesha heard that the expedition from Blackthorn was in sight, she climbed her favorite tower on the east side. She knew the view from her secret outlook on the battlement was the perfect place to watch their arrival without being seen. She had a clear view of the road all the way to where it dropped into Fox Hollow and disappeared.

She leaned across the sill of the crenel and looked for the billowing dust on the road beyond the trees but did not see it. She remembered hiding on the balcony of the great hall thirteen years ago the first time her rude half nephew had visited. She was amused and a little chagrined that she still felt the need to hide like she had as a little girl.

The sun slipped through the clouds that hung across the fjord of Dragon Deep and touched the sea. The light kissed the bleached grass of late summer and turned it to gold. The fields east of the moat were cut into strange shapes by the purple shadows of turrets, walls, and towers. The leaves of the sycamore along the creek shimmered in the warm light, reminding Meesha of the mythical golden forest in the legend of King Noloos.

Where are they? Was the gardener mistaken? She hoped not. For all her worry, there was something exciting about the expedition's arrival.

Unpleasant as she knew it would be to face her father's other son and her half nephews, they were not the only ones coming to Stókenhold Fortress. It was an entire expedition, and Meesha's curiosity about who else was traveling with the prince heightened her anticipation.

What manner of men might they be? However awkward the evening and days to follow might be, seeing new faces will be interesting.

Meesha walked south along the parapet to a crenel where she had a better view of the road. There was still no billowing of dust that she could see. Patience was not among her better qualities. She wriggled a chunk of broken mortar from a joint of rock, leaned forward as far as she dared, and dropped it into the moat. She watched it fall and counted. *One old dragon, two old dragons, three old dragons, four . . .*

The sound of a trumpet stopped the count, and Meesha looked up. Flags of the bannermen rose from the crest of the road where it climbed up from Fox Hollow. The expedition was closer than Meesha had imagined, hidden by the swale of the hollow and density of the trees. The moon moths in her belly took flight, and Meesha stepped away from the opening and watched, half hidden by the higher wall of the crenelations.

It was a magnificent parade. The finest Meesha had ever seen, but then, she had been isolated in Stókenhold Fortress for most of her life.

She did not recognize Kadesh-Cor from a childhood memory nor from Valnor's description. She knew him at once by his elegant attire, fine horse, and position of honor at the head of the procession. She loathed to call him prince because of his history, but seeing him on his magnificent courser, arrayed in the hand-tooled leather of finest grade and adornments of the hunt, she could not help but think of him as royal.

The carriages followed, rising from the road behind their prancing horses like beautiful creatures being born. The man in the first and most ornate of the carriages was no older than a boy.

That can't be him, Meesha caught herself thinking. *Sargon would be older.* She scolded herself for doing so but searched the entourage for a glimpse of Princeling Sargon.

Is that him? The man at the window of the coach behind? Her moon moths flittered again. *Could it be Chor? The older brother? Perhaps.*

She narrowed her eyes as if it would shorten the distance. No childhood memory of a boy melded with the features of the man in the coach. *Little wonder,* she shrugged. *It has been many years.*

The last of the coaches passed. It was the color of plums. The curtains were drawn, and the passengers hidden from view. The procession passed into the long shadow of the tower as the road crossed the field and swung south along the row of trees growing parallel to the moat. When the parade emerged in the swath of sunlight, she saw glints of golden light from the armor of the kingsriders riding guard beside the carriages.

Six Huszárs followed the coaches, each riding a fine horse. One rider looked to be no older than a teenaged boy.

Meesha could hear the rumbling wagon wheels and clopping hooves of the heavy draft horses even before they rose from the crest of the road. There were so many of them, and a drove of wranglers driving a remuda of spare horses not far behind.

A grand perch to watch a grand parade, Meesha thought. She looked back at the window of the polished black coach trimmed in burnished brass. *What must Princeling Sargon look like as a man?* she wondered, then scolded herself again. *Ah, why must my childhood nemesis dominate my thoughts?*

She returned her gaze to the horde of wranglers and horses at the end of the parade. Without the boiled leather and iron of the kings-riders or the ostentatious raiment of the Huszárs, the horsemen looked more like the men of Westgarten. The sight of them calmed her, and she liked them more than the rest.

She watched the wranglers and horses until they entered the shadow of the castle. The parade was over.

The fading light made her suddenly aware how long she'd lingered in the tower. Her governess was surely frantic to dress and groom her for the formal reception of the visitors. She hurried along the parapet to the tower, but before she set foot upon the steps, she stopped and leaned through the crenel for a final look at the expedition.

The front of the parade was hidden by the bartizan that protruded from the sloping walls of the chemise, but she could see that the bannermen and prince had passed beneath the portal of the rampart and halted at the footbridge of the outer barbican.

A movement on the south road at the edge of the hollow caught her eye. The first of the chariots rose from the crest of the hill. Chariots were rare, and she turned her attention with unusual fascination. Except for the black horse ridden by the prince, the trio of coursers drawing the last of the chariots looked to her to be the finest of the expedition. They were dirty white and ruddy to their bellies from the red dust of the road.

The chariot moved from the shadow into a shaft of sunlight between the tower and the keep. As the reinsman left the shadow, he looked up at the parapet as if beckoned by the light.

He looked up at Meesha.

Can he see me at such a distance? See my face? Meesha drew a quick breath and pulled back into the shadow of the battlement. She felt a strange connection with the man gazing up from the chariot below. *Is he looking at me? Did he see me?*

She shifted her position to get a better look at the man driving the chariot. He was closer now and in full sunlight. He was tall with broad shoulders. The contours of his arms rippled as he guided the horses and adjusted his grip on the reins. His blouse and vest were open to the waist against the heat. The muscles of his chest and hard stomach were wet with sweat and glistened in the flaxen glow of the setting sun. He was striking, even at the distance, and when he turned again she saw it. The iron collar around his neck.

The man driving the chariot was a slave.

The corset felt like long fingers crushing her ribs. Her waist was cinched so tightly her breathing came in short little gasps. Waiting in the great hall for Kadesh-Cor, his sons, and the men of the wild horse expedition was discomforting enough without her body being squeezed into a shape never intended for it. To her grave chagrin, the corset accentuated the curves of her bosom at the edge of the bodice.

Meesha squirmed, hoping to ease her discomfort, and tugged at the neckline until she caught her mother's frown and tried to be demure.

Her governess insisted it was her father who'd requested the elegant wardrobe, but Meesha suspected it was more likely a conspiracy between her mother and the governess. She could hardly imagine the dear old woman would still want to pair her with Princeling Sargon in one of her romantic matchmaking fantasies.

Surely she knows me well enough to know I would never stand for such a thing, the wishes of the king be damned! She bit her tongue at the thought with a flush of guilt.

In spite of her mother's disapproval of Tolak's hospitality, it was her mother's nature to please her husband. She expressed her opinion, he had listened, and now she willingly abided by his decision.

A grand and gracious lady, Meesha mused, *but a woman I could never be. I could never bear such submission. I shall never marry.*

Tolak waited alone in front of the large doors that opened to the outer hall. Stókenhold Fortress had no slaves, bonded servants, courtiers, or the military presence one would expect in a manse of royal blood. Tolak had been allowed to bring his steward and favored staff from Blackthorn, but otherwise, Stókenhold Fortress was kept by hirelings from the village—a kitchen staff, maids, stablemen, groundsmen, and a few private guardsmen. King Orsis-Kublan had boasted it was "an act of great benevolence" to allow a man shamed and exiled to have servants at all, even if the man had once been called a son.

The kingsmen assigned to the prison were quartered in the oldest part of the fortress and isolated from the main complex.

Tolak and his family understood that, besides looking after the prison, the keepers were there to spy and report and enforce the privation of exile as suited the king.

Exile of a royal person to an obscure province or humiliating circumstances was deemed, by tradition, a more acceptable punishment for dissent and disloyalty than prison or execution. There were no bars on Tolak's chamber, and he and members of the family were free to come and go as they pleased within the dominion of Westgarten, but they were always watched. It was rarely spoken, but everyone understood that Tolak and his family were prisoners of the king.

Meesha waited with her mother and Valnor's wife, Sarina. Valnor had married Sarina on the day she had turned sixteen. Tolak had arranged the marriage without the blessing of House Kublan. Valnor and Sarina had already been acquainted, and their love had flourished. Now she was pregnant with her third child. Meesha knew Valnor loved his two little girls, but she also knew her brother wanted the new child to be a boy. She reached behind her mother and squeezed Sarina's hand and offered a reassuring smile. She knew what Sarina was thinking.

I also wish Valnor was here. She longed for the feeling of well-being that came when her brother was close. It was Valnor who kept her hope alive that the great wrongs wrought upon them by the king would be righted and their father redeemed. If such a miracle occurred, Valnor—not Kadesh-Cor—would be heir to the throne, but her brother never spoke of it. Not even to Meesha.

The women waited at the far end of the long table that was set for the lavish banquet. Forty-four places—the count of the expedition—plus three seats of honor for the prince and his two sons.

Victuals were prepared and waiting in the kitchen, ready to be served. Hirelings from the village were working as waitstaff. Ignorant to the intrigues of the highborn, the village girls were aflutter at the prospect of serving the prince of the North and his royal, handsome sons.

Meesha saw two girls peeking from the kitchen with wide, expectant eyes and shook her head. *To the lowborn,* royal *means* handsome *no matter how ugly.*

Meesha looked at her father, who waited at the door. His shoulders were slightly slumped. She felt a rush of anger and left her place at the table. She walked quickly to her father, slipping her hand into the crook of his elbow and standing beside him. She knew it should be Valnor standing beside their father to greet the guests, but he wasn't there. She didn't care what people might say. Her father looked old and tired, and she wanted to put her arm around him.

He didn't look at her or speak, but a flicker of a smile appeared at the corner of his mouth at her touch.

The rattling of armor and a commotion of voices echoed from the hall. Meesha fixed her eyes on the doorway as the moon moths took flight once again. And then she had a strange and unexpected thought. *Will he be among them? The man in the chariot?*

CHAPTER 31

Sargon was hidden from Meesha's sight as the visitors entered the room. Tolak stepped forward to greet Kadesh-Cor and his sons, and Sargon appeared from behind his father. He was no taller than she. His hair was a rage of flaxen curls. His face was a bit puffy but clean-shaven and as pallid as the bottom of Meesha's feet. The whites of his eyes had a taint of yellow. His face was well-proportioned and not unattractive, but there was something unpleasant about the way his brows were fixed in a perpetual scowl of arrogant condescension.

Meesha had an uncomfortable sense of déjà vu. She was shaken by the feeling she had been here before, in this precise moment, but it was as if she were in a dream. She saw Sargon's eyes flit to the dark side of her face, then away. As salutations were exchanged and introductions made, Kadesh-Cor's voice echoed somewhere in the back of her head.

"Do you remember your nephew Princeling Sargon, son of Kadesh-Cor, of House Kublan?" Kadesh-Cor spoke to Meesha, but his scornful smile was aimed at Tolak when he spoke the name of their common house.

Meesha clenched her jaw to suppress the surge of contempt she felt.

"Oh, how could I forget my dear, sweet half nephew Sargon?"

Meesha's words dripped with dark honey, and before her good sense could stop her, she stepped forward, gripped his face between her hands, and kissed him on both cheeks as was tradition. But Meesha went far beyond tradition. She held his cheek against the marked side of her face until he jerked back in shock and dismay.

In some strange collision of emotions, the horror on his face was softened by the fluttering of his eyes and what, for a moment, was a dazzled look of infatuation.

———

"And what does pretty Meesha think?"

They sat in their places around the long table. Sargon's voice rose above the drone of conversation.

Meesha found little interest in trivial bantering. Her thoughts drifted to the tower where she remembered standing at the crenelations of the east wall and looking down at a man with the iron collar of a slave around his neck. He was not among the few who came to the hall with the prince. *Why would he be? He is a slave.* The sound of her name brought her back.

"Meesha?" It was her father. "Sargon posed a question for you."

Meesha looked to where the grinning princeling sat in his place of honor at the end of the table.

"Your opinion? It would please me to hear your thoughts on such matters. I have particular interest in the opinion of a lady of such grace and beauty." Sargon's flirty compliment was tainted by sarcasm.

Flirting? How can that be? Meesha shivered at the thought.

Such grace and beauty. Sargon's words hung in the air. Meesha regretted the impulsive kiss that had invited such familiarity, and yet his flattering words were enticing. And his flirtations? *Is that what he intends, or is he more cunning than I and mocks me with subtleties all can see but me? Is he so detested by the girls of Blackthorn he would trifle with a girl who has a face that . . .* A knot tightened in her stomach. *No. He mocks me.* She could not escape the fleeting felicity of flattering words, but favoring anything about Sargon only increased her ire, and she flushed the compliment from her head.

"Meesha?" This time it was her mother. "Please."

"I'm sorry," Meesha said. "I fear I was in a lightness of being. What was your question, Sargon?" Her omission of his title was obvious.

Tolak, sitting beside Prince Kadesh-Cor at the end of the table, rescued the moment. "We were discussing the dangers of travel on the King's Road and—"

"No!" Kadesh-Cor cut him off with a sharp gesture. "You misunderstand me. There are dangers for commoners and peasants, but I and my companions travel without the slightest concern for the lowborn riffraff."

Meesha noted that each time Tolak spoke, Kadesh-Cor interrupted to oppose his point of view or tell him he was wrong. The thick discord between them was palpable. There was tension in every twitch of their expressions. Feigned courtesies. Guarded words. Pretended interest in the vacuous conversation.

Her elder half brother hardly looked at Katasha, and when he did, their eyes met for only a moment. Katasha smiled, but Kadesh-Cor flushed and looked away.

Meesha knew her father had hoped for some small measure of reconciliation, but none seemed likely. Since the visitors had arrived not a single word had been spoken about what was painfully obvious. Meesha's loathing of Prince Kadesh-Cor and his sons worsened.

"You travel with a great company," Meesha said, flitting her eyes to her father for approval. "What bandit would be brave enough to attack a royal expedition of House Kublan traveling under the protection of the king?" She spoke the name of House Kublan as if it were rotted cabbage. As an afterthought, she glanced at the captain of the kingsriders accompanying the expedition and added, "And under the protection of the notorious kingsriders." Her smile made it sound like a compliment.

Tolak's forehead wrinkled as he raised his brows and looked at Katasha. She used a napkin to cover a smile.

Meesha locked eyes with the burly captain without intending to. Ill-mannered as it was to stare, she could not pull her eyes away. He was a rough-looking man with a history of violence written on his face in ragged scars.

"Not by our choice," Sargon glanced at his father for validation. "We've a large enough company and are able to protect ourselves without the kingsriders."

Meesha saw the captain's contempt for Sargon. He was likely the worst of men, but in their mutual contempt for the pampered princeling, they were kindred souls.

Tolak broke the uncomfortable silence and spoke to the prince. "Indeed, and we await the men of your company with high expectations. I trust they are hungrier than we." He laughed softly and touched his stomach. "I am eager to call for the food. Will they join us soon?"

"Is that why we sit before empty plates?" Kadesh-Cor scolded. "All who are coming are here. By the gods, be a gracious host and call for the food. We are famished."

"As are the men of your company, I am sure." Tolak smiled. "The moment they take their place at our table, we shall begin. There is a fine feast prepared, despite our circumstances."

Kadesh-Cor pushed his chair back from the table and scowled at Tolak. "You expect us to share the table with those who accompany us as servants?"

"Whatever the status, caste, or station of the men of your expedition, m'lord prince"—the title was clearly bitter on his tongue—"to us they are travelers on the King's Road, no one of them better or worse than another, and by custom they are entitled to my hospitality. We have invited them, and they are welcome to my table." Tolak gestured toward the thirty-three empty places at the long table. "We have prepared for all."

Kadesh-Cor's lips soured in a sneer. "Why do you persist in this stubborn stupidity? Have you learned nothing? You grow more foolish as your years slip away." He extended his hands, palms up, like a parent perplexed by a pouting child. "The privilege of royal blood is ours by the will of the gods. It is as old as the earth and will continue ten thousand years after your body is burned and the saga of Tolak, son of Kublan, the man who might have been king, is forgotten. Your contempt for the rule of kings makes you nothing more than a naked fool wallowing through a thicket of blackthorns."

Kadesh-Cor leaned forward with one hand on the table. "Despite what you may think, I have not come without purpose. We have much to talk about." He took a deep breath, visibly trying to calm himself.

Meesha felt a surge of hope. Perhaps they had finally come to what was important above all else. The reconciliation of father and son. A healing of old wounds. For her father's sake, she hoped it would be so.

"My grandfather has sent a message that I wish to discuss with you in private." He paused before continuing. "I wish to speak to you as . . . as your firstborn, if only you will show some deference to . . ." Kadesh-Cor stood up and waved his arms as if his unspoken words were a swarm of bees. "Pray, call for the food and let us feast as family, and then we may retire as men to talk about things of importance." There was a rumbling of tankards hammering the table as was the tradition of Blackthorn.

Tolak nodded and raised his hand. The steward came quickly to the table. "Please ask the cook to have the trenchers placed and the platters prepared to serve. Have the servers take their places."

Kadesh-Cor smiled and nodded to his company.

"And shall we bring the food, m'lord Tolak?" the steward asked.

"In the very instant the rest of our guests arrive."

Meesha was suddenly aware that her mouth gaped open and closed it. She had never loved her father more. Had *this* been his intention from the beginning? Was *this* why Tolak insisted in hosting his son? Meesha felt certain that it was. Was it better that he yield to the demands of Kadesh-Cor in the hopes of reconciliation or for him to remain firm in his convictions? She knew the answer. Words tumbled out of her mouth before she thought them through.

"I've yet to answer your question, dear half nephew Sargon," she said, her eyebrows raised and her eyes bright, "I am eager to meet the men who keep you safe from the bandits on the King's Road. Perhaps you should run and fetch them?"

Sargon slammed his palm on the table in a concussion of rattling pewter and stood up. "What insolence is this! My father is prince of the North and heir to the throne. The men of our company are unworthy to sit at a table with him. With any of us! Even you"—he pointed a shaking finger at Tolak—"disgraced and dishonored as you are!"

It was only a flashing thought, but Meesha imagined leaping to the table with her sword and closing the princeling's arrogant mouth with the point of her blade at the end of his nose.

"The men who drive the wagons and carry our burdens are lowborn," Sargon continued. "Drudges, gillies, drovers, and servants. Even slaves."

Slaves! An iron collar. A bared chest and rippling muscles, glimmering with sweat. Meesha saw him again in her mind's eye and gasped a short breath. *The corset is the cause of it,* she lied to herself to justify the flutter in her stomach.

Sargon wasn't finished. "If you feed a lowborn a leg of roasted swan with butter and sweet cloves when his gut is used to eating bread crusts and pork rinds, he'll retch for a week." Sargon's vulgar imagery stirred a ripple of laughter.

Kadesh-Cor growled at Sargon. "Sit down."

Sargon sank into his chair, his pallid skin tainted with a flush of pink. Chor, the older son, was more like his father than his brother, and his chagrin at the blathering of his younger brother was telling.

Kadesh-Cor inhaled deeply then turned to Tolak. "Those seated at your table are the only guests you shall accommodate this night."

Meesha scanned the company present. The six Huszárs were seated at the table, including the exuberant lad who rode with them. Horsemaster Raahud and the kingsriders sat farthest from the hosts. Beyond them the places were empty.

"And I, once again, welcome you to Stókenhold," Tolak said. "I regret that you disregard the tradition of the King's Road and refuse the conditions of our hospitality, but none shall eat at my table unless all who are hungry are fed. Pray, call for the men of your company to join us."

Kadesh-Cor clenched his jaw. "I have sent them to quarter with *your* keepers of the prison. They shall be fed there."

Meesha was certain Kadesh-Cor knew her father had no access or influence over the keepers consigned to watch after the prison. She also knew that quartering with the keepers meant the men of the company would be bedded down in the old stables that lay a level below on the southwest side.

As youngsters, she and Valnor had explored the lost and forgotten corners of the old fortress. She knew the discomfort the drivers, drovers, and reinsman—and the man in the iron collar—would suffer in the old stables. From the tower they were nobles in a royal parade. To the prince and his arrogant boy they were little more than the animals that pulled the wagons. *Will the keepers share their ration of food, or will they feed the company rotting fruits and spoiled meat?*

"The keepers are ill-prepared to feed such a throng," Tolak offered, as if hearing Meesha's thoughts. "Your animals will go hungry as well as your men. Let us feed the men of your company here at my table and send our stablemen to help with your horses."

"The men are cared for." Kadesh-Cor pointed at the steward. "Bring us the food."

Tolak shook his head.

The steward stood as still as an iron post.

"It is not a suggestion," Kadesh-Cor bellowed at the steward. "It is a command of the prince of the North and heir to the Peacock Throne. Are you fool enough to defy a royal command at the bidding of this man who is without kingdom, rank, or honor?"

"A man in exile is a kingdom unto himself," Tolak said.

The only sound was the dripping of water and fire that crackled at the far end of the hall.

Tension filled the room like smoke. Meesha held her breath.

Were it not for his thumb thumping the wooden table in cadence with the echoing drip drip drip, Kadesh-Cor might have been a statue of an ancient king. After a time, he rose to his feet. "Is it any wonder our omnipotent and sovereign king disavowed your blood and sent you here?" His nostrils flared with noisy breathing.

Tolak rubbed his neck in sudden weariness. "There are none here who will heed your command unless put to the sword. Surely even you would not act so shamefully."

Meesha caught the contemptuous smirk on the captain's lips. When she looked at Kadesh-Cor, it was evident he'd seen it as well. Every eye was upon him. His face flushed. Heat and hubris rushed to his head. He drew his sword and laid the point of it against Tolak's chest.

Katasha gasped and brought her hand to her lips. The captain of the kingsriders shook his head at the prince's foolish action and moved his own hand to his sword. The Huszárs turned to stone.

Tolak stiffened but showed no fear, even though he bore no weapon.

"You misjudge my willingness to enforce a royal command." Kadesh-Cor jutted his chin, but his voice wavered.

"Have you fallen so far?" Tolak asked.

Meesha knew the pain in her father's voice was not from the sword on his chest but from the wound in his heart.

"Stop!" She leaped to her feet, her legs bumping the table and tumbling the tankards.

"Stop indeed!" A strong voice boomed from across the hall.

Meesha whirled around and gasped. "Valnor!" She left the table and ran to meet him.

The broad-shouldered man striding from the open door was taller than Kadesh-Cor. His hard stomach and thin hips were wrapped with the leather belts and weapons of the hunt. His square face was framed by a tangle of hair the color of straw along with locks of brown and sun-bleached white. He stared at Kadesh-Cor with cold, blue, unblinking eyes.

A enormous sea eagle was perched on his left arm. Her head was covered with a hood that had a plume of feathers and a pom-pom of red wool. Her wings were outstretched, her feathers feeling the air for balance. Her talons gripped the thick leather glove protecting Valnor's arm.

"Lower your sword, *brother*, and do it quickly." Valnor's demand was quiet and calm, but his right hand gripped the handle of his sword.

"Keep him at bay!" Kadesh-Cor barked to his kingsrider, but the point of his sword did not move from Tolak's chest.

The command caught the captain in an awkward position. He moved lest he disobey the grandson of the king, but slowly lest he escalate the foolish conflict.

"Katta!" Valnor barked and, with a forward swoop of his arm, put the huge bird in flight. The hood pulled free. Bells dangling on the jess rang as the eagle thrust upward on powerful wings. The feathers of her head were stark white against the rich brown of her body and the black tips of her wings. She looped high, then rolled and dove at Kadesh-Cor with talons poised.

Kadesh-Cor stumbled backward. His heel caught the edge of a stone, and he fell in a humiliated heap. His sword rattled away.

The kingsrider captain laughed out loud. Meesha suspected he would suffer a reprimand later but was grateful for the moment that broke the tension and ended the madness. The Huszárs tried not to snigger, but the lunacy of the blustering prince blown over by an eagle was too much as their mirth escaped in a rumble of chuckles.

The eagle reached the high vault with a few thrusts of her powerful wings, then swept over the floundering royal before returning to Valnor's arm. Valnor dug a fish head from his bag and rewarded his remarkable raptor. By then Valnor was standing over Kadesh-Cor with Meesha at his side.

"I see your manners have not improved in the last thirteen years, brother." Valnor extended his right arm to help Kadesh-Cor to his feet.

Kadesh-Cor rejected the offer and reached for Chor, who helped him from the floor. "Nimra!" he barked as he stood.

A squire hobbled forward on a misshapen foot rolled inward at the ankle, forcing him to walk awkwardly on the side of it rather than the bottom, but he showed no evidence of pain. He seemed oblivious to his misfortune.

Meesha recognized him as the boy in the coach and found herself staring at his foot. *Me, of all people,* she scolded herself.

The squire was young. Eighteen? Nineteen, perhaps. He was shorter than Meesha by a handbreadth and slight of build. As thin as the squire was, his sinew was taut and his muscles hard. It was as if the gods had given him a fine, strong body to make up for the mangled foot.

The squire retrieved the fallen sword. Kadesh-Cor returned it to his scabbard with a sharp clank of brass against quillon. "You make a grave mistake," he said, his gaze moving from Meesha to Valnor to Tolak. "We will retire to our chambers. You have until the ninth hour to prepare the table for us. My squire will remain to bring us word. I trust you will come quickly to your senses. It is treachery to refuse a chosen vessel of the king his wish."

Kadesh-Cor turned to go, then paused as he brushed past Tolak's chair. He leaned down, his voice a guttural whisper. "I had thought to offer you a royal pardon if you were yet alive when I take my place on the Peacock Throne, but by the gods you are remorseless and un-changed. Your blood is a blemish in my body. You are not my father nor have you ever been."

Prince Kadesh-Cor's words were punctuated by a rumbling of movement and scraping of wood on stone as his entourage pushed their chairs from the table and strode from the hall behind him.

The youngest of the Huszárs shrugged his shoulders in an apology and walked in a wide arc to steal a breaded trencher from a kitchen maid before strolling away to catch his comrades. He winked at the girl, and she blushed.

CHAPTER 32

"Is everyone all right?" Valnor asked.

The guests were gone. Valnor passed the eagle to falconer Fooloo, who whisked the bird away.

"Well enough," Tolak said as Katasha helped him to his feet. Valnor knew his father didn't need help, but he appreciated how his mother was always at his side. "How was your hunt?"

"Dull compared to the homecoming." He smiled, clasping fore-arms with his father.

Tolak motioned for the steward, who had barely begun to breathe again, and turned to Kadesh-Cor's young squire. "The steward will take you to the kitchen and give you whatever you'd like. Afterward, he will find you suitable quarters. You needn't wait for us to change our minds." He took Katasha by the arm and left the hall.

Sarina rushed to Valnor and put her arms around him. "I'm so glad you're back."

When Sarina finally let him go, Meesha stepped in for her turn. "You always have been the master of the grand entry," she teased.

"I came a bit too early." He smiled. "I suspect you were about to use your marvelous talents to put the prince in his place." He winked at her, and Sarina, who knew of Meesha's training with the sword, laughed. He put one arm around his sister and the other around his wife, and strode toward the kitchen for something to eat.

———

Valnor's first memories of his years at Blackthorn were of Meesha. He met her before she was born. His mother teased him that her swollen stomach came from swallowing a watermelon, but then she held his hand against her skin.

"It moved!" Valnor gasped in wonder. He was three years old.

"It's the baby kicking," she had said. "It must not be a watermelon after all."

He was disappointed at first. There was something wonderful about a watermelon in his mother's stomach. She had held his hand against her stomach a long while. Even now he remembered how vigorous the kicks had been and how he had worried about his unborn brother being trapped. It never occurred to him that the wriggling lumps beneath his fingers was a girl. No one talked about baby girls. No one seemed to want one, which made sense to a little boy.

He sat with his mother on the day she'd curled up in the great chair with her hands clasped to her stomach. She gazed out the window but seemed to be looking at nothing. Tears wet her face.

A few days later the baby was born.

He'd been told his baby brother was a girl, though he was not allowed to see her for a long time. When he finally saw his little sister, his father held him close and whispered in his ear, "The beautiful color of her face makes her a special child. You are her brother. It is your duty to look after her."

Valnor was six years old when the family was exiled to Stókenhold Fortress. For a young boy, it was all a grand adventure. It was during the arduous journey from Blackthorn to Stókenhold Fortress that he took Meesha under his wing.

He held her hand when the short-legged horses clambered across deep ruts in the King's Road and the jolting carriage gave her discomfort. Valnor discovered that he and Meesha could walk almost as fast as the caravan traveled. He preferred walking, and so did she. She loved to hold his hand and walk at his side. The villages, open fields, dark forests, and rolling hills looked different on foot than they did from the carriage windows.

Valnor and Meesha found particular delight in walking beside the biggest of the wagons. Its wheels were taller than a man. Valnor showed her how to drag a stick across the wooden spokes and hop-skip to the rhythmic chatter. Every day was a new adventure.

One afternoon, when the caravan stopped to rest and Valnor's mother and Meesha were sleeping, he slipped out of the carriage and walked to the end of the caravan. He wanted to see his father, whom he was told was riding with the kingsriders at the rear. He had not seen his father since they'd left Blackthorn. When he finally saw his father on his horse, he ran to him but was stopped by a hard-looking man on foot.

"Go back to your mother's carriage, boy," the gruff man said. "And do not come rearward again! You hear?"

Standing there with the hard-looking man hurting his arm, Valnor stared at his father, who nodded reassuringly.

"Get on back with ya now!" The gruff man pushed him so hard he stumbled.

On the way back to the carriage, he wondered why his father rode with the kingsriders instead of with his mother. He knew the man who would know. The blacksmith, Rusthammer, seemed to know everything

The old blacksmith had become his friend the year before when Valnor had run away. He couldn't remember why he had been so angry with his mother, but he remembered the kindness of the blacksmith. The old smith had found him hiding in the hay, and, with a twinkle in his eye, had put a finger to his lips in a promise to protect their secret.

The blacksmith had picked him up, sat him next to a horse, and told him a wondrous tale filled with mythical beasts. He whittled a piece of wood as his words created a fanciful world. Every twitch of his lips and crinkle of his face brought the characters of his story to life. By the time the tall tale had ended, the lump of wood had been carved into the very dragon the story was about.

Valnor did not find the old blacksmith in the caravan and got nothing but shrugs the two times he asked after him. It was almost an hour later before he caught up with his mother and Meesha.

Valnor dug the wooden dragon from the bottom of his bag. "Why didn't the blacksmith come with us?" he asked his mother when the caravan started to move again.

Her face tightened with sadness. "Only a few from our household were allowed to come with us. Most were commanded to remain at Blackthorn."

Valnor was intrigued by the huge campfires around which the men of the company gathered for the night. His mother's tent was always set a distance away. When Valnor asked if he could go to the fire with the men, his mother knitted her brows and shook her head. "Men talk about things that six-year-old boys should never hear," she said, then pinched her lips as if that would censor whatever was spoken of at the fire. She might as well have poked the curious boy with a sharp stick and told him not to jump.

More than once, Valnor sneaked away when his mother and Meesha were asleep. He crept as close as he could to the fire, hoping to hear what six-year-old boys should never hear. Slithering over rocky ground in the dark left him with scabs on his elbows and scrapes on his knees. Sometimes he got close enough to hear voices and laughter, but that was all. Mostly because he got caught every time and sent back to his mother's tent with a cuff to his ears or boot to his buttocks. Every time but one.

He had crawled to the edge of the fire and laid in the grass a long time listening to the muted voices. The night was cold, and he wanted to sleep. Just before he disappeared into his dreams, he heard one of the men speak his father's name.

"Tolak's a bloody fool."

"Done it to himself, sure enough," another scoffed.

"A prince w'out'en a castle is no better 'en a pauper w'out'en a pot!" The first man belched, and the others laughed.

Valnor was never sure if what he heard that night was the vulgar talk his mother had warned him about. He dared not ask. Whether it was or not, he remembered the aching sickness in his stomach when the men laughed at his father.

He never crawled to the fire again.

When Meesha was too tired, Valnor walked alone beside the kingsriders on their elegant, long-legged destriers. He stepped to the cadence of the iron shoes that hammered the hardened road in a shimmer of feathered hair above the massive hooves. He listened to the dissonant clank of music made by metal touching metal and the groaning creaks of boiled leather. He squinted his eyes when the banners passed before the sun, their bright colors bursting into flame. When he saw that the sigil of his father was missing, he wondered if the king's bannermen had forgotten to bring it.

On one of the days Valnor walked beside the kingsriders, the darkening clouds burst with rain. The road winding west from Knight's Tower was churned to mud. Clumps of wet clay clutched at his feet and pulled him deeper with each step. In the instant he felt doomed to succumb to the relentless monster of mud, a strong hand gripped his arm and lifted him onto the rump of a warhorse.

Valnor sat astride the woolen pad across the coupling and gripped the high wooden cantle with both hands. He could smell the boiled leather of the kingsrider's armor. He felt like a warrior of the first order.

"What is your name, boy?"

"I am Valnor, son of Tolak." And then in case the warrior didn't know, he added, "My grandpa is the king."

At that the kingsrider put a gentle hand on the boy's shoulder. It felt safe and comforting.

Valnor rarely walked again, even when the sun was shining, which made Meesha sad, but he couldn't resist riding proudly on one of the beautiful horses.

For a lad of six years, the journey from Blackthorn to Stókenhold Fortress seemed to take a year. Valnor could hardly remember what it was like to sleep in a bed, though he wasn't certain he ever wanted to again. He remembered the night he announced he was going to sleep outside like the kingsriders instead of in his mother's tent next to his sister.

To his surprise, his mother was pleased. She stood beside him at the opening of the tent, staring at the night sky and the canopy of stars. She placed her hand on his shoulder.

"If you look very closely, your future can be seen in the stars," she told him. "Some say they can even see the writings of the gods."

He was never sure where to look for the writing of the gods, but he loved listening to the men talk about the eleven monsters created by the goddess of the ocean and seeing the pictures they drew of them from the stars in the night sky.

On all but a few nights, Valnor curled in his furs and stared into the endless vault of heaven. The points of light filled him with such wonder they lifted his thoughts until he felt as if he floated in the air above his body. He could never remember when consciousness ended and the dreams began.

— —

Within hours of their arrival at Stókenhold Fortress, Valnor and Meesha began exploring their new world. Their explorations were cautious at first, lest they got lost, but once begun, they never ended. The two only became more daring as they grew older. Over time, they discovered and explored towers and turrets and the labyrinths of passageways with endless doors and chambers, gateways and stairways. There were great halls and tiny rooms. Much of the old fortress was in ruins. There were areas in such a state of deterioration they'd been abandoned, blocked off and boarded up.

Meesha and Valnor were never supposed to go to these places, but being forbidden made the exploration even more enticing. Valnor and

Meesha made up stories about the men and monsters that still lived in those secret, undiscovered places and shivered with delight.

The one place they did not go was the catacombs below the damp and musty cellar where the ancient dungeons were again being used as a prison.

One day a keeper of the prison snagged them by the scruff of their necks and warned them of a secret pit with a trapdoor where naughty children were put. It was enough to keep them clear of the lower levels of the old fortress, even though they were sure the story was nothing but a scary tale.

They discovered it by accident. They had stumbled into a secret passage concealed behind the stones of a fallen fireplace in a chamber below the north tower. The passageway descended in a steep, stone stairway to the burial crypts in the limestone caverns deep in the cliffs. In the flickering light of their torch, the burial chamber was the scariest place they'd ever been.

"I want to go back!" Meesha said without breathing.

"Just a little farther," Valnor encouraged.

"Only to the edge of the light," she agreed.

Before they had taken a second step, they heard an anguished human cry.

Meesha didn't wait for the light. She turned and ran and struck her foot and fell. As Valnor helped her scramble to her feet, the light of the torch washed across a nearly rotted trapdoor made of wood. The ghastly sound was coming from below. They ran and didn't look back.

There was no better place on earth for a boy like Valnor and a girl like Meesha to grow up than Stókenhold Fortress. It was not until they were much older that they realized their family's exile was intended as a punishment. It had never seemed so to them. From the day they loaded the great wagons at Blackthorn to this very day, it had all been a grand adventure.

CHAPTER 33

When Valnor was twelve years old, he went to Rokclaw to be trained by his mother's brother, Romonik. Given the history and conflict between Tolak and her brother in earlier years, Katasha's suggestion was unexpected, but much had changed over the years.

Tolak agreed there was no one better than Romonik. "If Valnor can endure the rigorous training of his body and tutelage of his mind, he will have an advantage over other men for life. Romonik's severity and discipline will serve him well."

Romonik, son of Mersoon, was not an easy man to be around. The hardened lumps of skin that scarred his body told of tragic tales of war. His face was a pitted remnant of the pox and held in a perpetual scowl by scars that wouldn't heal.

Romonik was born of common blood but rose to become ruler of House Dressor, a minor house of Rokclaw. His mother was a peasant girl from Village Red Nullah, and his father was an itinerate fletcher, who taught him the craft of making arrows. That was before the war. Before the rebel Orsis-Kublan killed his parents and seized the Peacock Throne from House Romagónian.

Rokclaw was a settlement since ancient times. Other than the small wharf at West River where the water emptied into the fjord—a dock considered too dangerous for all but the smallest ships—Rokclaw was the only access to Dragon Deep from the lands south.

When the Mankins discovered blue crystal in the caves of Aktodas on the west slopes of the Mountains of the Moon, hordes of Mankin miners came in bullhide boats from their ancestral home at Harven to work the mines. The harbor at Rokclaw grew into a busy port and a dangerous place, taverns and brothels springing up along the waterfront like noxious weeds after a dousing.

When Kublan moved the Peacock Throne to Kingsgate, Rokclaw became the port from where the king's share of bluestone, gold, and other gems from the pits of desolation could be shipped to the end of the Akeshen fjord where the king was building a colossal castle at Kingsgate.

Because of its strategic location and access to the open sea, Rokclaw was a battleground in every skirmish fought in the rise and fall of kingdoms from the beginning of history. Control of the kingdom depended on control of the southern access to the sea, which was controlled by Rokclaw.

In the war of rebellion, annum 1024, Age of Kandelaar, the rebel warriors of Orsis-Kublan marched on Rokclaw. It was the first day of the Beaver Moon of Rah Kislimu, season Kīt S'atti. The battle of Rokclaw lasted seven days and left the harbor stained in blood. Some said the water of Dragon Deep ran red.

Romonik's mother and father fled with their two children when their house was set aflame. They took refuge in the woods lying just above the coast but were discovered and ran to the village where they were chased down by a warrior on a black horse with spikes on its iron shoes. Romonik's father died with a sword in his hand. His mother was killed.

Romonik escaped by slithering into the sewer and disappearing into the tunnels that ran from the village to the sea. The putrid slurry sickened him, and he retched until he fainted and fell into dark dreams.

It was winter and bitter cold, and though it rarely snowed in

Rokclaw, standing water froze and by morning, the trees were laden with frost.

When he woke—frightened, hungry, cold, and alone—it was nearly dark. He crept back to where his mother and father lay dead. The cobblestones glistened in the drizzling rain. He dared not look upon his mother. He fell across the body of his father and cried. Besides the pattering of rain and gurgling of the water in the drain below, there was no sound. The invaders were gone, gathered at the tavern in a drunken celebration of their bloody victory.

Then a baby cried. The boy's heart leaped. Could it be that his sister, Katasha, had survived? With trembling hands, he pushed on his mother's shoulder until she rolled onto her back. He kept his eyes away from her face. She was rigid and stiff, and, even through her wrap, felt as cold as a frozen pond. The baby girl was bundled tightly and protected by her body.

Romonik was seven years old.

Finding someone to care for his little sister was easier than he had imagined. There were so many dead, so many loved ones lost and so much sadness, the miracle of a child who survived was a glimmer of light in the darkness.

"Yab el cárim," the woman cried out in the ancient tongue when Romonik placed the baby in her arms. "Miracle child," she said again, then wept. Her own little girl had been killed. The woman wrapped Katasha with a blanket and looked at Romonik. "Better she never know," the good woman said.

When Romonik left, he knew he would never see his sister again.

Romonik was not the name given on his day of blessing. It was the name he picked for himself. It meant "forsaken" in the ancient tongue.

He survived in the streets and stayed hidden in the stables. He stowed away on the boats that transported Mankin miners to Harven. He stole their food and drank the ale left in their cups. When he could, he'd lift a purse or steal a coin. Though Romonik was tempted to steal one of the precious bluestones, called Savin's Fire after the Mankin who first found them, Romonik never tried.

Bluestone was highly prized and guarded by Mankins wielding swords and clubs and wearing strange armor. Mankin miners were short and squat and walked with a curious dodder, but they were as strong as bulls. They were known to cut a man's legs off at the knee with a single slash of their two-handed blades. "'Tis the Mankin's way a' bringing an enemy down to where he can look 'em in the eye," Romonik had heard one crusty Mankin sailor say.

When he was ten years old, Romonik formed a gang of orphans, beggar children, and abandon boys. By the time they matured into young men, the army's ranks had grown to more than a hundred. They sought apprenticeships with blacksmiths and forged crude weapons in the cover of night.

Romonik taught them to make arrows. They learned to fight, not with the fancy skills of highborn boys trained for the tournaments but with the deadly skills required to survive at any cost. They worked at being inconspicuous, invisible. They swore an oath of secrecy sealed with spit and blood. They were children forced into maturity beyond their years. They lived by their daring but also by their wits.

The king enticed village locals to be his eyes and ears. In the eyes of Romonik and his band of orphan warriors, quislings and colluders with the King were worse than lowborn. They were betrayers of their own kind. Traitors. Romonik and his clandestine army of rebels were never found out. The mysterious disappearance of the king's informers quickly changed what some thought would be easy coin to a deadly profession.

Romonik's Army of Orphans was driven by revenge. They had all lost parents. They had all had their childhoods ripped from their bloody fingers. They refused to acknowledge Kublan as king. They were sustained by the idealism of youth and the optimism of ignorance. The young freedom fighters truly believed the day would come when they would march to the Romagónian castle of Rockmire Keep, drag the rebel king to the public square and put him in the stocks until the flesh fell from his bones.

That day never came. Instead, Romonik and his Army of Orphans marched to Passage to face the son of the king and a march of kings-riders. It was the day everything changed. The earth shook. The battle never came. A marriage was ordained that ended the fighting, if not the hatred.

— —

Nearly half a century had passed before Valnor arrived at Rokclaw to begin his training under Romonik's instruction.

Tolak made sure Valnor understood his years at Rokclaw would be punishing. He would be pushed to the limits of mind and body. He was also cautioned that, despite the family connection, he was not to call Romonik "uncle."

On that first day, Valnor spent long hours wrestling with the other apprentices while Romonik watched. He knew that the way he distinguished himself in the first few days would determine his training and what consideration, if any, he might be granted by the tough old warrior.

On the second day, Romonik gave Valnor the biggest rock he could carry.

"This is your comrade-in-arms," Romonik said. "You are responsible for him. You are to keep him with you at all times. Carry him with you wherever you go and sleep with him at night." Carrying the dead weight of his "comrade-in-arms" all day made sleeping at night easy under any circumstance.

On the first day of the second week, the rock was replaced by a bigger one, and again for the third week, until Valnor was able to carry a rock very nearly his own weight. Even on the run.

He rode horses every day without a saddle until he could whirl them in circles with nothing but his knees.

"Earn your horse's trust, and he will run for you until his heart gives out," the warrior taught. "Then make sure it never does."

He learned to ride the destrier and to use the lance, though jousting was for tournaments, which held little interest for Valnor. Riding the long-legged coursers or heavier warhorses was far more demanding than the ponies he learned to ride in the shallow surf on the beach of Dragon Deep. He loved to ride and was willing to spend as much time in the saddle as possible, partly because it was the one place his stone "comrade-in-arms" did not go with him.

Valnor's training at arms was concurrent with his education under the tutelage of the masters of Rokclaw. He learned the history of the realm and was tutored in the legends, myth, and mystery of the gods. An old man from the village taught him the language of First Man. He learned the way of the royal court. He even learned to dance and sing from a lady who came often to visit Romonik and would sometimes stay for days.

When he was fourteen, Valnor spent a year as Romonik's personal squire. He had done well, and being chosen was a high honor. He dressed him in the morning, served him meals, maintained his armor and weapons, cared for his horse, and cleaned the stalls. The tedium of physical tasks was forgotten. The lessons learned were mental and emotional. Discipline and self-control. Obedience and diligence. They would serve him well in the training that meant the difference between life and death.

Valnor's training with weapons was extensive. He learned to use short swords, arming swords, two-handed great swords, long swords, broadswords, and the foil. He mastered archery with both the longbow and the short bow. He was startled to discover that the exquisite arrows he was given had been fashioned by Romonik himself. He took it as a silent statement of approval.

He learned to use a shield and how to fight with a variety of pole-weapons as well as weapons made to bludgeon and cleave. Among them were strange and horrible instruments of battle that Valnor had never seen and never wished to use. When he said he saw little purpose in learning to use a weapon he would never choose to use, Romonik explained that it was important for a warrior to become familiar and skilled with every weapon there was.

"You don't want to see a flail with a spiked ball on a chain for the first time in the hand of a man running toward you," Romonik told him.

One of Valnor's favorite memories of his training was the day his cousin, Hiskim, had come to watch.

Hiskim was an angry, troubled boy of seventeen. Romonik's wife had died in childbirth, so the boy was raised by a gaggle of nursemaids and servants. For all his prowess as warrior, Romonik had no interest in being a parent.

Hiskim took as much malicious delight in tormenting Valnor as he did in inflicting pain on other living things. He often came to torment or heckle Valnor during his training.

Valnor was practicing against the quintain—a large, heavy sack of sand shaped like a man. It was fitted with a shield like an armed opponent and hung on a pole fastened to a central pivot. When struck, the quintain spun around with great force, demanding he move quickly to avoid being knocked to the ground.

Hiskim circled the quintain's pivot to make sure Valnor saw him making vulgar gestures and rude remarks.

Valnor took his stance and tensed himself to strike as if he didn't see his archenemy at all. Rather than strike, though, he dropped the sword and slung the bag with both hands, full force.

Hiskim saw it coming but could not clear the circle in time. The heavy sack knocked him on his buttocks. In his anger to get up, he stumbled and was hit again by the swinging bag.

The inevitable retribution was stopped by the sound of Romonik's voice. He had been watching from the balcony overlooking the yard.

Valnor almost wished Hiskim's double-fisted advance hadn't been stopped. He was ready to test himself against the arrogant older boy. Romonik never said a word to him about it, but Valnor was excused that evening from his duties in the kitchen, and, when he retired to the loft, there was honey cake to eat and goat's milk to drink.

He thought for a long time the feeling he enjoyed that night was the pleasure of revenge. In time he understood it came from knowing Romonik knew and cared. After so many years, the hardened old warrior had finally let him know he approved of him, even though he said it without words.

It was one of two times Valnor felt like kin.

The second came near the end of his training. He was invited to dine with Romonik. He assumed he was one of several invited to feast with the master, but he was the only one. Not even Hiskim was there. The pang of hungry anticipation was replaced with a knot in his stomach that felt like a stone. He had remarkable respect for Romonik, even affection, though it was not a feeling he'd confess, even to himself. He wondered what he should say or whether he should speak at all.

Other than the expected formalities of welcome and appropriate grunts of satisfaction to compliment the cook, they ate in silence.

Romonik had never spoken about himself, his past, his exploits, or how he got his scars. There were plenty of stories, but none of the boys knew which of them were true and which had grown into legend. Valnor had heard all the stories, but there was one he desperately wanted to hear—needed to hear—from his uncle's own lips.

After Romonik finished his third tankard of wine, took a deep breath, and breathed out with a smile, Valnor dared his question.

"How did you find your sister again? My mother?"

"She never told you?" His look of surprise turned to a wrinkle of smiles that Valnor had never seen. Romonik chortled.

"I've only been told you saved her as a baby and spared her tragedy as an adult, but I don't know what that means."

Romonik laughed again. "You don't know your mother at all, I'd say," he said, the smile never leaving his lips.

"Tell me," Valnor begged.

"You'd best ask her."

"I have, but she said she doesn't like to talk about it, and I don't even know when you found her again and—"

"I didn't find her. She found me—found us. She searched for our Army of Orphans and joined with us. She must have been fourteen. I bragged in those days about escaping, going back, and saving my sister. That's how she knew who I was."

"She knew you were her brother?"

Romonik nodded. "She did, but I had no idea who she was. After a few weeks, there were some who became curious about how similar we looked. That's when she finally confessed—a bit of pride in being kin, I like to think."

"What did she mean that you 'spared her'?"

"I refused to let her fight or carry weapons or task a target." Valnor had heard stories about what happened to the members of the army who ratted out for coin and knew better than to push for details.

"And when you marched with Ormmen and Army of Orphans against my father?"

"She stayed behind. She was not happy, but I demanded she remain behind. I did not want her to die, but it was more than that." Romonik inhaled deeply. He closed his eyes, but the wrinkles that covered them quivered. He expelled the air through his nose with a sound like wind through dry grass, and then opened his eyes. "I did not want her to have to kill." He paused for a long time, and Valnor could see the burden of regret and guilt, even though he could not begin to understand the depth. "I did not want her to ever experience the horror of taking the life of another. I spared her from that tragedy."

He looked at Valnor. "In the life of every man there comes a day that defines who he is. I was fortunate to have two such days. The day I saved my baby sister and the day I stopped her from marching to Passage." Romonik shook his head, and Valnor thought he heard a chortle hidden deep within his throat. "And to think she would one day marry the man I'd marched off to kill." He returned his gaze to Valnor. "If you remember anything of my training, remember this: What you do when your day comes—and sure as the sun will rise in the east, it will come—it is what you choose to do that determines who you are. Nothing else."

Valnor nodded in solemn understanding. "I am most grateful you failed that day in the battle of Passage."

"Call me uncle," he said.

The following day, Valnor and those who had trained with him were honored in a traditional ceremony. It was all very proper and very stern, but when the laurel wreath was place on his head, Uncle Romonik winked.

CHAPTER 34

The king coughed blood. It left a crimson stain in the grizzled white of his beard. He wiped it away with the heel of a frail hand. Tonguelessone moved quickly to clean him with her woolen rag, but he pushed her hand aside.

The sky was dark, the air wet and cold. The heavy rain had passed and left behind a persistent drizzle, lashed about by the winds blowing in from the fjord of Akeshen.

"If there be one of you here assembled who decries the justice of this sentence, let him speak." It was hardly a trial, but the offer soothed the king's conscience. He scanned the solemn faces of the men who huddled like sheep at the scent of a wolf. They were brothers of the secret order of mystics: the Wizard of Maynard, Magus Zuwor, Vorrold, Bawork, the Mankin, and Than-lun, the alchemist who was about to die.

Than-lun was stripped to the waist with his hands tied behind him. His chest was pressed to a thick stump, his neck exposed. His hair was black in the rain and dangled from his head like the yarn of a dirty mop.

The cult of mystics was gathered in an abandoned courtyard in the old section near the north wall to witness this clandestine execution. Weeds grew in cracks, and the stones were matted with wet leaves. It was a place rarely visited and seldom seen. In ages past, it had been a wing of the ancient castle of Akeshen.

The old king coughed again. His body trembled. He gagged and nearly retched. A gurgle of blood and bile choked up from his throat. He spat it out and wiped his mouth. His hand was a bony claw covered with translucent skin. His fingers were frail, his nails long and yellowed.

His dark eyes peered from sockets of wrinkled skin. He stared at his blood as it mixed with the rain with a strange fixation, as if the swirl of pink stain disappearing between the stones was a part of his essence being sucked away. *An omen of my death?*

The unsavory affair taking place was entangled with the king's preoccupation with death. Not the death of the man on his knees but his own inevitable demise. Orsis-Kublan thought of death as an enemy to be conquered, a foe to be vanquished, like the hundreds of others he had faced and fought and crushed.

How could it be otherwise? He ruled by divine right. He declared it. Demanded it. Commanded that it be repeated in every council, spoken in every prayer, and recited in every ceremony: His Greatness, Orsis-Kublan, Omnipotent Sovereign and King, ruler by the will of all the gods, is vicegerent of the gods upon the earth, and thus whatever he wills, he can do no wrong.

The mantra of his divine right to rule, though of his own invention and written by his own hand, became so deeply embedded in his brain it had hardened into truth. It *was* the will of the gods that he should be king.

Why would they appoint him to die like a common man? They would not. Not Enlil, god of air. Not Enki, god of water. Not Anu, the great sky god, lord of constellations and king of gods, spirits, and demons. He heard their voices in the darkness and even saw them sometimes in his dreams or when his blood was thick with spiced wine or his mind soared on opium wings. He heard it from his trusted counselors, from his wives and concubines. All things affirmed that his quest for immortality was the will of the gods, as surely the sun would rise.

The king standing in the cold drizzle of the abandoned court was aged and aggrieved, hardly a shadow of the young idealist who had overthrown the tyranny of the Romagónians sixty years before. The once-joyous chant of "Orsis! Orsis! Orsis! Savior of the people!" was only an echo in the failing memory of an old man whose omnipotence was not enough to keep his life from slipping away. Mortal decay deepened his bitterness and drove him to madness.

The bitterness and madness merely stiffened King Kublan's resolve to find the secret of perpetual youth, the immortality granted to Tishpiin.

I am the king. Omnipotent. It is my destiny. So why am I surrounded by such fools? Why have my men failed me?

The old king sloshed through the puddles to where Than-lun knelt.

Tonguelessone scurried to hold the parasol over him and keep the drizzle from wetting his robes.

Orsis-Kublan had been a tall man in his youth. Even hunched with age, his stature gave him presence. He leaned down, bracing himself with his hands on his knees.

"You promised me an elixir that would keep me sleepless for seven days and seven nights, but you poisoned me instead." He leaned closer. "You should not wonder there are none to step forward in your defense. Or did they encourage you to poison your king?"

Kublan stood upright and held his arms tightly across his body. He looked at those gathered. They were sworn to a blood oath of secrecy. Five magi, the alchemist on his knees, the high pontiff, Raven to the King, and two men-at-arms chosen from the elite guard of kingsmen. One to convey the alchemist from his chambers, the other to chop off his head.

There were no counselors or officers of the court. By tradition such matters should be handled by trial in the great hall with punctilio, debate, and a hall of gawkers. But this affair could not be handled in open forum. Who could he trust? Not the number of courtiers who thought him mad and whispered treason behind his back. Not his wives or concubines. Maharí's betrayal had twisted his mind and left a wound in his heart that would never heal.

Thus he had ordered this gathering in the old north court with only these few in attendance.

Even still, other than the Raven, he trusted none of them completely. The king looked from face to face. *Which of these within the walls of Kingsgate might whisper to my enemies?*

The wrenching pain in his bowels got suddenly worse in a wave of urgent discomfort. Paranoia gnawed at him like hungry rats.

They are all complicit in the alchemist's failure, but if I kill them all, as they deserve, who will be left to find the plant of endless life?

He rested his hand on the alchemist's shoulder. A small part of him regretted the loss of his transformer of elements, but he believed it was necessary for the others to witness the results of failure.

"No one speaks for you. Will you speak for yourself?"

The condemned man looked up. Strands of sodden hair stuck to his face, giving him the appearance of a wild creature. He tried to shake it aside, but it clung wet and flat. "I plead your mercy, oh great and honorable king. I confess it is by the will and pleasure of the gods that you are destined to an endless life and to rule forever." The alchemist choked back his terror. "I have taken the oath and drunk your blood and swear the only purpose of my life is your desire and your destiny."

Orsis-Kublan coughed again and blood flecked his lips. "It was not an elixir of immortality you gave me to drink, but a poison potion. But for the will of the gods who favor my destiny, I would be dead!" He coughed again and then spat blood toward the others, implicating them all.

The alchemist leaned against the stump. "I sought the ancient secret from the wickkans of Loonish, who sent me to the sorceress of Dragonfell, but I found—"

"Dragonfell!" The king cut him off, the dread of conspiracy fluttering through his head like bats trapped in a cave.

"I found nothing but shadows and folktales," the alchemist

continued, "but then I found a recipe among the archaic writings eluci-
dating the epic poem of Melgeshrabin. A wondrous potion of jade and
cinnabar and gold. It claimed to be the elixir of sleeplessness required
to prepare one for endless life. Before I began, I sought the blessing of
the gods and the guidance of the high pontiff of Anu."

The high pontiff moved away from the huddle of mystics lest the
alchemist's words implicate him in his failure.

The man on his knees gasped for air and fought to gain control of
his emotions. "We conjured spirits and invoked the ancient incantations to ensure the elixir would bring sleeplessness for seven days and
seven nights."

"I have hardly been awake since you gave me your poison!"

"I have done my best, but I will try again. I will not rest until I give
you what the gods will."

The king turned to face the mystics. "A man who does his best in
battle and fails is just as dead as the coward who holds no sword." The
words hovered in the sodden air like a winged harbinger of fate. The
silence was broken only by the gusting wind and the hiss of rain that
had started again.

"High pontiff of Anu," the king said with an air of disturbing piety. "As spiritual advisor and voice of the gods, I leave it to you to
adjudge whether this act be right or wrong, lest I betray my pledge of
benevolence as omnipotent king."

The high pontiff stood in the damp, cold air, a humble slope to his
shoulders. He recited the words the king wished to hear. "You are vicegerent of the gods upon the earth and thus whatever you will, O great
and Omnipotent Sovereign and King, is right. You can do no wrong."

The king nodded and held out his hand. "Then, by the oldest of our
traditions, he who suffers an offense worthy of death is he to whom the
right of the ax be given."

The faces of the mystics twitched in shock and disbelief. While the
tradition was known, it was rarely exercised.

The kingsman put the double-bladed ax into the king's hands and
pushed the alchemist's neck across the block. The weight of the weapon

caused the king's hands to tremble as he rested the blade across the alchemist's neck. He adjusted his stance. The weight of the steel broke the skin and a trickle of blood wriggled down the man's throat, drawing a line for the blade to follow.

"Mercy!" he croaked. "By all the gods, I plead for mercy!"

The king tightened his grip for a moment, then relaxed. "I shall grant mercy," he said.

A gush of emotion escaped from the man on his knees.

"I am sick because of the poison you bade me drink. My hands are cold, and my grip is weak. It is unlikely I could separate your head in a single blow. You cry for mercy, and I am a benevolent man. Thus I relieve you of the prolonged pain I would inflict were I to wield the blade." He nodded to the kingsman, who moved immediately forward. "I relinquish the ax to one who will remove your traitorous head with a single fall of the blade."

As the king pulled the ax away from the man's neck, the blade sliced deeper in the alchemist's flesh. He handed the ax to the waiting kingsman, then turned and walked toward the narrow stairs on the south side of the court. Tonguelessone held the parasol without looking back.

The dull crack was like breaking a melon with a brittle shell. It was muted by the incessant patter of the rain. It was followed by the hollow thud of something heavy splashing onto the stones.

The king turned on the second step of the ascending stairway. None of the others were looking at their fallen brother. Two had turned their backs. The Wizard of Maynard was on his knees, retching. The high pontiff had backed himself into the wall and lifted his face to the rain.

The king cleared his throat and spat out the bitter taste of bile and blood. "I regret this had to be," he said, his voice rising against the rain. His eyes were dark holes in the falling light. "I call upon you to fulfill the oath you have sworn by my blood. Bring me the secret of everlasting life. Whatever it may be. Wherever it lies hidden. Whoever holds it in their hand. Find it. And bring it to me."

He paused as the kingsmen dragged the headless body from the court.

The king shook his head with what might have been genuine sorrow. "From this day forward you will abandon the bonds of your order," he said to the remaining mystics. "You shall travel your separate roads. You shall each rely on your own sorceries in the search of this preeminent treasure. The one who succeeds shall be rewarded beyond imagining. Whatever you desire shall be granted tenfold."

The Wizard of Maynard looked up and wiped the vomit from his chin.

"Those who fail . . ." Kublan glanced to where the kingsman had disappeared with the headless body and let the words hang in the cold, wet air. He pressed his fingers to his forehead to stay the jolt of pain in his head, then, after a moment, said, "You have until the first day of Samna in season Mis'il S'atti. By the Moon of Falling Leaves, I will realize my immortal destiny! Do *not* fail me again!"

The Raven to the King watched and listened and waited. He was not among those challenged or warned, but he knew the king's last look at those assembled would end with him. It always did.

When the king's eyes found him, the Raven furrowed his brow to insure an expression of profound wonder. He offered his approval with an exaggerated nod of his head. This silent ritual at the end of every gathering was a predictable pattern.

This time, the king's look to the Raven was longer than usual. Something unspoken. Something unnerving.

The Raven repeated his reassurance with another vigorous nod of his head and a small gesture of his hand.

A smile quivered at the corner of the king's mouth, and then he turned and climbed the stairs. Tonguelessone gripped his arm and helped him ascend without the slightest shift of the umbrella.

The Raven watched him go but did not move or breathe more than a shallow breath until the king passed through the high portal and vanished from sight.

Sounds that had seemed muted and far away were suddenly deafening. A rumble of thunder. The splash of pelting rain. The slosh of feet through puddles. The guttural murmuring of the condemned. The Raven turned to watch the frightened cult of magi hurry from the court.

He knew they were destined to fail. They sought a plant found only on the trellis of mythology. As the thought surged through him, he felt a strange premonition. *Where there is history, there is myth, and where there is myth, there is history. Because there is no plant of endless life at the bottom of the sea does not mean* all *the stories of immortality are false. It may only mean they are searching in the wrong place.*

The court was empty. The wind blew across Akeshen fjord, driving the rain against the battlements of Kingsgate like tiny pellets of iron. Even as the storm raged and the skies turned black, the Raven remained where he stood. He knew the road of destiny was not a single path through tranquil woods. It was a rocky road that forked repeatedly. Often at the least convenient times.

An idea erupted from the mysterious darkness of his mind. It was more than a concept of reason. Something beyond. An outrageous impression billowing up from his chest. An obsession, far more preposterous than the youthful fantasy of years long gone. Fear consumed him in a cloud of dark confusion. His heart pounded, and his head swirled with euphoric intoxication, even as he argued within himself.

It is impossible! It is not your task.

But if I succeed . . .

If you fail, the king will have your head.

Where there is myth, there is history.

A plant of endless life? No truth in it.

Then perhaps an elixir or an enchanted chalice. An incantation or magic stone. Perhaps it is the will of the gods.

Hypocrite. You deny the gods.

Perhaps there is another god we know not of. Perhaps there is a secret of endless life that's not been found.

The rain turned to ice and stung his face. There were a few times in a man's life when he felt truly alive. For Raven, this was one of them. His internal war ended, and his thoughts flowed with singular clarity.

He breathed in the icy air but felt as if his feet had left the cold, wet stones.

If there is in fact such a truth, if endless life is indeed possible by some mysterious power, then he who possesses that secret will possess a power greater than all the kings of earth.

In the black of night and pelting rain, the Raven stood at a fork in the rocky road of destiny.

CHAPTER 35

"Shh!" Meesha put a finger to her lips and lifted the lantern. In the half-light of the flame, the blemished side of her face disappeared into the darkness. She waved the girls through the narrow archway and coaxed them down the steps. The stones were ancient, unevenly worn, and the footing was precarious. The seven girls moved as quietly as they could, burdened as they were with their secret lading: platters of food wrapped in loosely woven cotton, linen bags filled with bread and cheese, baskets of fruit, and flagons of wine. The aroma of roasted meat and sweetbread collided with the dank odor of animals and rotted hay that wafted up from the stables.

The clandestine procession floated downward in eerie silence. Except for the padding of stocking feet on the stones and the swish of cotton skirts, there was no sound. Their shadows flitted across the walls like dancing fairies. It was three hours after midnight.

The woman leading the cortége was Selmaas. She was a plumpish attendant to the cook and older than the other girls by a score of years or more. She was one of the few family servants who'd made the journey from Blackthorn to Stókenhold Fortress. Meesha had always been her favorite, and Selmaas could deny her nothing.

She had listened to Meesha's plan, shook her head, and declared, "It's outrageous and doomed to failure," then added quickly, "but if that is what you want . . ." After that, she recruited the girls she could trust and sneaked into the kitchen.

When Selmaas reached the leading edge of the light, Meesha hurried forward with the lantern to light the next stretch of the narrow passage. She had on the leathers she wore when fencing with Valnor instead of her high-fashion gown. Without the constraint of the corset, she was as lithe as a cat. Only a step behind Selmaas, she encouraged the girls with a nod and a reassuring smile.

Meesha had not told Tolak about her plan to take the food prepared for the feast to the men of the Kadesh-Cor expedition in the middle of the night. Surely it was her father's intent from the beginning to feed the entire company. She was confident he would approve, and she would tell him soon enough—*after* the expedition was gone from Stókenhold.

Her biggest worry was whether the men of Kadesh-Cor's company would keep their surprise feast a secret? *Were there spies among them?* She changed her mind. She would tell her father in the morning. Better he hear it from her than someone else.

She had told Valnor, though.

"It's a dangerous idea," he had said before breaking into a grin. "Dangerous but brilliant. And delightfully ironic to give the grand feast prepared for the prince to his drudges while he and his sons sleep with empty stomachs."

The rhythmic snoring from the open portal to the keeper's quarters erupted with a gagging snort. Meesha felt a surge of adrenaline and motioned for the girls to hurry. The idea to feed the servants, drovers, drivers, *and slaves* had come to Meesha during the conflict between her father and Kadesh-Cor. It was the right thing to do. It was something she must do.

She knew it was a dangerous idea. She would not be her father's daughter had she grown into a woman without understanding the truth of tyranny. Valnor had offered to help, but she shook her head.

"If we are caught, it will be discounted as the misplaced sympathy of foolish girls. If you are with us, it will be seen as defiance and aggression. There are times when being 'a silly, foolish' girl is a benefit."

The girls descended the last of the stairs and followed Meesha's lantern across the open court.

———

"You there!"

Meesha whirled toward the harsh voice that barked from the darkness. The girls stuttered to a stop behind her with a rush of gasping breaths and squeaks of fear.

A large man emerged from the shadows and strode toward them. Leather knee-high boots stepped into the lighted circle of the lantern. His face remained in darkness. "What is your purpose at such an hour?" The light of the flame glinted on the blade of the short sword in his hand.

Meesha swallowed the lump in her throat and recited the terse homily, memorized and well-rehearsed in case she and her band of kitchen maids were caught by the keepers of the prison or worse, a kingsrider. "I am Meesha, daughter of Tolak, the master of Stókenhold Fortress and most gracious host of travelers on the King's Road. We are come to insure the comfort of our guests." She remembered it perfectly and spoke with confidence. "With whom do I converse, good sir?" She lifted the lantern to light the face of the man who could jeopardize her ambition and maybe her life. She stopped breathing.

"M'lady Meesha?" Shadows fled as the man stepped closer to the light. "I did not recognize you . . ." He slipped the sword into his belt with some chagrin.

"Horsemaster Raahud!" she gasped, recognizing him at once. He was among the men of the royal entourage who sat at Tolak's table. One of the men who'd been sent to the chambers with an empty belly . . . and he looked very hungry. She swallowed hard. Was it his growling stomach she heard and not the croaking of the night frogs?

"Did you not find the bed to your liking?" She regretted the trifling question as soon as the words left her tongue.

"I prefer the company of horsemen to princelings," he said. "I was honored by the invitation of Prince Kadesh-Cor to share the feast with him and his royal companions, but . . ." His serious expression broke into a broad grin and he laughed. "It would seem a sour potato with the likes of us is better than the empty pewter of the prince."

Meesha exhaled with a chortling sigh. "The men of your expedition have eaten?"

"Very little and poorly."

Meesha waved one of the girls forward and lifted the loosely woven cotton from the platter of roasted goose baked with onions, garlic, and herbs. "Better a leg of a goose than a sour potato or empty pewter. There is enough for all, but eating the prince's feast without him must be kept a secret."

"My wranglers first, if you please," he said, and Meesha liked him more than she ever could her royal half brother or the spoiled Sargon.

———

A fire was built for heat and light in the open yard of the stables. Raahud roused his wranglers and bid them spread the word. Before the fire was fully ablaze, all but a few had gathered. Drovers, teamsters, coachmen, gillies, cooks, servants of the camp, and reinsman of the chariots.

All but one, Meesha noticed.

The men rubbed sleep from their bleary, unbelieving eyes as the girls served the sumptuous feast. Only a few men seemed to notice Meesha's face, or perhaps it was not so easily seen by the light of fire. Flagons of wine were passed about and quickly drained. Meesha kept one aside. She crossed to where Raahud had settled with the horsemen. "Where are the kingsriders?" she asked.

"Looking after the wagons and coaches in the upper court." He nodded toward a ramp of cobblestones that swept upward at the far end of the stable. "And watching out for the girls, I suspect," he added.

The girls? Meesha flinched, and, seeing her reaction, Raahud offered a rueful shrug of regret that it had slipped from his tongue.

"Hmm, 'companions' of the prince."

Meesha had heard rumors of such arrangements in the taverns and from the chatter of blushing village girls. "Were they given something to eat?" she asked. He didn't know. Meesha waved Selmaas to her. "There are others in the upper court," she said. "Gather what remains and prepare a platter for them. We will go to them."

"The kingsriders will not likely keep your secret," Raahud warned.

"Perhaps, but they travel the King's Road and shall have my father's hospitality."

"Even if he doesn't know," Selmaas added.

"Why are there none like you and your father at Blackthorn?" Raahud asked with a smile.

Meesha wondered if it was possible Raahud did not know her family's history. "Oh, and I meant to ask," she said with nonchalance. "The reinsman in the last of the chariots? I have not seen him here."

Raahud bit into the knuckle of a leg bone, sucked the marrow, and raised his eyebrows.

"I was high on the wall, a good distance away, but it looked as if . . ." She unconsciously put her hand around her throat as if it were an iron collar. "As if he wore . . ."

"The collar of a slave." Raahud nodded. "And you wonder why we've a slave who drives a royal chariot?"

Meesha nodded and hoped her blush was hidden by the darkness.

"There's only one, but he is the best. He drives by my request, to the great displeasure of Princeling Sargon I might add," he said with a twinkle in his eye.

She smiled at him.

Raahud put an onion in his mouth and laughed as he licked his fingers. "The driver is also above." His wry smile let Meesha know he suspected her thoughts. "They demanded I keep him with the chariots rather than with the men."

Meesha nodded a quick thanks and slung the flagon of wine over her shoulder. "I'm sure he'll be hungry," she said.

"He will." Raahud smiled.

Meesha motioned to Selmaas to follow her with her kitchen maids and the food.

"His name is Qhuin," Raahud called after her. "A'quilum Ereon Qhuin." The way he said it gave the otherwise lowly title a tenor of dignity. When Meesha turned back to look at him, he shrugged as if he had said nothing, but his smile betrayed his affection for the slave who drove a chariot.

———

The upper court was a clutter of unhitched wagons and coaches arranged in no particular order. The chariots were parked in a row along the low wall that opened to the fjord below. There were two kingsriders on night guard. Both asleep, or drunk, perhaps.

The ripe plum paint of the common coach was the color of a dried prune by the light of the lantern. The reflection of the flame danced across the burnished brass trim. The curtains remained closed. Meesha could see the richness of the fabric and floral patterns of gold brocade as she drew near. She knocked on the door. The coach shivered as someone stirred within. She knocked again. Delicate fingers moved the curtain aside.

The girl who opened the door was younger than Meesha. She blinked sleep from her eyes and squinted at the strangers. She was confused and frightened.

"I pray, forgive our intrusion," Meesha said kindly. "We've brought you food and something to drink, if you desire it."

"Oh," the girl gasped and touched her fingers to her full lips still smudged with a reddish stain. Her eyes darted to the dark side of Meesha's face, but only for a heartbeat. "Oh, yes, yes, you are most kind." Her hair was a tousle of honey-colored curls. "Effy, Effy, wake up," she said to someone else in the carriage and pushed the door open all the way. "They've brought us something to eat."

The other girl was older and not quite so pretty. She gathered herself from the velvet plush of the seat and let her woolen blanket slide away. She put both hands across her stomach. "May you be blessed by the spirits above and below," she said in a hoarse whisper as the kitchen maids gave them half a goose in a basket filled with bread, cheese, fruit, and utensils.

The girl reached into the basket. "Ouch!"

Meesha turned.

The younger girl had cut her hand on the knife in the basket and her blood spilled in a rush. She gripped the wound and started to cry.

Meesha tugged a handkerchief from her pocket and reached for the girl's bleeding hand. "Here! Give me your hand."

"No, no, m'lady, you mustn't," the girl said in tears. "It will soil your beautiful handkerchief."

"It will wash," she smiled and wrapped the girl's hand tightly to stop the bleeding. The delicate handkerchief had been a gift from her governess to celebrate her eighteenth day of blessing. It was silk and fine linen, embroidered with tiny symbols in a swirl of graceful lines: *She Who Lives*—the meaning of her name in the ancient language.

"Thank you, m'lady, but how shall I ever return it?"

"No need." Meesha smiled. "Keep it."

"Perhaps someday I shall have the pleasure of seeing you again."

"Perhaps." She leaned forward and embraced the girl with genuine affection. Drawing back, she asked, "Where are the kingsriders?"

"There, through the portal," the girl said.

Meesha slung the flagon of wine across Selmaas's shoulder. "Give the rest to the kingsriders," she said.

"Are you certain?"

"Begin with the wine and perhaps they will keep our secret," Meesha said.

Selmaas took the lantern from Meesha and hurried for the portal on the far side of the court. The kitchen girls followed.

Meesha gathered a small basket of leftovers for herself. There was one man yet to feed, if only she could find him.

CHAPTER 36

The chariot rode above the billowing dust like a bird with giant wings floating on the wind with wheels carving graceful lines in the clouds with nine white horses running side by side in teams of three and flying with the rippling of reins and cords of light glimmering across their flanks igniting an explosion of white and a whirling wind with flowing hair surrounding the face of a woman calling to him in a voice singing with the exaltation larks, Master Qhuin?

"Master Qhuin?"

Qhuin erupted from his dream and bounded to his feet. The chain attached to the shackle on his ankle dragged over the iron edge of the footboard. The piercing clatter of it fractured the night. Drowsiness fled in the rush of adrenaline that prepared him to run or fight. His fingers flew to the leather pouch next to his hip, checking to make sure his precious treasure had not been stolen while he was dreaming.

The woman standing before him stumbled back at his violent reaction. She clasped a hand across her chest and tried to regain her composure. "Pray, pardon me for awakening you in such a manner," she said.

Qhuin had been curled up on a deerskin hide on the footboard of the chariot. The hide was poorly tanned and brittle in spots but softer

270

than the flat stones of the court. The loosely woven afghan that covered him fell away when he jumped up. It was old and frayed around the edges.

"Pray, pardon," she said again, "but I have brought you food. My father is lord of Stókenhold Fortress. The others of the company have been fed. We had only a little left." She offered him a basket. "It's for you," she said.

Meesha studied Qhuin as he considered the basket of food. He stood rigid against the chariot, his eyes curious, if not suspicious. He was tall and, given the added height of the footboard, towered above her. When she looked up at him, he averted his eyes, but then slowly raised them until they rested on her face.

My face! She felt an unexpected heartache. She had come to Qhuin thinking only of the strange connection she'd felt when she had seen him from the wall.

When Qhuin didn't look away, she smothered the ache in her heart as she always did. *Even a slave cannot stay his curious eyes from the blemish of my face.*

She suffered the thought but returned his gaze with a confidence she did not completely feel. She was suddenly aware how striking Qhuin's appearance was. His features were chiseled by the shadows of the stark light falling on his face. His eyes were dark beneath strong brows, and hard shadows defined his cheekbones, his nose, and the full lips of his wide mouth.

He studied her face too, but not with the morbid curiosity she had experienced so often. He looked at her as if he was seeing something hidden in her very soul.

Qhuin knew he should not hold the gaze of a woman of noble blood, but he could not pull his eyes away. With the moon behind

271

her, she was a silhouette, rimmed in a halo of honey-gold where the soft light kissed her hair. It was not the wine-red stain on her face he saw, it was the deep pools of her eyes that glistened as if with a spark of starlight. There was a tinge of her scent in the damp night air. It was not the sickening sweetness of the perfumes worn by the ladies of Blackthorn but a fresh and subtle fragrance like a flower in the morning dew or a meadow after the rain. He flushed and wondered who she was, feeling shy that she had come.

He offered an awkward smile but held his gaze.

———

Meesha flushed and looked away when he smiled at her. Her eyes darted to the shackle around his ankle and the iron collar hanging from the cowling. *At least they were kind enough to grant him slumber without the collar,* she thought, and in the same instant, *The lessening of abuse is better than not, but hardly a kindness.*

"How do you know my name?" Qhuin asked.

"The horsemaster told me where to find you."

"Raahud knows you are here?"

"He does."

Qhuin looked toward the lower court as if his eyes could see through stone. He stepped from the footboard and accepted the basket. "Thank you, m'lady." He nodded graciously but made no move to eat.

"Are you not hungry?"

Qhuin nodded.

"Well, eat. Go on."

Qhuin picked up a dark red fruit and examined it with curiosity.

"It's a pomegranate. Have you never eaten one?" By his expression she knew the answer immediately. "It's the fruit of the gods, I'm rather sure of it." She smiled and took it from him. She sliced open the leathery skin using the sharp edge of the shackle.

He smiled as he watched.

She peeled the pomegranate open, lifted a cluster of seeds, and handed it back to him. He put half a dozen seeds in his mouth, puckering slightly at the tart sweetness. She laughed gently at his expression, and he rewarded her with a broad, embarrassed smile.

Meesha knew she should return to the manse before she was discovered, but asked instead, "Wouldn't you rather sit down to eat?"

"Only after you, m'lady—if you wish to stay," Qhuin said.

"Oh, I'm sorry, of course." Meesha sat on the wall with her back to the fjord. There was a perpetual breeze blowing inland from the sea—sometimes with a raging fury, sometimes gentle as the fluttering of fairies' wings. Like tonight. The wind swirled Meesha's hair softly across the dark side of her face. She made no effort to brush it aside.

Qhuin sat on the footboard with the basket and continued his feast.

Meesha watched in silence, taking pleasure in the way he savored each morsel whether the red pomegranate seeds, the soft bread with hard crust, the dark cheese, or the succulent flesh and crisped skin of roasted goose. He ate with his fingers as was the custom, but with a refined manner she had not expected from a slave.

She inhaled the cool damp air and listened for the whispering of the wind. She knew the stillness of the night was never an empty silence but a melodic symphony of tiny creatures chirping, calling, crying, and croaking. In the midst of the music of the night, the mournful hooting of an owl came from the darkness somewhere above.

Meesha wondered why she felt such calm. *Because he is a slave to the prince, and I am slave to my face.* It was a curious thought. She felt the heat of her face and wondered why he hadn't seemed to notice it at all.

Laughter floated through the portal on the far side of the court. *Kitchen maids and kingsriders*, she smiled to herself. *Blessed wine.*

"I regret I had no wine to bring," she said.

"I am beholden tenfold for your generosity and kindness."

"It is the way of the King's Road."

"Indeed, m'lady, but . . ." Qhuin lifted the chain, then let it slide through his fingers and rattle to the ground. "A slave is without privilege on the King's Road, and yet you have shown me such kindness."

The nighttime symphony suddenly faded with nothing remaining but the hush of the wind. Meesha's eyes followed the tumbling chain, and the nonsensical verse of her childhood bounced into her head.

With fingers crossed
And eyes shut tight
I ask the fairies of the night
To hear my wish
And come to stay
And make my wish come true today

The fairies of the night had never come to take away the wine-red stain of her face, so it was unlikely they would hear her wish and cut these chains and set him free.

"Why does the daughter of the lord of Stókenhold Fortress treat a slave with such kindness?" Qhuin's question brought her back from her private thoughts.

"To me you are not a slave." Even as she said it, she realized it was more than a patronizing token of conversation. "Prince Kadesh-Cor or my vulgar nephew might only see the chain, but Master Raahud told me who you really are. You are not just like any other man, but the best of them, he said."

Qhuin wrinkled his forehead and lifted his chin to the sky. The shadows fled from his face. His azure eyes were luminous in the cold blue light of the moon.

Meesha took a short breath. Raahud was right. He was *not* like any other man.

"There are no slaves at Stókenhold Fortress," she explained. *Only as thinking makes it so.* It made such sense. It made no sense. "My father does not believe a man should be privileged or condemned by birth or blood but by his deeds."

"Who is your father?"

"He is Tolak."

"Of what house?"

Meesha was reluctant to declare her father's blood and kinship to the king, but she could not withstand the urgency in Qhuin's voice. "Of House Kublan," she said, "but he claims no royal blood and no privilege."

"You are the granddaughter of the king."

Meesha tightened her jaw and waited for a chasm of contempt to open wide between them.

Qhuin stood slowly and pushed his fingers through his thick hair. "Your father is Tolak?" He spoke the name with intensity. "Tolak, Baron Magnus of Blackthorn and prince of the North?"

She swallowed the fear that threatened to constrict her throat. "Many years ago," she said. "Before . . ." She was confused by the intensity in his eyes and said no more.

Qhuin shook his head slowly, then settled back on his haunches. His intensity became a look of delight. "Your father is the one who spared my life, who took me in as an abandoned babe."

"My father?"

"As I've been told the story by the blacksmith who found me."

"But how did my father come to . . ." Her mind raced and her mouth moved, but there was no sound. Finally she managed to say, "'A'quilum Ereon Qhuin' means 'man of unknown blood,' does it not?"

Qhuin nodded. "It does, m'lady, and I know nothing of the woman who gave me birth or the man who . . ." He shook his head. "I was found at the door of a hovel in Village Darc and taken to Blackthorn."

"Found by a blacksmith?" Meesha raised her eyebrows as if the story was suddenly a fairy tale.

Qhuin laughed. "Yes. Leo Rusthammer, by name. He took me to your father, and your father took me in. He was the mighty Baron Magnus of Blackthorn and yet had compassion for an abandoned, low-born boy—most likely a whore's bastard." The dark possibility of his birth was barely a whisper. "I was suckled in his house by a servant woman whose baby was born dead. She became the only mother I ever knew."

Meesha was puzzled. "Whatever the circumstances of your birth, my father would never have made you a slave!"

"No, not he. Your father was a kind and good man."

"And remains so." Meesha smiled with pride.

"Indeed!" Qhuin looked at the ground for a moment, then raised his face again, "I was raised among the servants, but when your family left Blackthorn, I was taken from the woman who raised me and given to the stables as a slave."

"By Kadesh-Cor!" Her eyes flitted to the chain. The evidence of her half brother's villainy brought bile to her throat. "Do you know why my father left Blackthorn? What happened to our family?"

He shook his head. "Only the gossip of the stables, m'lady."

"I am not 'm'lady' by the way." She smiled. "I am Meesha, so unless you wish me to call you 'Grand Lord of the Chariots,' you should call me by my name."

Qhuin smiled at her ludicrous suggestion, but Meesha could see the very idea of it stirred a resolute sense of destiny deep within him.

"I wonder if my father ever knew what became of you," Meesha said as she rose from the wall and circled the chariot. She traced the ornate pattern of iron that trimmed the top of the cowling as if looking for the answer to a riddle. When she turned back, her face was in full moonlight. She continued to caress the swirls of iron, but she looked at Qhuin. She could not see his eyes but could feel them on her. *On my face.*

"You are Meesha?"

"Yes. That's much better, thank you."

"Pray forgive me, m'lady—Meesha—but may I know how many years have passed since your day of blessing?"

"You must never ask a lady her age," she scolded with teasing in her eyes.

Qhuin bowed his head from long habit, truly contrite. "Pray forgive me, m'lady. Perhaps you can tell me how old you were when your family left Blackthorn."

"Three!" she said with a lift of her chin. "And it's Meesha, remember?" she said with a forgiving smile.

Qhuin's eyes glistened as a mischievous smile came to his lips. "Then we have met before," he said.

The simple words took the breath from her.

"I was a child living among the servants at Blackthorn when you were born," he said.

"We never played with the children of the servants, so I . . ." She stopped and offered a soft apology. "My father has changed since then, I'm sorry I . . ."

"We met only once." Qhuin smiled. "You came down to the kitchen."

"How can you recall such a thing? You were a child, a little boy, only . . ."

"Five."

"But we only met once? How could you remember?" *How could a little boy ever forget a little girl with a face like mine?* The thought pounded in her head like thunder. She was suddenly aware of her fingers on her face. She drew back and forced her hand to retrace an iron swirl on the cowling.

"It is not your beauty I remember, m'lady, it was your kiss."

Meesha's eyes came up and her mouth fell open. She touched her bottom lip in utter surprise and stared at Qhuin in a daze.

"You sneaked into the kitchen looking for the honey cakes. You told me your name was Meesy and that you were hungry. I climbed to the bake box in the cupboard and stole three honey cakes. I might have stolen more for you, but it was all I could carry and still climb down."

"And I . . . I kissed you?"

"Three times. Right here." He touched his cheek at the edge of a wide smile. "One for each honey cake." Qhuin picked up the basket and leaned over the cowling opposite Meesha. The gossamer mist whirled away, and his face brightened in the half-light of the moon.

"I'm sure you've had many honey cakes and kisses since then." She laughed to hide the flutter of wings in her stomach.

His sigh was more a lament than a laugh. "You know little about the life of a slave. The kiss of a child is a precious memory."

"You've not been kissed again?" Meesha was incredulous.

Qhuin shrugged and used the tail of his shirt to buff away a tarnished smudge on the trim.

Meesha stepped close beside him. She took the basket from him and plucked a stray pomegranate seed from the fruit.

"I have stayed too long," Meesha said, pressing the sweet juice from the seed between her teeth. "The girls will be worried, and we must be gone before the keepers rise."

"Your kindness here tonight will be spoken for many seasons."

"I hope such telling can wait until the prince and his sons are far from Stókenhold Fortress." She smiled.

Qhuin laughed softly, then bowed his head. "You have repaid the honey cakes a hundredfold, m'lady," he said.

"I am Meesha, the girl who repaid your kindness with a kiss."

When his face came up, she was closer to him than she expected. She leaned forward slightly and offered the smooth white skin of her cheek in the customary greeting for a kinsman.

Qhuin looked like a man who had faced many fears and never trembled, but he was trembling now. He kissed her softly on the cheek, then gently turned her chin and kissed the dark crimson of the other side.

Meesha blushed as she stepped back. So did he. Their eyes met, and Meesha knew she would never forget the way the slave of Blackthorn looked at her. She could see the light in his eyes. He was looking at her face, but he saw only her soul. Her fingers touched the lingering heat of his kiss on the dark side of her face. She was certain the warmth of it would never go away. Then, without intent or thought, she leaned forward and kissed his cheeks as well.

She hurried away, but when she reached the pattern of dark stones, she turned to him again. "What was her name?" she asked. "Do you remember? The servant woman who mothered you in your early years?"

"I called her Mor, but the others called her Selmaas."

CHAPTER 37

The wagons, horses, and chariots were staged and waiting to take their places in the procession already winding its way from the central court of Stókenhold Fortress. Both the bannermen and Kadesh-Cor were beyond the outer gate, riding eastward to the King's Road. The rest of the expedition was strung out from the wall of the ward, through the double barbicans, over the bridge, and under the portcullis.

Qhuin heard Horsemaster Raahud shouting for him. His words were smothered by the hammering of hooves on cobblestones and the grinding of iron wheels. Raahud moved the last of the wains into the procession and waved for the wranglers to follow with the horses.

Qhuin rippled the reins, and the horses pranced forward to take their position at the end of the procession. He glanced over his shoulder from habit lest an unexpected rider, wagon, or chariot approach from behind. There was no one there except for the mounted kings-riders on rearward guard.

To keep disgruntled drudges from running away—and slaves from escaping, he reminded himself.

Qhuin's three-up team of coursers was rested, fed, and eager to run. They were perfectly groomed, and their whiteness shimmered in the morning sunlight as they danced in their traces. "Lassooommm, lassooommm," he called to the milk-whites in the language he spoke to them. The breaching, belly bands, and the leather of their harnesses were oiled and the sounds of them almost silenced. The brass rosettes, couplings, and buckles were polished, and the ornate iron trims were without a smudge. The cowling and wheels were scrubbed clean as new.

Qhuin matched the stony stares of the kingsriders. Holding the secret of his past, whatever it may be, in the pouch at his hip gave him a curious sense of superiority as he gazed at those whose lives were pledged to the king by blood. Was there so much difference between them?

He searched their faces wondering if they knew that he knew. Wondering if they had kept the confidence of the girls who'd brought them wine and food and laughter in the middle of the night. He hoped they had for Meesha's sake. The thought of her tingled through him.

"Hold!" Raahud shouted to Qhuin again as he reined in beside the chariot. He shouted to the kingsriders waiting rearward. "Ride on and stay with the flank. We've a repair to make." His face cracked with a tiny smile. "We'll catch up with you at the outer wall."

The kingsriders were eager to get on the road and spurred their horses forward without question. It was Qhuin who wondered what was going on. An iron hand tightened its grip around his gut. The links and couplings were in perfect order. He had smeared the axles of the inner hub with pig fat. He had replaced one of the groupers. It hadn't broken, but he thought it unduly soiled.

"Pray tell me, what—" Qhuin began, but Raahud held up his hand.

"Wait here," he said with a look that told him to wait until the kingsriders were beyond hearing. With the tumult of departure it was a short distance. Without explanation, Master Raahud rode forward as if the procession were a drove of bovine and he the lone wrangler.

A slave lived every hour with the uncertainty of knowing their life was not their own. Only two things were constant. Obedience or punishment. Qhuin had suffered more punishments than most. The mindless obedience expected of slaves was impossible for Qhuin to maintain, but he knew his survival depended on his mastery over his nature. It was an onerous, ever-present gnawing in his gut.

Except last night. After Meesha was gone, Qhuin realized it was the first time in as long as he could remember that he felt the calmness of real joy and a feeling of hope.

The ache in his stomach returned. Why had Horsemaster Raahud told him to wait? *Had the secrets of the night been discovered? Am I to be the scapegoat?* It didn't seem like something Horsemaster Raahud would do, but Qhuin had learned by beatings and bleeding that a slave could not presume that any small kindness held meaning beyond itself.

Perhaps the master of horses has no choice. Perhaps Kadesh-Cor is looking for someone to blame, or the pampered Sargon has demanded revenge for sleeping with a hungry belly. A tyrant had a smorgasbord of excuses with which to do whatever he fancied. To remind a slave of his station. To show power. To save face. To enforce discipline or simply punish one in the name of royal expediency. Whatever their whim. Whatever their caprice. Whatever their hunger or lust.

It was hard for Qhuin to contain his hatred.

As worrisome possibilities whirled in his head, a yet more dreadful thought appeared. Had the lord of Stókenhold Fortress been told that his daughter was seen with a slave in the middle of the night? *Am I to be condemned to the prison of Stókenhold Fortress?* There had been nothing untoward in his behavior, but Qhuin knew the truth would not matter. Men had been put to death for less. The word of a slave was little more than chaff blown away by hot wind. *But Lady Meesha will tell the truth of it.* Iron fingers tightened their grip around the knot in his stomach. *Will she not?*

Qhuin scanned the portico that surrounded the grand plaza on three sides. With the sun straight above, the open hallways were in shadow. He squinted into the dimness in search of the keepers of the prison who were surely coming for him. *Will I have no chance to plead or for Meesha to explain?*

Qhuin swept his eyes from the portico to the plaza in search of Horsemaster Raahud and found him sitting astride his horse in the middle of the court, watching the procession leave the plaza without him. Once the kingsriders had followed the coaches through the portcullis on the far side, Raahud turned and looked at him. At such distance, his expression was difficult to read.

Then Raahud looked up and nodded with an obvious suggestion for Qhuin to follow his gaze.

Qhuin looked up at the broad balcony, high on the north side. It was covered by a curtain of colorful silk rippling in the soft breeze. The sun was bright and the shadows dark. Three figures stood in silhouette. One of them stepped forward into the full sunlight of the balustrade. It was Meesha. Qhuin could see by the look of delight on her face that this was not the day he would die.

— ‑ —

Meesha acknowledged Qhuin's gaze with a fluttering of her fingers, and he bowed his head slightly, taking care to keep his place.

She cast her eyes to the rear of the plaza where a woman approached the chariot. She was plump, older than Meesha by a score of years, and wearing the frock of a kitchen maid. She favored her right leg and moved with a limp as she hurried past the pillars supporting the west portico. The closer she got, the faster she hurried. She shuffled under the arch of the portico and then broke into a loping, limping sprint across the open court toward Qhuin and his chariot.

Qhuin did not see the woman coming. He was trading glances with Raahud, trying to sort out what was going on.

Meesha held her breath as she watched the scene unfold, her fingers to her lips in expectation.

The horses threw their heads and pranced in warning—or welcome—as the woman approached. Qhuin turned, and the woman stopped.

Despite her high vantage, Meesha could not see the expression on their faces nor hear their words, but neither were needed to understand.

The woman covered her mouth with both hands and her shoulders heaved as she sobbed. She struggled to catch her breath.

Qhuin wrapped the reins on the stay and stared at the woman, rigid as a stone. Neither moved for a long moment. There was a simple exchange of words. Questions asked and answers given, and then, a marvelous dawning.

Qhuin leaped from the chariot and ran to the woman. He gripped her shoulders and held her for a long time. When he stepped back and looked at her again, she was laughing in joyous sobs. He shook his head in disbelief, then scooped her into his arms and lifted her from the ground.

She wrapped her arms around him, and Meesha wondered if either of them would ever let go.

Meesha brushed a tear from her cheek as she watched A'quilum Ereon Qhuin embrace the only mother he'd ever known—Selmaas, the kitchen maid who had suckled an abandoned child and loved him as her own.

When Meesha had asked Selmaas to come to the plaza and told her why, the kitchen maid couldn't believe it.

"I have wondered my whole life what happened to my little son," she said and began to cry. "I've clung to the unimaginable hope that this day would come." Even before she finished speaking, she gave Meesha a hug that nearly smothered her.

Meesha's eyes were fixed on Qhuin, and when he looked up from the embrace of his mother, she knew the joy and wonder on his face was a vision she would never forget.

The gratitude in his eyes left her feeling loved in ways she'd never felt before.

—◦—

Tolak and Katasha moved from the shadows to join Meesha in the sunlight of the balcony. They too had watched the reunion with great delight. Selmaas was like family and had been with them a long time.

Tolak's delight was dampened by a sleepless night. His meager hopes for a reunion with Kadesh-Cor were lost. He and his son had not spoken again. His modest expectations of reconciliation and healing were crushed by the same conflicts that had fractured the family and splintered House Kublan more than two decades before. It was unlikely to change, and the reality saddened him. Perhaps his idealism was foolish. Certainly not worth the loss of his life nor the joy of his soul.

He put his arm around Katasha and looked below. There was one good thing that had come from the sojourn of kinsman, and it was taking place in the court below. A wonderful, happy, unexpected thing.

Tolak smiled. *Even in the depths of darkness, there is always light.*

CHAPTER 38

The shadow of the obelisk rippled across the calendar stone as the sun passed over the Mountain of God. Great masses of clouds rose up from the western fjords. Ashar and the Oracle had been in the holy sanctum for three days. Priests came and went with wine and food but would not speak of what they saw or heard.

The Blessed Sages waited patiently for the Oracle to bring them word about the boy who claimed to be the blood of the Navigator. They filled their waiting with endless debates. The loquacious Sage Hakheem had begun with one of his predictable pontifications.

"The blessing of age is wisdom. The curse of wisdom is pride." He spoke as if every word was precious. "When men are learned they think they are wise. They suppose their knowledge comes from themselves, and thus they are easily snared by the prideful presumption that their opinions are enduring truths." He excluded himself, of course. It was his way of underscoring his insistence that there were no blood descendants of the Navigator. His gnarled brows moved up and down like bobbles of gray yarn, rising to punctuate his perfect logic or scrunching to a furl of wrinkles to emphasize his point.

It was challenging to break into Hakheem's garrulous soliloquy, but when he finally did, Sage Ahmose said, "I agreed in principle with Sage Hakheem, but I believe on the matter of—"

Ahmose was interrupted by a great bird passing low over the temple court, which Sage Hakheem took as a sign his discourse had the blessing of Oum'ilah and began to quote from the Codices of the Navigator once more.

"The Immortal Crown is blind. That which is lost shall be found. To be gathered in the righteous hand by the child of pure blood by the strength of a sword he cannot hold. And returned to the crown of endless life, and endowed with the power of godliness to evil or to good in the age of chaos and the saga of kings."

Hakheem paused for breath, but before he could continue, Sage FarzAn said, "But the full meaning of the prophecy has been lost in the confusion of language from the time of the tower to First Landing."

Sage Ahmose grunted his agreement.

"A canker among the ancestors," FarzAn bewailed. "Seeds of malevolence that allowed the secrets of darkness to survive!"

"Agreed," said Sage Armu-Tukic, who rarely engaged in argumentation.

"And I," opined Sage Laehus, who like his brother, Sage Armu-Tukic, found the endless collision of ego and enlightenment curiously entertaining but of little value.

Sage Batukhan disagreed with all his wizened peers and recited the entire prophecy verbatim. He twisted his face into a scowl and chewed on certain words with such gravitas the truth of it was obscured even further. By the end of his recitation, he was wagging a finger toward the top of the mountain since no one was listening.

The Mankin, Sage Kurgaan, broke his silence. "I have listened patiently to your wits and words. As we Mankins are little in size, so tend we to be little in word." He chortled softly to himself. "I thank you not so much for your wisdom, as we all confess in rare moments of clarity that we are aged billows of hot air, but because your dissensions have filled the time and eased my impatience." The smile on his large face was punctuated by a guttural rumble of humor. "If the importance of what is taking place in the sanctum as we blather away the hours is not obvious to you from the lofty heights from where you look upon the world, I can tell you that close to the earth, the truth of it is clear."

Sage Hakheem began to speak, but a boom of thunder silenced him. A shadow crossed the gateway to the holy sanctum. The Oracle emerged from the portal and stepped into a shaft of sunlight that pierced the rumble of gray clouds at the precise moment he appeared. The Blessed Sages stopped where they stood.

The Oracle stepped aside, revealing Ashar, who wore the amulet of the temple around his neck: twelve tiny crystals encircling an eye of gold. It matched the amulet around the Oracle's neck.

The eyes of the Blessed Sages remained fixed on the Oracle. There was an unmistakable glow of contentment on his face. He gestured for Ashar to stand beside him. The Oracle's voice sounded like a clap of thunder rolling over the Mountain of God.

"Ashar, son of Shalatar, is the son of Ilim, son of Worm, son of Issens, son of Syn, son of Corus, son of Kotar, son of Qaqos, son of Tsak, son of Izek, son of Ashar." He closed his eyes and tilted his face to the heavens. "And Ashar is son of Naesh, son of Faron, son of Palan, son of Joram. We thought the bloodline of Joram was broken and lost, but this day it is found. Joram *is* the son of the Navigator, and Ashar is of his blood." The Oracle bowed his head and stepped backward.

A murmur of awe fluttered among the sages. Hakheem was the first to step forward. He choked back his emotions and lowered himself to one knee. "Ashar, scion of Joram, blood of the Navigator. As the voice of all present, I ask your pardon and seek absolution of our misjudgments."

Sage Hakheem's voice sounded faint and far away. Ashar wanted to respond, but a burning vision rushed into his head.

Sanctum. Stones of light. The cold warmth. A bloody palm. The light. The healing.

Ashar dropped to one knee, his mind disappearing in darkness.

--

Ashar floated in a dark void and the shining stones were out of reach and the dragon came and her breath was fire and his mother cried and her tears fell in great drops and splashed as blood upon the stones and the dragon took her into darkness and he tried to follow but his feet were mired in mud and the blackness strangled him and the breath of the dragon burned his skin and the flame was the shining of the stones and his terror was swallowed by the light and Master Doyan cried that fear and faith cannot abide and he felt hope and with hope came faith and with faith his fear was swept away in a pelting wash of rain and he knew his mother was not lost in the darkness but would be found and ascend to the clouds of the blessed and Celestine appeared in a shining crystal with a tremor of joy and the exquisite sweetness of total abandonment to his destiny and the will of Oum'ilah.

Ashar opened his eyes. He was still on his knees. What seemed an enduring dream had been no more than the blinking of his eye. He pushed the puzzling vision from his mind and rose slowly to his feet. He was startled and embarrassed to discover Sage Hakheem still bowing before him. He had no idea what he was supposed to do. He was the least among them, and yet it was he before whom Sage Hakheem was genuflecting.

He closed his eyes and inhaled deeply, eager to access the bluish essence of his mind where he could hear the whisperings of the still, small voice. What he should do came in a calming wave of warmth.

He reached out and took the old sage by the hand. Hakheem looked up with a smile that consumed his face. His eyes sparkled. They were bottomless black pools of wisdom in a swirl of wrinkles.

Ashar was struck by the joyous thought that he would be privileged to sit and learn at the feet of the Blessed Sages. *In time I, too, will learn what it means to be wise.*

Ashar tugged on Hakheem's frail hand and, using his other hand to steady the old sage, lifted him to his feet.

A concussion of air pounded Ashar's ear. The sound of the arrow as it pierced Hakheem's chest was the crash of a wave upon a rock, as final as a thump on a drum. The arrow had sliced through the Sage's heart. An iron spike protruded from his back, and there was blood and flesh and torn threads of flax on the ragged point.

Sage Hakheem's raised brows were frozen in disbelief. The furrows on his forehead stretched flat in astonishment. His eyes were wide in shock and confusion, the light in them turning murky. His fingers clenched Ashar's hand, and pain shot up the boy's arm.

One moment Sage Hakheem was alive and staring at Ashar, his muscles taut and trembling. In the next, he was dead in a clump of woolen robes at Ashar's feet, his eyes open, his mouth agape. For what seemed like a long time, Ashar was unaware of anything other than the weight of the old Sage crumpled against his legs.

The other sages whirled about in a panic, crying out in shock and terror. Sage Ahmose teetered on his staff and turned to flee, but with his first desperate stride, his fragile legs failed and he fell. He threw out a hand to catch himself, but his wrist buckled and his face struck the stones of the courtyard.

Violence reigned. Deafening. In the midst of the chaos, the quiet voice came again. Ashar heard and understood. He pulled his hand free from the death grip of Sage Hakheem and ran to the Oracle. He pushed him backward over the wooden bench and dragged him under the heavy planks.

Sages Butukhan helped Sage Ahmose to his feet, and together they stumbled toward the steps of the temple. An arrow from the upper terrace struck Butukhan in the chest. He grabbed Ahmose's arm as he fell, and both tumbled to the ground in a pitiful heap.

Ashar whirled to where the arrows had come. There were four archers atop the walls on either side of the courtyard.

An arrow struck Ahmose in the neck. The shock of it paralyzed him for an instant. He gripped the shaft and tried to pull it out, but the barbed spike did not move. Another arrow pierced his chest and a third into his heart. His soul ascended to the clouds of blessing before his body crumpled dead upon the stones.

The other sages scrambled for the gate, their arms wrapped about each other, but there was little hope of escaping the archers' rain of death.

Ashar pushed the bench against the pillar of the arch that opened to the temple steps, protecting them from the archers on the west wall.

"I must get to the holy sanctum," the Oracle said, struggling to move from cover.

"No!" Ashar gripped his arm without regard for the chasm separating their status.

"I must," he said, calm in the midst of the chaos. "And you must come with me."

Ashar felt compelled to obey in spite of the raging terror, but he knew they would be killed if they abandoned their cover. He searched for the archers on the east wall. They were gone. He risked a glance around the pillar in the other direction. No archers on the west wall either. He gripped the Oracle's arm and prepared to dash to the temple steps when the clatter and shouts on the far side of the plaza stopped him. He looked up.

An army of outlaws jogged through the east gate and up the broad steps that led to the silk-covered plaza of the holy sanctum. The men were fearsome shadows in the bright sunlight of the open court. Their armor was dirty brass and black leather—a stark contrast to the soft fabrics and colorful robes of the sages. Most of the men advancing had drawn their swords. Some carried glaives or poleaxes. A second rank of soldiers followed them and formed up as rear guard. No one would escape the gate.

Ashar narrowed his eyes. The sun glinted from polished armor and breastplates that bore the sigil of the king. He had seen kingsriders before on his errands in the markets of Candella, but why would kingsriders come to the temple with weapons drawn? It made no sense. *Have these men come by order of the king?*

He watched in shock as the band of brigands in dark armor herded the Blessed Sages to the center of the courtyard, like dogs gathering sheep to protect them from wolves. Only today it was the wolves that gathered the sheep.

Ashar lifted the Oracle to his feet and started for the sanctuary of the holy sanctum.

"Wret'ka!" The word was shouted in a foreign tongue. *Halt!* The command came from a bowman who leaped forward from behind the east pillar. His bow was fully drawn, his arrow aimed at the Oracle's heart.

Ashar stepped in front of the Oracle to protect him even as another archer ran toward them from the east wall with an arrow nocked on his bowstring.

The plan was suddenly clear to Ashar. Bowmen from the west side were coming toward them, arrows nocked and ready.

Ashar circled slowly with his back to the Oracle. He had never thought of death. Like every young man, he thought he would never die.

The sages left alive were forced to kneel. The rest had been killed, all but Sage FarzAn, who lay wounded near the gate. A warrior pressed his short sword to the fallen sage's heart, but the fatal thrust was stayed.

"Let him live!" The man who spoke was a dark silhouette framed in the archway of the gate. His face was in shadow, but his eyes reflected fire. The stark command that rolled across the plaza was followed by silence. Even the fluttering of leaves and the hum of bees had been stilled. The man withdrew his sword and joined the other invaders, who formed a passageway in double ranks for the man striding forward.

Beyond the soft light of the billowing silk canopies, the sun's glare cast the man in a rim of hard white light that glinted off his armor in spite of the tarnished brass. He wore a bloodred cape that swept across his chest and flowed behind him like the wings of a dragon.

Ashar swallowed hard, certain that he was looking upon the face of the bandit king who had been terrorizing the countryside.

CHAPTER 39

The Oracle's life teetered on the trembling fingers of the bowmen who stood behind Ashar and the Oracle in a loose half circle. Each archer had his bow fully drawn and the spike of the arrow pointed at the Oracle's head or heart. With the flip of a thumb ring, the highest of high priests of the temple of Oum'ilah on the Mountain of God would be dead. It was unthinkable.

And I shall be dead as well! The thought shuddered through Ashar as he watched, wide-eyed and unblinking.

The bandit king passed through the gauntlet, not to the blows and distain of punishment, but to gestures of adulation and murmurs of deference.

The imposing man stopped three strides from the Oracle. Ashar edged forward by instinct as if doing so could somehow protect him.

The Oracle stood straight and stared into the bandit's face. He showed no sign of fear, only deep sorrow.

When the bandit removed his helm, the archers let down their bows and released the tension of their bowstrings.

"I am Drakkor, Blood of the Dragon." His voice was as coarse as a boot crunching grit along the river.

Ashar's muscles tightened when the bandit moved closer to the Oracle. A multitude of odors reached his nostrils: the oak tannin of leather, the sweat of horses, the acrid smell of iron weapons, and the stench of blood.

"I know who you are by the cry of the fatherless children and the widows who mourn." The Oracle's eyes were hard, but he spoke with a quaver of resignation in his voice. A sense of the inevitable finally upon them.

The words of the prophecy were clear in Ashar's mind: *The seal is broken. The ancient evil is come again.*

"And I know you, grand master of the mountain of a god who is naught." Drakkor swirled his red cloak and bowed to mock his vanquished foe. Then, rising, he said, "I share your grief for the useless deaths of these learned old men."

Ashar's eyes darted between the bandit king standing before them and the Blessed Sages who had fallen. Blood crept across the porch and disappeared into the cracks between the stones.

"Nothing can justify the murder of the old and helpless and most blessed among us," the Oracle said. "The consequence of this evil is upon you. The blood of these men will cry to the God of gods for vengeance, and His judgments shall fall upon you and your seed to the seventh generation."

Drakkor laughed softly but not without a margin of respect. "You are precisely the old fool I was told to expect." A demeaning laugh rumbled from deep in his throat. "Were it not for the promise I have made to my men, I might have appeared to you as a fabled winged spirit of your mythical god and accomplished my purpose without bloodshed, but you must understand, these men who ride with me have a lust for blood and the pleasures of the flesh." He shrugged, and Ashar followed his gaze to where one of the archers marked his forehead with the blood of a fallen sage, then touched his tongue. "They measure their worth by the tally who die by their hand." Drakkor leaned forward as if sharing a confidence. "They believe we are here to create a stronghold against the rising aggression of Kingsgate. They wish to make of your temple a grand castle and of this humble man before you a king."

Drakkor's smile sent a chill down Ashar's spine. "They do not understand who I am, nor can they comprehend my destiny. But you, the source of light and wisdom, as your ignorant pilgrims believe," he taunted, "must know my purpose and why I have come." He touched the sacred amulet that hung around the Oracle's neck. "And why you are yet alive."

He has come for the stones of light! The thought sent a jolt of pain through Ashar as if an archer had pierced him with an arrow.

"You may triumph for a season," the Oracle said, "but you will not escape the wrath of Oum'ilah."

"I have no fear of the wrath of the old gods of the tower. Why should I fear a god that is naught?"

"You are blinded by the evil that has overtaken you. There is but one true god and that is Oum'ilah, God of gods and Creator of All Things."

Drakkor reached out and closed his fingers around the Oracle's throat. He pulled the frail man closer.

Ashar started forward on a protective impulse but was stopped by the archer.

"I did not come to match wits," Drakkor said and relaxed his grip. The Oracle gasped for breath.

"Why do you seek the relics of a god whom you say is useless and naught?"

Drakkor paused and narrowed his eyes. "Ah, so you do know why I have come. The look on your old face confirms the rumors are true. You possess the missing stones of fire."

"The stones you seek are lost." The Oracle jutted his chin in defiance. "They are no more."

Ashar was startled by the boldness of the lie.

"Then how is it that I hold one in my hand?" Drakkor reached beneath his tunic and pulled out a stone. He held it up. The crystal was black but strangely translucent and shimmered in a shaft of sunlight.

Shock and fear passed over the Oracle's face

Ashar did not understand. *The Oracle should be laughing.* The stone could not be a stone of light. It was dark and discomforting to look upon.

But it was Drakkor who laughed as he held the stone higher.

"The stones of fire, hidden on this mountain, do not belong to you. They are not the relics of your god. They were not touched by the finger of your god as you stupidly believe. They were stolen by the Navigator. Your 'great and mighty' voyager who created a great lie to cover his crime." His voice was the rumble of a beast. "The stones are the eggs of she-dragon, buried in the ocean of chaos, hatched in the darkness, and ignited by the fire of the dragon's breath. They are the shining stones that light the way from the darkness of the world to the power of renewal and endless life."

The bandit's words were blasphemous, but it was fear not faith that surged through Ashar's head. In his memory, he saw Master Doyan's face, his mouth covered by the putrid gauze. His words were spoken to his mind. *"By the God of gods? You really think there is such a being? The mythical Oum'ilah, Creator of All Things?"*

"'That which was lost shall be gathered,'" Drakkor gloated, "and so I have come to claim what belongs to me. And I will not be denied."

The Oracle's face twisted when Drakkor recited the words of the prophecy.

Ashar felt the dark power of the man. The overpowering evil. Drakkor's voice echoed from the walls of the temple as if his very presence sent tremors into the bedrock.

"Your quest is vain!" the Oracle said. "Even if the stones were here, they can never be gathered in the hand of evil."

"And yet I hold one in my hand," Drakkor scoffed.

"To your destruction," the Oracle warned. "You hold the Swayyus Stone, stolen from the temple in ancient times by the cult of she-dragon and desecrated by the sorceress of Dragonfell."

Drakkor blanched at the Oracle's clear knowledge of things he couldn't know.

"It is a stone of visions, but in your hand it has become a stone of deception. You have perverted the power to penetrate the minds of other men to an evil purpose. The whiteness of the light is gone from it."

"It is blackened by the fire of she-dragon's breath."

"Using the power of the stones of light for an evil purpose is a desecration of unfathomable consequence to the wicked who willfully commit such blasphemy."

The Oracle's voice was strong, but his body quivered. "Return what you have stolen to the temple that it may be purified to righteousness again. I beg you to depart this holy place."

A breeze rippled through the shrouds of silk. A trio of bees buzzed about Drakkor's face as if the sunken scar were the blossom of a noxious weed. He swatted them away.

"The stones were touched by the finger of God as a symbol of His goodness. A remembrance of the great voyage." He inhaled deeply and let the breath out slowly. "They shall be gathered by the hand of righteousness. Only one with the blood of the Navigator may be consecrated to endless life by their power."

Only those with the blood of the Navigator? Ashar shuddered.

"You weary me with your babbling. Take me to where you have hidden the stolen stones of fire," Drakkor said.

Their eyes locked in combat: a dark face of fury with a scar of purging against a bright face of faith with gossamer skin.

The rustle of the silken shroud and buzzing of the bees were gone. Silence returned as the shadow of a cloud passed before the sun.

"You shall never have them," the Oracle said.

Drakkor narrowed his eyes. His cape swirled in a red smear the color of blood as he turned and strode to where the Blessed Sages huddled with Master FarzAn. Drakkor grabbed the wounded sage by his hair and dragged him to his knees.

The old sage looked up in a confusion of pain and fear. There was no time to pray.

Drakkor drew his long sword from the scabbard on his back and, in a single sweep of the doubled-edge blade, cut FarzAn's head from his body. It thumped to the stones and rolled away. The torso tumbled forward, and the stones of the temple were stained by blood.

Ashar gasped for breath and choked at the bitter taste that filled his mouth. He swallowed to keep from retching. His heart hammered in his ears. The sages were paralyzed in shock and horror.

Drakkor faced the terrified old men. He motioned for the Mankin to step forward. "You! Come here!"

Another execution? Another murder in cold blood? Ashar was desperate to look away, but his neck would not move and his head would not turn.

Master Kurgaan waddled forward, his face resolute. His eyes remained fixed on the sword in Drakkor's hand. When he drew closer, Kurgaan closed his eyes, stopped breathing, and began to pray.

"No, no, little man." Drakkor laughed softly and stroked the Sage's head as if petting a dog. "I lament that your imprudent Oracle has made this demonstration necessary." He wiped the blade of the bloody sword across Krugaan's shoulder, leaving a crimson stain on the Mankin's woolen cassock. "I much prefer that the wisest among you join with me rather than die as a nameless martyr to a god who is naught." He waited for the wind to carry his words away. "Your wisdom can keep you alive. Your secrets are valuable to me, and I have much to accomplish." His words were gracious, but there was no mistaking the ultimatum: betray your faith and deny your God of gods or suffer an ignominious death.

Drakkor returned the sword to its scabbard and walked to the Oracle. "Bring me the virgins," he said to his men holding the girls behind the pillars. The terrified daughters of the temple were ushered forward. Celestine was among them, struggling to keep the brigand's groping hands from her body.

A spike of fury slammed into Ashar's heart.

Drakkor looked west and shielded his eyes against the sunlight as if none of the chaos was taking place. He turned as the girls were pushed into a ragged row before him. He looked at the Oracle to make sure he was watching.

Ashar could hardly restrain himself from wrenching loose of the strong hands that held him to attack the monster with nothing but his outrage, but he knew that doing so would be certain death. For him, the Oracle, and Celestine.

"As I have told you my men are driven by a hunger you and I can't understand. They feed on the spoils of conquest and . . ." Drakkor lifted a handful of Celestine's silken hair and let it flow between his fingers. "The pleasures of the flesh."

The Oracle moved toward Drakkor, pleading with arms extended, "In the name of all things holy, I implore you! Do not—"

Drakkor trampled on his words. "No, no, of course! I also find the lust of these men appalling. To allow them to violate the virgins of the temple is unthinkable." Drakkor turned toward the sun again. It had escaped the wisp of clouds, and the light fell on his face. "If the stones of fire are gathered in my hand before the sun's last rays are lost in the endless sea, I will protect the honor of these cherished creatures." He laced his fingers through Celestine's silken hair a second time. "And there will be no more blood staining the stones of my castle." He looked up at the gleaming towers of the temple with the reverence of a pilgrim, then turned to the ashen face of the Oracle.

"Which will it be, holy man? Blood or virtue?"

CHAPTER 40

The Oracle held Ashar's arm as they climbed the stairs to the sanctum. His whole body trembled. "I have no choice," he whispered under his breath. "May the God of gods forgive me."

Drakkor followed the Oracle with three of his men, one of whom had Celestine in his grip. The others ushered the trio of remaining sages: Armu-Tukic, Laehus, and Kurgaan.

Ashar knew the hostages were being brought lest the Oracle forget the high stakes of Drakkor's impossible proposition. He pleaded silently with Oum'ilah as the evil men entered the holy sanctum of the temple.

—–—

Ashar removed the silken shroud from the box and opened the coffer as the Oracle instructed.

Drakkor leaned over the plinth and stared into the box. His dark hair glistened in the sunlight that fell from the disc of polished copper above.

"They are white!" Drakkor scowled.

"As I have told you," the Oracle said.

Drakkor tightened his jaw. "Where are the rest?"

"Lost," the Oracle said.

"You lie!" Drakkor pointed at the Oracle. "You have until the next beat of my heart to tell me where you have hidden the rest."

The Oracle looked up with pleading eyes. "I tell you the truth."

Ashar's head pounded in cadence with the pummeling of his heart. He stopped breathing.

Drakkor dragged Celestine to the center of the chamber and ripped away the thin fabric of her gown. "Who will have her first?" he shouted at his men.

Ashar charged Drakkor in a blind rage. He was knocked to the stones by the iron hand of the brigand who had stepped forward to take the girl.

Through a blur of blood and whirling fog, Ashar saw Celestine pushed to her knees. She covered herself with her arms across her chest.

The Oracle stepped forward and put both hands on Drakkor's chest. "I swear by the holy ground on which I stand, the other stones are lost, but . . ."

The Oracle's voice changed, and Ashar ripped his eyes from the girl and looked up at him.

"But these are enough."

The brigand had Celestine by the wrist and was about to pull her to her feet, when Drakkor said, "Wait!" His voice was calm.

The brigand scowled and let her go.

Drakkor kept his eyes on the Oracle. "They are enough?"

"I know what you seek. The magic power of these stones will be enough."

Magic? Ashar touched the throbbing pain in his head. His fingers came back sticky, wet, and red. He crawled to Celestine's side and wrapped the silken shroud across her trembling, bare shoulders. Celestine thanked him with a blushing, fleeting glance.

Ashar's attention returned to the Oracle. Something about him had changed. Color had returned to the holy man's face, and he moved with unexpected vigor. *What is he going to do?*

"You do not know the prophecy," Drakkor said. "All of the stones must be gathered in the hand of might by him worthy of the blood!"

The Oracle raised his chin. "You embrace a corruption of the ancient sayings, but I say again: I can give you what you seek."

"The stones of fire?"

"No. A life that does not end," the Oracle said.

Drakkor narrowed his eyes, and his face twitched as skepticism collided with vain hope. Then he cackled a scornful laugh. "You expect me to believe *you* have such magic?"

"It is not by magic such a thing is wrought."

Ashar could feel a strange power emanating from the Oracle.

Drakkor shifted his stance and stepped closer. "You ask me to believe in the power of a god that is naught. Is it a game you play with me, old fool?"

"Does the prophecy not say endless life comes by the power of the ancient secret?"

Drakkor nodded, but Ashar was confused. Those were *not* the words of the prophecy.

"As I said, these stones may be enough, but *only* if bound by the secrets of the ancients. Do you carry the book of ancient spells? The ancient grimoire that contains the conjuration of the ancient mysteries? You do have it, do you not?" The Oracle's tone was mocking.

Drakkor's face darkened and, though he tried to hide it, his expression confessed that he had no idea what the Oracle was talking about.

"Did your Navigator steal that as well?" he said.

The Oracle closed his eyes briefly and said, "I am guardian of all things pertaining to the stones of light."

In a flash, Ashar remembered the thick black planks of hardwood wrapped in a chain and sealed with wax that he had seen earlier that day in the chancery. *Could it be?*

"You have the ancient book of spells. You know this ritual." Drakkor's voice retained some skepticism.

The Oracle held Drakkor's eyes, but did not speak.

"And you would trade this secret for old men and children?"

The Oracle nodded. "If you swear by the blood of she-dragon that you will leave the Mountain of God and never return." He held Drakkor's eyes, and Ashar could almost hear the silent prayers the Oracle offered. "With endless life, you will not need these ancient walls as a fortress. You will be king. You can have whatever castle or kingdom you want, or all of them."

"Where is this book of spells?"

The Oracle tapped his forehead with three fingers and smiled.

"How can I believe you?" Drakkor's chortle cracked with disdain.

The Oracle waved a frail hand toward the armed brigands and hostages. "Our lives are in your hands. You stand with a force of arms. We are old men who bear no weapons."

Ashar's mouth was dry.

"If you deceive me, you and every living soul on your mountain will die." He let the warning hang in the air for a moment. Then he said, "What must I do?"

"First, swear your oath that you will leave this mountain when it is done."

He grimaced. "By my honor and the blood of she-dragon, I swear it," Drakkor said.

CHAPTER 41

Selmaas! Mother! Qhuin's thoughts were far behind the parade of wagons, men, and horses moving south. They lingered instead in the courtyard of Stókenhold Fortress. He had never expected to see again the kitchen maid who'd nursed him as a child. He could still feel her arms around him. He would never forget the look of joy and wonder on her face. The scent of her: the pungent blend of sweet and sharp; hot baked bread and steaming broth. Breath sweet as a nip of honey from the combs. The memories brought a surge of delight and, with it, the face of Meesha smiling down. The moment she entered his mind, she filled his head and seized his thoughts.

Meesha: the woman he had known as a child, the woman who had brought him food and shared the night, the beautiful woman who'd kissed him. The memory of her whirled through him in a flutter of happiness. *How shall I ever thank her?* Qhuin wondered. *What power has given me such good fortune?* he wondered. *Truly the winged spirits of the God of gods is watching.*

His reverie was shattered by an angry voice.

"Move ahead, bondsman!" the kingsrider bellowed at Qhuin as he rode alongside the chariot. The expedition had kicked up another storm of dust on its way across the dry lake basin north of the Tallgrass Prairie. Qhuin had fallen back for cleaner air, but the kingsrider riding rearward this day was more diligent than others. The man held his place and breathed the dust and demanded Qhuin do the same. The chariots ahead were little more than shapes in the billowing dust.

"Pull up the slack! Move on!" he yelled again.

Having felt a sense of freedom on the journey, the kingsrider's demand was galling. He was a soldier, not a nobleman nor a master over Qhuin. By what right—Rusthammer interrupted Qhuin by whispering in his head as he often did. *"To do, not to think, is the burden of bondage. You must never forget—the burden of bondage does not keep you from being free!"*

Qhuin squinted against the whirling sand, then, trusting his horses, he closed his eyes. Rusthammer grinned in the darkness as if their conversation never ended. *"Masters and high-born dare not consider the mind of a man in bondage might be brighter and better than their own. They dare not allow that a slave is capable of intelligence, thinking, or emotions that bring pleasure or pain as real as their own."* It was almost as if Rusthammer stood beside him in the swirling dust. Qhuin's thoughts drifted to the stables of Blackthorn. To Rusthammer.

———

If the blacksmith Leo Rusthammer had a noble lineage, it had been lost. He never knew his father, and his mother died when he was very young. By tradition, only those with a legacy of smithing, working metal, and making accoutrements for the royal house were worthy to forge armor or weapons for the king. The importance of lineage was fundamental to the perpetuation of royal privilege. Rusthammer's legacy should have kept him from the blacksmith station of Blackthorn. It didn't.

For all his failings, King Orsis-Kublan had the good sense to acknowledge Rusthammer's extraordinary mastery of the forge. The king bequeathed him a worthy lineage and charged the scrivener to create ten generations of noble ancestors. Rusthammer never looked at it, but the document satisfied the pedants of protocol who cared deeply about such things.

Most of the highborn of Blackthorn thought the blacksmith mad. "Suffering the curse of a demented mind," some said. His irrational way of thinking and the impractical ideas he proposed were deemed by many as clear signs of a descent into madness.

As long as the arms and armor emerging from the anvil and forge of Blackthorn continued to be splendid, however, the blacksmith was safe in the king's royal shadow.

Qhuin knew the blacksmith's eccentricities were not madness but evidence of a brilliant mind. He also knew that Rusthammer did little to dispel the rumors that he was an eccentric out of touch with reality. It ensured that no one paid attention to what he did with his metal and forge beyond making weapons.

Qhuin had seen many of the secret inventions the blacksmith had created, including Rusthammer's most magnificent machine, kept hidden in the catacombs below the south end of the stables. Qhuin believed it was only a matter of time before the old blacksmith's invention would be finished: the Iron Eagle, he called it. A machine that could fly, allowing men to soar into the sky alongside the birds.

One evening, as they were finishing a lightweight chariot for the hunt, Rusthammer suddenly volunteered something that had nothing to do with their work. It was personal and spoken with utmost secrecy.

"There is something you should know about me," he had begun without looking up from where he secured the cowling. There was a long pause before he continued. "I do not believe in the gods of the ancient tower. I have come to understand the old gods are the creations of men, spawned from their fearful imaginings. They are idols with no more significance than the wood and stone from which they are made."

To be complacent about religion was not uncommon. To reject the beliefs of the king was considered a path to trouble if not ultimate demise. Qhuin understood his old friend's need for secrecy.

Rusthammer continued. "As a boy, I was fed the mythos of the old gods of the tower. When I began to think for myself, I was drawn to the religion of the Navigator and Oum'ilah, God of gods and Creator of All Things. I became a pilgrim, and"—he paused as if considering whether to share his secret, then smiled with confidence—"for a brief time I lived at the temple on the Mountain of God. While there, I was befriended by the keeper of the chancery and given access to writings handed down a hundred generations. By his leave, I was allowed to make copies of the ancient works."

Qhuin was spellbound. His mind was racing and reaching and wanting to know more.

"When you return," Rusthammer said, "I will take you to where I keep these sacred writings hidden and teach you how to interpret them. I will show you wondrous things."

———

With the conversation still echoing in his mind, Qhuin adjusted the covering over his mouth and looked back at the kingsrider to see if the man might have changed his mind as the dust thickened. It did not appear so.

Qhuin felt a surge of anticipation about his future. The feelings of freedom on the road had raised his expectations. Of what, he wasn't certain, but even as the rush of optimism came, the weight of the iron collar around his neck mocked the hopeful feeling and pushed it from his mind.

Like the unfinished Iron Eagle, it was not yet his time to fly.

CHAPTER 42

Ashar watched in breathless fascination. He strained to hear the thoughts of the Oracle. He'd been taught the ways of mediation and speaking mind to mind, but the intensity of focus it demanded was elusive and difficult. He was distracted by the throbbing from the blow to his head.

Drakkor had been stripped of his armor and wore a simple loincloth. The last rays of sunlight reflected by the copper disc fell over him. He was thick in the chest and narrow at the waist, and his stomach was a rippling of muscles. His skin was stretched tight and looked pale against the dusky bronze of his face. The tail of the black dragon tattoo encircled his neck, then slithered over his shoulder and under his arm. The body of the fire-breathing beast curled from the deep scar of his navel to the hardened muscles of his chest.

Drakkor stood at the topmost point of a pentagram drawn on the floor of the chamber. A stone was placed at each of the other four tips of the five-pointed star: three white stones from the temple and the blackened stone of Drakkor.

Had he not been there in person, watching with his own wide, unblinking eyes, Ashar would not have believed such a ritual could take place in the temple. It was puzzling. He had never seen a pentagram among the symbols engraved on the walls and monuments on the Mountain of God. He remembered Master Doyan's lesson on ancient symbols; he had said the pentagram was used by the cults of black magic.

There is so much I do not know, so very much.

Ashar's eyes slipped past Drakkor to the sages held as hostages. From the bewildered expressions of the sages's faces, Ashar wondered if this was the first time they had seen the "ritual of endless life." The sages watched with hollow eyes, looking sick and old and more frail than Ashar remembered.

The Oracle has no choice. He is violating the sanctitude of this holy place for them. Ashar looked to Celestine. She was curled against the wall, her legs tucked under, the sacred silk wrapped tightly around her. *He is doing this for her.*

Ashar's eyes continued to move around the room. Drakkor's bandits stood on three sides, swords in hand. Drakkor had ordered his men to slay them all at the slightest provocation.

The ritual was short and mysterious. Drakkor drank an elixir that sent him into a haze of euphoric oblivion. The Oracle began the conjuration with an incantation chanted in a language Ashar had never heard. He finished in the common tongue. "And thus by the power of the ancient secret, it is done."

Drakkor blinked his eyes and rubbed his temples as if trying to squeeze the fog of the elixir from his brain. He shook his head to chase the dizziness away. "It is done?" His tongue was thick, and his words slurred. "That is all?"

Ashar could see the bandit remembered little of what had taken place.

The Oracle sighed. "Yes, and may the God of gods forgive me for the desecration of the sacred stones."

Drakkor straightened his back and pushed his fingers through his hair. He faced the Oracle.

Ashar tensed at the inevitable confrontation between the victor and the vanquished. *Will Drakkor keep his word or kill us all?*

Drakkor opened his mouth to speak, and the room plunged into gloom. The last ray of the sun was swallowed by the endless sea that flowed to the edge of the world. The reflection from the polished brass illuminating the chamber was gone.

Drakkor seemed suddenly seized by a sense of vulnerability. *Little wonder,* Ashar thought. The sudden gloom of darkness. Standing nearly naked. A brume of opiates still swirling in his head.

Ashar ignited an oil lamp that filled the room in a half-light and cast grotesque shadows onto the walls.

"Gather the stones," the Oracle said.

Ashar knelt and reached for the black stone first.

Drakkor stooped, gripped his wrist, and plucked the stone from Ashar's hand. "Put the rest into the box and bring them to me," he said. "We shall know the truth of this masquerade soon enough."

Ashar stared into the blackness of Drakkor's eyes. His face was close, and his breath was sour. The odor of his sweat-soaked body was strong. "Yes, m'lord," he said, regretting the slip of his tongue. He carefully gathered the other four stones.

Drakkor put on his linen shirt and trousers, then slipped the black stone beneath his padded doublet. "Other than a thousand needles stabbing the backs of my eyes," he growled as he pulled on his boots, "I feel no different now than before." He fitted the cuirass of boiled leather to his chest.

"You will sense the change soon enough," the Oracle said, inhaling deeply and holding out his hand. "You took an oath to return the stone to the temple to be purified and cleansed."

"Soon enough! Do you take me for a fool?" Drakkor scoffed and continued dressing. "How do I know this is more than a cheap magician's trick to delay your death?"

Ashar took the stones to the box. As he turned his back, he felt the Oracle touch his leg. The movement was hidden from Drakkor's view by the Oracle's body. Ashar glanced down at the Oracle's open hand. A shimmering of blue behind his eyes. A clarity of thought. He understood what he was to do and slipped the last of the stones into the Oracle's hand.

"If some great change has taken place, why do I feel nothing?" Drakkor demanded.

"The life of the flesh is the blood, and blood sets the limit of life," the Oracle said. "You will remain the same, only the essence coursing in your veins will be changed. By the power of the ancient secret and ritual of conjuration, the stones have the power to purify your blood and transform it to the finer substance of enduring life. It takes time. You must be patient. It may not be until morning. You must keep your word and leave."

"Until morning! You expect me to leave the mountain on the pretense of such babbling? What proof do I have that I have not been deceived? How do I know your white stones are more than cobbles from the brook? Give me a sign."

The Oracle smiled, and when he turned, the shadowed side of his face fused with the darkness. He appeared to be a mythical creature floating in the air. "Give me your hand," he said.

The Oracle's visage gave Drakkor pause, and he hesitated before extending his left hand. In a single, sudden movement, the Oracle slashed his dagger across Drakkor's palm.

Drakkor whirled away and stumbled back. He seized his long sword from the mound of armor and laid the point of it against the Oracle's throat. He gripped the hilt with both hands.

The Oracle touched the sword. A cold white light shimmered down the blade, enveloping the hilt and Drakkor's hands. As the quivering glow radiated between Drakkor's fingers, he lowered his sword and opened his wounded hand. The lacerated palm was oozing, but there was no blood. A translucent substance shimmering with a thousand tiny specks of light emanated from the wound. As Drakkor stared, the wound healed itself, and the light retreated back into his body.

A surge of wonder and terror passed across his face. He held up the healed hand and turned it slowly. His lips moved, but there were no words. He looked at his men, their faces pinched by superstition.

In the long silence that followed, Ashar studied the Oracle's face, searching for answers to the questions pounding through his head.

Drakkor fitted the final piece of his armor but could not fasten the buckles, and the straps hung loose. He wagged a commanding finger at Ashar. "Bring me the stones."

Ashar's eyes darted to the Oracle.

The Oracle shook his head. "The stones belong in the temple," he said. "I have given you what you asked, and you have sworn your oath to leave."

"The stones, boy!" Drakkor yelled.

"No!" the Oracle said, and moved to block the dais with his body.

Drakkor scoffed loudly and pushed the Oracle aside, but as the old man stumbled back, he seized the box and clutched it to his chest.

Drakkor grabbed it with both hands and jerked with such violence that the Oracle was thrown to the floor. The box crashed open, and three stones bounced out like living creatures escaping a cage. The Oracle reached for the stone he had hidden, but it wobbled from his fingers when he fell.

Drakkor stomped his boot on the Oracle's wrist, crushing it.

Ashar hurled himself against Drakkor's leg. "Stop!"

Drakkor swept down and lifted the boy to his feet with an iron fist around his throat. "Gather them!" he growled in a voice as feral as his animal eyes. He threw Ashar to the floor, but in doing so lifted his boot from the Oracle's arm.

Sage Laehus rushed to the fallen Oracle and helped him to his feet. He kept him from falling with an arm around his waist.

Ashar gathered the stones and returned them to the coffer.

"Give it to me," Drakkor said.

"You swore by your gods!" the Oracle said, stepping forward with the help of Sage Laehus.

"I am my own god," Drakkor said and took the coffer from Ashar. He spoke to the Oracle in a way that included all present. "You and any one willing to join us are welcome to stay. Otherwise you must leave the mountain before the sun reaches midday on the morrow." He looked at his hand healed by magic. "Unless, of course, I awaken with no sure sign of the endless life you claim to have given. Then . . ." He shrugged an apology for his murderous threat.

Drakkor put the box beneath his arm and turned toward the door. With a sudden and violent movement, the Oracle lunged forward and grabbed the box, then whirled away.

The room erupted in chaos.

From where Ashar stood, it looked more like a dance than a fight, a graceful ballet that could only end in death.

The momentum of seizing the coffer spun the Oracle in a sweeping arc. Drakkor's arms followed like ribbons blown by the wind, but his grasp fell short. The Oracle circled the plinth and ran for a portal arch. Drakkor's reaching hands circled around and returned with the sword in their grip.

Celestine seized the moment of confusion. She sprang to her feet and bounded from the room like a gazelle escaping a lion.

Ashar saw her from the corner of his eye and felt a surge of hope.

Sage Kurgaan struggled up and tried to block Drakkor from chasing after the Oracle, but the warrior knocked him down with single blow.

The old sage cried out, and the Oracle turned back. Empathy was his undoing. It gave Drakkor the one blink of an eye he needed to slash the Oracle across his back and shoulder. The blow would have been fatal had Drakkor not tripped over the toppled dais and stumbled as his blade came down.

The Oracle sprawled forward and landed on the box, his blood running out. He clutched the precious relics to his chest and dragged himself forward.

With the warrior's attention turned, Sages Armu-Tukic and Laehus grappled to escape the chamber with the wounded Kurgaan. Drakkor's men chased after them.

With a growling curse, Drakkor scrambled to recover his feet and lifted his blade to end the Oracle's life and might have but—

Smash!

Ashar pounded a wedge of marble into the side of Drakkor's head. He had snatched up the broken corner of the dais without the slightest forethought.

Drakkor went to his knees, and the would-be fatal blow of his blade clanked harmlessly on the edge of the archway.

Now I am going to die, Ashar thought. He backed away with the ragged chunk of marble still clutched in his hand. He expected an explosion of anger and slashing sword, but Drakkor remained on his knees, stunned.

Drakkor looked over at the Oracle crumpled in the portal behind him. No longer moving. He raised his fingers slowly and touched the ridge of bone above his temple. There was no translucent flicker of light. No mystical substance of immortality. Only a ribbon of blood.

Drakkor touched a bloody finger to his tongue. His face darkened with the realization. In the same moment, Ashar also understood. The elaborate ritual had been a charade. An elaborate deception by the Oracle to trick the bandit into leaving the mountain. Give them time. Allow them a chance to escape. Get help. Survive. It had failed.

Ashar gulped air to catch his breath and glanced behind him. The Oracle lay as if he were dead, the box of stones clutched to his chest.

Drakkor rose slowly to his feet and twisted his neck with an audible crack. The flickering glow of the oil lamp deepened the hole in his face. "Who are you?" he asked Ashar. His voice was level, soft and deadly.

A conversation with the monster was the last thing Ashar expected. *Fear and faith cannot abide.* Ashar tried to visualize fear as a creature fleeing from a warrior that embodied faith. He felt a curious sense of courage, but it did not come from the imagined warrior of faith in his head. It came from the broken chunk of marble in his hand.

"I am Ashar, son of Shalatar, postulant to the Holy Order of Oum'ilah, God of gods and Creator of All Things."

Drakkor laughed. It was chilling and disdainful. "That may be who you think you are, Ashar, son of Shalatar, but you are mistaken."

Ashar tensed.

"Since I gained the summit of this mountain, you are the only one with the courage to challenge me." He laughed again, scoffing. No longer chilling. "A boy in a woolen robe with a rock in his hand and the courage to stand against a warrior clad in armor with a sword. You are not who you think yourself to be."

"You promised to leave."

Drakkor looked at the blood on his fingers, then turned his hand toward Ashar and raised his eyebrows. "Where is the essence of endless life your holy man promised me?" His words were cold. "There will be more blood spilled before the night is over. Only those who bow will be allowed to live. And what of you, son of Shalatar? Will you stay alive and follow me? You do not belong in the crumbling temple of a mythical god." He looked to where the Oracle lay atop the box of stones. "With these stones, I will have the power to be King, and as King, I will gather the rest of the stones, and when I am immortal, I will reign as a god on earth. Join me, Ashar, son of Shalatar, and stand beside me in my glory."

Ashar stood unblinking. Then he set his jaw and shook his head.

Drakkor swept his blade forward and pushed the point of it against Ashar's throat. "Put the rock down."

Ashar felt the pinprick of pressure at his throat. The chunk of marble thudded to the floor. Fear splintered through his head like breaking glass. The pressing point of the steel blade made it hard to breathe.

"Where are the rest of the holy stones?"

"I don't know." Ashar tried to swallow but his mouth was too dry.

The point of the blade went deeper, and he could feel warm blood trickling down his neck. Tiny sparkles of light fluttered at the edge of blackness as consciousness slipped away.

He was ripped from the edge of darkness by the rattling clank of metal crashing over stone.

A warrior clad in armor smashed into the wall and landed in a broken heap on the pentagram. A second man flew in from overhead as if thrown by a catapult. He landed headfirst on the stone floor. Dead.

The point of the sword against Ashar's throat vanished, and he dropped to his knees, gasping for breath.

Drakkor whirled with his sword in both hands. Too late.

Rorekk, the giant, stepped over Ashar in a single stride and grabbed Drakkor by his breastplate. At close range, the sword was useless. Rorekk lifted the bandit off his feet, whirled him in a half circle, and slammed him against the wall. Rorekk was a forearm and a half taller than Drakkor and thicker by twelve stones. Drakkor fumbled for the dagger in his belt, but Rorekk crushed him against the wall a second time.

Three of Drakkor's warriors stormed into the room. The first of them plunged a short sword into the giant's side. Rorekk flinched and lost his grip on Drakkor, who tumbled to the floor in a semiconscious stupor.

Rorekk pulled the blade from his side in a rush of blood. He seized his assailant by the wrist and flung him in a circle, like a battle flail of flesh, bones, brass, and leather. The bandit's airborne body struck the next attacker in a violent collision that drove him face-first into the wall.

The third bandit leaned back to evade the whirling death, then lunged at the giant with his ax. The iron spurs on the boots of the man Rorekk swung like a human flail caught him in the neck and slashed his throat.

Drakkor struggled to his feet with fleeting glances at the giant's rain of death. He scurried for the door with his back against the wall. The giant whirled the hapless bandit in a third arc of destruction. His iron spurs hit Drakkor in the chest, tearing across the leather breastplate, but not deep enough to wound. He was thrown backward into the passage. As he struggled to regain his feet, he kept one hand over the blackened stone of fire.

Several brigands rushed into the hallway of the sanctuary. One threw an arm around Drakkor and helped him toward the entrance.

Rorekk lifted his human bludgeon over his head and hurled him into the confusion of men who charged toward the doorway with weapons drawn. He didn't wait to watch the calamity of bodies crashing into bodies but seized the ornate iron door and dragged it shut. The rusty iron hinges shrieked a wailing cry. He dropped the heavy crossbar as the door slammed into place.

Ashar followed the giant to where the Oracle was struggling to rise. "Leko wessnos brelisaa." The giant spoke with a broken cadence in a language Ashar had never heard, but when Rorekk pointed at the coffer, he understood. *Rescue the stones.*

A moment later, the thud of a heavy object slammed against the iron door. The shouts of angry men slithered under the crack. The rusted pins holding the hinges to the stone wall jolted in a crumble of mortar and stone.

The pounding grew louder and more determined. At first Ashar thought it unlikely the warriors could break through the iron door, but the weight of whatever they had found to use as a battering ram and the incessant pummeling was wrenching the hinges from the wall.

Ashar knelt by the Oracle and removed the stones from the box. He wrapped them in fur and pushed them deep into a leather satchel. He looked up as Rorekk lifted the Oracle into his arms as if the holy man weighed no more than a child.

Ashar followed the giant through the portal. He looked back at the dust from the commotion on the other side of the door. The pounding was punctuated by the profane shouts of the men. Above the rest, he heard the distinctive rasp of Drakkor's voice.

"Kill them and bring me the stones!"

The Oracle's limp arm was draped over the giant's shoulder. The fingers moved, and the old man's hand grasped the giant's leather vest. He was alive! Ashar thanked the God of gods and Creator of All Things.

A wondrous realization came in the midst of chaos. *My destiny is beyond what I have imagined.* With the thought came the sobering reality of how ill-prepared he was to survive in the world beyond the temple.

He had the strange sensation that the chunk of marble was still in his hand and the fighting had only begun.

CHAPTER 43

The portal opened to a circular antechamber with no windows and no door. Tallow candles with double wicks in a ring of wrought iron sconces gave the room an orange glow.

Rorekk's shadow rippled across the hip of the vaulted arch as he crossed to a circular mosaic on the floor in the center of the room. "Em'ot fesloc dants."

"I don't understand," Ashar said, failing to understand the words or glean meaning from the movement of the giant's head and eyes.

Stand close to me. The meaning of the giant's words appeared in the bluish glow somewhere inside his head. He hurried forward and pressed against a leg as massive as a tree. Until that moment, Ashar had not realized how huge the giant was. He glanced up to see an amused smile on Rorekk's broad face. Ashar realized he was staring with his mouth agape. He snapped it shut with a silly smile.

The tumult of pounding from the other room rumbled into the antechamber. It grew louder as the bottom hinge broke away and the bottom corner of the door twisted partially open. One of the bandits dropped to his belly and struggled to slither through the opening.

The floor beneath Ashar's feet began to move. He clutched the leather satchel to his chest and grabbed Rorekk's leg to keep from falling.

The abrasive grind of stone on stone joined the cacophony resounding from the walls of the chamber. The mosaic circle on which they stood stuttered downward. Even in the dim light, Ashar could see that a shaft had been cut through the solid rock.

Their descent into the catacomb below the holy sanctum was swift and ended with a violent jolt that knocked Ashar to his knees. Rorekk cradled the Oracle in his arms and spoke to him in soft whispers. He seemed oblivious to the wound in his side that was still bleeding. Rorekk stepped through an opening in the wall, and Ashar followed.

The moment Ashar stepped off the stone disc, it rumbled upward. He could see it was lifted by a complex mechanism of cogged wheels and iron-strapped timbers that rose from a pit filled with water. The slab bunged into the hole in the floor, hiding the secret of their disappearance.

The masonry of fitted stones opened to a natural cavern. The air was damp and pungent with the biting smell of sulfur. The muted sound of distant shouts was joined by the tranquil music of water dripping into pools. Fingers of stone reached from the blackness above; others rose from the floor. As they emerged from the man-made passage, Rorekk nodded toward a brazier of glowing coals.

"H'crot e'kathe," he said over his shoulder as he continued forward, his strides long and confident.

Ashar followed his eyes to the torches. He grabbed one and laid it on the glowing red coals of a brazier. The suet-soaked rags burst into yellow flame.

Ashar ran to catch up. Shadows raced past him on the walls as the torchlight passed through the enchanted forest of calcium spindles. The path had ascended slowly from the time they entered the cavern, but now it rose abruptly and threaded its way around an underground lake. The water glowed with a strange luminescence the color of gingko in early spring. Water gurgled from a tumble of rocks on the far side and fell, frothy white, to the lake below.

The warm light in the cavern cooled and brightened as the trail rose steeply up a fall of rock. Ashar saw daylight beyond.

Rorekk adjusted his arms around the Oracle. He never faltered, and his pace never slackened. He stepped from boulder to boulder as if the rocks were a stairway made for giants. Perhaps it was. The rocks were slick with moisture and moss. Ashar fell twice and dropped the torch. Rorekk did not look back.

When they emerged from the caverns, it took a few moments for Ashar's eyes to adjust to the light. The sun was still in the sky, even though it was beginning to sink behind the Mountains of Deepmore. They had climbed higher than Ashar had thought.

Rorekk gave Ashar a moment to catch his breath, then continued along the trail. Ashar threw the torch aside and hurried after him. The path wound upward through a thicket of brush to the base of the monolith of stone.

The sheer wall erupted from the hogback ridge and rose a thousand cubitums to a perpetual swirl of clouds, the sign that Oum'ilah was present. At least that's what Master Doyan had taught. The thought sent a ripple of pain to his stomach, where it collided with a sudden pang of hunger, reminding Ashar he had not eaten in two days.

Ashar climbed to the top of a boulder that looked like the shell of an enormous turtle. He had a mostly open view of the village and temple below. It was a great distance and hard to see any detail in the fading light. Numerous fires punched holes in the blue twilight. Smoke hung over the ridge in a dusky pall. There was a large fire in the central court. Silhouettes moved back and forth through the flickering light. It appeared that the bandits were sorting votaries into groups and rounding up pilgrims who had come to the temple on the wrong day.

Ashar could hear the cries of agony, even at the great distance. *There will be more blood spilled before the night is over.* Drakkor's promise pounded in Ashar's head. *Only those who bow will be allowed to live.* Ashar understood. Only the fainthearted, the sympathizers, the traitors to Oum'ilah willing to bow to evil. Ashar could not condemn those who were too frightened to resist, those who would do what they needed to do to spare their lives. The outrage twisted his heart until the screaming came from within, an anguished cry of lost innocence. The man who called himself Blood of the Dragon had taken the temple. The purge of the righteous had begun.

Ashar started up the trail, but turned around when an impression pulled him back. *Where is Celestine?* He stopped breathing and narrowed his eyes, hoping to penetrate the fading light. His eyes flitted among the moving shadows in a desperate search, but he could not find her.

Then the flowing white of her gown caught his eye. A flicker of light in the darkness. She was running east, to where the trail to the Tears of God left the courtyard. *She is alive!* He thanked the God of gods in a silent prayer. When he opened his eyes, he saw two men chasing after her. Talons of fear gripped him. *We have to go back!*

"Master Ashar?" Rorekk's thick voice was urgent.

Ashar turned from the horror below and caught a glimpse of the giant as he vanished behind a tumble of boulders.

"I have to go back!" he yelled. "Do you hear me?"

His voice was swallowed by the sounds of angry shouting. Not from the village below—closer! He whirled around. Torches emerged from the black hole at the entrance of the cavern. The warriors had found the hidden passage. There was no going back. The realization pounded through his chest like a war lance.

The pale, pure face of Celestine filled his mind. Terror constricted his throat. He turned to where Rorekk had disappeared. A glimmer of sunlight on the clouds that shrouded the summit of the monolith caught his eye, and it was as if the light spoke to him. He stared into the clouds that marked the hiding place of Oum'ilah.

He is taking us to the hallowed fane.

"The hallowed fane is sacred, not secret." Ashar could almost hear Master Doyan's voice. His lessons on the subject were intended to dispel the mystery of the most holy of holy places. The orthodox story was that the hallowed fane had been built by the Navigator and the people who had come with him. A Blessed Sage, long since passed away, was

often quoted as having said that the holy fane was the altar built by the First Man and already there when the Navigator came.

He was so close to the sheer rock wall he could not see the top of the mountain. Even if he could have seen it, the mystery was hidden by the clouds. The wondrous anthology of stories, mythos, gossip, and speculation was vivid in his mind. For Ashar, with his inquisitive nature, creative disposition, and abundant imagination, it could hardly be otherwise. Was today the day the mystery would unfold?

What was it that glimmered through the wisp of clouds in the sun's last golden light?

He was jolted back to the harsh reality by the shouting of the bandits and the clamoring of iron.

CHAPTER 44

Dusk was slipping into darkness by the time the Raven to the King reached the Tavern at Leviathan Deeps. In contrast to the quiet, cold blue of twilight, the tavern was clamorous, crowded, and warmed by firelight.

The Tavern at Leviathan Deeps was a tumble of buildings where the track to the village crossed the King's Road. It stood a stone's throw from the banks of the inland sea that stretched eastward to Stone Island.

According to local lore, the rocks and the rough-hewn timbers of the tavern had once been part of a fortress that kept sea monsters from coming ashore at the narrow bridge of land that divided the south from the north. There was hardly anyone who called it "the Isthmus" in spite of the name of the village. For most, the narrow neck was simply "the Narrows."

As he reached for the tavern door, the Raven was struck by how foolish he was to be lured to this place by nothing more than a note given to him by an old woman on the road to Village Isthmus. She had appeared suddenly, mumbled incoherently, and then stuffed a scrap of parchment into his hand. It was scribbled with charcoal and hardly readable.

COME TO THE TAVERN AT THE CROSSING.
I KNOW WHAT YOU SEEK.

Giving the cryptic message any credence conflicted with his instincts, but his errand was urgent. If he succeeded, he'd have a power greater than kings. If he failed, he'd likely lose his life.

Even as his heart thumped faster, he felt a strange sense of calm. Intuition? Destiny? Curiosity? He couldn't be sure. He gripped the hilt of his sword and stepped inside the tavern. He stood by the door and looked for the stranger he'd come to meet.

It was impossible for an emissary of the king or a person bearing the sigil of the Peacock Throne to move among the common folk asking questions without igniting a flurry of gossip as quickly as a firebrand in a field of dry grass at high summer.

An emissary of the king traveling without the protection of kingsriders had cause to be wary. As one privy to the king's secret cult of mystics, even more caution was required. Vanity had not allowed a completely convincing disguise, but he had exchanged most of his elegant wardrobe for the less-striking attire of a nobleman. Perhaps it would be enough.

His errand was one of unusual sensitivity. He needed to move freely and make his inquires without stirring significant curiosities. But traveling alone on the King's Road was dangerous, whether or not he was an emissary of the king, so a pair of kingsriders followed at a distance with orders to rendezvous at a prearranged location every third day. They had missed their last appointment.

The Raven searched the faces of the tavern patrons for a telltale look. A signal. A subtle gesture from the one who sent the message. The tables were mostly occupied by common folk, mostly travelers stopping for the night, a few soldiers, and some who had the look of highborn nobles. Peasants from the village crowded around tables at the far end where the roof was so low a normal man would need to stoop.

Likely local folks who gather every night to dull the pain of labor with cheap ale, the Raven mused. Ale, home-brewed by the innkeeper, was available for meager coin. It was bitter and tasted bad, but after two gulps, the taste didn't matter. It loosened tongues and enlivened the burden of living.

Anything to brighten the sparsity of their meager lives, the Raven thought.

The clamor grew louder as he shouldered his way toward the rear, but no one looked his way or showed him any interest. He stood by the door with his back to the wall. He noticed a band of men at a large table by an alcove at the back. Big men mostly. Swarthy. Unkempt, yet strangely disciplined. They carried weapons not often seen. Some wore armor. Not the tempered metals of the kingsriders but iron, leather, and brass.

Brigands? Drakkor's men? The Raven shuddered at the thought of what the ruthless bandit had done to an entire march of kingsriders.

The men huddled over a leg of pork, black bread, cheese, sugared apples, and jackfruit. They took flagons of wine from the tavern wench and waved her away. The biggest of the men sat with his back to the door. At a nod from the man across from him, he turned and looked at the Raven. It was a hard look. Intense, cold and unnerving.

The Raven held his eyes. Was this the stranger he was sent to meet? Tiny claws of fear pricked his neck, but the man nodded cordially and turned again to his companions.

A woman hurried from the kitchen with a flagon of ale. Her movement caught his eye. She looked at him as if he were a wild creature let in by mistake. The message in her eyes was clear: *I am the one you are here to meet.* Her face was ashen and her lip trembled. She was a sturdy woman, plumpish with a bodice tight and low, and older than most of the girls who served the room. She glanced about as if someone was watching, then turned away to fill a woodsman's mug.

The woodsman got an eye full when the woman leaned down, and he muttered a crude remark. He was a churlish fellow, drunken, disheveled, and dirty from the mountains. His tunic bore the sigil of a minor house, or a league of huntsmen, perhaps.

The woman glanced up at the Raven as she poured the ale. The mug filled too quickly, and the liquid spilled over the top. The woodsman laughed and clutched the woman in a handful of cloth and flesh and pulled her to him.

She tried to keep her balance, but his hand was tight and his arm strong. She stumbled and landed in a clumsy sprawl across his lap. The flagon fell to the wooden board and burst into shards. Spiced ale spilled across the table, sending the man's companions leaping to their feet in an eruption of toppled benches and foul cursing.

The foolery brought a wave of laughter, but it was quickly swallowed by the tumult of voices, the song of the jongleur, and the rattling of copper and tin.

A woodsman groping a tavern wench was not an uncommon sight in a tavern on the King's Road. Given different circumstances, the Raven would hardly have noticed, but the look she had given him could not be mistaken. *This is the woman who sent the old crone with the note. She has something to tell me. But how can she know what I am after?*

The Raven circled to a small table in a corner on the other side of the room. He kept his eyes on the woman. She watched him but was distracted by the groping hands of the woodsman. Whores were common in many alehouses along the King's Road, but she did not have the look of one. In times past, whoring was shamed and hidden in dark corners, but under the reign of Orsis-Kublan, the boundaries between right and wrong had been badly blurred. Depravity in the royal house was a persistent source of gossip, providing tacit approval to whatever bad behavior the common folks pursued.

More an innkeeper's wife than a tavern wench. The Raven knew more than one innkeeper who had become wealthy by obliging a wife and brood of children to cook and clean and serve and, if required for extra coin, behave a bit unseemly. He tried to imagine what she knew and why she'd called him here.

The Raven felt sorry for the woman, whoever she was, but his sympathy passed quickly. He was on an errand of great importance, but it was not the anxious, gray face of the king that drove him. His thoughts vacillated between the promise of power if he succeed to the promise of death if he failed. But he was a stargazer, and the heavens foreshadowed his triumph.

The woman pushed the woodsman's hands aside and tried to recover whatever dignity remained. "I've got to mop up the mess, m'love," she said with a spurious smile, glancing up to capture the Raven's eyes again. "I pray you let me go." The woman flirted but without disguising her disgust.

How was it possible this woman knew he sought the secret of endless life or that he was Raven to the King? At best, she was merely an innkeeper's wife. "I know what you seek," the note had said. Was it an offer to help. Or was it a trap?

Two of the king's mystics had already died. Killed by one of their own? No one knew. Another had not been heard from since he left for the north. *Which among us would murder another for the sake of the prize?* The answer was unsettling.

The king had shown them the fruits of failure with the execution of the alchemist. There were few men for whom greed did not trump loyalty, or for whom power was not stronger than any bond of brotherhood.

The Raven lamented the fact there was so little honor left in the dominions of Kandelaar.

Guilt pestered him with a dreadful thought. *I am the king's trusted counselor, and yet . . . I am no better.* He pushed the truth of it aside.

The woodsman still held the woman on his lap and slobbered kisses on her neck.

She gripped his fondling fingers with a vigorous twist and pushed his face away. "Let me be! Let go of me!" She struggled to get up. He pulled her back.

"Not without another kiss," the woodsman slurred. His companions guffawed and pounded their mugs on the board. The woodsman gripped a fistful of the woman's hair and twisted her face toward him.

"No, m'lord, please. I pray, let me go!" The woman's voice pierced the clatter and commotion.

Like a shadow come alive, the Raven was suddenly upon the man. He gripped him by the throat and pushed him backward, toppling him from the bench. The thud of the man's head striking the floor was louder than the thud of the wooden bench striking the hardwood planks.

"I am in a hurry, and you, sir, are keeping this woman from serving me."

The woodsman's companions stumbled up in awkward panic. The larger of the two pulled out a short sword, but he clearly had no intent of using it.

The Raven put the hand with the two-fingered ring in the woodsman's face. The man blanched and waved his companions off. Striking an emissary of the king would result in imprisonment at Stókenhold Fortress, a fate many considered more onerous than death.

The Raven knew that showing the royal ring emblazoned with the sigil of the king was a risk, but hubris overcame caution.

The woman stood breathing hard with one hand across her bosom and the other tugging at her skirt. The Raven looked at the woman with a confirming nod. She turned away to wipe the ale and gathered the pieces of the broken flagon, then hurried to the kitchen with her sodden rags and shattered bits of porcelain.

The Raven expected a glance back. There was none. Had he been wrong? Had he misread the woman's look? As one whose mind was consumed by mystical combinations of the stars and planets, he knew better than almost anyone that what was imagined and what was real were rarely the same.

He watched the woodsman and his companions swagger from the tavern in a clomping of boots and slurry of profanities. They bumped their way through the door and into the night. A moment later, the woman came to the Raven's table with a flagon of ale as if nothing had happened.

"How may I serve you, m'lord?" She glanced about, then smiled and held his eyes.

"With something more than a tankard of cheap wine," he said, studying her face for a sign.

"We've a barrel of spiced ale with cinnamon from the brewery at Kingsgate, if ye'd rather, m'lord."

"I've not come for drink," he said. "My curiosity is stronger than my thirst." He placed the scrap of parchment on the table and moved his hand away, revealing the two-fingered sigil of the king.

She inhaled deeply, leaned forward to whisk crumbs from the table, and plucked up the note. Her face was close to his and her whisper soft.

"There's place for the horses behind the inn." She flashed a practiced smile and hurried away.

CHAPTER 45

Ashar scrambled upward through a fall of rocks to catch up with Rorekk. The trail followed the ridge that swept around the west side of the mountain. The overhang made the climb difficult. The rocks were sharp and loose, the footing precarious. Ashar managed with nothing more than minor abrasions on his elbows and knees.

Rorekk laid the Oracle on a slab of stone. He cradled his head and gave him water. The high priest's mouth was slack, and water dribbled into the white of his beard.

Ashar stared at the bloodstain on the Oracle's back. *Did he die?* He fought the feelings of foreboding that hammered through his heart. The terror of the attack and the deaths of the Blessed Sages had left him in shock. His skin was pallid, his breathing short. He felt cold. The knot of hunger was gone, but he was desperate to quench his thirst. At the sight of the water flask, he licked his parched lips.

Rorekk offered the flask to Ashar. He took a few quick gulps, sucked in a long slow breath, and raised the flask again.

The giant plucked it away. "Sele'esk!" Rorekk furrowed his immense brow and clenched a fist to his stomach. "Sele'esk noi tomo."

Too much too fast is not good. Ashar understood, though he wasn't sure how. Rorekk offered a wedge of dried venison instead. The smell of hickory smoke and pepper sent a shudder of anticipation through Ashar's shrunken stomach. He savored the briny smell before gnawing his way into the leather-tough jerky.

Rorekk wrapped a leather strap around the Oracle's legs and lifted the unconscious patriarch to his shoulder. The Oracle's head and upper body were cradled across the giant's chest. Ashar had never seen a man carried that way.

The sling holding the Oracle allowed Rorekk to use both hands to climb. The trail was little more than a ledge of rock rising steeply toward the north face.

Ashar's breathing came in short gasps. He turned to look at the trail behind them. How had the bandits discovered the hidden passage? He knew what they wanted. He gripped the satchel and squeezed the soft leather to confirm the stones were still there. The warmth he had felt in the sanctum returned with startling clarity.

The clank of weapons and gruff voices reached him on the breeze. His reverie was shattered. In spite of the surge of optimism he felt with the stones in his hand, the sounds of evil filled him with dread—not for himself or his companions on the mountain but for those he'd left behind. *Master Doyan and . . .*

Celestine's face appeared in his mind's eye. He took comfort in the fact that he had seen her running toward the Tears of God. *Had she escaped the men who chased her? Was she still alive?*

Once again, he had fallen behind. At the sound of the brigands on the trail below, Ashar scrambled upward and looked for Rorekk. He caught sight of him far ahead. Seeing the Oracle in his arms soothed his fears. Nothing could be more important than saving the Oracle. But had they saved him or was he already dead? The thought drowned his calm in a wave of dread.

Ashar forced the image of the awful scene below from his mind. Faith chased fear away, and for a fleeting moment Ashar felt blessed by the God of gods. He looked to the top of the mountain and hurried his pace. The narrow ledge rose steadily and steeply as it wrapped around the west side of the mountain before turning north.

From the temple courtyard, the monolithic mountain appeared to be nothing but solid stone. Ashar was surprised by the crusts of lichen and thick moss the color of emerald. There were bushes and flowers growing from the tiniest of cracks. Here and there a tamarack twisted from a fissure, its roots slithering into pockets of humus brought there by the winds.

The ledge ended at a sheer wall that protruded from the main face like a huge slice of bread pushed from the loaf. Steps, rough-hewn from solid rock, wound upward through a narrow fracture where the slab had slipped away. The cleft was passable for a normal man, but barely wide enough for the giant. Ashar clambered through the cleft. He touched a stone so cold he thought it must be close to the ice that never melts.

The ascent was torturous. If there had been a trail in the past, it was long gone. It was evident that no one had been here recently. The moss and gray-green lichen was undisturbed, and there was more of it now and fewer patches of flowers.

They reached the north side of the mountain. Two thousand cubitums straight down was the river, a skinny scrawl of reflected sky scratched in a charcoal-green night, like a squiggle drawn by a child.

Where the stones steps ended, a ladder made from slender trunks lashed with steps of corroded iron lay against the wall. Ashar gasped for breath. He closed his eyes to fight his fear of falling. *Fear and faith cannot abide.* He recited the mantra, but fear wore many masks, and he wondered if Master Doyan had ever walked up a near-sheer incline of rock holding nothing but a thin chain.

Rorekk moved the swaddle to protect his wounds and adjusted the straps of the cradle. He spoke softly to the Oracle, then gripped the rungs of the ladder. Ashar watched in wonder as the giant tested the iron steps and began to climb. The rusted iron was lashed to the rails with sinew. They bowed with each heavy step but held.

Ashar couldn't see how the ladder was attached to the stone and expected it to break loose at any moment. He shuddered at the vivid image of the giant and the Oracle plunging to their deaths. *And I will follow.* Ashar felt light-headed and realized he was holding his breath.

At the top of the ladder, the route turned sharply east and followed a jagged ridge, the top of which was no wider than half the height of a Mankin. In a few places, a length of rusted chain was looped between spikes hammered into fissures in the rock, but most of the posts were either loose or missing. The trail fell away to a chasm on the right where a massive section of the monolith had sloughed away. The other side was an escarpment of loose rock extending to the edge of a sheer drop straight to the river. If they fell, their bodies would end up on the ragged rocks jutting from the north side of the monolith like shards of glass.

Where the ridge ran into the sheer face again, a precarious walkway protruded from the walls as if hung there by hemp from heaven. *Who could have put it there? Guardians from another time? Or were they likewise borne up by the winged spirits of God?* The air was thin, and Ashar wondered if he was thinking clearly.

Iron rods pounded into cracks and fissures stuck straight out from the sheer face, each one higher on the vertical wall than the one below. Bamboo poles had been lashed together, spanning the gaps between the rods. Smaller bamboo poles were laced crossways by twisted hemp, creating a steep ramp barely two cubitums wide and suspended in nothing but air. The rise was so steep in places the ancient builders had left gaps between the bamboo slats to create steps.

In places the trail was almost vertical. Ashar gripped every cavity or pocket of broken rock along the face. He tried hard not to look down, but it was impossible. The abyss beckoned with a strange power that felt like someone tugging at the hem of his robe. When he wasn't looking down, his eyes were fixated on the shreds of rotting hemp and splintering bamboo. His ears filled with the creaking, groaning protests of the ancient walkway.

Ashar pressed his back against the rock and edged upward, his fingers fumbling for purchase. His heart pounded, and his breath came in ever shorter bursts. He dared not breath more deeply, lest any sudden movement send him plunging to his death.

Fear and faith cannot abide. He recited it over and over in his head and tried not to look down. *Fear and faith cannot abide. Fear and faith cannot abide.*

Whichever wise sage penned such wisdom in ages past had never been here. He could not have written those words while fighting phantoms of fear and clinging by his fingertips to a crevice of a rock.

Ashar grit his teeth, closed his eyes, and allowed his faith to fail. He had no choice but to abide his awful fear.

The faith required to believe in the doctrines of the codex was, at that moment, completely disconnected from finding the confidence to navigate the walkway. He recited the dogma of endlessness instead. He knew it well. *All that is, has always been, and will forever be, and who we are and were before not only is but will always be and continue through endless time.* It didn't help.

Ashar cautiously increased his pace and caught up with Rorekk and the Oracle. He stayed as close as he could. Close enough to touch. *Close enough to grab in case I fall,* he confessed to himself.

Somewhere in the swirl of disjointed thoughts, Ashar wished for a winged servant of God to pluck him from his frightening perch and fly him to the hallowed fane. Or whatever it was they would find at the top of the monolith of stone. *If we survive!*

Suddenly the bamboo broke. His legs smashed through the splinters, and Ashar plunged toward the river.

CHAPTER 46

The wild mares broke to the right and raced toward the setting sun. Qhuin looped the leather around his wrist and pulled his trio of horses into a dangerously tight turn to chase after them. The iron wheel of the chariot slashed a deep wound in the wild grass and threw up a storm of red earth.

The Princeling Sargon stood beside Qhuin in the hunting chariot, gripping the rail with both hands and fighting to stay on his feet. His knuckles squeezed white; his breath came in short bursts.

One wheel lifted off the ground and the chariot skidded sideways. Qhuin adjusted the tension on the reins and held the horses in the turn. The chariot teetered precariously before the wheel slammed to the ground again.

"Get me closer!" Sargon screamed, his voice more fearful than excited.

The chariot settled, and the traces pulled straight. Qhuin gave the milk-whites their head. With a gentle rippling of the reins, the geldings lengthened their gait. At the sound of Qhuin's voice, they raced faster to catch the fleeing tarpans. They would run to the edge of death for this master.

The six Huszárs raced after the fleeing horses. It was their assignment to contain the herd and keep the wild horses circling to the left. It allowed the chariots to run the outside of the oval and gave the hunters more than one chance to capture a horse.

The hunters carried birchwood lasso-poles twice the height of a man. A noose of woven horsehair and sheep gut hung from an iron fitting at the tip. The cinch ran the length of the pole, held in place by iron rings and fastened at the end of the handle. The pole was attached to the rider's horse by a saddle strap tied to the iron ring at the end of the handle. A quick pull of the rope would tighten the noose once it was around the horse's neck.

———

The night before the hunt, Horsemaster Raahud tactfully suggested that Prince Kadesh-Cor and his guests go after the wild herd on horseback instead of in chariots, which would be difficult and dangerous. Kadesh-Cor rejected the suggestion. There were incredulous glances, but none dared challenge the prince.

When the folly of catching wild horses from chariots reached the Huszárs, they saw the humor of it. "'Tis a fair enough plan," laughed one, "but mark my words, the prince will tell 'em to go left, and the wild ones will go right and show 'em nothing but their tails and arses!"

There was humor enough to go around, but some saw the idea of the wild horses' refusing to obey the prince as something more profound. Wild creatures doing what they chose stirred an instinctive sense of freedom in the hearts of most men.

Free will is the order of the universe, Qhuin mused as he considered the words later that night. It tickled a notion that sometime and somewhere he would have the courage to go right when the prince said left and show him nothing but his arse.

———

As predicted, the wild herd broke right to keep from being trapped. The circle had been broken almost as quickly as it had been formed. The Huszárs waved their coils of hemp to turn the horses back without the slightest result. Three riders on the right spurred their horses to catch up, but they were no match for the wild tarpans of the Oodanga Wilds.

Qhuin glanced back. None of the other chariots had attempted the dangerous turn.

Princeling Chor's chariot was a colorful blur as it swung in a wide arc around a copse of cyprus and a curtain of hanging moss. Chor shouted at his reinsman, who pushed his team with the lash of a whip.

Horsemaster Raahud drove a chariot that was lighter and faster than the others. He was less experienced than his reinsman, Jewuul, but had traded places for his own pleasure. He required a wide circle to return to the chase, and by then he was far behind. Jewuul held the lasso-pole, but any chance of catching a horse was lost.

Kadesh-Cor's chariot crossed a shallow depression and nearly turned over. It slowed and, a stone's throw farther on, veered away from the chase. The reinsman, Jehu, turned his black horses in a wide circle and pointed the chariot toward the crest of a hummock. From there the prince would have an unobstructed view of the swirling melee of riders, horses, men, and chariots.

Qhuin felt a twinge of disappointment when the prince abandoned the chase, but he was not surprised. It was impossible for Kadesh-Cor to keep pace with wild horses in a gilded chariot designed for the paved road of parades, not the broken ground of the hunt.

The Baron Magnus prided himself on his hunting prowess. The humiliation would not settle well. Qhuin had been near enough the night before to hear Kadesh-Cor brag that he himself would be the one who would catch the finest of the wild horses.

Qhuin raised a fist in a salute and a promise as he watched them go. *I will catch you a horse.* He held his fist aloft until Jehu glanced behind and caught his eye. Jehu saluted back.

Qhuin thought of Jehu as a friend, even knowing the chasm

between them was too wide and deep to give the word much meaning. Jehu was hardly highborn, but his lineage was known. He was Jehu Lochneer, son of Nacle. Knowing your father and your father's father and the endless chain of one's lineage distinguished one man over another other in significant ways.

Rusthammer and Qhuin had discussed it many times. Crossing the chasm of tradition was an impossible journey, especially for a slave of unknown blood. Ethnic derivation, bloodline, and the length of ancestral lines were important. Over time, an odd construal of royal lineage seeped into every level of society, like poisoned water into the public cistern. Perhaps it grew from the commoner's contempt for royal privilege for the sake of a name. Perhaps it was the universal longing to be royal.

If royal blood and the lineage of kings had the power to do evil and count it good, to revere insanity as wisdom and excuse moral degeneracy as a divine right of rule, why shouldn't the ancestry of common folk, real or imagined, also be the measure of a person's worth? Why should the pride of bloodline and breeding not be used to gain advantage, demand privilege, and excuse behavior?

Highborn men paraded about in fine apparel, competing in adornments with their fellowmen until the gaggle of royals was arrayed with an obscenity of bangles, bobbles, ringlets, and precious stones of outrageous cost and bad taste. Those who could tolerate the pain decorated their bodies with elaborate tattoos, puncturing the skin with needles dipped in lampblack and oil.

Irrational as it was, society demanded a man not be judged by his actions or who he manifested himself to be, but only by whose blood flowed in his veins and what honor, nobility, or notion of grandeur could be attached to it.

Rusthammer told Qhuin that the values held in high esteem at the time of First Landing that measured the true character of a person were lost as society was segregated by prejudice, pride, and power.

Many of the horsemen in the Blackthorn stables were like Jehu—freemen with a respectable lineage but without the nobility of a great house. They were employed by Blackthorn and paid a modest wage. They had families and, from time to time, left for a life away from the stables.

Qhuin often tried to imagine what it meant to be a "freeman," but Jehu and the others kept it private, as if sharing any part of what went on in their small stone houses in the village might diminish the sanctity of it or risk its existence.

The rush of pride Qhuin felt in besting Jehu was expelled by the envy that tightened around his heart. *Who am I to indulge in such vanity? I am A'quilum Ereon Qhuin. A man of unknown blood. Jehu is free, and I am not.*

"No one in the reign of kings is truly free, not even Jehu," Rusthammer's voice said in his head. A person was so easily condemned by the company he kept that the risk of friendship was great. The suspicion over misplaced trust was inevitable and the danger of betrayal absolute.

"Free will and self-determination are illusions," the blacksmith said. "Choices are made by the overlords in a perpetual feast for power. What little remains is spat out only by the good pleasure of the sovereign lords who rule from their great houses and grow fat on the labor of the poor."

The roar of iron over broken ground and the pounding of hooves brought Qhuin back to the moment.

Sargon was shouting at him, but he heard no voice. Even the sounds of the horses and chariot were faint and far away.

Instead, his inner voice spoke louder than his thoughts. He had heard it before, and he knew he should not listen. It filled his head with ideas that pounded inside his skull like a prisoner trying to escape.

Qhuin knew the smallest thought of rebellion was perilous. Allowing the secret voice expression, even if only in the privacy of his mind, was dangerous. It spoke from the depths of his soul and came from a place that would never be silent.

The voice also filled his head with images. "Your mind's eye," Rusthammer called it. "The place of wondrous creation." But the images in Qhuin's mind were not wondrous. They were wretched. Emaciated men in stocks for alleged offenses against the king. Women stripped, shamed, and humiliated in the public square. Heads impaled on wooden spikes and black-winged creatures plucking out their eyes.

Why could he not rid himself of such horrors? Were they a warning? A foreshadowing of his fate?

Qhuin felt a rush of emotion that left him with a strange sense of hope. So he listened to that inner voice and allowed himself to imagine living a different kind of life.

— —

The herd of wild tarpans galloped into the shallow end of a deep wash and disappeared in shadow. The vast plains of rolling grass shimmered in the last long shafts of golden sunlight.

Qhuin looked west at the barrier of mountains that divided the lands southward and protected the grasslands and forests from the sands and desolation that ran from the west slopes of the mountains to the sea.

The sun hovered at the rocky crest as if reluctant to send the shadows of night across the grasslands. Qhuin knew the Great Barriers by their ancient name, the Mountains of the Moon. Rusthammer had once told him the legend of a shrine in the mountains and of a hiding place of mysterious and sacred things. Qhuin remembered laughing at the story, but now he thought of the stone tucked into the secret pouch by his hip and wondered.

"We've only two hours before it is too dark!" Sargon shouted above the rushing wind with all the authority he could muster while clinging for life and limb to the railing of the hurdling chariot.

"We've an hour at best," Qhuin said. "Speak when spoken to" was the rule, but the princeling was wrong. He intended no rudeness, but correcting a royal always ended badly. "The darkness will come even sooner down there," he said and nodded toward the swale where the horses had disappeared; it was already in gray light.

"Use the whip!" Sargon yelled close to Qhuin's ear.

"They're not trained to the whip, m'lord."

"I said use the whip!"

Qhuin nodded, but his jaw tightened and he made no move for the whip.

"Have you forgotten who I am?" the princeling shouted, jutting his chin forward and leaning even closer to Qhuin's ear.

"You make it easy to remember . . . m'lord." The pause held a caustic edge of contempt.

Sargon lifted the whip from its cradle and held it out. "Then do as I command and use the whip. I've a wager with my brother who'll get the first catch." The cords in the princeling's neck bulged beneath the tight white skin. "Should I lose because of you, bondsman, I will take my losses from your hide, and you can be sure that I will—"

Qhuin turned his head so suddenly and his gaze was so intense that Sargon swallowed whatever else he intended to say. The stark blue of his eyes surrounded by the rich brown of his skin gave him a mystical quality. A soothsayer. A teller of fortunes. A diviner of men's minds. His brow was pinched into a scowl.

Sargon inhaled sharply and pressed his body into the side of the chariot, a spoiled boy pretending to be a man. It took him a moment to recover, but then he lifted his chin with authority. Still, when he rubbed the back of his neck and fumbled with the collar of his jerkin, his fingers trembled. "I will have you flogged," Sargon finished his threat with a voice that cracked. The final word came out in a pathetic squeak.

Qhuin took the whip from Sargon's hand and shoved it back into its place.

"Just be ready with the lasso-pole," Qhuin said.

The princeling's eyes turned black.

CHAPTER 47

"Over here, m'lord!" The woman was waiting in the shadows when the Raven exited the tavern. He could only see half her face in the glow of the lantern.

"What is it you have for me, woman? Tell me quickly!"

"There is word about the village that you are a man willing to pay them that can help you."

"Perhaps. If the help given warrants it."

"You are the Raven to the King, are ye not?"

How could she know? He had moved with such care and stealth and secrecy. Before he could recover from his surprise, she continued.

"And the rumor in the village is that the king seeks to live forever, is that true?"

His mouth moved, but he didn't speak.

She took his silence as affirmation. "And you are looking for the magic stones, ain't that so?"

Magic stones? How could a tavern wench possibly know something the eyes and ears of the king did not? He was discomfited by his ignorance but felt a burst of hope in her words. This was what he had been hoping to find: Something more than a legend. Something real. *Does the woman truly know of such things?*

He regained his composure and scowled at her, fiddling with the laces of his cloak to buy time.

"Magic stones? And I suppose you are here to sell me your 'magic stones' for a heavy purse of coin. Do I appear to be such a fool?"

"No, m'lord, but I—"

"How can a tavern whore know of such things?" He cut her short.

Even in the low light, the Raven saw her neck turn red. She curled her arms around her middle. "I was not always what you see, gracious lord. I was abandoned by my husband and left in despair. He journeyed to the West River with two cousins and a fisherman, but they never returned. It's been nine years since. The cousins returned but said they knew not what became of him. One later claimed that he drowned, but I don't believe . . ." Her voice faded away. "Because I am of common blood, once he was gone, I was taken from what little privilege I'd been given."

"Enough of your babbling," the Raven said. "Your existence is of no interest to me. Tell me of these magic stones. I will reward you well enough if what you have to offer is of value." He patted the money purse fitted snugly under the broad leather belt around his waist.

She stared at the purse. The long silence was discomforting. A sound came from the darkness. A footfall? He glanced behind him. The distance between the inn and the dark shadows of the stable made it a fine place for thieves. He remembered the man with dark eyes inside the tavern, and he gripped the pommel of his sword.

"I've three children who stay with my mor while I'm working," she said, blinking away an unwanted emotion. "I know little more than what I have told you, but there is such a thing, and the legend is true."

He wanted her tale to be true, but it couldn't be. It made him angry. "And how can you vouch for something about which you know so little? Or nothing at all, as it seems?"

"I have spoken with one who knows it from an ancient source— even where the magic stones are hidden."

Hope gripped his throat, but only for an instant. "Who?"

"A holy man."

"What to you mean 'holy'? Where do I find him?"

"I pray, m'lord, but if you please . . ." She held out her hand.

"Do you not trust a man who wears the sigil of your king?" He held up his two-fingered ring.

"I'm sorry, m'lord." She looked down, but her hand did not move. "I trust only what I've learned by being cheated."

"You try my patience!" the Raven barked, but he lifted the purse and dropped two coins into her palm.

"Only two, m'lord? Is it not endless life your king seeks?"

"Greed will not serve you. How can I be certain you speak the truth about this holy man and his knowledge of these magic stones?"

"I had a fourth child. A boy. My oldest. My husband took him to the mountain and gave him to the priests of the temple. I pleaded with him to leave the child with me, but my husband was a cruel man. He resented me because I had loved someone else before. He never accepted the boy as his son, and he demanded I never tell the boy the truth."

"What truth? Speak plainly."

"My husband was not the father of my firstborn child." She raised her face without shame. "The boy's father was the son of a nobleman. He was the only man I ever loved. He intended to marry me and make me a fine lady, but—"

"A nobleman?" The Raven cut her off.

"Of House Edom. A minor house, m'lord, very old, almost gone now." The flickering light of the lantern made the tear on her cheek glisten like a diamond. "It was not long after my husband took my boy away that he disappeared with the fisherman."

The Raven expelled a gust of breath. "I don't care about your sorry life. Tell me about the holy man," he demanded.

"A year ago, an aged man who'd been beaten by bandits and left for dead was brought to my mother's cottage. She's a wisewoman of the old tradition and knows the secrets of the healing herbs. When the poor man could finally speak, he said he had come from the Mountain of God."

The Raven wrinkled his brow. "Beyond Village Candella?"

She nodded and continued. "He said he was given to the high priests of the temple as a child, and, in time, became an enlightened master and Blessed Sage. He came down from the mountain to proclaim his God of gods and Creator of All Things 'to all mankind,' he said. We cared for him. In spite of our disbelief." She smiled and shook her head. "In spite of our impoverishment, we shared all we had with the prophet."

"You call him a prophet?"

"He was called such by the villagers who found him and brought him to my mor."

"And this 'prophet' has these magic stones of endless life?"

The woman continued as if she had not heard the Raven's question. "I asked him what became of the children given to the temple. Whether all of them lived to be old men filled with great wisdom, like him. He said not all, but when I told him of my son, he said he remembered a boy I feel certain was my child. 'If he is your boy,' he told me, 'he is gifted in spiritual things.'" She paused a long time before returning from where her heart had taken her. "It was many years ago. If my boy is yet alive, he would be a young man now. Quite handsome now, I'm sure, and so very, very bright." She tapped her head.

"Yes, yes, but the magic stones—what did the prophet say?"

"He never told us about them, exactly, not in a way that—"

"By the gods, woman! If he did not tell you, how can you presume to—" The Raven gripped her arm. The lantern swung, and the light of it wavered across her face. "If you do not tell me something of value, and quickly, I will take back my coins and your lying hand with it!"

The woman dug her sharp nails into the back of his fist and twisted away. "You don't think me foolish enough to meet you here alone?" she said and glanced at a stack of timbers no more than a dozen paces away.

The man looming in the shadow would have remained invisible had he not shifted his stance and adjusted his grip on the club in his hand. When he moved, the light from the window fell across his face. It was the man Raven had seen in the common room of the tavern.

"My apologies," the Raven said while looking at the large man. He raised a hand in a gesture of calm, then turned again to the woman. "I am eager to know all you can tell me."

"The prophet was beset by a fever for many days, his mind muddled."

"So what you heard of magic stones came from a man in delirium and madness?" He chuffed loudly.

"He spoke of the stones and their mystical power only in his worst of times, as if caught in a nightmare by day."

"An illusion, then?"

"No, m'lord. They were secrets that could never otherwise be spoken. No words are truer than those spoken by an unguarded tongue."

The Raven pinched his face to ponder the wisdom of that. "And what did he say of their magic?"

"*Magic* was not a word he used, m'lord, but from his uttering, I found out that whoever possesses the stones will live forever with no fear of death. And there was something else. About light that caused them to shine. He said that . . ." She pursed her lips as if she dared not speak another word.

"And what? Pray continue, woman!"

"He said the stones were touched by the finger of God."

The Raven to the King and the woman of the tavern stood in the island of lantern light in a black sea of silence.

"He said they were the sacred stones of light of ancient days," she whispered.

"And he had them?"

She shook her head.

"They were taken by the thieves who attacked him on the King's Road?"

"No, I think not, m'lord. He never said such a thing."

"Did you ever learn his name? Where is he now?"

"I long to tell you where he is, gracious lord, but I am a despairing woman. I have lost a husband and a son, and I have naught to feed my mor and little daughters." She reached out her hand. "Forgive my shameful begging, but . . ." She bowed her head, but her hand remained steady.

"You are a foul woman," the Raven scowled, but he opened his purse and dropped half a dozen coins into her hand. "Where do I find your so-called prophet? What is his name?"

She looked at the coins in her palm, then brought her other hand forward, cupping them together. "I swore to him I would never reveal his name. If I must dishonor what little is left of me, it must be for coin enough to cover my shame and feed my children until they can care for themselves."

The Raven's jaw muscles twitched. He resisted the urge to strike the woman down. But what if it was true? What if there was a holy prophet who knew of magical stones of light with the power of endless life and where they could be found?

He emptied the contents of his purse into the bowl of her two hands. "Very well, but I tell you now, if your prophet is not where you send me, or if he is unable to give me what I require, or unwilling, you will find me in your tavern again, and what 'little of you is left' will be cut into pieces and fed to the pigs." He stuffed the empty purse into its place. "Now, by the gods, tell me where he is!"

"The prison at Stókenhold Fortress."

The Raven's eyes caught the flame and blazed bright. "He's a prisoner? What are his crimes?"

She shrugged her shoulders. "He was taken from us in the night." She shivered against the cold damp creeping in from Leviathan Deeps.

"How do you know where he was taken, then?" The Raven narrowed his eyes.

"I heard the soldiers talking. One of them said they were taking him to the prison of the old fortress. The only place called such is the dungeons of Stókenhold Fortress."

The Raven's guarded smile broadened to soft chortling. "Indeed."

He turned from the stable but stopped at the entrance and looked back. "I fear I have been too harsh. I apologize for my rudeness."

She smiled and lifted her hands, heavy with gold coins. "No need, m'lord. You have saved my precious ones."

"Your boy," he asked her. "The one taken to the temple. What was his name?"

"Ashar, m'lord. The son lost to me was named Ashar."

CHAPTER 48

Ashar fell. A rusty rib of iron slammed beneath his armpit and stopped him with a painful jolt. He dangled at the end of the rod that suspended the walkway from the side of the cliff. It bounced slowly up and down. His legs swung free above the bottomless chasm below.

Rorekk looked back at the sound of the cracking bamboo and broke his stride. "Pu flesroy tegethen," he yelled as he twirled a thick finger.

Ashar squinted, searching for the strange essence that helped him understand what the giant was saying. He held the iron rib in a death grip that turned his knuckles white. He dared not look down but could not help himself. The river was a faint curve of gray in the dark mist of the valley below. The sun had fallen below the Mountains of Mankin and cast all but the top of the world in a haze of blue twilight.

"Help me!" he cried, but Rorekk stood where he was.

"Pu flesroy tegethen," he said again.

I can't come back! Ashar understood Rorekk's words, but the realization made his heart hammer faster against his ribs. His understanding went beyond what was said. *Even if he could come back, his weight would send us both to our deaths. The safety of the Oracle comes first.*

Then Rorekk swung his right leg up and slowly turned in half a circle to show Ashar what to do.

Ashar understood, but the thought of doing what the giant was suggesting terrified him. Moving at all in his precarious circumstance meant death. He was sure of it. The iron slipped a notch downward and undulated slowly. He had no choice.

He clenched his jaw, gripped the rod more tightly, and swung his foot toward the brace. He missed. On the second try he managed to throw his knee across the bar and lock it there. The violent movement jerked the bar farther out from where it was pounded into the wall. A fistful of broken rock tumbled into the gloom.

Rorekk started forward but stopped himself. "Eres, eres!" he yelled and pointed behind Ashar and to his right.

Ashar could hardly breathe, and his heart sounded like a hollow stick being dragged over pickets. He twisted his head around. When he saw it he understood. He reached for the hemp that laced the bamboo slats together, taking care to move slowly. His weight shifted, and the iron rib slipped again. He gasped and froze. His eyes clamped closed. He dared not move again.

Fear and faith cannot abide.

He opened his eyes and cautiously stretched his fingers for the braid of fiber. Touching it with his fingertips, he teased it into his fist. He tugged on it to assess its strength, then swung his leg over the bar and grabbed for the rope with his other hand. His feet slammed against the wall of stone.

"Pu seos doog. Doog!" Rorekk shouted, his voice elated.

Ashar's focus remained on climbing the wall. He pulled himself to where he could sprawl across the broken walkway. He gripped the bamboo slats and slithered on his belly until he was on an unbroken section of the walkway. His escape from death had taken less than two minutes, but Ashar was certain he had dangled over the edge for more than an hour.

—-—

Even the heights were fading into darkness by the time they reached the tombs. The summit of the monolith and hallowed fane were still far above them, hidden by both cloud and darkness.

The walkway ended where a column of rock arched from the wall like the handle of a jug. Beyond the portal, the walls gave way to a broad, flat landing overgrown with moss. Tombs had been carved into the sheer cliff wall. They rose as high as he could see in the fading light.

Ashar stared at the tombs in wonder. He had heard of the tombs of the blessed, but he had never imagined their exquisite beauty. Ascending the cliff face, they looked like a disorderly stack of ornate buildings. The burial chambers were hollow rooms hewn from the solid rock. The oldest of the tombs were carved to resemble houses made of timber and had ceilings of unhewn tree trunks, some of which had rotted and fallen away. Others tombs were patterned after temples, with columns, epistyles, pediments, and ornate architraves. Intricate relief carvings and engraved drawings covered every workable surface. Funerary feasts. Banquet scenes. Animals and hunting. Some had been painted rather than carved, and all but a trace of the pigments had weathered away.

The guardians of the hallowed fane go up but never come down. The chilling thought sent a shiver down Ashar's spine.

A slot canyon split the wall of rock on the other side. Stones cut in a pattern of concentric circles flared from a concave scoop at the bottom of the cliff. They were defined by the green and living things that had taken root and survived in the tiny cracks between the stones.

An ancient obsidian altar sat on a protrusion of rock that hung over a cliff with nothing below but the river, now vanished in the gloom. From the density of the flowering vine and thick sponge of moss on the north side of the altar, Ashar suspected it had not been used in many seasons. The carved symbols and inscriptions were largely covered, but a particular motif caught his eye: thirteen egg-like ovals with emanating rays, strange vessels with peaked ends, and great winged birds.

Ashar helped Rorekk lower the Oracle to the large round dais at the center of the circle. His body was limp, his jaw hung loose, and his eyes were closed. Ashar gripped his hand. "Honorable master?" he whispered. Fear gripped his throat. The Oracle couldn't be dead.

Ashar rubbed the old hand vigorously. He didn't know what else to do. The Oracle's hand was growing cold. He put his ear to the Oracle's chest. Silence. Ashar looked at Rorekk for some hope, then shook his head, refusing to accept what he knew to be true.

There is life beyond death. The righteous ascend to the clouds of blessing. There is a state of endless being. The teachings of Master Doyan swirled through Ashar's head but brought him no comfort. He looked up at Rorekk again, surprised to see that the giant who had saved them both showed no emotion.

Ashar turned at the sound of something rushing as if in a wind, but there was no breeze. He lifted his eyes to the mist above his head. A basket as old as the tombs descended on a length of braided hemp. The wefts were woven from fiber, weathered and cracked. The warps were willow wood no thicker than a child's finger. The basket was suspended by a quadrangle of twisted hemp attached to the corners. The rope vanished in a swirl of clouds the color of bleached bone.

Rorekk lifted the Oracle as a mother would a child and placed him in the basket. He lifted the bundle of stones wrapped in black fur from the satchel slung over Ashar's shoulder and tucked it under the Oracle's limp hand.

The sound of boots clattering on bamboo grew louder. Ashar whirled about. Shadows thrown by the bandit's torches darted across the archway and danced among the tombs. The bandits burst into a sprint to reach the portal before it could be closed.

Rorekk bolted to the arch in seven great strides and threw his weight against the massive stone gate. From the size of the granite stone and struggle of the giant, Ashar surmised that sealing the gateway to the tombs was rarely done.

The sound of stone grinding over stone melded with the rattling of bamboo and the wild cries of ferocious men who screamed when they saw the entrance closing.

Ashar ran to Rorekk's side and threw himself against the massive stone. He pushed so hard that his leg muscles cramped into spasms. He howled at the shooting pain but rolled from his shoulder to his back and strained with every muscle in his body to help Rorekk close the gate.

The stone rasped in grating protest, but slowly the immense stone moved. The opening narrowed.

The first of the warriors reached the arch and started through.

Rorekk threw his weight forward into the stone with one last heave.

The warrior dove headlong into the rapidly narrowing crack. Too late. His left arm, leg, and upper torso were caught and crushed as the colossal stone gate crunched into the slot on the opposite wall. His howl of pain became a rattle of death as his bones were broken and his body crushed.

Ashar saw the torch fall to the ground. The flame bloomed like an orange flower. The wails of the warriors faded to a hollow echo, distant and far away. Ashar collapsed. The exertion had sapped the last bit of strength from his starving body. Exhausted, used up, and sinking into a dark void, he slumped to the ground, his cheek slamming against a flat stone. The crush of wet moss was pungent. He watched the bandits push the stone as if in a dream that was pierced by tiny explosions of light.

So many of them. Strong. Fierce.

They were strange creatures moving sideways through a darkening fog.

With muscles, spears, and the strength of ten, the bandits moved the stone enough for the dead man to tumble out. The gap was wide enough to give the warriors access to the landing. They scrambled through with weapons drawn.

Rorekk retreated to the basket and took a protective stance.

The warriors gathered at the gate, though two of them remained without. Perhaps too superstitious to transgress the tombs of the legendary city of the blessed dead on the holy mountain.

Ashar struggled to see through the darkening tunnel of his consciousness.

The brigands rushed the unarmed giant, but broke stride when Rorekk seized the first man, lifted him over his head, and hurled him back into the charging horde. It was delay enough. The basket trembled as the hemp tightened and began to rise.

The warriors surged forward to stop it. Rorekk was nearly overwhelmed by their numbers, but his will was greater even than his strength. He fought and flung and fended them off until the basket rose beyond their reach.

From the fleeting edge of consciousness, Ashar saw the basket containing the Oracle's body swallowed by the clouds. He saw Rorekk fighting, flailing, and falling to one knee only to take up a sword in a slash of blades and rush of blood.

The last thing Ashar saw before his eyes closed and his mind swirled into unconsciousness was three men striding toward him with swords and bludgeons. Their faces were contorted by vicious growls, but the sound was swallowed by the strange darkness.

—

Celestine reached for him and her face glowed in a shaft of sunlight, and she laughed and the light struck her tears and was a stone of light in the palm of his hand, and glimmering shafts of white light streaked into the darkness igniting other stones that marked a path and beckoned him to follow, but the way was hedged by a many-headed monster that swallowed the light and he was afraid but fear and faith cannot abide, and he reached down to grasp a hand thrust up from the darkness and lifted the man into the light and the man wore the collar of a slave and held the sword of a warrior and he slashed the belly of the beast and the light of the stones within exploded in a profusion of color and the monster was no more, and the man with the sword knelt before him and offered him a shining stone and the shimmer of light was blinding and he closed his eyes and was lost in the darkness, and wraiths from the tombs flew at him on leather wings and their eyes were the color of blood and their faces were covered with scales and the sound of them pierced his skin and spikes of teeth roared with thunder and the lightning was a ball of fire and the fire was the breath of the dragon and the dragon was Drakkor and he tried to run but the bamboo rotted beneath his feet and he fell and he cried for help but armored men with bludgeons and a howling of beasts came and the giant tried to stop them and was cleaved in two and his blood was black and he fell in a drowning darkness and sank into oblivion, and the stone of light was in his grasp and the man with the sword stood watch and a great hand caught him, and he floated upward through the darkened mist of clouds the color of bone to a warmth and brightness that was sunlight falling on his face.

CHAPTER 49

Qhuin ignored Sargon's angry pout. He slowed the team only slightly before turning them toward the shallow end of the ravine. The slope was rutted by erosion, exposing lumps of hard rock. The ground was steep and broken, which slowed the wild horses. Following them in the chariot looked to be impossible. Striking a hoodoo with a wheel would shatter the spokes or topple the chariot.

Qhuin was about to rein in when he saw the slickrock escarpment to his right. It was bold and dangerous but their only chance to stay in the chase. He rippled the reins and called to his horses in the language they understood. The milk-whites surged ahead with confidence. Qhuin loved his horses.

Princeling Sargon stiffened and prepared to jump.

Qhuin gripped his arm to stop him and pulled the team hard right. Iron hooves and iron wheels slipped and skidded across the steep slope of smooth rock and jolted to a hard landing in the sandy wash at the bottom.

The team regained its footing and surged forward without a command. Twin rooster tails of sand sprayed up from the wheels as the milk-whites stretched their necks. The dry bed twisted to the bottom of the broken slope.

The wild horses had picked their way down the ragged slope. Most of them had reached the bottom by the time the chariot burst from the wash on the canyon floor. Eyes wide and nostrils flared, they scattered in confusion as their wild instincts screamed for them to flee.

The mares still on the slope turned back. Their hooves slipped on the loose gravel. Some fell to their knees. Others bolted for the flat ground where the walls fell away and the canyon splayed wide.

"Be ready," Qhuin shouted and turned the team toward the heart of the wild herd. The milk-whites ran stride for stride with the tarpans galloping on either side. Qhuin picked the largest of the wild horses, a reddish brown mare with patches of white, her neck stretched out. He eased the chariot to the left and matched her pace. Her head stayed straight, but her eyes rolled back.

"Now!" Qhuin shouted.

Sargon stood on the footboard with his feet spread and his thigh pressed against the cowling. He advanced the lasso-pole hand over hand, careful to keep his balance. The ground was uneven with crusted sand and clumps of sage. An exposed turtleback of rock protruded from a pool of sand. The chariot lurched. Sargon lost his balance and stumbled.

Qhuin caught him by the leather strap across his chest and pulled him upright. "She'll break away. Take her now!"

Sargon adjusted his stance and thrust the lasso-pole over the neck of the running horse. He was so eager to tighten the noose that he fumbled the line before the lasso looped under her nose.

The mare dipped her head and thrashed to the right. The lasso skidded over her ears, tangled in her forelock for an instant, then slipped way. The pole fell and hit the chariot's wheel, flying out of Sargon's hand. It dragged behind on the safety line, flopping like a fish on a flat rock.

"What are you doing?" the princeling yelled. "You've got to get me closer!"

The painted mare shied away when the pole fell. She broke from the pack and ran alone to escape the strange beast chasing her. The milk-whites followed. Qhuin watched the panicked mare galloping away and worried she might be injured. For a moment it was as if their thoughts connected in the dusty air and merged and he was her. He felt her fear and knew her mind.

Predator with horse's heads. Three that run as one. I must escape!

"The loop has to be in front," Qhuin shouted over the tumult of rumbling wheels and rushing air that howled around their ears.

Sargon recovered the lasso-pole. "It was in front," he shouted back.

"Put her nose in first and get it all the way over."

"You've got to get me closer!"

"We're as close as we can come. You've got one more chance. If she reaches the trees, you've lost her . . . m'lord."

"Then drive like you're supposed to!" Sargon screamed.

"Of course . . . m'lord."

The mare ran for the wall, but Qhuin knew that at any moment she would break right and run for the shelter of the trees. He pulled the rein right and pointed his horses to where their paths would cross.

Sargon adjusted his stance and his grip on the lasso-pole. "What are you doing? Why did you turn?"

"Just be ready!"

The princeling fumbled with the noose, opening it up and tightening it again.

The mare reached the rock wall and broke right toward the trees just as Qhuin knew she would. The distance to the woods was less than a stone's throw. If she reached the trees, they couldn't follow. Qhuin pulled up beside her.

"Closer," Sargon shouted. "You've got to get me closer!" He leaned forward with the lasso-pole. The hub of the wheel was less than a cubitum from the mare's thrashing legs.

Qhuin held his course. He would not break her legs or end her life for the sake of an inept princeling.

"In your hands, m'lord."

The right wheel dropped into a rutted furrow and jolted out again. The footboard lurched in spite of the cushion of leather and cotton. Qhuin pulled hard left to avoid another burrow some critter had gouged. The meadow was a ruin of craters.

Qhuin knew the folklore about carnivorous rats that lived in the Tallgrass Prairie. "Bigger than dogs," some said. There were grizzly rumors that the rats gnawed off the limbs of infants as they slept. The enormous burrows made him wonder if such creatures were more than myth.

He prayed to the gods that the horses would not stumble or catch a foot or break a leg. *Do they even listen? The gods?* The thought emptied his head, leaving nothing but an echo of doubt.

Sargon tried to steady himself on the lurching footboard. He gripped the rail with one hand and reached for the horse with the other. The loop on the lasso whipped back and forth above the horse's head as Sargon fought the bucking chariot.

The trees loomed closer. Qhuin looked at the racing mare. Her nostrils were flared and filled with blood. He calculated their distance to the trees. Out of time.

He loosened the reins and wrapped them twice around the spindle. He grabbed the lasso-pole from Sargon and, in one smooth motion, swept it in front of the mare's head, over the muzzle, the poll, and around her neck.

Sargon gripped the pole and snugged the rope. The noose tightened. Sargon kept his hand on the pole as Qhuin lashed the leather straps of the handle to the iron ring, securing it to the brace of sycamore wood outside the cowling and tethering the captive horse.

"Samma, samma, samma," he shouted to the milk-whites, pulling the bronze bits against tender mouths. They slowed, shook their heads with triumph, and then stopped.

The wild mare pivoted around the point of the pole and thrashed her head. She pulled against the noose, but she was tied to the chariot by the rope and iron ring. The weight and strength of the milk-whites kept her from dragging the chariot away.

Sargon leaped down and strode toward the horse.

Her eyes ignited in a flash of fire. She lunged and chomped at him with her teeth and nearly took a bite from his face. The princeling stumbled back against the side of the chariot. He tried to grip the wheel, but he stepped into a rat hole and landed in a humiliating heap at Qhuin's feet.

Qhuin found it hard to believe the princeling was stupid enough to think that catching a wild horse subdued her wild instincts. "Let her settle!" he barked. "She's frightened enough. Back away."

"What did you just say?" Sargon gasped as he struggled to his feet. He brushed dirt from his silks and tried to regain a regal stature.

"I'm sorry, m'lord. I misspoke. It's best we give her time to calm."

"Calm? It's a wild horse! What's best is to teach the cursed beast who its master is!" Sargon glared at Qhuin, who did not miss the double meaning. Sargon grabbed the whip and lashed the mare across the face.

"No, m'lord, you must not—"

Sargon lashed the horse again. "I think you've forgotten who is master and who is slave! I command you to stand aside!" The princeling kept his distance from the captured horse but taunted her with the snapping whip.

The mare jerked her head against the pole with each pop of the lash. The noose tightened around her neck.

"See," he said with a nervous laugh. "She learns quickly that her life is in my hands." He lashed the wild horse across her knees and cannon as if training her to the high step favored in parade. The wild mare pranced to get away.

"No, m'lord! You mustn't!" Qhuin stepped forward with his hands outstretched.

The princeling lashed the whip across Qhuin's open palms and giggled like a child playing games.

Qhuin jerked his hands away, and the princeling snapped the whip at his knees and shins.

"Let's see if you can king-step as well as your horses."

Anger surged in a rush of blood to Qhuin's head and, with it, a flood of dark memories.

— —

He had been at Blackthorn all his life and had known the princeling as long as he could remember. Though close in age, the princeling never noticed him. Why would he? Qhuin was an orphaned slave. Nothing more than a possession. Sargon, on the other hand, was the son of Kadesh-Cor, Baron Magnus and prince of the North, raised from birth to believe he was superior to everyone, coddled and over-indulged.

The princeling's abuse of animals was a topic of frequent conversation among the stablemen. As a youngster, Sargon had killed chickens with his bow and arrow, sometimes dogs. Everyone knew, but no one dared comment or complain. Qhuin suspected Kadesh-Cor knew as well but still let the boy do what he liked. More worrisome than dead chickens were the whispers he heard in the stables: "If the 'right people' died, Sargon would end up king."

Rusthammer's words remained with Qhuin. "In a saga of kings, the uncertainty of who will live and who will die looms on the horizon like the black clouds of a coming storm."

When Sargon was fourteen, his cousin's Alaunt went missing. The dog was found many days later, tied up and starved to death in an abandoned cellar of the keep. One of the servants was flogged and set in the stocks for neglecting the dog, and that was the end of it. But everyone knew it was Sargon's work. The hound had nipped him on the hand, and he had taken his revenge.

Qhuin could still remember the smirk on the princeling's face as he watched the flogging of the servant from a balcony above.

— —

Qhuin jumped away from the strike of the whip. The welts swelled red.

The princeling's laugh was high-pitched, childlike, even girlish. He scowled at Qhuin and lashed the horse a savage blow. Then again.

Qhuin grabbed the princeling's wrist with such sudden, unexpected force that Sargon was thrown to the ground. He wrenched the whip away. It took Sargon a moment to comprehend what had happened.

A feeling of dread washed over Qhuin. He regretted his impulsive action even before the princeling spoke.

"You are going to die for that," Sargon said as he clambered to his feet. "You insolent, stupid imbecile!" He drew his short sword from the scabbard at his waist.

Qhuin stood his ground as Sargon laid the point of his blade on the soft flesh of his throat.

"I've the right to kill you for touching me. Do you understand, you ignorant fool?"

Qhuin tensed every muscle and clenched his jaw. He cursed himself for the burst of rage that had put his life in peril. He struggled to control the fury still seething inside. It was a flaw he'd struggled with from his earliest years.

Sargon put pressure on the blade until the point of it pierced the skin. A trickle of blood stained the top of Qhuin's tunic. "But I'm not going to kill you," he said and lowered the blade. "I want to teach you a lesson so you and your kind don't forget what you are. Put out your hand!"

Qhuin glared at Sargon until the princeling flushed and looked away. "Give me your hand, slave!" he shouted like an adolescent in a tantrum.

Qhuin knew cutting off a body part that offended a royal person was an old tradition. The slave who cared for the hogs had a stump instead of a hand.

Sargon raised his sword. "By the gods, put out your hand and bear your punishment or I shall cut off your head!"

Qhuin put out his right hand, but not as he was told and not as Sargon expected. It came fast and jabbed straight into the princeling's

362

chest with all of Qhuin's weight behind it. In the same motion, he seized the quillon of the sword with his left hand and wrenched it free.

Sargon flew backward, striking the wheel of the chariot. His mouth hung open in surprise. When he spoke, his voice was pinched. His eyes bobbed from the cold stare in Qhuin's eyes to the short sword in his hand.

"No! No, don't. Please, I wasn't really going to. I was only trying to frighten you, as a warning, a reminder of your place. You know that slaves are not allowed to touch a royal person, so please, I was just . . ."

Qhuin walked forward slowly, the sword comfortable in his hand.

Sargon tried to keep a defiant lift to his chin and stop the trembling of every limb, but he could not.

"I know my place, m'lord," Qhuin said in a constrained and respectful voice. "You know me only as a slave of Blackthorn, and I am that. But I am also a horseman in the stables. I am the driver of your chariot. I have given you first catch and won for you your wager. I have put the welfare of the horses first and, in doing so, m'lord, have been obedient to your father, whose expedition this is." Qhuin paused, picking his words carefully. "But you err, m'lord. Whether you or your father—the king or the gods themselves—*may* not allow me to touch you, as you suppose, you'd do well to understand that I *can*."

He placed the point of the sword on the creamy flesh below the princeling's quivering chin. "I, and others like me, *can* touch you. And I, and others like me, will—whatever the consequence—if pushed too far." He paused to let the fear take root before he finished. "I think it wise for you to leave the care of the horse to me, and our disagreement forgotten." He held the princeling's eyes, and when he spoke again, his tone was mocking. "M'lord."

Sargon nodded in vigorous agreement, but his smile was disingenuous, his acquiescence a lie.

Qhuin dropped the sword on the ground and turned to the wild mare. He whispered to her as he haltered her head and removed the choking noose of the lasso-pole. He tied her to a high tree limb lest she wrap the tether around the trunk and become tangled in the rope.

—-—

A claw gripped Sargon's gut. He dared not confess his envy of the slave, even to himself. He wanted to be like him: confident, courageous, skilled. *No! He is a bondsman. A slave.*

He hated Qhuin for making him feel small and insignificant. He would kill the thing he envied, destroy the prowess he coveted but could never claim. He would see the slave's head on a spike.

Sargon, son of Kadesh-Cor, jutted his chin forward and vanquished his humiliation with a single thought: *The slave is going to die!*

CHAPTER 50

"Open your gates in the name of the king!" the Raven growled. He thrust his fist through the iron crosshatch of the portcullis so his two-fingered ring was close to Meesha's face.

She stood with the gatekeepers and guardsmen at the entrance to Stókenhold Fortress.

"Lord Tolak, the master of Stókenhold Fortress, and my mother, Lady Katasha, and my brother, the noble Princeling Valnor, will return from the village before the sun is down, m'lord. No stranger may enter Stókenhold Fortress except by their invitation." Meesha cared little that her family's titles had been stripped in exile.

"Are you blind? Can you not see I wear the sigil of the king?"

"I see, m'lord, but these are strange times with rogues about. No man can be trusted. I've met scoundrels in the markets of Westgarten who peddle forgeries of that very ring."

"I am Raven to the King!"

"With apologies, m'lord, I've no way to know that is the truth." Meesha shook her head.

"I demand you allow me to enter. Send word to the captain of the prison that the Raven to the King demands his presence. There is a prisoner here that I must see at once!"

"I pray your forgiveness, m'lord, but you arrived without herald or dispatch. I have never known an emissary of the king to come without a harbinger of his arrival brought by royal courier. And from what I know of such things, it is most unusual for an emissary of the king to ride without a kingsriders' escort." She peered through the gate to affirm he was alone. "Is it not, m'lord?"

"My visit to Stókenhold Fortress was unplanned, but it is a matter most urgent. I demand that you open the gate!"

"I may not, m'lord, but I would be pleased to have refreshment brought while you wait."

The Raven gripped the iron bars, his knuckles white. He lowered his face, and his eyes disappeared in black shadows. Then he threw his cape across his shoulder, opened the top of his linen blouse, and exposed the bare skin.

The sight of the lumpy flesh took Meesha's breath away.

The sigil of Orsis-Kublan had been burned into his chest. The peacock and her bloody arrows were a pitted scar just below his collarbone. His hairless chest was pallid compared to his swarthy face. The brand was fresh, and the ridges of seared flesh were purple with dried blood.

There were whisperings about the king's secret oath of fire, but Meesha never imagined it might be real. *How could the king—my grandfather—engage in such a depraved ritual? Am I truly the flesh of his flesh and blood of his blood?*

Meesha had been told whoever bore the mark had sworn themselves to the king. Not as a soldier or a servant or a slave but as a votary having pledged their life and surrendered their soul to the king's wishes.

Before me is a man who has traded the very essence of his breath for the pride, the pleasures, and the possessions bequeathed by the throne of power. He has sworn an oath of blood and ritual of fire unto death. She shuddered at the thought.

The Raven stood straight. "By the power of this mark, whether by my voice or the voice of the king, it is the same. My command is his command. My mind, his mind. By my word, I have power over your life and your death!"

Meesha's mouth was dry. Her lips moved, but no words emerged. She traded looks with the gatekeepers and the guardsmen. They awaited her order. Her eyes moved to the outer gates, hoping beyond hope to see her father and brother returning.

The Raven buttoned his blouse slowly as if the flesh were still tender and the pain of the branding lingered.

Meesha was afraid to open the gate, but she was more frightened by what might happen to her and her family if she refused. Having seen the mark, she knew he must be who he claimed to be. She raised a hand to the gatekeeper. "Let him in." Her voice was weaker than intended.

The men threw their weight into a synchronized winding of the two-handed winch, and the heavy grate of the inner gatehouse began to rise.

The screech of rusted iron over iron sharpened Meesha's fear that letting this man into Stókenhold Fortress was a mistake.

―――

The echo of leather boots on stone rolled through the vaulted tunnel. The Raven followed the keeper of the prison through the winding passage that sloped downward to the lower dungeon. The jailer was a corpulent oaf of a man with fat hands and thick lips. His ruddy cheeks seemed out of place for a man who lived like a mole. The patch of hair on his chin was color of mud. He carried a torch of rags soaked in sheep tallow and oil. It stank.

Meesha followed at the edge of the light. The Raven insisted she come as a witness to affirm the propriety of his official visit to a prisoner, but she knew it was a lie. Following the confrontation at the gate, she knew he dared not let her out of his sight.

Meesha listened to the Raven describe the prisoner to the jailer as they moved through the passage. "He's an old man," he explained. "There are some in the villages south who call him 'the prophet' . . . or did." The Raven dragged his hand over his beard and twisted the two-fingered ring with his thumb, making sure the keeper saw it clearly.

Meesha's stomach burned, and her mind whirled with dark expectation. She tried to calm her pounding heart. It was all she could do to keep from running away. *Is it possible the Raven knows?*

"Hmm," the jailer mused. "This prisoner have a name?"

"He must surely have a name," the Raven answered, his disdain unguarded, "but I know him only by what he is called by the pilgrims—'prophet' or 'holy man,' perhaps."

The keeper's laugh rumbled through the chamber, crude and unpleasant. "Half the wretched souls we got down here come from among the pilgrims. Most likely all of them think they're holy." He guffawed again. "But I know the one yer after! Crazy as a loon, that one. Couldn't shut him up from his ranting blasphemies, so we put him in the pit."

Bile rose in Meesha's throat. Her eyes flitted to the Raven, who turned at that moment and looked at her. *He knows,* she thought. *Will Father and Valnor get here before it is too late?*

There was a labyrinth of passageways beneath Stókenhold Fortress. The ancients who'd raised the first castle atop the cliffs had discovered a honeycomb of natural caverns and made them into catacombs. Later occupants cut passages to connect the caverns, adding walls and floors of stone and brick until it was a dungeon.

It was a pitiful place, made worse for the wretched souls condemned to a cell no larger than a crypt and imprisoned where other men were buried. Ceilings had crumbled. Walls had fallen. Sections were blocked off.

Along the main passageway were quarters for the keepers of the prison, a tumble of small cells, and a place for torture. Beyond that there was a dark and dangerous maze of forgotten stairways, pits, and passages.

The oubliettes were at the lowest level. Deep pits lined with mortared rock, and walls too smooth to climb. They were covered by a wooden trapdoor in the cell's ceiling.

The jailer used his torch to light an oil lantern, then stuffed it into an iron sconce. He tied the handle of lantern to a length of shaggy hemp and walked to trapdoor marked III.

The jailer lifted the heavy covering and let it fall open. Wood thudded on wood, and the putrid smell of rot and human waste wafted up from the hole. The Raven gagged at the rancid stench. Meesha covered her face with the sleeve of her blouse.

"Wake up, holy man," the jailer bellowed as he lowered the lantern. He breathed as if the stink were a fragrant garden breeze instead of the foul air of human misery.

The Raven pressed a hand across his mouth, looking into the hole and squinting against the darkness. The sway of the flame sent eerie shadows slithering over the wet stone walls like evil wraiths fleeing from the light. A colony of rats gnawed on moldy crusts. All but one scurried into cracks at the sudden light. The biggest rat stood its ground with a hump of bristled hair and snarl of rotted fangs.

The jailer gasped. "He's gone!"

"Gone? How can he be gone?" the Raven asked.

"I do not know, m'lord, but he isn't there!" The keeper licked a blister on his trembling lower lip, then chewed until it bled.

"That's impossible!" the Raven said.

The jailer's eyes grew large as his reason was ingested by his superstition. "They said the old man was a mage." His voice trembled, and his eyes darted to the shadows as if to see an evil spirit.

"Not even a sorcerer with the powers of Aka'mainyu could escape such a pit," the Raven began, but his voice quivered.

Meesha could see by the fleeting look of fear on his face that he wondered if the missing man was indeed endowed with supernatural powers.

"The rats must'a eaten him," the man said with conviction. "Better hungry rats than black magic, but where are the bones?"

Meesha shuddered at the thought of a man being gnawed to death by rodents. She clenched her jaw to stop the tremors. *Even if the Raven to the King finds out* . . . She felt a surge of optimism.

The Raven scowled at the mumbling jailer. "You imbecile. You've clearly forgotten which pit." He went to the adjacent oubliette and jerked the trapdoor open, turning his head to avoid the rush of putrid air. "Here!" he said. "Look here!"

The keeper hurried with his lantern and lowered it into the pit.

Meesha peered into the dungeon even knowing the prophet was not there, and then wished she hadn't. The man curled up in a muddy mix of straw and his own filth was hardly more than a skeleton. He raised a bony hand in a pleading gesture.

"It's not him, m'lord," the jailer apologized.

The lantern was lifted, the door slammed shut, and the wretched creature returned to the darkness of his living death. Meesha swallowed hard to quell the urge to retch. She stiffened her resolve and felt a surge of courage. Even if what she and Valnor had done was discovered, she would do it again.

The Raven lifted the door on the last of the oubliettes. "That one's dead, m'lord," the keeper said.

"Is he the one I'm looking for? Can you see?"

The jailer lowered the lantern and shook his head. "The prophet's hair was white as milk. Even with his scalp mostly et away, you can see this'n's was dark."

"Then where is he? He has to be somewhere!" As the Raven raged at the jailer, his eyes flitted to the rotting carcass. He gagged and slammed the heavy door closed. He stood for a long time as if he could still see the man at the bottom of the pit.

Is it possible there is compassion beneath the frightful scars on his chest?

"You have mistaken him for another," he said finally.

"I think not, m'lord," the keeper said.

"You keep a register of prisoners?"

"It's how I knowed where he was. I put him here myself." He hacked a gob of phlegm from his throat and spit on the floor. "I remember 'cause he tried to put a hex on me. Said I'd suffer the wrath of Oum'lah, whatever that's supposed to be."

"When was he put here?"

The keeper dragged a hand across his muddy beard. "Two, three seasons maybe."

"When was the last time you saw him *here*—in the pit?"

"We drop 'em bread every day. Most days," he added with a shrug.

"With the lantern?"

The keeper scratched the stubble on his neck. Something crawled away from his fingers as he shrugged and shook his head.

"Who might have moved him from here? Who has that authority?"

"Captain and me, but . . ." He furrowed his brow and shook his head. "Once a man is thrown to the pit, we don't ever take 'im out."

"Even after they're dead?" The Raven's face twisted in disgust, and he glanced at the first pit.

"If we get time, m'lord." He chortled and added, "But what's it matter if a traitor has to share the pit with the last man 'til he rots away?"

Meesha knew from his sniggering such a horrible thing had happened before.

The keeper of the prison misread his visitors' sensibilities. The Raven straightened the leather strap across the big jailer's chest like a commandant preparing a kingsrider for inspection. "Pray tell me," he said, his voice cold and threatening, "if the keeper of the prison loses a man put in a pit, who should go there in his place to eat all that bread leftover from the rats?" He looked at pit III lest the dullard misunderstand. The burly keeper was reduced to a quivering rabbit.

Meesha saw the Raven staring at the trapdoor of the dead man's pit. His lips were curled in disgust. She could hear the whispering of his mind: *No man deserves to die in such depravity!* She spoke almost without thinking.

"No man deserves to die in such depravity," she repeated.

The Raven looked at her sharply.

"Am I wrong, m'lord?"

His face remained hard. It was not the reaction she'd hoped for. *I have misjudged his sympathies. Revealed myself.* Meesha flushed and held her tongue. She knew nothing of the man other than what he claimed. She had seen the ugly scars of the ritual oath of fire. *Is it enough?*

The Raven held Meesha's eyes. She could feel him reaching into her head, a tentacle that pierced her skull and slithered into the privacy of her thoughts. She broke his gaze and looked away, but he gripped her chin and lifted her face. His eyes were dark and cold.

"You know something of the missing prisoner," he said with the chill of an icy wind blown over a frozen lake. It was a pronouncement, not a question. "Tell me what you know of this old fool, and tell me quickly!"

Meesha caught her breath and, with it, her courage. "Why has an emissary of the king come so far just to see a man condemned to the pit?"

"You are a cursed child!"

Cursed? Witchchild. Even in the midst of their confrontation, Meesha felt the pain of his insulting words, and heat flushed over the dark side of her face.

"If you did not bear the king's blood, I would throw you into the pit for such insolence."

His unwillingness to harm her bolstered her courage. "What do you want of the one they call the prophet?" she asked.

"It is not for you to know the business of the king," he snapped, his patience spent.

"It is my father's place to know the business of Stókenhold Fortress, including the hapless souls condemned here by your king." It wasn't entirely true, but the confidence of her declaration made it so.

"Has your impudence no bounds?"

"I stand for my father in his absence. What is your true purpose here, m'lord Raven to the King?"

He turned away, but Meesha could see his face redden. He clenched his jaw. The plume of peacock feathers on his velvet hat rocked like a boat in a ripple of waves. His demeanor changed. "I have come to give him his freedom," he said after a moment. "The king has need of him."

Meesha was surprised and studied his face for any sign of deceit. "You speak the truth?"

"Would you challenge the word of the Raven to the King?"

Meesha said nothing but answered the question with a twist of skepticism on her face.

"It is the truth, but no one can know of this arrangement. It is an unusual circumstance." He raised a warning finger and glanced at the keeper of the prison. The man's head bobbed in promised compliance.

"You have come to set him free?" Meesha said it slowly. *There must be no misunderstanding.* The Raven nodded, and Meesha took a deep breath. *Perhaps I have misjudged him.* But even as the hopeful thought swept through her mind, she couldn't shake the feeling there was something amiss.

CHAPTER 51

The canyon had fallen into twilight by the time Qhuin and Sargon left the mare and wheeled to the end of the valley where the rest of the tarpans had run. The left wheel of the chariot dropped into a burrow with a jolting thud and bounded out. Qhuin saw something scurry in the darkness, and he glanced back. For an instant he was eye to eye with a giant rat standing on its hind legs at the edge of its hole.

The creature curled its purple lips and hissed at the intruders. Its mouth was a snag of yellow teeth with fangs protruding from the upper jaw. One of them was broken. Dried blood dangled in crusty clumps below the rat's chin.

The sight of it gave Qhuin a sickening sensation. It was the ugliest creature he had ever seen. The size of it was shocking. As the skies darkened, a horde of rats emerged from their burrows and prowled into the dark.

The legendary carnivorous rats of the Tallgrass Prairie are real. And with Qhuin's musings came the thought, *If the creatures are more than legend, then what of the rest of the horrid tales?*

—-—

"It's too dark," the princeling complained.

"Almost, m'lord," Qhuin agreed. The words were hardly out of his mouth when a mysterious glow spread over the red dirt and reflected from the walls. Sargon glanced at Qhuin, who looked up. A column of cumulus clouds boiled high and caught the last rays of the sun. Reflected light accounted for the gloaming.

It was serendipitous good fortune. The horses were contained by the steep walls of the box canyon, and the lingering light meant they had one last chance of catching another wild tarpan.

Qhuin saw the prince standing at the rim of the vale. Jehu was behind with a tight grip on the bridle of a black. He must have driven the prince to the edge of the canyon so they could see into the valley floor.

How long has he been watching? How much did he see? Did the prince see me strike his son? The possibility filled him with dread.

If the prince had seen the altercation with Sargon, there was serious trouble ahead. Qhuin's threat had frightened Sargon when they were alone, but he knew the moment the princeling was back in the company of kingsriders and kin, what had happened would not be forgiven nor forgotten.

Retribution and punishment were inevitable. *This very night? After they returned?* The fleeting thought that he may never see another sunrise sent a shudder through his being. The lump of stone in his gut turned to ice.

He cursed himself for losing control. *"Always remember the difference between feeling free and being free."* Rusthammer's wisdom was always there inside his head. *"Temper has its place, but only when perfectly controlled. Overcoming your own nature is the greatest of all challenges."*

Qhuin knew he had crossed a line from which there was no retreat.

He reined the milk-whites left to avoid a sinkhole created when a burrow of the giant rats collapsed.

Chor and Horsemaster Raahud left their chariots near the edge of the swale where Qhuin had entered the ravine. They picked their way down the rutted slope of stones and moved on foot across the valley with lasso-poles and coils of hemp in hand.

Four of the Huszárs dismounted and moved swiftly down the slope to join the other men. The other two remained at the top of the swale. The youngest of them was only sixteen. Seventeen at most.

"Baaly, son of Mesqulick, is second cousin to the princelings," Horsemaster Raahud told Qhuin, pointing.

When Baaly saw Qhuin and the chariot on the valley floor, he spurred his horse down the dangerous slope with whooping bravado. Stepping the horse slowly made the ascent a reasonable possibility. A trot was dangerous. A gallop was a death wish.

The iron shoes skidded on the loose rock. His pony lost its footing and skidded down the slickrock on its side. Baaly's leg was trapped between the pony and the rock, but he pulled it free as the horse rolled over.

Baaly tumbled to the bottom in a graceless splay of flying legs and grasping hands. With no weight on its back, the pony found purchase, regained its legs and half stepped, half skidded to the bottom where it galloped away.

The young Huszár winced as he struggled to stand on one leg. His bravado was gone. Or was it? He raised both hands and let out a bellowing crow of exhilaration.

The prince laughed out loud from where he stood watching from the rim.

— – —

The wild horses had run to the far end of the valley and were trapped by steep walls on three sides. There was only one way out of the box canyon, but the hunters moving toward them blocked their escape.

Qhuin and his trio of milk-whites wound their way through the rat craters on the valley floor in a three-beat gait. The runaway pony hurtled past the chariot with startling speed and headed for the wild herd. Horsemaster Raahud, Chor, his reinsman, and four Huszárs moved forward in a well-spaced line with ropes and poles, and way behind, Baaly hobbled to catch up.

Qhuin looked to the rim where the prince was making his way down a rockfall. He leaped from rock to rock with surprising agility. Jehu followed with a leather satchel strapped to his back, two coils of hemp, and a long lasso-pole wrapped in leather.

Growing up and serving in the stables of Blackthorn, Qhuin had longed for the prince to notice him. The slightest acknowledgment. A grateful nod. A word of "thank you" or an almost unimagined "well done." It never came, but he could not help himself from trying to please the man who owned him. It angered him that he felt the need, and yet, the old longing for approval had never gone away.

Was he watching? Did he see that it was I who caught the painted horse? He pushed the thought away, but not before the irony struck him and he almost laughed aloud. *If the prince saw me lasso the wild horse, then he also saw me knock his son to the ground.*

— —

The wild tarpans ran back and forth at the base of the cliff, looking for a way to escape as the chariot rolled and the hunters strode toward them. Eager as the hunters were to wade into the herd with hemp and poles, Horsemaster Raahud shouted for them to move slowly, stand steady, and let the tarpans adjust to their presence. The horses gathered in a hollow of the cliff face that looked like a giant bowl half buried in the sand.

Qhuin positioned his chariot in the center of the human barricade and held a tight rein.

Sargon stepped from the footboard with the lasso-pole in hand even before the milk-whites stopped.

Chor and his reinsman were on the right flank where the dry riverbed ran along the base of the cliff. Seasonal storms had left a ragged wash. It was where Qhuin thought the wild horses would most likely make their break.

Jewuul and Raahud were next in line. The rest of the hunters spread themselves between the chariot and the tumble of broken rocks by the canyon wall.

Sargon stepped ahead of the others and moved toward the wild horses that milled about in nervous confusion. *Eager to redeem himself in the eyes of his father,* Qhuin surmised. He wanted to stop him but restrained the impulse. The trouble for him was deep enough without humiliating the princeling further.

"Stand steady, m'lord." Horsemaster Raahud spoke loudly enough to be heard above the rumble of hooves and nervous whinnies.

Sargon glanced back at the phalanx of hunters who watched him with displeasure.

"If they spook, they're gone," Raahud warned. "Let them settle. We should wait for your father . . . m'lord."

Let them settle. It was the same thing Qhuin had said to Sargon. The princeling pressed his lips into a thin line, but to Qhuin's surprise, retreated to the line with a half nod.

Qhuin felt Sargon's eyes on him but resisted the urge to look at him. Whatever his expression, the spoiled princeling would construe it as a haughty show of triumph. There was no retreat from his trouble with the princeling. No reason to make it worse.

Kadesh-Cor and Jehu had reached the bottom of the escarpment and moved toward the line of hunters standing steady, waiting for the herd to settle.

Had Qhuin not known the royal status of the man striding toward them, he might have taken him for a huntsman. A man among men, responding to instincts passed down since the high gods were begotten of Apsu and Anu and set the universe in order. It affirmed again why many commoners felt a curious kinship with the Baron Magnus of Blackthorn.

The prince reached Qhuin's chariot and motioned for Jehu to join him.

Sargon chewed at a fingernail, already bitten to the quick. "I got one, did you see?" he said with guarded enthusiasm. He crossed and uncrossed his arms. His eyes flitted to Qhuin, then away.

"How did you miss it?" Kadesh-Cor said. The question was simple, but the tone sharp. The kindness Qhuin had seen in the prince's eyes when they met on the King's Road was missing.

"I didn't miss. I caught it," he protested. "I tied it to a tree back where—"

"It was your reinsman who made the catch!"

The wish of a nine-year-old boy to be noticed by the most important man in the world came racing from somewhere in the back of Qhuin's memory. He felt foolish and angry, but also a tiny flush of pride.

"The reinsman didn't hold the course," Sargon insisted. "I was ready to drop the loop, and he let them break away." He poked Qhuin in the chest with the lasso-pole. "Didn't you?"

Qhuin locked eyes with Sargon and for a moment had a vague suspicion they were negotiating a wholly different matter. Knowing that Prince Kadesh-Cor had watched the entire event from the ridge gave him a sense of calm.

Qhuin said nothing. Kadesh-Cor shifted his attention from his son to the bondsman. When their eyes met, Qhuin did not look away.

The rasp of Rusthammer's voice whispered so loudly in Qhuin's head he wondered if the prince could hear. *Three things cannot be long hidden: the sun, the moon, and the truth. Do not seek to be great. Seek to tell the truth, and you will become great.*

"You broke away too early, didn't you?" Sargon demanded with another poke of the pole.

Qhuin breathed deeply. "We didn't break, m'lord. We held the course." He could see the prince was startled by his audacity in challenging his master. Clearly Kadesh-Cor had expected a humble concession to the princeling's lie in spite of what he'd seen.

"Are you calling me a liar?" Sargon gripped a fistful of the rough weave jerkin Qhuin wore and pushed him against the cowling of the chariot. His confidence waxed high in the protective shadow of his father.

"No, m'lord," Qhuin said. "The ground was rutted. You caught her on the second pass."

Sargon relaxed his hand and strained to see the ruse behind Qhuin's eyes.

"Your hand was on the pole. First catch is yours."

Kadesh-Cor narrowed his eyes in admiration and something else Qhuin couldn't measure.

"We best move on the horses, m'lord. Darkness will soon be upon us," Horsemaster Raahud said. "The pick of the herd is yours, m'lord prince, but I suggest the chestnut. She's sixteen hands at least and young enough to give you many foals."

"Hemp or pole, m'lord?" Jehu asked as he stepped forward.

Kadesh-Cor nodded toward the lasso-pole without taking his eyes from the large chestnut mare. Jehu put it in his hand.

"You may wish to slacken the loop just a bit, m'lord," Horsemaster Raahud said as the prince walked slowly forward. The horses retreated to the concave wall of rock and crowded into a defensive clump as the circle of hunters closed in around them.

Qhuin eased the chariot forward, keeping pace with the men and filling the break in the line.

Sargon walked in front of the milk-whites with a coil of hemp in his hand.

Kadesh-Cor stalked the chestnut with stealthy, nimble steps.

The mare turned to her left, then jumped back, confused by the hunters moving closer, tightening the circle. She broke right, and the prince followed. She stiffened her legs and skidded to a stop, then turned back and bolted away.

The prince lunged forward at the same instant and stopped her flight. He moved forward again with the pole extended, jabbering at the horse nonsensically.

Qhuin watched with such intensity he felt as if he was the one taking the last few steps toward the chestnut mare. *Move to her left.*

The chestnut stared at the prince and pawed the ground. Her hooves threw up a storm of dust and desert crust. She threw her head back with her nostrils flared. The other horses bolted to the left.

The prince sprang forward as the chestnut whirled to follow the herd. He swung the pole to where she was going and dropped the noose perfectly around her neck. He jerked the hemp tight and wrapped it twice around his waist. He dug his boot heels into the ground and fell back with his weight on the pole.

"Go!" Horsemaster Raahud screamed. Jehu and Jewuul broke from the line and ran to where Kadesh-Cor was being thrown about by the thrashing horse. The big mare fought the tether with such force she reared over backward and landed on her haunches. Before she could regain her feet, Jehu looped a lasso of hemp around her neck; Jewuul added a third loop. The chestnut scrambled to her feet and reared again, but she was caught in the triangle of ropes.

She had a small head for her size and a blaze of white on her face. Her forelock was a shag of wild silk. Her legs were long and her body elegant. Her mane and tail were black and swung in graceful swirls as she pranced to escape her captivity.

"He's got her!" Sargon exclaimed to Qhuin in a burst of delighted excitement.

Qhuin smiled and, leaning toward him, said, "Your painted mare's the better horse."

Caught by surprise, the princeling flushed with pride before turning away.

The horses swarmed together in confusion. The sun was gone. The glow from the high clouds had lost its warmth, and the last light of the twilight sky descended into gray. There was still time. Qhuin knew that with Kadesh-Cor as their leader, the hunt would be triumphant.

CHAPTER 52

Sunlight fluttered through blossoms of begonia flowers and danced on Ashar's face. He opened his eyes. The magnificent blooms climbed a trellis made of glass. Pink petals glowed in the light. The sun was warm on his cheeks, and light replaced the darkness.

Ashar was curled in a ball on a mat of thick moss, his legs drawn up and his arms folded across his chest. His mind was muddy and his memory blurred. He was in a bower of trees, climbing plants, and a medley of flowers.

The arch of the roof was a tangle of aged limbs of lemon trees laden with ripened yellow fruit the size of a man's fist. Their thick trunks were as gnarled as the olive orchards planted by the Navigator that still grew at the temple.

The bower opened onto a pavilion with a domed roof covered by a rainbow thicket of climbing roses. The ornate iron of the imposts was entwined with grapevines heavy with green and purple fruit. An altar of stones stood at the center of the pavilion at the top of thirteen steps.

The hallowed fane of Oum'ilah. The reality of where he found himself sent a shiver up Ashar's spine and left a tingling in his head. *How did I get here?*

Ashar rose slowly to his feet and looked about. Three bowers extended from the pavilion. A smaller pavilion at the end of the west passage opened to a garden that was wild compared to the groomed botanical bowers.

His stomach growled, reminding him that the only food he'd eaten since the beginning of his cleansing fast was a chew of venison. *The cleansing fast.* The thought ignited his memory with a sputtering of fireflies. *The testing. Master Doyan. Blessed Sages. Drakkor, Blood of the Dragon. Murder, blood, and death. The stones of light!* His hands tightened on the leather satchel across his chest. Even knowing the stones were gone, his fingers felt for the lumps beneath the leather.

"The stones of light are safe." The voice behind him stopped his heart. He whirled to see a man hobbling toward him. The shafts of sunlight bathed his hair in a gossamer glow of white. His face was in shadow, but as he drew closer, Ashar saw who it was.

"You're alive!" His shock was replaced by a surge of joy. "You are *alive!*"

The Oracle nodded. He looked older. Weary. Discouraged but not defeated. There was no trace of blood on his robe from the near-fatal wound he had suffered.

"You have the sacred stones . . . is that how . . . ?" He dared not ask.

"The stones of light can heal the wounds of our bodies but not the wounds in our hearts." The Oracle turned his head slightly as if he could see the temple and his fallen brothers far below. His face was pinched with sorrow.

"I thought you were dead," Ashar stammered in wonder and disbelief.

The Oracle offered a strange and haunting smile.

He was *dead!* The truth came to Ashar in a gasping thought. *And he is alive again.*

The Oracle gestured toward the small pavilion at the garden end of the corridor. "Eat and renew your strength. Then we will talk."

— ‑ —

Ashar sat at the ornate table in the pavilion of the wild garden. Fruit, bread, cheese, and the sweet juice of ripened grapes were prepared and waiting.

Ashar ate alone. He gorged the first of the morsels to satiate his gnawing hunger and gulped great swallows of juice to quench his thirst. Eventually he slowed, relishing the succulent flavors and delicious tastes.

"Are you refreshed?" The Oracle's voice startled Ashar for the second time.

Ashar's thoughts were on all that had happened, and he had not heard the Oracle approach. *Or did he just appear?* Ashar wasn't sure.

"It is so good," he said and swallowed his last bite whole. "The finest food I have ever eaten." Ashar stood to show his respect.

The Oracle chuckled. "There are few things better than the fruits of creation with none of our vain embellishments." He waved Ashar back to the stool.

"How did I come to be here?" Ashar asked. "I remember we were set upon by the bandits who chased us up the mountain, and I was . . . Where is Rorekk?"

The Oracle furrowed his brows and shook his head, then laid his fingers on Ashar's brow. His thumb and smallest finger gently closed Ashar's eyes. The touch of the Oracle's hand was cool, but it kindled a quiver of warmth and, to his amazement, he could see all that had happened as if he were watching through a lens of amber glass.

— ‑ —

The basket containing the Oracle's body rose into the clouds beyond the reach of Drakkor's men. Rorekk rose with a sword in one hand and a bludgeon in the other as the fallen few recovered and a second assault of bandits charged. The fighting was awful. A slashing of swords and collision of clubs. Their blows bounced off the giant like a stick hitting stone, but their blades drew blood.

A bandit reached Ashar and raised his sword. A great howl of rage stayed his hand. It echoed among the tombs as if amplified by the gods of war and spirits of the dead. The bandit whirled around. The thunderous bellow came from Rorekk, who erupted from the pounding mob of men.

Blood gushed from a head wound. His slashed tunic was sodden with blood from a gash in his side. He swung a wooden cudgel, dropping seven men like a reaper with a scythe, then parried the thrusting of swords with his other hand. The violence was astounding. His war cry was shrill and piercing.

Ashar had seen Rorekk's strength in the holy sanctum. He could not help but think that whoever Rorekk was and whatever life he had lived before his service at the temple, he was not the man the Blessed Sages imagined him to be.

Rorekk seized a man who stumbled backward to escape the whirling mass of destruction. He lifted the bandit above his head as if he were a half-sack of flour and hurled him at the man about to end Ashar's life.

The bandit clambered to escape the catapulted body, but stumbled as the flying man in heavy armor crushed him.

Rorekk grabbed Ashar by the arm, and carried him to the wall. He wrapped a rope around his chest and beneath his arms. Almost before the knot was tied, the rope pulled tight and lifted him away.

At the same moment, the bandits swarmed over Rorekk, who stood with his back to the wall. It was the last image Ashar saw as his vision ended in a mist of clouds the color of bone.

—

The Oracle removed his hand, and Ashar opened his eyes. He felt the warmth of the sunlight. He looked up at the Oracle in wonder and confusion. *How is it possible for me to remember what I didn't see?*

The Oracle answered the unspoken question with a smile. "All that happens is, and thus will always be, and our minds can thereby know things that our eyes have never seen."

Ashar didn't understand the workings of such mysteries, but his last vision of Rorekk, unarmed and under siege, gripped his gut. "What happened to the giant?" he asked.

"I do not know," the Oracle said.

"But I thought . . ." Ashar protested, confused.

The Oracle shrugged an apology. "If he traded his life to bring you to the hallowed fane, we can be sure it was for a greater purpose. His will be a grand mansion in the clouds of blessings."

Ashar swept his gaze across the wonderful, wild garden. "It is very different than I imagined," he said at last. "I had been told the hallowed fane was a monument to the God of Gods in marble, gold, and precious stones."

The Oracle laughed softly. "Ah, the vain imaginings of men. There are but few who truly understand the meaning and purpose of this place. The hallowed fane is not a mysterious shrine of relics that too easily take the place of God. It is an altar of gratitude to the God of gods and Creator of All Things. It is a place of praise to Oum'ilah, whose true and blessed name we must never speak, in thanksgiving for the wonders of the heavens and the earth.

"A tower of marble and gold and precious stones, no matter how finely wrought, is still a creation of human pride and foolishness. The Codices of the Navigator tell of men of ancient days who aspired to the creative power of God and, in their vanity, tried to build a tower to heaven."

"Which was destroyed by the fierce winds," Ashar said. "We were taught this story as part of our preparations."

"The ancient evil has come again. The secret works of darkness return from their hidden places. But there is hope," the Oracle said as he opened the bundle of black fur on the table. A shaft of sunlight illuminated the clear white stones until they glistened with a thousand facets. "Do you know the story of the sacred stones of light?"

"Only what I have been taught by Master Doyan." The Oracle nodded, so Ashar continued. "The Navigator went up to the mountain of Sheseem and did molten out of a rock thirteen small stones. He prayed to the God of gods, who touched them with His finger to light the way of the ships during the great voyage."

"And what do you know of these stones of light after the time of First Landing?"

"Only that they were lost."

"I will teach you what you must know. When the voyages ended, the stones of light were taken from the boats and placed into a crown of pure gold, representing Oum'ilah and His ever-watchful eyes upon us. The Immortal Crown was worn by the high priest on holy days and in the temple to invoke the visions of God. To penetrate the veil separating us from the unseen world." He paused and placed a hand on Ashar's shoulder. "When the stones are found and restored to the Immortal Crown, the kingdom of light will come again."

"How were they lost?" Ashar asked.

"By the ancient secrets of evil that crossed the great deep." The Oracle's face filled with sadness. "From the time of the great tower, a record of secret oaths and signs and combinations of murder was kept. It was supposed to have been buried in the sea, but those entrusted with that task were seduced by evil. This grimoire—and its dark secrets— was hidden on one of the vessels, and brought to the new land.

"In the time of First Landing, the God of gods was cherished. It was the time of the kingdom of light. But by the fourth generation, the Way of the Navigator had been weakened by avarice, pride, and the struggle for power. People returned to the gods and superstitions they knew from the times of the dark tower. Governing councils degenerated into a clamor of rival sovereigns, princes, and lords. Boundaries were drawn and dominions established. Men proclaimed themselves kings by the divine right of the gods. They levied taxes, imprisoned and enslaved their people. They murdered the innocent to appease their superstitions. They sought power and possessions. They were lifted up in pride and seduced by the pleasures of the flesh.

"By the third century, the dominions of Kandelaar were in the midst of chaos. The stones of light were taken from the Immortal Crown to be traded, bought, and sold as ordinary gems. As their strange powers became known, they were sought by witches and sorcerers and workers of dark magic. The codices of ReMoetr-Gakahn record that the stones of light were gathered by a brotherhood of religious zealots and hidden, lest any man become immortal." He looked at the glimmering stones on the table. "We believe that the sanctum on the holy Mountain of God is one of four shrines built by the zealots to hide the sacred stones."

"Where are the other shrines?"

"No one knows. Some believe they were erected equidistantly from the ancient altar used by the Navigator himself. But the distance is unknown and the location of the altar is lost, if indeed there was such a place. We do not know how many of the other stones of light have been discovered."

"You knew the bandit's stone was once possessed by the sorceress of Dragonfell. You knew its name. The Swayyus Stone."

The Oracle nodded. "I knew by his claim of the power to enter the minds of other men, and also by its color and the quality of the light it gives. A sacred stone perverted by the hand of evil can no longer radiate the pure light of its power. It cannot blaze white because it is tainted by darkness."

"Does each stone possess a different power?"

The Oracle nodded slowly. "According to the oldest copies of the Navigator's writings, twelve of the stones are endowed with the six powers of godliness: power over body, power over mind, access to the realms of spirits. Dominion over the elements of earth, the boundaries of time, and the limits of space. Two stones endowed with each power."

"What of the thirteenth stone?"

A glimmer of light escaped the deep pools of the Oracle's eyes. "The thirteenth stone is the god stone. There is little said of it other than it is preeminent over the rest and the keystone to restoring the promise and power of the Immortal Crown."

Ashar studied the shining stones, squinting against the brightness. "How does one discern which of the stones possess which power? They are so similar—"

The Oracle's laughter stopped him. "Is there no end to your questions?"

"Forgive me, honored one." The rote apology bubbled up from years of humble submission. "I've misspoken."

"No, it is right of you to ask."

"Do you believe the seven remaining stones are hidden or . . ."

"I have faint hope the missing stones rest safely in an undiscovered sanctuary. I wish it is so, but I fear it is not."

"How is it possible that stones touched by the finger of God and endowed with the powers of godliness can be used for evil?"

"At the dawn of creation, the God of gods endowed his human creatures with intelligence, discernment, and the power of choice. In the hand of evil, the power of the stones comes from darkness, where all things are done in secret.

"It is only in the hand of the righteous that the stones of light shine with the light that comes from God."

CHAPTER 53

"What is to become of me?" Ashar asked.

"Can any of us truly know our destiny except by faith and walking beyond the threshold of knowledge? You are who you are, and were before, and you will always be through endless time." The recitation of the tenet was spoken with familiar cadence, but the Oracle made it personal with his choice of *you* instead of *we*. Ashar felt the reality of his endless existence in a way he never had before.

The Oracle's voice hardened. "Evil is a force that can change the course of eternity only as we allow it. The Creator of All Things has given us the power to choose our destiny."

"What must I do?" Ashar wondered aloud.

The Oracle's face softened. "You must do what only you can do. What only one with the blood of the Navigator has the power to achieve." He looked at the stones on the table. The crystals refracted a pure white light onto Ashar's face. "Faith is a hope in things not seen that are true. I know you will be tested and tempered, and I have faith you will find the strength to rise to your destiny and the wisdom to triumph over the challenges that await you."

"Challenges, honored master?" Ashar ventured.

"The powers of darkness can only be defeated by the glory of light," the Oracle spoke in a reverent whisper. "You must find the missing stones of light and return them to the Immortal Crown. You must fulfill the prophecy and open a way for the kingdom of light to come again. You must gather them before more of them fall into the hands of evil."

Ashar shuddered. The evil countenance of Drakkor was clear in his mind's eye. In that moment he knew the day would come when he would stand face-to-face with him again.

"But I am just a boy," he said.

"Many years ago, I sent Blessed Sage Granswaan to gather the missing stones of light. For many seasons, he sent us word of his progress. They were hopeful and informative words, but his writings were without detail lest a dispatch fall into the hands of villainous men. His last message, brought by a pilgrim who had seen him in the village, was a cryptic communiqué that left me certain he had found some of the missing stones."

Ashar's eyes brightened, but only for an instant.

"Then he vanished, and I've have had no word of him. I fear he is dead. I called him to the task, believing he was 'the one,' but it was a decision of the mind and not the spirit. I was mistaken. My vanity blinded me." The Oracle placed a hand on Ashar's shoulder and held his eyes. "Now the task has fallen to you."

Ashar trembled.

"You must never allow the stones to be gathered in the hand of one deceived by that darkness. In depriving evil, you will save the world from the greatest of all calamities: an immortal man controlled by the forces of darkness with the power of renewal and endless life."

Ashar paced the garden like a caged lion. "I have lived on the mountain since I was a child. I am ignorant of everything beyond the walls of the temple. The ways of the world are unknown to me except from books and the teachings of the enlightened masters. How is it possible that I should be the one who—"

"You are of the blood of the Navigator! That knowledge came to you for a purpose. I believe you are the fulfillment of the prophecy recorded in the Codices of the Navigator." He paraphrased the familiar passage. "When the ancient evil is come again, that which was lost shall be found and gathered in the righteous hand by the child of pure blood, by the strength of a sword he cannot hold, endowed with the powers of godliness, and returned to the crown of endless life. And in that day, the kingdom of light will come again."

Ashar could feel the Oracle's eyes looking into his soul.

"I believe that you, Ashar, son of Shalatar, are the child of pure blood."

The Oracle wrapped the stones in the bundle of fur and slipped them inside the satchel around Ashar's neck.

"From this day, *you* are the keeper of the sacred stones of light."

"I am but a boy!"

"In this hour, the God of gods has made of you a man." The Oracle leveled his eyes with Ashar's and took the young man's hands in his. "There is no one else."

In the same way the knowledge of his lost lineage had presented itself as he stood before the Council of Blessed Sages, the words of the Oracle entered his mind on a beam of light, and he knew the words were true. He had no understanding of what it meant, but he felt the blood of his ancestors coursing through his veins and the spirit of the Navigator surging through his being.

"You must find Blessed Sage Granswaan, if he is yet alive," the Oracle said. "If he is alive, he will join you. If he is not, perhaps he left a clue behind. He most surely knew that someone would eventually come looking for him. The kingdom of light cannot come again until all the stones are returned to the Immortal Crown. Do you understand why?"

Ashar spoke before this thoughts were fully formed.

"The shining stones remind us that the finger of God can touch our hearts and minds, fill our lives with light, and enable us to believe in things not seen." It was not the recitation of a postulant. It came from a light within illuminating his understanding.

"Even the most devoted feel a need for something to touch—the sacred relics. Or smell—the burning incense. Or adorn—our robes and vestments." He was startled by the words flowing from his lips as if he were a Blessed Sage.

The Oracle smiled and nodded. "Our finite minds crave reconciliation with the infinite. The stones of light help us across that chasm. They allow us to soar as if carried by the winged spirits of God. The stones of light are a miracle beyond our understanding. The finger of God has touched you here." The Oracle's fingers tapped gently over Ashar's heart as he pushed himself to his feet. "With this man of evil and his army occupying the holy mountain, there is grave danger that the order of Oum'ilah will never rise again. It might even vanish from the earth unless you are successful. I know it is a great thing I ask of you." He paused. "That Oum'ilah, the God of gods and Creator of All Things asks of you."

The gravity of it had not left Ashar's mind. "You expect me to combat evil and find the stones and face the Blood of the Dragon, but . . ." He took a deep breath and crossed the boundaries. "You performed the ritual of endless life! If he cannot die, he has no fear of death. How can I stand against such a man?"

To Ashar's surprise, the Oracle smiled as if the answer was as light as a hummingbird. "Perhaps I should be ashamed of this, but . . . I lied to the liar in the hope we might escape his fiendish intent. I have deceived him, but he shall discover it soon enough."

"You mean you didn't . . . ?"

"I recited a poem in the ancient tongue. Did you not wonder why there was no shining?"

"But the wound in his hand, and the light . . ."

"The healing and the shining was through me. The stone was in my hand, thanks to your quick thinking."

Ashar blushed with a rush of pride.

"May the guilt of it be smothered in the mercy of the God of gods." Not the slightest twinge of guilt was present in his voice. "Our one hope is that the power of the stones requires that all be gathered in the hand of righteousness and returned to the Immortal Crown."

Ashar remembered something the Oracle had said to Drakkor in the court. He flushed at the thought of asking the question lest the Oracle misunderstand, but he gathered his courage.

"Is it true that only those with the blood of the Navigator may be consecrated to endless life?" It was a question of curiosity. A question that frightened him.

The Oracle's smile came slowly. "Some of the Blessed Sages believe that the blood lineage matters. Others believe that nothing more is required except that the stones be gathered in a single hand. Yet the stones have not been in one place or in one hand since they were stolen from the Immortal Crown many centuries ago and lost. So I do not know."

"Were there any given immortality who might still be among us?"

The Oracle closed his eyes as if listening to a voice that Ashar couldn't hear, yet in the long silence, Ashar heard the answer, "Yes."

"Will you guide me in this holy quest?"

The Oracle shook his head.

"I cannot do what you ask of me without your guidance," Ashar said.

"My time has ended, and I must prepare to go the way of all the earth."

"No! You must never leave us. If I am truly the one of pure blood, as you believe, I will not rest until I gather the stones of light and bring them to you so you will never die."

Ashar saw affection in the Oracle's smiling eyes. "The prophecy is hopeful but only predicts what *may* be, not what *will* be. The gates of iniquity are wide, and the jaws of the dark world gape open. Drakkor will destroy all who oppose him in his quest, but the prophecy he follows is corrupted. He does not know that the endowment of endless life is only possible when all thirteen stones of light are returned to the Immortal Crown, each according to its proper place about the god stone."

"And what of the Immortal Crown? Is it also lost?"

"For now, yes."

"Where is it?"

"Hidden in a secret place inside the temple."

"Where the man of evil now walks in blasphemy," Ashar whispered.

There was a long silence between them. Then Ashar clenched his jaw and lifted his chin as courage flowed into him. "I will find Sage Granswaan, if he is yet alive, or learn what he discovered, if he is not. I will go wherever the stones of light may lead me. I will find the ancient shrines, if that is where the sacred stones are hidden, be they north or south or a place unknown, and I will unravel the riddle of the Immortal Crown. I swear by the God of gods I will do all that you have asked of me, or die in the quest."

"Dying is not your destiny." The Oracle turned as if listening to a voice that Ashar could not hear. The old priest inhaled deeply and closed his eyes. His lips quivered in a faint smile as he turned again to Ashar. "You must trust nothing until it is confirmed by the quiet voice that speaks in your heart. There is something here to give you hope." The Oracle turned to the thin sheets of hammered brass in the ring-bound codices on the table. "Can you repeat the words of the prophecy?"

"Much of it, but you have spoken many words that I've not heard before."

The Oracle turned the book toward Ashar. "Read from here." He pointed to a spot on the page.

Ashar searched the Oracle's face, then looked down and began to read. "'That which was lost shall be found, to be gathered in the righteous hand, by the child of pure blood by the strength of a sword he cannot hold—'"

"There!" The Oracle tapped the page with a slender finger.

Ashar shrugged. "I have not the strength to hold a sword, nor the skill."

"Again," the Oracle said. "Just there."

"'By the strength of the sword he cannot hold.'" Ashar read the words again.

"I have read this many times, but not until this moment have I understood. It is not *you* who shall hold the sword that will protect you from evil. There is another called to such a purpose."

"Who?"

"In the day you need the sword, you shall know, and so shall he."

CHAPTER 54

Qhuin felt the sound before he heard it. It reverberated from the walls of the narrow canyon like a rolling wave of thunder before the sky exploded. Everyone could hear it, but no one knew what it was. A fearsome roar shattered by a piercing scream. The mares erupted in a frenzy of hooves hammering heavily over rock.

The chestnut whirled toward the sound and fought the triangle of ropes that held her in place. The muscles beneath her reddish hide quivered with expectation. A pounding crescendo raced toward them. The herd of wild mares parted.

An enormous stallion burst from the twilight shadows of the canyon wall and plunged down the escarpment toward them.

He was the most magnificent horse Qhuin had ever seen. More majestic even than the great warhorses of legend. He was the color of smoke with a speckling of gray. His muzzle was black and matched the mask across his eyes. The mane and tail were black and rippled in the wind like a banderole streaming into battle.

His head was perfectly shaped, and the elegant arc of his neck flowed into heavily muscled shoulders. His black eyes were alert and all-knowing. His legs were long with large hooves and fetlocks covered with silken hair the color of night.

The colossal stallion charged forward, splitting the herd and hurtling toward the captive chestnut mare with all his power.

Qhuin watched the magnificent beast in awe and admiration. Was it possible the idea in his head was true? He mouthed the word that would not leave his mind: "Equus."

There was no time to think. The great horse had erupted from the shadows into being. By the time Kadesh-Cor and the men holding the chestnut comprehended what was happening, it was too late. Jewuul whirled as the stallion approached but clung to the rope on the chestnut with determined courage. Obedience overpowered instinct. He tried to avoid the gnashing teeth and pounding hooves, but was confined by the length of hemp and could not escape.

The stallion smashed into the reinsman and knocked him down.

Jewuul tried to crawl away, but the horse turned back and trampled him.

Qhuin grabbed the lasso-pole from Sargon and ran toward the chaos. The stallion whirled toward the prince. Jehu hurled his coil of hemp in an effort to turn the horse. It struck the stallion's muzzle with no effect. With two of the ropes hanging lose, the mare bolted.

Kadesh-Cor was jerked forward and pulled to the ground. He fumbled with the rope wrapped around his waist as he tumbled in a spiral at the end of the pole. The chestnut dragged him over the broken ground.

When he finally unraveled the rope, he tumbled to a stop in a heap of dust and blood. The stallion ran over him. A hoof struck his ribs with a crack. Another struck him in the face, ripping flesh from his cheek. The stallion pranced a tight circle and turned back to trample the creature that threatened his harem of mares.

In pain and barely conscious, Kadesh-Cor scrambled backward on all fours like a wounded crab escaping a voracious bird. A ribbon of red flowed down his face.

Sargon watched in horror, petrified by fear. Qhuin leaped over the prince and faced the wild stallion with both hands raised. He spoke to him in the special language he had for horses. Urgent. Soothing.

The stallion thrashed his head, but enraptured by the soft voice and strange words, he halted his advance. His silk forelock swayed over his forehead. The stallion was clearly puzzled by the creature facing him with nothing but a piece of pole and a ragged length of hemp.

Time slowed. Qhuin felt as if there were only two creatures on the earth, and he was one of them. *Is this the horse of legend or a beast of flesh and blood?* A torrent of impressions passed through his mind in the space of a heart beat. *If one man could not hold the chestnut, this horse will drag me to the end of the Oodanga Wilds.*

The stallion surged forward with deadly intent. Qhuin returned to the moment. He cracked the stallion on the nose with the pole and yelled, "Pace o' a nona equis."

The stallion skidded to a stop. Gusts of steaming vapor burst from his nostrils. His hooves pounded the ground.

Qhuin lunged toward the prince, Jehu rushing to join him. Kadesh-Cor lost consciousness and crumpled to the ground. Qhuin and Jehu gathered him up and half dragged, half carried him behind a mound of rock, safely away from the thrashing horse.

Qhuin watched the stallion. What he saw would never be forgotten and not easily believed.

The stallion ran after the chestnut and used his teeth to rip the nooses of hemp and pole away. He ran a wide circle around the mares until they ran with him, a spinning cyclone of dust and thunder.

Then the stallion turned up the rocky slope the way he had come. The herd of horses followed.

Had they escaped into an unseen cleft in the face of the cliff or been swallowed in the shadows? It was difficult to see in the darkness. The mystery would mingle with the myth, and the legend of Equus would endure.

A heavy silence fell over the vale. The horses of the Oodanga Wilds had vanished.

CHAPTER 55

"Fly from the cliff?" Ashar stared at the Oracle with wide, unblinking eyes. "Is that what is written?"

"'Carried by faith on the winged spirits of God.'" The Oracle traced the markings incised on a sheet of hammered brass as he read from the codices of the Navigator.

"I don't remember reading that," Ashar said. "Are you certain of the meaning?" He tried to moisten his lips, but his tongue was dry. "You are sure"—he could hardly say it—"that I must leap from the mountain's edge to prove my faith?"

Ashar and the Oracle spent long hours together in the wild garden. Ashar listened and learned.

The Oracle's words filled his head like light filling a darkened room. As he walked with the Oracle to the north side of the monolith, he caught a glimpse of the guardians of the hallowed fane. They wore curious habiliments, unlike anything he had seen in the temple below. He found it curious that none of them seemed to notice him or the Oracle as they made their way across the flat stones of the summit.

By the time they stood at the precipice, clouds had formed and the bright morning had faded. The sun was a glowing orb diffused in a swirl of mist.

"It is written that the powers of the stones are wrought by heart and mind. Believe in your heart. Desire in your mind. Abandon yourself to your faith. You have heard the voice and felt it in your heart."

Ashar's face paled. "We are taught to believe beyond our doubts, but . . ." His voice trembled. "How do I know it's a promise from the God of gods? What if you are mistaken—" He caught himself. "What if I am not the one you imagine me to be?"

The Oracle raised his grizzled eyebrows. "There is no time left, and there is no other."

"But is"—he could hardly say the word—"*flying* from the mountain the only way?"

"The winged spirits of God will carry you."

Ashar was filled with fear; his faith had fled. He glanced about, hoping to see the legendary messengers of heaven, even knowing he wouldn't. He asked the question he knew he shouldn't. "Have *you* ever been carried by the winged spirits of God?"

The Oracle tapped his finger on the ancient record. "*Real* is a relative concept when dealing with our eternal nature and dimensions of endless time. The winged spirits of God are as real as your faith in things unseen."

"Pray, forgive me honored master, but my fear of things unseen leaves little room for faith to fly." His face pinched tight at the thought of it.

"Such feelings and fears are not unexpected. You have only begun your quest, and your burden is great." The Oracle's eyes drifted away with memory. What came next was deeply personal. A confession? Ashar had clear impression the Oracle had faced his own extreme test of faith and gained an understanding not easily explained.

"If you find the courage to vanquish your fear of death, if you conquer your doubts with conviction, if you embrace the destiny to which you are called and surrender yourself—body, mind, and spirit—to trust in the God of gods, and the powers He has given us, you will be endowed with a force and faculty you cannot comprehend."

In spite of his trepidations, Ashar knew he must face his destiny, however grave or fearsome. He knew he must take that first bold step on the dangerous odyssey before him.

"First bold step" was a familiar cliché among the postulants, but it took on a whole new meaning for Ashar as he shuffled forward, taking care to keep his balance. He settled one foot on solid stone before advancing the other. His steps grew smaller as he approached the rim. When he finally arrived, he leaned forward and looked over the edge. There were no clouds blocking his view of the river. It was a thread of silver in a sea of emerald shadows two thousand cubitums below.

The muscles in his stomach tightened and his legs quavered. Was the Oracle's outrageous instruction to step from the cliff only because the path was blocked by Drakkor's men? *Or is it a test of faith I must endure if I am to succeed?* Master Doyan's voice spoke in his memory: "Enlightenment requires the courage to face your greatest fears."

Ashar felt nauseous as he stared into the void and certain death. Fear gripped his gut with a burning fist. His extreme and irrational fear of heights made him dizzy. He stumbled backward and fell at the Oracle's feet.

"I can't," he muttered.

"You carry the stones of light touched by the finger of God. The blood of the Navigator flows in your veins." The Oracle touched Ashar's head and then his heart. "It is here and here that a man is empowered for good or ill. In your hands, the stones of light are a force for good you cannot comprehend."

Ashar tightened his grip on the satchel and pulled it closer to his heart as the Oracle helped him to his feet. His fingers settled over the lumps beneath the leather to confirm the presence of the stones. They were all there. He experienced a sudden rush of confidence.

"Does one of these stones hold dominion over the earth? The power to fly?"

The Oracle looked at him with furrowed brows but didn't respond. The answer was clear. He didn't know.

Ashar turned his eyes from the Oracle back to the edge of the rock. This time there was no shuffle in his stride. He reached the edge and looked at the river again. A filter of thin clouds slipped by beneath him. The sky opened above, and the sun felt hot on the back of his neck. Light entered his mind, and he felt a strange desire to fly.

The Oracle put his arms around Ashar and held him close. He whispered in his ear, "Fear and faith cannot abide. The God of gods is with you."

Ashar was surprised, but as the Oracle's arms tightened around him, he returned the embrace and wept. It was the first time he'd been shown such tangible love since the day his stepfather had taken him from his mother's arms.

"Remain here and stay well until I return with the Immortal Crown and *all* the stones," Ashar said.

He retreated half a stone's throw from the precipice, then ran as fast as he was able and leaped into the swirl of clouds that had gathered again at the top of the Mountain of God—the sign that He was there.

CHAPTER 56

Confusion reigned in the darkness following the appearance of the mystical stallion and the disappearance of the horses. The prince was unconscious, his face ripped open, and Jewuul was dead. A damp coldness enveloped the canyon. It was too dark to see, and the encampment was more than a league away.

Qhuin made a torch from strips of cloth torn from his tunic and a smear of lard from the lubricated chamber of the chariot's hub. He held the flame low over Kadesh-Cor, who lay unconscious on the ground. The fire cast a ghoulish yellow-orange light onto the anxious faces of the men who surrounded the badly injured prince. There was something oddly disconcerting about seeing the prince at the edge of death. He bled like an ordinary man, and his exalted rank no longer seemed important. If he died, the mighty Baron Magnus of Blackthorn and prince of the North would be nothing but a box of bones. The memory of him no more than a name chiseled into a rock and soon forgotten.

Qhuin watched as Horsemaster Raahud staunched the flow of blood from the gash on Kadesh-Cor's face with skill and confidence and replaced the flap of skin the best he could. He bound the wound with a wad of wool and a strap of leather.

The prince never moved.

Raahud held his ear close to Prince Kadesh-Cor's nose to measure the depth of his breathing. He nodded slowly, but his face was grim. "We must get him to camp immediately. He must be purified and sewn at once."

"By who?" Sargon blurted. "No one is allowed to touch him but the royal surgeon."

"He will not last the night if we do not get him back and sew the wounds." Raahud rubbed his nose with the back of a bloody hand as he stood. "The prince will ride in the chariot with . . . Jewuul." He paused to look at his dead friend, his face broken with sorrow. "Wrap his body with your cloak," he said to Chor's reinsman. "Qhuin is the best of the drivers, so he will drive the whites with the prince and—"

"Who are you to give us orders, Horsemaster?" Sargon demanded as he shouldered past his brother.

"Your pardon, m'lord. I didn't mean to—"

Sargon cut him off. "My father is not going to ride in a chariot with a dead man. Leave the body of the hireling." His tone made it clear he considered Jewuul of no importance.

A murmur swept through the company.

"With respect, m'lord," Horsemaster Raahud said, "we cannot leave him. The rats will clean him to the bone by morning, and I'm sure your lord father—"

Sargon cut him off again, louder this time. Disdainful. "My lord father is insentient, and though we pray to the gods he shall recover, my brother and I—" He straightened slightly and narrowed his eyes as he sought the right words. "It is *we* who now preside as your sovereign lords." His face brightened at the sound of his own words, delivered with a sense of pride and power. His eyes glistened. He was ten feet tall with a crown on his head.

"By the gods, shut your mouth, brother, or I shall stuff it full of bloody rags!" Chor snapped. The disgust on his older brother's face shrank Sargon back to normal size.

Chor turned to his reinsman. "Do as Raahud says. Wrap the poor lad's body and put him in the chariot with our lord father, and do it swiftly."

"But—" Sargon's protest was cut short by Horsemaster Raahud, who nodded respectfully to Chor while making no effort to hide the smile at the edge of his lips.

"Move swiftly," he said to his men. Turning to Chor, he said, "Thank you, m'lord." Baaly and two of the Huszárs hurried to the fallen reinsman while others of the company shuffled about, but none dared touch the prince.

"Wait!" Sargon held up a hand and shouted at the reinsman. The urgency of his demand cut a hole in the din. He took a long, slow breath and bowed to his brother, bending low with outstretched arms in an exaggerated gesture of feigned respect. "Lord Chor, your greatness, if I may?" His words oozed with sarcasm. "I say we camp here for the night. Better our lord father rest than be shaken to his death on this rutted field. The horses will be unable to climb the rocks in this darkness. The chariot will be lost, and, as eager as you are to become Baron Magnus of Blackthorn, I do not think we should hasten the death of our lord father. Do you, brother?"

"He must be purified and sewn immediately, m'lord," Horsemaster Raahud repeated. "He cannot wait."

Chor scooped his hands beneath his father's shoulders. "Stop acting like an imbecile, Sargon, and help me put him into the chariot."

The flush on Sargon's cheek was visible even in the flicker of firelight. He stood motionless while Raahud, Chor, and three of the Huszárs lifted the prince. They followed Qhuin to the chariot. The shrouded body of the dead reinsman was placed on the footboard.

"We will never find our way up the cliff," Sargon moaned. His arrogance thinned to the whine of a child.

"The horses will lead us," Qhuin said. "They can see in the dark."

"That's a myth, you ignorant fool," Sargon said, but everyone ignored him.

Qhuin stepped into the chariot and handed the torch to Jehu. "Form a column behind the chariot. Take hold of the person in front of you, and we'll all make it fine." He looked to Chor for affirmation that he had not overstepped his bounds. The older princeling nodded.

Sargon approached the chariot and was about to step in when Qhuin stopped him. "You'll need to walk, m'lord. We're already heavier than we ought be for the grade."

A tidal wave of animosity crashed upon the rocks of Sargon's ego. He glared at Qhuin.

Qhuin held the look but shuddered at the promise of retribution so clearly burning in the princeling's eyes.

— - —

The milk-whites were the only ones that didn't falter or stumble on the climb from the canyon. Horsemaster Raahud helped Baaly, whose wounded leg made it difficult for him to climb. Sargon slipped and fell three times. Chor gripped his arm to help him, but the younger brother pulled away.

Once they were out of the canyon, Kadesh-Cor was moved from Qhuin's hunting chariot to the larger quadriga, where he was bedded on a cushion of harness pads taken from the other teams.

Qhuin was right about the horses—they could see things in the dark that men could not—and the crossing of the Tallgrass Prairie was without incident.

Sargon rode with his father in the quadriga. Qhuin felt the princeling's eyes on him even in the darkness. He knew better than to hope his subtle threat would dissuade Sargon once the princeling was surrounded by the kingsriders and Huszárs. He prepared himself for the worst.

The hunters' return with the injured prince consumed the attention of the camp. Qhuin, Chor, and Horsemaster Raahud carried Kadesh-Cor from the chariot to the entrance of the royal tent with the help of a young kingsrider who cast his helm aside and assisted without a command from his captain.

Prince Kadesh-Cor's hunting dogs ran from the tent to sniff and prod and lick their master's hands. Horsemaster Raahud scolded them away, but they would not retreat. A kingsrider gripped them by their collars and pulled them away. Their howls of protest dwindled to a mournful whimper, which added to the fear encircling the camp.

Qhuin looked for Sargon; he had not seen him since they arrived at the edge of the encampment. He had expressed such grave concern in the canyon that Qhuin was surprised he was not hovering over his injured father and barking commands.

"Which of you can attend to wounds?" Horsemaster Raahud asked the gathered crowd in a loud and urgent voice.

"Speak up," Chor commanded, lest none dare respond to Raahud in the presence of the princeling. There was silence.

"I'll do it, m'lord!" Nimra, Prince Kadesh-Cor's squire, hobbled forward on his twisted foot. Even filled with concern for the prince's welfare, the squire's face was cheerful.

Qhuin had seen Nimra for the first time when the boy had come with the prince to the stables at Blackthorn. He had seen him a few times during the journey—once returning from a hunt with a short bow slung across his shoulder and a quiver of feathered shafts hanging on the leather belt about his middle. The squire always seemed hopeful and optimistic.

Qhuin thought it odd that the prince had chosen a crippled boy as his squire. Prince Kadesh-Cor could have named anyone in the dominion of Blackthorn. Why pick this hobbling youth who could hardly care for himself, let alone the demands of his lordship?

Chor clearly disapproved of his father's choice of squire. He dismissed Nimra's offer to help with a wave of his hand. "You've not the skill." He scanned the faces in search of someone he could trust with his father's life. "Is there none of you who—"

The squire stepped forward again. "I have attended the royal physician . . . m'lord." His voice was soft but firm, and the honorific was only added after an unusually long pause. A squire attending the royal physician? That was unusual.

Chor glowered at Nimra, and, though nodding his acknowledgment, added, "Attending is not training, and watching is not doing."

"He gave me training," Nimra said. Then, in a tone that revealed something dark and hidden, he added, "Personally, m'lord." The mystery of the squire deepened.

The hum of conversation was replaced by a tense of silence. Nimra stood with a confidence Qhuin had not expected. There was a connection between the squire and the princeling that was not what most imagined.

Horsemaster Raahud turned to the squire. "Are you certain you can do what must be done to save his life?"

"And spare him the ugliness of scars," Chor added.

Qhuin thought it odd the princeling was thinking about his father's outward appearances when his life was in grave jeopardy.

"The prince is my responsibility," Nimra said. "I shall do my very best." He looked at Chor meaningfully. "You know I will, and why, m'lord."

Chor nodded, his jaw clenched tight.

"Then may the gods guide your hand," Raahud said.

"For his sake and yours," Chor added as he stepped aside. His voice was as cold as the winds of Icenesses.

"Who here fosters the craving?" the squire asked, turning to the men gathered near the entrance of the tent. "Come, come. When the prince awakens, the pain will be intense."

A bannerman came forward with a pouch of dried poppy leaves. Then a kingsrider grimaced and stepped forward. "I've a poke of cannabis," he said and lifted a sticky wad of yellow resin wrapped in oilcloth from beneath his broad leather belt. The warrior glanced at Chor but handed the narcotic to the squire-turned-physician's attendant.

When no one else was forthcoming, Chor gave a curt nod to Nimra, who entered the tent, followed by Qhuin and the others who carried the prince in their arms.

The courtesans in the tent helped settle the prince on a bed of fur robes and woven wool. One of the girls brushed against Qhuin as he helped lower the prince to his berth.

Aside from his encounter with Meesha, Qhuin had never been so close to a woman, and when their hands touched, a tingling sensation shot to the top of his head. He pulled his hand away, but not before she looked at him and smiled.

Princes called them courtesans, but the stablemen at Blackthorn called them whores, though Qhuin disliked the bitter taste of the word. He also disliked the bawdy stories the stablemen told and their rude laughter. He had never been with a woman, and his innocence made him an easy target for the ridicule of the other men.

Qhuin had never even seen a woman without clothing. Well, once, but he had only been fourteen at the time. He had happened upon a gaggle of girls from Blackthorn bathing in the pool where he took the horses for water. The girls screamed when they saw him and ran for the water in a blur of white skin.

He had turned away and stopped breathing. He could hear their girlish giggles of embarrassment. He knew he shouldn't look back, but he could not stop himself, and when he did, one of the girls stood straight up in the waist-deep water and threw her arms above her head to squeals of scandalous delight from her friends.

Qhuin abandoned the horses and ran half a league before he dared stop. To this day, the vision of her remained in his head as clear as the day it happened.

The prince's courtesan was young, delicate, and pretty. She knelt beside the prince and washed the blood from his face and neck. After she finished, she smiled at Qhuin again as she exited the tent.

He flushed and bobbed his head, turning swiftly and bumping into Nimra. "Pray, forgive me, m'lord," Qhuin said, bowing his head. The apology tumbled over his lips without thought. The words of survival. Bondsmen, slaves, and even lowborn freemen were forever begging pardon, asking forgiveness, and showing obeisance to their masters in the hope of leniency and mercy.

"I am hardly a lord." The squire smiled. There was a sparkling light in his dark eyes. "You are A'quilum Ereon Qhuin," he said, nodding slightly in a show of respect. "The word about camp is you are the one who saved the prince from the phantom horse."

Qhuin was startled that the prince's squire knew his name. He felt a flush of pride, but it was guarded. Suspicious.

Nimra's face illuminated in a smile. He put a firm hand on Qhuin's shoulder and squeezed. "You have a lion's heart."

Qhuin exhaled the breath he'd been holding. "I regret I was unable to spare him his injuries."

"But he is alive," Nimra said. Then, leaning close with a confiding whisper, he added, "And if it be the will of the gods, he shall stay that way."

Something behind Qhuin snagged the squire's attention. His eyes stretched wide, his expression changing from hope to horror. In the same instant that Qhuin turned his head, he was seized by the iron hands of kingsriders. Two of them pinned his arms and a third looped a chain around his neck, dragging him backward.

———

Rusted iron cuffs cut into his wrists. His hands were shackled behind a tree with his arms twisted backward. His boots had been removed in order to chain his ankles together. The iron slave collar, removed for the hunt, was clamped around his neck.

The ground he sat on sloped down, so he used his legs and feet to brace his back against the trunk, hoping to lessen the wrenching ache in his shoulders. A jagged knot of bark bit into his skin. He moved to a different position to alleviate the pain, but it only made it worse.

Qhuin jerked forward and tried to pull his hands through the iron bands. A paralyzing jolt of pain spiked up his arms. Rather than fall back, he pulled harder. The self-inflicted agony was penance for the stupidity that had put him in this awful circumstance. He'd been warned against his temper. He jerked again, this time with even greater force—and pain.

Wresting the whip from Sargon was an offense of such enormity that it merited cutting off Qhuin's hand. Wresting the sword was an even greater offense of humiliation. The princeling's retribution would be calamitous. Worse than death.

Qhuin shifted his position in a vain effort to find relief from the needles of pain that pierced his wrists. He recognized the warm wet creeping across the back of his hand. Blood.

———

Qhuin hovered in a fog of agony and exhaustion, revisiting his folly over and over in his head.

If only . . . if only . . . But what else could I have done?

He had taken the whip for the sake of the horse. He had taken the sword for the sake of his hands. Qhuin had known many slaves over the years who were submissive to the point of their own destruction. Unlike them, he refused to be a bull led to the slaughter.

Rusthammer purged Qhuin of what he called "ignorant acquiescence"—*"Obey to survive, but survival is greater than obedience."* The old smith's quiet wisdom was a comfort in the grim discomfort of his circumstance.

Qhuin had seen enough in the stables of Blackthorn to know that punishment was capricious, swift, and always ghastly. Justice varied greatly from manse to manse depending on the clemency or cruelty of the ruling lord.

How will Sargon choose to punish me? Qhuin's thoughts passed through a gauntlet of frightening possibilities. Arduous labor? Flagellation? Prison? Exile to the mines of desolation? His hand cut off? His tongue cut out? Burned at the stake? His head on a spike beside his friend's on the King's Road?

Would none of what happened in the valley distract the princeling from immediate vengeance? The painted mare. The mysterious stallion. Rescuing the prince from deadly hooves.

Rusthammer's voice whispered courage. *"Even the darkest night will end and the sun will come again."* The thought gave Qhuin hope. Even in bondage, he clung to a curious sense of freedom. He refused to believe his destiny would forever be defined by Blackthorn, Prince Kadesh-Cor, or the pathetic princeling Sargon.

Qhuin exhaled slowly and closed his eyes. He remembered seeing the prince standing on the high ridge. The memory came with a surge of hope. The prince had been watching!

Surely he knew the truth of what had happened. Surely he would not allow his callow son to mete out punishment so undeserved.

He pulled against the chains, looking around the tree. He was in a copse of gumwood trees and undergrowth that kept him out of sight of the camp. In a clearing beyond, silhouettes of men and horses moved past a fire blazing as high as a man. Three men stopped at the edge of the light. They were faceless black shapes against the flame. One of them pointed. He was short and slight and wore no armor. The other two nodded and looked in Qhuin's direction.

Prince Kadesh-Cor might know the truth, but he was unconscious, and Qhuin's fate was in the hands of his son.

CHAPTER 57

Ashar floated in a dream. He had no sense of falling except for the rush of wind on his face. Even though the river did not appear to be getting closer, he was filled with dread and fought to keep fear away. *Fear and faith cannot abide.* He closed his eyes and cried out to Oum'ilah, the God of gods. "If the kingdom of light is to come again, and if I must do what must be done, thou canst not let me die!" The words rushed from his mind, whirled away in the buffeting winds.

He gripped the satchel and wrapped his fist around the lumpy leather covering the stones. They quivered in his hand. Or was it the wind? *The power over body, mind, and spirit. The elements of the earth, the boundaries of time, and the limits of space.*

A warbling shrill rose up in the whistling of the wind. It grew louder and came closer. Ashar turned his head and his body rolled. The wind fluttered against his back, his face free of the rushing air. He opened his eyes and stared up in surprise and wonder.

A colossal bird dove through the mist of clouds, its wings folded back like a falcon diving for its prey. Ashar had loved to watch the falcons that nested in the temple cliffs, but the winged creature was not a

414

falcon. It was as pure white as the clouds and as big as the dragon that lived in his imagination.

Before Ashar could recover from his bewilderment, the giant bird reached for him with its talons. He tensed against the power of the claws, certain it was his moment of death.

The crushing never came. The talons did not pierce his body or crush his bones. They embraced him like gentle hands with long, curved fingers of whitened bone. The great white bird unfolded its wings, caught the wind, and swooped from a dive into a gentle soaring. The warbling began again.

Ashar wrapped his arms around the talons and found purchase with his feet. It was like flying inside a great cage. *The winged spirit of God is not a spirit at all.*

The Mountain of God was more wondrous than he had imagined.

The bird soared down the north face of the monolith of stone and flew into the sunlight on the east side. It continued downward until they were flying lower than the ridge of the temple. Tendrils of smoke from smoldering fires snaked skyward. Ashar was too low to see from where smoke was coming, but the sight of it rekindled the horrors of the siege.

What if Drakkor finds the stones before I do? He tightened his grip on his satchel of stones. *What if he discovers the hidden location of the Immortal Crown?* Ashar knew where it was, or believed he did. He had seen it in his mind when the Oracle revealed the most perilous secret of all.

The mountain of stone and the buildings of the temple looked different from the air. They were magnificent beyond anything he had imaged. He no longer wondered what this creature was, or by what means he had been spared, or how any of what had happened could be explained. It simply was. The mysteries of the God of gods were not for him to know.

The great winged creature turned toward the mountain. Its feathery wingtips fluttered in the air as it rose on a draft of wind, then soared across a broad shelf jutting from the cliff. The talons opened, and Ashar toppled out.

The landing was a painful tumble on a padding of thick moss. He rolled to a stop and scrambled to his feet. He looked up, but the great bird was gone, leaving behind nothing but a swirl of mist.

It took Ashar a moment to sort out where he was. The great bird or winged spirit or power of the stones had brought him to a place not far from the Tears of God.

He strained his ears for the rattling of armor or footfalls of iron on the trail to the courts of the temple. He heard none, but found little solace. The roar of the waterfall inside the grotto would surely drown out the sound of men approaching.

Ashar found a place to hide in the fall of rock that had sloughed off from the outcrop above. He needed time to think. He was about to take the first step of a journey predestined by the council of the God of gods before the world was. *No, my second step.* He smiled to himself. His first had been into thin air from atop the Mountain of God.

The sound of water made him thirsty. He followed the hand-hewn steps across the slick rock to the Tears of God. He suddenly stopped. The fountain was the only source of water for the temple settlement. It was possible one or more of Drakkor's men was already here.

Trust in the God of gods, and you will be endowed with a force and faculty you cannot comprehend. The Oracle's voice seemed to whisper from the darkness of the grotto.

Ashar took a deep breath and sloshed into the pool. He ducked under the overhanging arch of rock and entered the grotto cave. The ceiling rose into darkness above him, and the falling water echoed like thunder. An army could approach the grotto cave and not be heard. He scooped up water with cupped hands and took a long cool drink. A rock splashed into the water behind him. He was not alone! He pushed himself along the edge. The deep water rose to his waist. He stopped to let his eyes adjust to the darkness and glanced over his shoulder.

A rock slammed into his head. The dull cracking sound was swallowed by a rush of black. Ten thousand tiny prickles of light danced behind his eyes. He crumpled sideways into the pond. The icy water jolted him to consciousness, and he pushed to the surface for a gasp of air. A biting pain erupted on the side of his head.

Celestine huddled in a crevice above the waterline with a rock still in her hand. Her face was smudged and her hair tangled. Her temple gown was ripped, but it glowed white in the light coming through the grotto's entrance. She stepped forward. "Oh! It's you, humble brother!"

Celestine's eyes were wide. She dropped the rock and covered her mouth with both hands.

Ashar could barely hear her over the roar of the waterfall. He pressed his hand to the pain on the side of his head. It came back red. He smiled through the fog of pain. He was so happy to see her. Two strokes put his feet on solid ground near the entrance. Celestine slipped into the water and swam to him.

"Pray, forgive me," she said as she climbed from the pool.

"No need." Ashar smiled. "I am grateful you're alive." He kept his hand pressed to his head to staunch the bleeding.

"How did you know to come here? What happened to—" She stared at the blood seeping between Ashar's fingers. "Are you alright?"

Ashar nodded. "We've much to talk about, but first we must find a way off the mountain."

Celestine followed Ashar from the grotto to where the stairs of mortared stone climbed the terraces of the vineyard. They paused to rest and listened for the sounds of soldiers. Ashar kept his hand to his head.

"I am so very sorry I injured you," Celestine said in a sudden rush of tears.

Ashar nodded. He knew the burst of sorrow was not for him. It was a rush of emotion from being alive. The solace of being rescued. A reprieve from the horror taking place. He hoped that after enduring so much loss and sadness, the tears were for the terror that had gripped the whole of her inner being.

"We'll make it off the mountain," Ashar assured her without the slightest notion of how he could fulfill such a promise or what would come next. His stomach fluttered in her presence in spite of their grim circumstance. "You'll be all right." His words recalled the memory of the first time they had met in this very place so many seasons ago. He had said those words to her when he had lifted her after she had fallen. He remembered the touch of her hand and the feeling it gave him. Did she remember it as well?

"Let me look at it," Celestine said, nodding to the wound on his head. She inhaled deeply and swallowed the last of her sobs. She pulled his hand away from the cut on his head without waiting for permission. She ripped a strip of fabric from her gown and wiped the blood where it had run past his ear. She ripped another and wrapped it around his head. Her gown was thin and soaked through, but she seemed unaware of it. Ashar tried to respect her modesty by only looking at her face.

When she finished wrapping his wound, she asked, "What are we going to do?"

He straightened his shoulders under the weight of the responsibility he now had for this girl. His instinct to help and protect those in need surged through him, but he knew it was more than that. "We must find a way off the mountain," he said. "I think we should hide in the vineyard until dark, then try to get to the road without being seen." He held out his hand, and she took it. The shiver he remembered rippled through him again. "There used to be a trail along the bottom of the old wall on the east side of the court."

He held her hand as they climbed to the first of the terraces. The path followed the undulating contour of the mountain and passed by vines heavy with grapes, the first blush of color kissing the tips of the leaves.

Ashar pulled a cluster of grapes from the vine and offered them to her. "Are you hungry?" The grapes were plump and purple and forbidden. Grapes were for wine, and wine was for rituals, and none but the votaries assigned to the task were allowed to pluck a single grape.

She looked at him as if he had suggested she steal the coins donated to the temple by the pilgrims. Her eyes revealed her hunger, and her finger twitched, but that was all.

"You will need your strength," Ashar said, then opened her hand and filled it with grapes. "The existence we have known has been ripped away. The expectations we have lived with all our lives have changed. Nothing will ever be the same for us again."

Celestine stared at the grapes, and Ashar could sense the conflicts of her conscience.

"The rules and rituals of discipline we have been taught are gone. We must pray to hear the whisperings of the God of gods. We must listen and do what we are told." Looking to the monolith of stone, he added in a whisper, "If the kingdom of light is to come again, we must survive."

Ashar plucked a grape and put it in his mouth. He picked another and held it to her lips.

She opened her mouth slowly, and he placed the grape on her tongue. She closed her eyes. When she opened them again, the sunlight turned her eyes to the color of bluestone. Her smudged face and disheveled hair made her all the more beautiful.

Ashar could not help himself and, for a fleeting instance, failed to avert his eyes from the rest of her beauty.

—–—

Four men came down the trail as the sun was going down.

Ashar and Celestine had climbed to the ninth terrace and found a good place to hide among the grapevines.

They watched through the thicket of leaves as the men came closer. If there were kingsriders among Drakkor's men, these were not they.

Each of the brigands carried a yoke with leather buckets. The rattling of iron made it difficult to understand what they were saying, but the tone of their voices made it clear. They were warriors on kitchen duty and not happy about it.

Ashar and Celestine crouched in the tangled shroud of vines as the men reached the ninth terrace. Ashar wondered if the men could hear the thumping of his heart. He held his breath.

"Hold up!" The largest of the brigands said as he flung the buckets from his shoulders. "I need'a stop for a misher." He unbuttoned his breeches, and took a few steps toward where Ashar and Celestine were hiding.

Celestine trembled under Ashar's arm, her face buried in her hands. Ashar stared at the man who stopped in a place where, with the slightest bob of his head, he would see them for sure.

It seemed like hours but was surely only moments before the man finished with a deep sigh and buttoned up his breeches. He stepped into the vines and plucked a handful of grapes.

"Well, would ya look at this!" he said.

CHAPTER 58

The stallion erupted from the darkness in an explosion of light and flames blew from his nostrils and the sky was on fire and his hooves shattered the rock into a splattering of shining pebbles that were the stars of heaven and his mane and tail were billows of silk that rippled in the wind unfolding as great wings from the stallion's side and the prince was astride and was lifted into the air and he felt the surge of power that rippled from his loins to his head and great crowds of peasants below him cried his name "Kadesh-Cor! Kadesh-Cor!" and their voices were music and he soared above their heads and was lifted into the burning sky and the fire consumed him and he twisted to escape the searing heat on his face and they cried m'lord, m'lord, m'lord—

"M'lord?"

Kadesh-Cor's hand spasmed as he returned to consciousness. His pain pushed through the dulling cloud of cannabis. The prince looked about, his eyes finally coming to rest on the girl who knelt beside him and held his hand, and his agony rushed out in a gasping moan.

The older courtesan hurried from the basin with a freshly moistened cloth.

"Praise be the gods, m'lord," Nimra said, who knelt on his other side.

Kadesh-Cor struggled to sit up. The courtesans moved quickly to arrange large pillows as a backrest. As he settled, Nimra offered him a goblet.

"This will take the pain, m'lord," the squire said. It was red wine heavily laced with cannabis and juice of the poppy.

The prince touched the wad of wool that dressed the wound on his face. Vanity triumphed over pain. "Is it . . ." he began, his expression a pleading question.

"It'll be fine, m'lord," Nimra said with an optimistic smile.

Perhaps he lied. Royal persons did not always want the truth.

"I want to see!" The prince said it in a way that made Nimra and the girls responsible for what had happened to his face. "Fetch me the glass!" He spoke to the older courtesan.

She sprang immediately to action and returned with a looking glass in a hand-carved wooden frame.

The prince moved it closer for a full scrutiny of his wounded face. Once again, he touched the woolen bandage that was wrapped around his ruined face. He pushed gently and winced. The infusion of alcohol and opiates had not had time to work their soothing magic.

"Take the swaddling away," he demanded, but his voice was diminished by uncertainty.

"As you wish, m'lord, but best you let the sewn skin fasten lest it be ripped loose," Nimra said. "Perhaps it would be wise to wait?"

The prince studied Nimra's face. He reached out as if to stroke the squire's face, but his hand faltered and turned into a fist. He thumped the boy's shoulder and moved away.

"It'll be all right, m'lord. The greater your patience the smaller the scar." The squire offered the prince a reassuring smile.

Kadesh-Cor clenched his jaw and discarded the mirror facedown. "Help me up," he said. Nimra and the girls helped him to the opening of the tent. He opened the flap to a narrow crack and peered out. His men were gathered around the fire in excited conversation.

———

"It was Equus!" Horsemaster Raahud's rasping voice burst from the purr of conversations like an explosion of sparks. The name of the mythical horse hung in the air in a void of silence.

"Equus is a legend," Sargon said with a scornful guffaw, "a myth." He tipped his leather flask and let the last swallow fall into his open mouth. He threw the empty flask to a camp gillie. "Bring me another," he demanded.

"Where there is history, there is myth, m'lord, and where there is myth, there is history. It is an old saying, but always proven to be true," Raahud said.

"It's an old wives' tale, and you're an old fool!"

The wine had loosened Sargon's good sense—what little there was of it—and Raahud shook his head. The boisterous antics of a noble were always awkward and discomforting.

"What is Equus?" Baaly asked.

A wave of laughter rippled through the company at his question. Baaly flushed. The gillie returned and gave Sargon a full flask of wine.

"The immortal horse created by the gods. He sired every horse on earth. Don't you know anything?" Sargon mocked. "Of course, there are no gods, so . . ." He raised the flask but missed his mouth, and wine dribbled over his chin.

Raahud had more questions about life than answers, but he was unwilling to condone the princeling's blasphemy against the gods. *Whoever they were and whatever they intended.* "The Princeling Sargon has it mostly right," he said to Baaly, smiling to minimize the princeling's reaction to an opposing opinion. "The story of Equus comes to us from our forebears from the time of the great tower as part of our creation story."

"Creation *myth*," Sargon chortled.

"Some believe it to be more, m'lord. Much more," Raahud said.

Chor moved next to his drunken brother and put a hand on his shoulder. To anyone looking on, it was a brotherly gesture, but Raahud knew the contentions between them and was satisfied the heckling had ended. He turned his attention to the larger group.

"Equus is a legend, some might say a myth, but if that were true, why are there so many stories about him told by so many over countless generations? As a boy, I heard an old man say that Equus lived in the unknown realms of the Oodanga Wilds. Until today I gave the story little mind, but . . ." He raised his eyebrows, unwilling to rule out the possibility the legend was true.

"The Oodanga Wilds lie beyond the Swamps of Dead Men," Baaly said.

"A realm of horrible beasts, behemoths, and dragons," the captain of the kingsriders said.

"And serpents that can swallow a man whole and keep 'em alive in his belly just for spite," another said with a sodden bellow that was clearly intended to mock his fellows.

Algord, son of Gorshon, was a heavyset warrior with a face ruined by fire. The melted flesh had hardened into crusty scars and frozen his expression in a perpetual glower of hate. His left eye peered over a lump of purple flesh. He was the kingsrider appointed by Kublan to look after Sargon, but Raahud suspected that early in the expedition the princeling had twisted Algord's allegiance to his own.

Sargon joined in the rude laughter. "You are all fools," he slurred.

"Perhaps, m'lord," Raahud said. "I was a horsemaster many years before your father brought me to Blackthorn. I have seen much, and I cannot easily explain why, but after what we've seen today, I believe the legend is true."

"Even if the horse we saw was this mythical stallion," Baaly asked, "what difference does it make? We can't go chasing after him across the swamp."

"Boy's right," the captain said. "The few men who've tried to get to the wilds south of the swamp were never heard of again."

Raahud squatted on his haunches and poked the fire with a long stick. Sparks erupted like a thousand fireflies taking flight. The flame reflected in his eyes. "While I lived at the stables of Rockmire Keep with my father, there was man named Kotar, son of Korlsis-Baan of House Murrain. He swore by the gods old and new that Equus was real. He said he knew the fables and folklore of beasts and wild men. He took an army of two hundred men across the swamps to look for Equus in the Oodanga Wilds. He claimed he found the horse, but . . ." Raahud twisted the stick and squinted into the flame. Another storm of fireflies. Most of the men had slowed their breathing to listen.

"But what?" the captain asked.

"Kotar returned a skeletal rag of a man with a fevered mind, mumbling incoherently. A strange state of madness, my father said, and yet . . ." Raahud paused and looked to the tent of the prince. Kadesh-Cor pushed through the flap, his wounded face illuminated by the light of the fire. He listened, his expression intense. Raahud nodded, knowing he was compelled to finish.

"Something horrible had happened to the man. I don't know what. My father said Kotar could never quite explain it, and when he tried, it made no sense. All two hundred of his men were killed, or so he said. I admit it is hard to know whether his recollections were the fables of a feeble mind or the memory of what he actually saw."

Even Sargon leaned forward through the fog of wine with a curious intensity.

"He spoke of ferocious beasts, behemoths, and a savage race of primitive half-men who ate the flesh of humans. My father heard it himself from Kotar's lips, and I heard it from my father."

No one spoke. No one suggested going south. No one talked of crossing the Swamps of Dead Men. The mandate of their expedition was not to risk death for the sake of a horse. A wave of relief rippled over the company.

Horsemaster Raahud sent another explosion of sparks into the night and dropped the stick into the fire as he stood. "I believe the gods created Equus," he said with such confidence no one doubted his words. "A preeminent immortal first horse to sire all the horses of the earth. The great Equus of legend. It is possible the splendid stallion we saw today might be him, but that is not what I meant."

Still no one spoke, but the emotional reaction to his words was as palpable as if the god Zéphuros had buffeted their bodies with a fierce west wind. Sargon inhaled to speak, but Chor put an arm about his shoulder and a hand over his mouth, holding it closed.

"Our stallion. Our Equus," Horsemaster Raahud said, "may not be the immortal sire of legend, but he is an 'Equus' just the same." He spoke the name with a heightened awe that was not missed by the men or the prince. "I believe there is more than one—a great sire appointed by the gods in every age. I believe the great horse we saw today is the Equus of our age."

―――

Kadesh-Cor watched from the opening of the tent and listened with pointed interest. The juice of the poppy flowed in his veins, and the pain was gone. He floated in a blessed euphoria and was consumed by a sudden desire to own the mythical horse.

It is not just a horse. Drifting in the stupor of the opiates, there was no question whether Equus was the sire of all horses, created by the gods. *Some things simply must be.* The thought swirled through the fantasies of his mind. A covetous passion to posses the great horse swelled in his chest.

As the sweet juice enveloped his brain and he sank again to his furs, the vision of his dark dream returned, and he flew into the heavens on the back of the immortal Equus. By the gods, he would have the great horse, even if it meant the death of every man in his company.

"Bring me my sons," he croaked to Nimra.

The squire stared at him longer than a squire should. The corners of his mouth quivered but refused to fall. "Your sons? Yes, m'lord."

CHAPTER 59

Meesha and the Raven followed the keeper of the prison and two of his men from the dungeon in the catacombs to the open yard of the bailey before crossing to the great manse of Stókenhold Fortress, where Tolak and his family lived.

"My brother and I came for the prisoner when we heard he was moved from the cells and thrown into the pit." Meesha glanced over her shoulder at the head jailer with a tiny shrug.

His mouth hung open, his face twisted and incredulous. Meesha knew what he was thinking. How could a prisoner be taken from the deepest levels of the catacombs without being seen?

Meesha took pleasure in the befuddled look on the burly man's face but tried not to show it. Because she and Valnor had spent their childhood exploring the entangled labyrinth of the old Stókenhold Fortress, she knew there were ways in and out of almost everywhere. She would never reveal her secrets.

"He is old and sick," Meesha explained to the Raven as they walked. "He did no wrong."

"No one in prison is ever guilty," the Raven said, his tone mocking.

"He was condemned by the jealousies of the high pontiff. You, who are so close to my grandfather, must surely know the high pontiff fills his ears with flattering words and blinds his eyes to what is right and wrong." She deliberately referred to the king as her grandfather, confident her bloodline gave her a measure of protection.

"You have described the high pontiff perfectly." He smiled, and Meesha had the curious feeling she could trust him.

She distrusted anyone who traveled beneath a banner of the peacock with bloody arrows in its claws, so why she trusted the man with the same bird burned into his chest she wasn't sure. She pushed the feeling away.

"The prisoner had been attacked by bandits on the King's Road and left for dead," Meesha said. "He was taken by pilgrims to a wisewoman in Village Isthmus."

The Raven nodded.

"You know?" She was surprised. "Do you also know he was taken from them in the night and cast into prison without a trial?"

The Raven wrinkled his brow and tilted his head. "What else do you know of him?" he asked.

"My father appealed to the king to undo the injustice and release the prisoner, but his letter was never acknowledged. The accusations of the high pontiff toward the prophet deepened the king's contempt toward my father—toward his own son!" She said it as if expecting the Raven to share her outrage.

The Raven remained silent.

Meesha continued. "The prophet endured the ignominy of prison in spite of being sick and aged. He was moved to the pit because he refused the captain's demand to blaspheme the god of the mountain. He was punished to amuse the keepers and relieve their boredom." She took a deep breath. "When my brother and I learned the poor man had been condemned to the pit, it was enough."

She led the Raven up a dozen stone steps to a small room off the corridor of private chambers on the third level of the manse. The small chamber was where she and Valnor had secreted Sage Granswaan when they took him from the prison. Meesha's governess had nursed the holy man back to modest health and continued to care for him in secret.

The governess was attending to Granswaan when the visitors arrived. She was immediately wary of the arrival of the man wearing the sigil of Kingsgate and moved closer to Granswaan as if to protect him.

"It's all right," Meesha said to the governess as she entered the room. Turning to Granswaan, she said, "This man is an emissary of the king. He has come to grant clemency and pardon. The king has asked that—"

The Raven cut her off and barked an order to the keeper of the prison. "Take the women out of here and guard the door."

"What do you mean? What are you doing? You said—I demand we be allowed to stay—" Meesha and the governess were seized by the keeper of the prison and his men and dragged from the room to the hall.

Two of the jailers blocked the door.

"Step aside," Meesha demanded.

"Don't go getting all red in the face." One of them poked the blemish on her cheek. The other laughed.

Meesha lunged at the man, but her governess grabbed her by the shoulders and ushered her away.

"I betrayed him," Meesha said. "I thought . . . I trusted . . ." she stammered, distraught. "I must make sure he keeps his word."

"You still can." The governess smiled. "I wonder if, perchance, there's a child about who has crawled the vents and passages of this drafty old house?" She raised her eyebrows.

Of course! Meesha and Valnor had played hide-and-seek in the ventilating shafts that brought air from the outside walls to the inner chambers. As a skinny child, she had wriggled through the warren of small passages.

She left the governess and ran to her bedroom, where she kept her sword. Taking the weapon was instinctive. Valnor's training had included long discussions about the psychology of combat. "The blade is a weapon intended to kill. Draw wisely." She gave little thought to the axioms of the warrior. All she was sure about was that from the moment the man with the sigil of King Kublan burned on his chest had stepped through the gate, she had wished for her sword on her hip.

There was a vertical ventilation shaft connecting the main chamber to the ceiling of Sage Granswaan's chamber. Meesha lowered the scabbard by the strap until it rested on the ornamental wrought-iron grate at the bottom of the shaft. The masons had been careless when they laid the stones of the inner passages, and she found good purchase on the irregular edges for her hands and feet. Slipping through the hidden passages had been much easier as a little girl, but Meesha was still lithe and flexible. When she reached the grate above the room, she twisted herself in an awkward crouch so she could see into the chamber below.

Meesha watched and listened from her hiding place. Neither the holy man nor the Raven to the King knew she was near. She would make sure the Raven kept his promise.

— —

"I do not speak of sacred things," Blessed Sage Granswaan said. He sat by the window in the warmth of the sunshine with a woolen shawl around his shoulders. The light ignited his white hair with a glorious halo.

"I can either grant you freedom or throw you back into the pit," the Raven said. "Do you understand?"

Granswaan merely looked at the emissary of the king and smiled.

"Tell me what I want to know, and you shall be free to the end of your days." The promise hung in the silence. "Your life is in my hand." He balled his fingers into a fist to punctuate his threat.

"Only the life of this old body. What then?" Granswaan coughed. "Would you be so kind as to get me some water? There on the stand. My legs trouble me."

The Raven flushed, his body tensing with impatience, but he crossed the bedroom chamber to fill a cup with water. He returned and gave it to the prophet.

"Thank you," Granswaan said and took a long sip. "You are most kind."

"The stones of light?" the Raven asked as he settled again. "It is important to the king you tell me all you know of them—where they can be found."

The old man gripped his cup with both hands and took another sip of water.

Meesha shifted her position. The tip of the scabbard poked through an opening in the grate. She pulled it back with a dull clunk.

The Raven glanced up, but only for an instant. He hadn't seen her. "The woman at Village Isthmus—the one who cared for you. She said you spoke of these magic stones in your delirium, and now you will speak of them to me." The Raven's face was flushed. His patience was growing thin.

Sage Granswaan smiled softly and shook his head, but said nothing.

"You told the woman whoever possesses the stones can live forever," the Raven repeated. "Is it true?" He drummed his fingers. "By what magic?" He stood up and loomed over the old man. "Speak to me, old fool! 'Touched by the finger of God'? What manner of riddle is this?"

The Raven gripped Granswaan by his blouse and wrenched him from his chair. He lifted him until their faces nearly touched. "In the name of the king, I command you to tell me where they are and how the king may possess them. Are they hidden? Tell me! Are they in the temple on the Mountain of God?"

The weathered old face twitched. His eyes darted away. Had he involuntarily revealed the hiding place of the stones? Meesha saw the subtle changes on his face and wondered if the Raven had seen them as well.

"Tell me," the Raven implored. "Let me set you free."

"By my sacred oath, I cannot," the old sage said, his voice both weak and strong. "Even if I were not so bound, I still would not, but this much you may tell your king. The light of the stones comes from the finger of God, and the power of endless life only to righteous purpose. There are those appointed to keep them from being gathered in the hand of evil."

The Raven shoved him back into his chair, and in a blink his dagger was pointed at the old man's eye.

"Are you so stupid to think I do not have ways to make you tell me what I want to know? I will push this blade into your eye, then cut off your ears and then your nose. I can carve you into tiny pieces while keeping you alive. Be sure, old man, that I can make you tell me what I want to know. I can save them the trouble of dragging you back to the pit. Tell me now, for when my count reaches three, your eye will be gone."

"One!" He gripped a fistful of Granswaan's hair and tightened his hold on the blade. "Two!" The tip drew blood from the lower fold of the prophet's eyelid. Three never came.

Instead, a screaming wraith of fury crashed from the ceiling. The wrought-iron grate clanked loudly on the floor and Meesha flew down like a winged raptor set for the kill. Her sword was in her hand.

The Raven ducked and whirled back and away, loosening his grip on the old man. His eyes were wide and his face frozen in surprise.

Meesha had landed in a swordsman's stance, prepared to lunge with her blade extended. "Get away from him," she demanded.

The Raven's face twisted from shock to mocking disbelief as his confusion cleared. "By the gods, what is this? A girl who plays with swords?" He laughed.

"You are finished here, m'lord. Pray, leave us now." Meesha circled to her left to stand squarely between the Raven and the old man.

The Raven laughed again, a guttural growl polluted with evil intent. He moved his dagger to his left hand and drew his sword. "Put your toy away, girl. Do not make me kill the granddaughter of the king."

Meesha's heart pounded. Would her kinship to the king not protect her? She was suddenly aware of the delicate necklace about her neck. It was one of the few token gifts from the king she had not given to servants or girls in the village. The tiny pearl set in silver hung like a heavy stone. She took a deep breath and stiffened her resolve.

Valnor's reassuring voice was in her head. *Read reactions. Watch for movement and foreshadowing of action. Be on the defensive.* A strange calm came over her even as an icy shiver made her tremble.

She had sparred with Valnor hundreds of times, but she had never imagined she would actually face a man with a sword in his hand willing to kill her. Never in her wildest imaginings had she ever faced a man with the sigil of the king burned into his flesh.

"Leave!" Meesha said to the Raven.

"Please," Granswaan added, "there is nothing you want that I can give you."

"Leave!" Meesha said again and ground her jaw shut.

The Raven nodded and turned slightly as if following her demands, but his feigned retreat became a sudden lunge, a deadly thrust of his blade aimed at her heart. His move was lightning fast, but it was an old trick, and Meesha saw it coming. She parried the ploy as calmly as clouds drifting across a summer sky. Her body moved with grace, even though her mind was screaming. *He intends to kill me!*

She swept her sword upward and caught the inside of his blade as if to parry it away. She also knew some tricks. She took a step closer and pushed her sword straight, taking the Raven's blade with her. With their blades still touching, she whirled her wrist and wrapped his blade, then thrust her tip in a sudden, swift movement to the outside of his blade and down. She waited for the fleeting second of advantage she knew would come, and when it did, she was ready.

She jerked both swords toward her with all her power. The Raven stumbled awkwardly forward as his sword was jerked from his hand, pommel-over-point, and rattled to the floor.

Raven caught himself and whirled toward her with his dagger extended. When his back slammed into the stone pillar, his body turned rigid.

Meesha pressed the tip of her blade against the hollow of his neck, drawing a trickle of blood.

"Are you fool enough to kill an emissary of the king?" His show of confidence faltered.

Granswaan stumbled from the chair and moved toward her from across the room.

Meesha stood fast and swallowed hard. Her mind dashed like a dog hungry for a bone. She had kicked through the grate in a rage of blind instinct when she saw the dagger at the old man's eye. She had had no choice, but neither did she have a plan.

"Probably," she said, then nodded. "I am."

"Withdraw your blade!" The Raven scowled. "I demand it in the name of the king!"

Meesha heart thudded in her ears. "Throw the dagger away!"

"You are not going to kill me."

She pushed the blade forward. More blood trickled into the ragged ridges of his scars.

"You're trembling," the Raven mocked. "You haven't the courage to take a life." He dropped his dagger.

Granswaan moved forward cautiously and picked it up with two fingers like something dead and foul.

"Because the king's blood flows in your veins, I will overlook your stupidity, but *only* if you withdraw your sword at once."

Meesha tightened her grip, and the tip of the blade sharpened its bite.

"If I call for the keepers, your life is over," he warned.

The keepers! Of course. The idea came in a flash of light. She slowed her breathing and her heart as the thought took shape. A smile found its way to her lips. Her nemesis had given her the next move. She pulled her blouse loose and ripped it from her shoulder as far down as she dared.

"Help!" Meesha screamed. "Keepers of the prison! Help me!" The keepers burst through the door. "This man is not Raven to the King!" Her eyes flitted from the keepers to the man at the point of her sword. "He is a rogue and a thief, and he attacked me . . ." She clutched her bare shoulder and offered a helpless sob.

The keepers reached the conclusion she'd hoped for, and their faces turned cold.

By the time the startled Raven framed his words, he looked very guilty indeed. "She lies! Look, look, I wear the authentic sigil of the king." He waved his double-fingered ring.

Meesha laughed. "A perfect forgery! He fooled me as well."

The Raven moved his hand toward his shirt as if to loosen it and expose the branding, but Meesha stopped him with the pressure of her blade.

"Ah, ah," she said and then ripped his shirt open herself. "And look. You see why I was fooled? Who could imagine a rogue clever enough to brand himself, though you can see it was poorly done."

"Don't listen to her, you fools! Seize her!"

The keepers of the prison flitted their eyes from one to the other. They favored the girl with the torn blouse and exposed soft, white skin.

"He tried to have his way with me." She choked back a sob in a performance worthy of a place with the troupe of actors who came in summer. "Had it not been for you . . ." She blushed and lifted the torn sleeve of her blouse to cover her bare shoulder.

"You fools!" the Raven screamed at the keepers.

"They are not fools! They are constant and courageous and loyal to his greatness, King Kublan, and he will reward them handsomely for saving the honor of his only granddaughter!" She pursed her lips and nodded gratitude toward the keepers. "I shall see to it."

"Stop this madness," the Raven cried. "Can't you see what—"

The blade went deeper.

"Whoever you are," Meesha said, narrowing her eyes at the Raven, "you are a fool to think you can deceive men of such valor and intelligence."

The keepers straightened their spines, accepting the heroic image of themselves that Meesha had given them. They crossed the invisible line she had drawn on the stones and turned their weapons on the Raven.

"Bind his hands and feet," she said. "Strip him of his two-fingered forgery and other emblems of the king. Tie him to his horse and take him as far as the King's Road, then slap the horse and send him north."

"Should the scoundrel not be put in prison, m'lady?" the ranking keeper asked.

"In time perhaps, but for now let him be an example to other rogues and bandits who so blatantly defy the king, and who would . . ." She fluttered her eyes at the keepers and blushed.

Meesha watched as the keepers bound the Raven hand and foot and stripped him of his royal garments. "The two of you may keep the raiment. It shall be our secret. I shall keep the ring as a reminder of your valor." Meesha smiled. "Best we not let your good captain know any of this."

"You are a dead woman," the Raven snapped.

"On the contrary, I am very much alive, besides which, I am generous and modest. I have left you with your breeches." It was true. He remained decent enough, but without the slightest semblance of his royal status, other than the lumpy scar on his chest, which was now stained with blood.

— – —

Meesha stood at the gate as the keepers tied the Raven on his horse.

"You are a witchchild," he spat. "You shall not escape punishment for this treachery."

"Is treachery the word you would choose for me? Is it treachery to challenge a man who would push a dagger into an old man's eye in the name of the king? An old man condemned to the horrors of the pit for nothing more than speaking of his god to bystanders in the marketplace?"

"By the gods, blood of the king or not, I shall see your head and ugly red face on a spike."

Of all the insults Meesha had endured for the blemish on her face, the Raven's words bothered her the least. She walked to him and gestured for him to lean down. She spoke softly so that none but he could hear. "I shall not speak of this to my grandfather. And you, m'lord Raven, would be wise to likewise hold your silence. Troubling rumors, once released, are not easily recalled." She let the thought hang in the air, then turned to the keepers, who glowered at the Raven, their faces flush with self-righteous triumph. "It is true there is contention between my father and the king, but you make a grave mistake to think my grandfather does not cherish his only granddaughter and prize her virtue."

Meesha stepped away and turned to cross the open court. She smiled in genuine appreciation as she passed the keepers. The younger of the two leaped forward with a holler and slapped the Raven's horse across the rump. The animal erupted in a gallop, racing for the gate and the King's Road.

Meesha did not look back but could see him in her mind's eye as the sound of the horse's hooves faded, and she mentally followed him to where the road dipped into the hollow.

As she recovered from the fright of the ordeal, another image came into her head. She stopped and turned, but there was no one there and nothing to see, but for reasons she didn't understand, she felt a sudden longing for the bondsman she had kissed in the moonlight.

CHAPTER 60

Qhuin twisted around the trunk of the tree as far as the chains allowed. The pain was still there but lessened by the numbness creeping into his arms and hands. By pulling against the shackles, he could see the camp in the clearing beyond the edge of the trees.

Horsemaster Raahud was a silhouette against the fire, his back to the woods. He was too far away for Qhuin to hear what he was saying or the murmured conversations of the men gathered around him. With a tiny burst of optimism, he imagined Horsemaster Raahud was either arguing for his release or pleading with the princeling not to kill the prisoner tonight.

———

That had been hours ago, and he was still alive. *Horsemaster Raahud was successful.* The thought gave him hope. The camp was settled for the night. The royals and guests had gone to tent. The gillies, drivers, and servants were camped a respectful distance away. The Huszárs and kingsriders each had their own encampments.

The only movement came from the kingsriders on the night watch.

Two of them sat by the dying fire, the glow of orange embers reflected in their armor. The other two men circled the perimeter of the tents in opposite directions. They both carried axes.

The shorter kingsrider let his weapon hang like an extension of his arm. The other had a sparth ax with the long haft balanced on his shoulder. The broad blade rested against the nape of his neck, which was protected by a curtain of mail that hung from the bottom of his helm.

A gibbous moon hovered behind a mass of clouds blowing west. Moonlight swept across the Tallgrass Prairie in sporadic swaths of light until the sky closed with a pounding of thunder and the earth went dark.

Qhuin slumped forward in exhaustion, but could not sleep. The thunder rumbled closer, and the rush of wind pushed before the storm pelted him with grit. The numbness in his arms and hands worried him. He pressed his back against the tree and wriggled his fingers in search of feeling. The motion caused his shoulders to cramp. His mouth was dry, and the knot of anxiety in his gut was heightened by pangs of hunger. He had not had food or water since the early hours before the chase of the tarpans began.

A jagged bolt of lightning made ghastly phantoms of the tangled limbs above his head. The explosion of thunder was so close it shook the ground. The cold rain came in a torrent, and he was drenched before a hundred beatings of his heart. A shiver shuddered through him, and with it an unreasonable surge of optimism.

He pushed hard with his legs and jammed his back into the tree, lessening the pressure on his raw wrists. He twisted his hands and wriggled his fingers. The odd sensation of dead appendages was replaced by a prickling rush of blood. Like a glove of thorns being ripped away, the tiny spikes of pain were replaced by a welcomed tingling as feeling came again. He felt the warmth of blood flowing from his wrists and dripping from his fingers.

An explosion of light and a shock wave of thunder came at once. The trunk of a nearby koompassia tree split and burst into flame.

Something moved in the flickering light. Qhuin saw it at the corner of his eye. The sounds it made were covered by the rain pelting down on the broad leaves of the tree. Qhuin stiffened every muscle and held perfectly still. The menagerie of creatures from folktales of the southern wilderness skulked from the shadows of his mind. He struggled to push his fears aside.

He squinted into the darkness without seeing. He strained to separate the alien sounds he heard from the racket of the rain. It was guttural and muffled like the grunt of a wild boar rooting up a storm of muck with tusks and snout.

Lightning flashed, and he twisted against the chains. Whatever it was, it moved again at the edge of his vision. His view was limited, but the sputtering fire of the nearby tree cast an eerie light. He got only a glimpse, but it was enough to ram a spike of fear into his chest. Whatever it was, there were two of them, and they were big.

The sounds grew louder. Footfalls in the layers of rotted leaves. The sour stench of overturned humus mingled with the scent of rain. Or was the rotted smell from whatever lurked in the darkness?

Qhuin was blinded by another flash of lightning and squinted against the blackness. He shook his head and fluttered his eyes to clear the rain away. The creatures were dark shapes moving in dark shadows. They circled right, then turned toward him—two bristled humps skulking closer.

The lightning came again. The shimmer of light lingered in the clouds, and he saw the beasts clearly. One was a few strides away. The other was closer. It was an ugly creature with red mucus oozing from its long nose and quivering nostrils sniffing at its prey. Its eyes were black holes surrounded by a web of blood. Long yellow teeth thrust up from the lower jaw and protruded from its snarling upper lip.

Wet hair clung to its body like the skin of a reptile. The animal was bigger than a full-grown Alaunt and twice as long.

The fetid stench came from them, and the rain only added to the stink of wet fur. The giant carnivorous rats of the Tallgrass Prairie had followed them to camp. The shimmering of sheet lightning ended. The rats disappeared in the darkness.

Qhuin squeezed his eyes tight to adjust to the loss of light, but he dared not leave them closed.

With a wet smack, the putrid slime of the rat's nose pushed into Qhuin's face. It stank of rotted fish or feces or something worse he didn't recognize. Bile erupted in his throat. He jerked back, slamming his head into the rough bark with such force that he suffered a rush of blackness. He shook the fog away and kicked at the animal with his shackled legs. His feet struck a glancing blow off its head. It shrieked in anger. His second kick was double boots to the chest, and the rat tumbled away.

Qhuin kicked again into the darkness where the giant rodent had been. He was breathing hard. The muscles of his legs were on fire. With every thrust of his legs, the shackles rubbed more flesh from his wrists. The rain poured over his face, making it almost impossible to see, but there was nothing to look at in the blackness. The latent image of the hideous flesh-eating rat glowed at the back of his eye. His kicking continued.

Another shimmer of lightning irradiated the battleground. The closer of the two giant rats weaved its head from side to side. The mucus of its nose was red with blood that gushed from a flap of flesh where its fang had broken off. Qhuin's kicks had done the damage. Its bulging eyes never wavered.

As darkness came again, Qhuin realized the rain had slowed and wondered if the second rat was gone . . .

It felt as if a rusty nail had been plunged into his hand. The giant rat's teeth pierced his bloodied flesh. Drawn by the scent of Qhuin's blood, the first rat had circled the tree.

Qhuin jerked his hand from the creature's mouth and writhed against the chain. He opened and closed his fingers as violently as he could in a desperate effort to frighten it away.

"Get away!" Qhuin growled. "Get away!"

Driven to a frenzy by the taste of blood, the rat bit Qhuin's other hand. It clenched its jaw and twisted its head. Qhuin shook his hand as madly as he could.

A shaft of moonlight burst through the tumult of clouds and fell into the woods. The broken blue light enabled him to see, but the chains would not allow him to escape.

The realization of what was happening enveloped him in a deluge of horror. He flung his leg backward around the tree as far as he could. He had to get the monster off his hand. Pain clawed the muscles of his leg as he stretched them beyond their limit.

In the moment of distraction, the bigger rat attacked from the front, aiming for his throat with its fangs.

Qhuin whirled back and ducked his head. One fang sank into the leather shoulder yoke. Another other dug into his neck. But the stub of the broken tooth and ragged wad of bloodied flesh didn't break his skin.

It was a small victory. The other rat still gnawed on his hand. The only thing saving it was the iron shackle and the wrap of chain.

The big rat wriggled itself free and clenched Qhuin's head with a clawed front foot and lunged for the other side of his neck. The putrid fang poised to puncture the artery in Qhuin's neck would have ended his life except . . .

There was a tiny rush of wind as the point of an iron arrow found its mark.

The arrow struck the giant rat in front of its ear. The point pierced its brain and ripped half its head away when it exited the other side. The impact rolled the creature away from Qhuin. It was stone dead with hardly a quiver.

Before he understood what had happened, a second thud and rush of air sounded from behind the tree, and the pressure of the jaws on his hand vanished. Qhuin twisted in the direction of the camp.

The bowman stood at the edge of the woods, his face in deep shadow, his body a silhouette. Dark clouds rolled away, and moonlight drenched the fabric of the tents behind him.

The night was perfectly still. The only sound was the melodic noise of droplets falling from leaf and branch into shallow pools of rain. The arrow had ended the deafening noise that Qhuin now realized was only in his head. Qhuin could not imagine who dared defy Princeling Sargon's orders that none go near the prisoner. He squinted against the darkness but could not see the bowman's face.

The archer nodded graciously, then, shouldering his bow, turned and walked toward the sleeping camp. He walked with a hobbling gait on the side of his ruined foot.

CHAPTER 61

"Horkus!" the kingsrider shouted to his companion. "Come lookit what I found." He bit into his handful of grapes, then cast them aside and took out his sword.

Ashar sat in the huddle of leaves with both arms wrapped around Celestine. He dared not breathe. He had a blurry view of the kingsriders through the patch of leaves.

The other kingsrider came for a look without removing his yoke.

"Ya ever see one like that?" the first man asked. He reached his sword into the vines and lifted a green snake across the blade. It was hardly the length of a man's arm and not very thick. It coiled around the blade with unblinking eyes and a flicking, forked tongue.

Horkus stepped back. "That one can kill you 'fore you can say 'Kiss the king's arse.' Kill it!"

The kingsrider flipped the deadly snake to the ground and slashed at the head, but he missed and the snake darted into the vines.

They laughed and turned back to the path.

The snake froze in the shadows broken by a patch of green the color of its squamous skin, then crawled across the stark white skin of the girl's leg.

"Don't move," Ashar whispered in Celestine's ear.

She might have screamed, but Ashar put his hand over her mouth. They watched in breathless terror as the deadly creature slithered up her leg and across her lap. It paused to taste the air with its flickering tongue.

Ashar glanced at the kingsmen. The bigger of the two settled the yoke and adjusted the buckets, and then followed the other kingsriders headed down the trail for water. The snake crawled away.

It was hours before Ashar and Celestine dared to move.

———

Beyond the Narrows, beyond Leviathan Deeps, beyond Stone Island at the edge of the great sea, the moon rose cold and gray. The light was faint but bright enough for Ashar and Celestine to escape— or for bandits and kingsriders to see them.

They waited as long as they dared, then ascended the broad stone steps from the last of the terraces to the central courtyard. They crouched beside the east wall that ran the length of the outer court and found a place to hide.

The wall was overgrown with climbing weeds and brush on either side of the gate but offered little in the way of concealment. It was built a century before when two celebrants fell from the open court during the festival of Yasribsóg. Their bodies were never found, and some believed their spirits walked the wall on moonless nights.

Ashar knew the local lore, but gave the spirits of the wall no thought. Every wall and building, monument and tower, and even misshapen stones had been given a place in folklore. Hauntings by the spirits of the dead were always the most engaging tales, and Ashar knew them all. The complex of the temple and settlement of priests was the world of the postulants, and boys with fine imaginations made the most of it.

Ashar shuddered as the reality of the past days finally settled over him. *The world I knew has ended in violence. A thousand years of peaceful worship on the Mountain of God—ended with the single sweep of an assassin's blade. An assassin against whom I am now pitted in a race to find the stones of light, lest the world be plunged into darkness and immortal evil reigns for ever.* The thoughts filled Ashar's head like hornets knocked from their nest.

He rose slowly and peered over the wall. A fire burned near the obelisk at the center of the outer court. Four men sat at the fire, roasting a dog on a makeshift spit. They passed around a goatskin flask.

From the boisterous tone of their laughter and vulgar speech, Ashar surmised the desecrators imbibed more than wine. Two of them looked more like men who might ride under the banner of the king, but if they'd once been kingsriders, they were bandits now.

A sudden gust of wind turned the smoke, and three of the men stumbled back, choking and cursing. The windstorm grew stronger, and the flames blew sideways in a flurry of embers and soot. The men scrambled to contain the blaze and braced themselves against the power of the gale. The storm continued to rise, and the roar of it drowned out the men's voices. Ashar had never experienced such fierce winds on the mountain.

From where Ashar and Celestine were hiding, the only path to safety was the stairs at the south end of the outer court. If the brigands remained camped in the courtyard throughout the night, escape would be impossible. Come dawn, Ashar and Celestine would have to retreat to their hiding place among the grapes. Among the snakes.

Ashar dropped back and settled against the wall. Celestine's hair was blown and tangled across her face. Her skin glowed in the moonlight. Her eyes were wide and expectant. Fearful. Ashar offered a reassuring smile and took her hand. He whispered loudly in order to be heard above the roar of the wind. "As soon as they leave, we will go," he said. "We are going to be all right." He squeezed her hand, and she smiled. With his other hand, he clutched the mysterious stones in the leather satchel.

— • —

Three hours passed. Ashar watched from where he and Celestine remained hidden by the wall. The men did not leave. Two had wandered away, but the others remained and were huddled now against the wind.

Perhaps they can't leave. The thought came in a jolt of realization. *They guard the entrance to where the others sleep and will stay the night.*

Ashar appreciated the unrelenting fierceness of the wind. He could see from the posture and actions of the guardsmen, they were unnerved by the strange tempest. Their fire had blown out. They huddled with their backs to the wind and hardly glanced around.

The temple kept no men-at-arms. Ashar was certain that whoever had not been killed had been herded away and put under guard. *What of the other virgins of the temple?* He glanced at Celestine, hoping for her sake that her sisters were still alive.

The windstorm drove patches of dark clouds across the sky. Moonlight chased shadows across the outer court. Celestine was curled up and trembling in the cold. She had fallen into restless sleep, her face drawn tight. Ashar knew they could wait no longer.

He awakened Celestine with a gentle hand on her shoulder and a finger to his lips. Though the howling wind would cover any sound, he took no chances. He pointed to the moon. As a tumult of clouds shrouded the light, Ashar lifted her to her feet and scrambled over the wall. With a firm grip hand in hand, they ran south along the inside of the wall.

Running in shadows gave them an advantage, but the darkness made them blind. Irregular blasts of wind made running perilous. Ashar kept one hand on the capstone of the wall as a guide and ran in a low crouch. Celestine remained straight and fairly floated over the stones of the court as if carried by the mystical wind. He knew it was movement that would catch the eye of the night watch, not the height of the couple fleeing the compound, but still he worried.

The swirling darkness of the cloud covering the moon was thin and brief, and when it passed, the court was awash in pale blue light. Ashar stopped and pulled Celestine down beside him. They crouched beside a decorative stone post that supported the wall. With no thought of propriety, he put his arm around her, and she huddled against him like a trembling chick beneath its mother's wing.

Celestine stared at Ashar. Ashar stared at the moon, the clouds all blown past. The sky was clear, and the orb of night hung in a vast black sea of stars. *The moon has never been so bright nor the winds so fierce.* Ashar was sure of it.

He felt exposed and moved cautiously until he could see the men of the night watch. One of them rose from the huddle and took shelter behind a pillar. Another man stood, then squatted, his back to the wind.

Leave! Move! Take shelter! Ashar willed the men to leave their post. The stairs at the south end of the court were less than a stone's throw away. If they could make it to the bottom of the steps, they would be at the labyrinth of passageways in the oldest part of the ancient citadel. It was a risk, but even if they were seen on their dash to the stairs, they could disappear in the warren of alleyways and reach the old road.

Unless . . . Ashar looked back.

Three of the men were up and braced against the wind as they hurried for shelter under the archway at the top of the stairs. Two of the men carried short bows with a quiver of arrows slung over their shoulders. A chill went through him. If the men got to the arch before they got to the stairs, there was no way they could escape. A person running to the stairs would be an easy shot for a seasoned archer who could take a bird from the air.

Ashar was suddenly grateful for the raging wind that would make hitting a running target significantly more difficult.

"We must run very fast," Ashar whispered close to Celestine's ear. He could feel her searching his face. The trembling was gone, her fear replaced by trust. "Are you able?" She nodded.

Ashar clutched the satchel of stones and lifted Celestine to her feet. They sprinted for the opening in the south wall. As they raced across the open court, he glanced back, even at the risk of losing his footing on the uneven stones. The men were shielding their faces against the wind. The stairs were awash in moonlight.

"Glosno!" The name was yelled so loudly it struck Ashar like a bolt.

A man ran at them from his post at the bottom of the stairs, his armor rattling.

Glosno leveled the blade of his pike at Ashar and Celestine.

An archer sprinted across the court behind them.

There was no going back. They were trapped on the stairs.

Ashar grabbed Celestine's hand and ran left along the length of the broad middle step. The raging wind slowed them as if giant stones were chained around their feet.

Kingsriders chased after them, shouting for them to stand fast, but their voices were lost in the deafening wind. They moved swiftly despite their armor. Glosno was catching up.

The step ended at a wide balustrade that ran the length of the stairs on a rank of ornamental balusters. The drop on the other side was a steep slope of rock with no place to land. There was no way to jump.

For an instant, he was falling free through the clouds from the Mountain of God.

Ashar moved when the impulse came and whirled toward the charging kingsriders.

The move saved his life. The fletching of the arrow brushed his neck as it passed. The archer at the top of the stairs nocked a second shaft. He had measured the drift of the wind and would not miss again. The moon cast him in an eerie rim of blue as if he was a spirit of the dead who haunted the wall.

Ashar swept Celestine from her feet and sat her on the balustrade. It was polished granite, steep and as slick as ice on a winter pond. In the blink it took Ashar to leap onto the balustrade behind her, Celestine was already sliding down with arms and legs flailing. It was a long ride to the bottom, and they flew as if shot from a sling.

Celestine used her legs to cushion the collision with the ornate carvings of the newel post, and Ashar cushioned his landing with her. They rolled to the outside of the balustrade in an awkwardly intimate tangling of arms and legs . . . and faces. Ashar had never been so close to a girl's body. She was under his arm, and they were tumbling one over the other. They were wrapped in each other's arms, and the fluttering in his belly made him feel as if there was nothing in the world but this moment.

Glosno changed that. He was closing in. He bounded the last few strides as they scrambled to their feet. He raised his pike to strike and . . . disappeared!

The body of the archer catapulted down the stairs in a violent tumble and crashed into Glosno. The two men were swept so suddenly from Ashar and Celestine's view it was as if they vanished in a magic spell. It was bewildering, but there was no time to solve the mystery. Another kingsrider was only a few steps above.

"Run!" Ashar yelled, pulling Celestine to her feet and heading for the warren of passages. She took one step and fell.

"My ankle," she cried and gripped it with both hands. It was already starting to swell.

We are finished. The ugly thought slapped Ashar in the face. *How can that be?*

At that moment another kingsrider flew over the balustrade and crashed into a stone wall with a clattering of iron and cracking of bones, then crumpled to a heap and lay still.

How can a man in heavy armor jump so high and fly so far . . . and into the wind? Ashar wondered for only an instant before he understood. The man was not flying by his own power—he had been thrown.

An enormous man leaped over the railing behind him, reaching them in a single stride.

"Rorekk!"

The giant smiled. His tunic was ripped and bloody and flapped madly in the wind. His chest was bare except for the leather strap from the large bag slung over his shoulder. His body was scarred by numerous wounds. Most were a crust of blackened scabs but some were red and wet. His surging muscles glistened with blood and sweat.

By what miracle had he escaped the mountain? The wondrous thought came to Ashar in a rushing assurance of destiny.

"Sentos et ice'orp da naidraug ruoy eb lliwon." Rorekk's voice roared louder than the wind. Eager to be understood, he scrunched his brow, searching for the few words he knew of Ashar's language and used his hands to speak. He tapped his fist across his heart, touched Ashar on the head, and pointed to the stones. "Rorekk, lliwon. Protector! You. Sentos et Oum'ilah. Stones of God."

"You are the protector of the stones?" Ashar thought he understood.

Rorekk shook his head and touched Ashar's head again. "Ashar lliwon sentos et Oum'ilah. Rorekk lliwon Ashar."

Ashar is protector of the Stones of God. Rorekk is the protector of Ashar!

Ashar realized he had understood the strange words of the giant's tongue. *"A force and faculty you cannot comprehend."* That's what the Oracle promised. He hammered his chest with his fist without knowing why.

The rattling of iron and shouting of men at the top of the stairs was added to the roar of the tempest.

"We must go!" Ashar said.

Without word or warning, the giant scooped Ashar and Celestine onto his back and tugged their arms around his neck. He held them there with one of his great hands and bounded into the night.

———

The archer climbed slowly to his feet. He reached for his bow, but his arm was twisted and his fingers were broken. He groaned with pain.

The kingsrider beneath him was a heartbeat from death. He gripped the archer with a desperate fist. Blood spilled from his lips as he stammered, "The boy . . . with the stones. Tell Drakkor!" They were the last words the man ever spoke.

The archer pushed the dead man's hand away and started the long climb back up the stairs, dragging a broken leg behind him.

And the pelting hail began.

451

CHAPTER 62

Kingsrider Captain Ilióss Machous watched from the shadows of thick timber on a ridge above the river. Nine horses stood knee-deep in the shallow water at the edge of the river, their muzzles submerged. A froth of lathered sweat smeared their dusty hides. They had been ridden hard. Seven of the nine horsemen were on their bellies with their faces in the water. The other two had quenched their thirst and were filling goatskin flasks.

Machous's promise to the king sounded in his head. *I will savor the stench of his blood when it flows from his neck and soaks into the dirt.* He could not return to Kingsgate without the head of Drakkor. *Nor will I!* The surge of will brought new resolve, but the men at the river's edge were not who he expected.

"There are only nine of them!" Machous scolded the young officer who sat astride a short-legged horse beside him.

"The informant at the tavern told us there were fifty." The man blanched at his misjudgment.

The sun had fallen behind the Mountains of Mordan. In the dusky light, and at the distance, it was difficult to identify the men at the river by their dress or weapons. They were clad in an odd mix of leather and cloth, and all of them were armed. Iron armor was tied to the saddles.

Stolen? Machous wondered.

The men did not appear to be bandits, at least not by any description given of the brigands he had heard. *Could they be soldiers from the secret militias of the great houses?* Private armies were forbidden by the king, but everyone knew they existed. *Why are they here? And why on the run?*

Machous exhaled his irritation over the wasted days, but it was not the first time he had followed the wrong trail. Getting lost on a wild pig chase was inevitable when searching for a man as clever and ruthless as Drakkor.

Machous had heard the report of Drakkor's horrific attack on the temple of Oum'ilah. A pilgrim had sworn that Drakkor's army had taken it as a stronghold, but the pilgrim had been wrong.

The temple was abandoned when Machous and his men arrived. The holy places had been ransacked and defaced, but the massive walls that had stood a thousand years were unchanged. There were no people on the mountain except for a few old men, a huddle of refugees, and pilgrims who had come to bury the dead. The crawling green of living things had already begun to creep through the cracks between the stones.

There was an outrageous rumor that Drakkor and his bandits had been driven out by an infestation of wild bees. Machous found the story more humorous than plausible. If Drakkor left the mountain stronghold, it was not because of bees. More likely, the bandit king had heard that a king's commander, renowned for his courage, was looking for him with a double march of kingsriders, and he was afraid.

Machous had no illusion that Drakkor did not know he was coming. It was not possible for an army of kingsriders to move without tongues wagging in every tavern, town, and market from the boroughs of Wug to the caves of Aktodas. Drakkor was no fool. Clearly he was ill-prepared to meet such a formidable force, and he had fled in order to take the inevitable fight to a place of his choosing.

A wild pig chase. Machous shook his head. How much time had they wasted in their cautious ascent to the temple of Oum'ilah? No matter. Relentless pursuit was the way of the warrior, and he knew he would find Drakkor.

The men at the river must be an advance scouting party. Even the cleverest of men could not move with an army of mercenaries and traitors without leaving a wide swath of evidence and rumors behind. Somewhere there was someone who knew where Drakkor and his army were. When they'd passed. The direction they were traveling. Where they camped. The location of their hiding place.

Where was the person who knew? The informant who would tell? Was it the man huddled in the dark corner of the tavern? The wench looking for some extra coin? A village blacksmith constrained to shoe their horses? The farmer in the field, or the peasant on the road, or the merchant awakened in the night to fill their flasks and baskets?

Even if he found an informant, Machous knew he would still have to make him talk. Few of the lowborn and oppressed trusted a kings-rider captain bearing the sigil of Kublan. To many of them, Drakkor was a hero. Anyone, however villainous, with the courage to defy the tyranny of kings was a champion of the common folk.

Machous left no stone unturned or rumor unexplored. Mistaken information, ignorant peasants, and brazen lies were unavoidable, but they only needed one person who knew. Loyalty was more like the sands of the desert than the rocks of the mountain. It drifted in the wind and wrapped itself about whichever boot trod upon it.

Machous also knew that secrets were hardest kept when a man's head was soaked with ale, so he had given his men leave to frequent the bawdy houses, inns, and taverns in search of the one who knew and would tell. He gave them coin enough to keep drinking until late into the morning.

"How drunk was the sot who gave you the information?" Machous knew the answer, but asked anyway. He remembered the man who slurred his words and punctuated every sentence with another quaff, drizzling frothy ale into his scruffy beard.

The young officer recounted his conversation at the Inn of the Purple Serpent. "The drink loosened his tongue, and he swore he saw a band of outlaws riding hard for the Mountains of Mordan. He told me they rode like demons were snapping at their hooves."

"And he was certain they were bandits?"

"'As dark and dangerous men as I've ever seen'—his exact words, Captain."

"For another tankard of ale." Machous scoffed.

"Yes, Captain."

"So are we chasing bandits or the blubbering imaginings of a drunk who bamboozled a kingsrider?"

The officer fought to keep his face from flushing red.

As he looked down on the men at the river, Machous hoped he had made the right decision. He trusted his instincts, but he was chasing a rumor and had ridden a long way. Most of his double march of kingsriders had been left behind to bivouac on Sniggle Creek near Village Mordan.

Machous reasoned the men he followed would stay in the mountains and cross the Turskín River somewhere above the falls. From there they could vanish into the vast and largely unexplored Plains of Loonish, where it would be nearly impossible to find them again.

To flank his quarry, Machous had left the winding trails of the mountains and led his force of fifty men along the road that ran below the foothills on the north.

Machous twisted in his saddle, trying to relieve the ache in his lower back. The men at the river were disagreeing about something, or so it seemed from the distance. Only one of them was mounted. The others stood in a ragged circle, arguing. One of them pointed to the sky and then to the east as though deciding whether to set up camp at the water or risk being caught by darkness. They did not appear to be bandits, but something about them teased at Machous as he tried to connect the pieces.

"Your orders, Captain?" The young officer gestured to kingsriders who waited in a shallow valley on the west side of the ridge.

Machous narrowed his eyes to pierce the gathering gloom. *No stone unturned.*

"Take them alive," he said.

CHAPTER 63

"I warned you it was too dangerous to wander about like a vagabond without allowing the yoke of kingsriders to protect you," Kublan scolded.

"Alone was the only way I could move about unnoticed."

Kublan gave a guttural cough of contempt. "It would appear you did *not* go unnoticed!"

"I was mistaken. Being assaulted on the King's Road was not because I was recognized as an emissary of the king. Common thieves, I'm sure of it."

"What good is a Raven to the King if he is dead?"

"Of little use, m'lord." The Raven tried to smile, but he was uncertain whether the comment was the jest of a friend or the mockery of a king.

"Of *no* use!" growled Kublan. "Nor do you know who it was who attacked you!"

"It was night and they fell upon me suddenly. I was unconscious until I was found by the kingsriders."

"You can be glad it wasn't that murdering bandit who calls himself the Blood of the Dragon who robbed you, or else the body they found tied to your horse would be without a head!"

"Of course. You are right as always, m'lord. It was you who insisted the kingsriders follow at a distance. When I failed to rendezvous, they came to where I had been and found me. I bow to your superior wisdom in all things."

"What if the robbers had killed you instead of stripping you bare and sending you back like a beaten dog?" Kublan thumped a bony finger on the Raven's chest with authority but whimpered like a child begging favors. "You are the only one left . . ." he stammered, then cleared his throat and twisted his face in sudden pain. "The only one I trust." He narrowed his eyes. "The rest of your esteemed order of mystics"—he spit the words with contempt—"are fools and some have disappeared."

"Two are dead, I've been told."

"More than two," the king snapped, then blanched.

Icy fingers danced across the nape of the Raven's neck. *Did Kublan know because he killed them? Had they returned without success and paid the price with their heads?* The calm he usually felt in speaking with the king eroded away like sand beneath bare feet in a swirling tide.

"You are the last, the only, the . . . You must find this plant of endless life, or by the gods, I swear—"

He had known this moment would come and he was ready. "It is not a plant, m'lord!" He interrupted the king from speaking the threat.

"What do you mean? The loremaster has told the story many times."

"Tishpiin and the plant of endless life are only a myth," the Raven said.

"No, that can't be so! You sound like all the others!" Kublan struggled to his feet, his voice rising and cracking with rage. "How dare you!" He slapped his hand on the table. The pewter rattled.

"Because I have found the truth of endless life, m'lord." The lie came easily.

The Raven had not spoken the truth since the kingsriders had found him a dozen leagues south of the outer gates the night before. He was dehydrated and sunburned. He was barely conscious when they cut the hemp that tied him to his saddle.

As soon as they arrived in Kingsgate, the steward rallied the servants to attend to him. After he was cared for, bathed, and dressed, he told a horrendous tale of bandits and beatings on the King's Road.

The awful events were reported to the king with such detail the story was never doubted. As the Raven gauged the reaction of those who served him, he was satisfied his delirium had been convincing.

With food and wine and a long night's sleep, the Raven recovered. He broke his fast with bread and fruit with the king in the small room adjoining Kublan's private chamber. Morning light streamed through the tall windows.

"I have found what you seek." The Raven's lies continued. Given the "disappearance" of the other mystics, it was the only course he believed practical. "At no small risk to my person," he boasted with a modest bow of feigned humility, "I have learned that the secret of immortality is not a mythical plant that grows at the bottom of the sea but rather stones of light touched by the finger of god."

The king's face filled with confusion, but his eyes sparkled with hope.

"If that is true, most honorable and trusted friend, then by those very gods you shall be rewarded beyond your capacity to receive." The king leaned forward across the table. "Do you have them? Have you brought them to me?"

"No, but . . ." There had been time enough to concoct a convincing story on the long and humiliating return from Stókenhold Fortress, but as the words of the elaborate fantasy reached his tongue, he was struck with an impulse to tell a lie much closer to the truth.

He inhaled deeply and began with a shrug of his shoulders and a burst of soft laughter. "The past few days are all so . . . Sitting here, I almost wonder if I may not have imagined what happened to me on the King's Road."

The king twisted his face into an impatient puzzle.

The pain in his gut worsened. *Am I a fool?* he wondered, but the thought was chased into the thicket by the story he had begun.

"I met a woman at the Tavern at Leviathan Deeps who knew of these things, and for a sack of coins, she told me where I could find the one who knew the secrets of the stones and where . . ." He was about to speak of the old prophet at Stókenhold Fortress but caught himself and bit his tongue. *Not too close to the truth,* he told himself. Meesha's words were silent thunder in his ears: *"It is true there is contention between my father and the king, but you make a grave mistake to think my grandfather does not cherish his only granddaughter and prize her virtue."*

"You know where they are?" Kublan demanded, bringing the Raven back.

"Yes," the Raven said, more comfortable in his lies. He dared not chance the king discovering what happened at the prison. What happened with his granddaughter. What the keepers might claim. What he might believe. No. Not now.

The Raven had hardly crossed beneath the outer barbican of Stókenhold Fortress before he had resolved to return with a double yoke of kingsriders sworn to secrecy and seize the old prophet. The smile on the ruined face of the witchchild mocked him behind his eyes.

"I found the keeper of this great secret," he said. "A holy man of an ancient order."

"Where is he?"

"He is in a cave—a cavern where he has lived for many years." Raven flushed as the tangle of lies spread in his head like the tendrils of a climbing vine. "He is a hermit, hiding to protect the secret of the stones of light."

"Where is this cave?"

"In the Mountain—" The Raven started to say the "Mountain of God," but switched mid-sentence to "the Mountains of the Moon." Too late, the Raven realized his mistake. He bit his lip.

"Does Ormmen know about this holy man? These stones of the gods?" Kublan asked with alarm.

The Mountains of the Moon were largely in Winterhaven—a land ruled by House Romagónian.

"No! No one knows of these things but me and now you, gracious king."

"What of the woman?"

"She is no more." *Lies to cover lies.* The Raven flushed as the thudding of his heart grew faster. He grimaced. "I regretted killing her, but the risk was too great—"

"No, no. You did right," Kublan said it with a dismissive wave of his hand. "It was necessary, and you are guilty of nothing. By your oath, I have given you the power over life. By my divine right as king, you are exonerated. It is good. No one will know, and by my word, you are absolved of any consequence."

"Thank you, m'lord."

"Where is he now? This 'holy man'? Why did you not bring him with you?"

"It was my intent he should return with me to Kingsgate, but when I left him to get a horse, the bandits fell upon me."

"The man with my great secret might have been killed?"

"It is unlikely. I am certain it is the will of the gods he remain safe."

"How can I be sure?"

"I engaged two hunters—trustworthy men—to stay at his cave and protect him." Each new lie came easier and more convincing than the last.

Kublan looked at the Raven with affection, then nodded slowly and rose from the table. He walked to the window, and the shaft of light enveloped him in an unearthly halo.

"What does he think of his king—this holy man and keeper of these stones of endless life?"

The Raven was surprised by the question and gave it careful thought. "He wishes to fall on his face before you and kiss your feet.

He has lived for that moment and believes, as I do, that you are destined by the gods to rule as immortal king."

"You must return to him at once, and this time I command you to ride with a double yoke of kingsriders."

"He is safe enough for the time being. With your blessing, m'lord, I think it best to wait until the time of your grand council at First Landing. The attention of the kingdom will be on your historic gathering. The ruler of House Romagónian will be in attendance and, in his absence, his patrols will slacken their vigilance. The holy man and I can travel unnoticed to where he has hidden the magic stones."

"In the Mountains of the Moon?"

Raven nodded, but his mind was elsewhere. A new and different plan was forming in his head. *Tolak and Valnor will be gone from Stókenhold Fortress for the council at First Landing. I will not ride to Stókenhold with a double yoke, but rather the few kingsriders loyal to me. I will not be thwarted by the witchchild again!*

It would be easy enough to explain that the holy man had been discovered and taken to the prison when word of it finally reached the king. By then it would be done. By then his granddaughter would have been killed when the rogues of House Romagónian fell upon her. Such a tragedy.

The joyous expectation on Kublan's face had soured.

"What troubles you, m'lord and friend?" the Raven asked.

"My nights are troubled by dreams of . . ." He spit rather than speak Maharí's name. "I fear the evil woman who betrayed me in my bed has told her Lord of Vengeance that I seek immortality. What if it was he who attacked you on the King's Road—not to steal your double-fingered sigil but to get the holy man and discover his great secret?"

"We have no reason to believe there is such an one as the Lord of Vengeance."

"You don't believe that he and Blood of the Dragon are the same?"

"Perhaps. All the more reason for me to wait to return to the cave of the holy man in the Mountains of the Moon."

"Look to the heavens, Stargazer. What do they portend of this monster who will not leave my dreams? Drakkor. Lord of Vengeance. Blood of the Dragon. Tell me he does not know of these secrets. Tell me he does not seek to rob me of my immortal destiny."

"The stars are aligned in your favor, your greatness. There is none worthy of immortality but you, cherished friend."

CHAPTER 64

Dawn broke in a cloudless sky. A thin mist wafted from the sodden grasses as first light swept across the Tallgrass Prairie. Drops of rain on flowers, leaves, and blades of grass turned the prairie into a glistening sea of diamonds.

By the time the royals and their guests were roused and assembled to break the fast of slumber, the cooks, gillies, and stewards had churned the rain-soaked camp into a morass of mud. Kadesh-Cor stepped from his tent, half his face wrapped in silk and gauze. His squire steadied him.

The captain of the kingsmen was the first to see the prince emerge. "Hail, hail, mighty lion," he shouted. His extolment was echoed by his men, and cheers swept through the camp on a rising wave of relief.

The prince let go of Nimra's arm and stepped away. It was a show of bravado to enforce the tradition of royal invulnerability, but when he moved, the pain of his ruined ribs made him wince. He gripped his side.

The prince, Chor, the Huszárs, and selected kingsriders were served breakfast in a tented shelter erected on high ground. The prince invited Nimra and Horsemaster Raahud to join them at the royal table.

Sargon's absence from the modest celebration of his father's providential recovery was awkward and apparent.

It was a simple meal by royal standards; a feast by any other. Bread and cheese and broth. Seasoned breast of wild turkey and other game birds killed by the gillies, and spiced mead served in ceramic tankards with hinged lids of brass.

The purr of conversation stopped as the steward filled the prince's tankard with fermented honey and water. A blue-winged warbler sang in the tree above. There was no other sound. Everyone waited on the prince to begin the meal.

When he looked up, he focused his one uncovered eye on Baaly.

The wedge of cheese in front of the boy was missing a corner, and, considering the bulge in his cheek, it was clear he had broken the protocol of the royal table. The other faces about the table punished the boy with scowling glares of disapproval.

The prince knew the Huszár boy's bad manners were simply ignorance and impetuousness. He had probably never sat at table with a member of the royal family before.

A wry smile played at the corners of the prince's mouth, and he nodded his forgiveness. Baaly's cheeks flushed red. He swallowed the cheese whole and slid lower on the bench.

Kadesh-Cor raised his mug and nodded to his squire.

Nimra stood, holding his own tankard of mead above his head. He pointed his face skyward. "Anu, Enlil, Enki. God of water, god of air, and god of earth. Look with favor upon his eminence Baron Magnus of Blackthorn and prince of the North and judge us well." He bowed to the prince and sat down.

"Planosis si Ea. Planosis si Ea. Planosis si Ea." The name of the collective gods was a reverent, murmuring chant around the table.

Kadesh-Cor took a long draught of sweet mead. On that signal, the company reached for the food in a single motion but froze when the rattle of iron chains shattered the tranquility of the morning.

Qhuin was dragged forward by Algord, son of Gorshon. His hands were shackled behind his back and covered in a crust of dried blood. The manacles on his ankles required him to shuffle. His boots were gone, and one of his stockings was missing. A chain was wrapped around his chest and dragged behind.

Sargon led the procession. He nodded and Algord pushed Qhuin forward.

He tried to take a step to catch himself, but the chain between his ankles was too short, and he tumbled forward. With his hands chained behind his back, he could not break the fall. He plummeted face-first into the mud at the edge of the enclosure.

"Get up," Algord growled, rolling him over with his boot.

Qhuin struggled to his knees. He was eye level with the top of the table. Those seated stared in shock at the slave with bloody hands and a face covered in mud.

The table was spread with platters of food. The pungent scent of roasted game and wild garlic tightened the fist of hunger in Qhuin's belly. He had not eaten since early afternoon the day of the hunt. A gillie fanned a kitchen rag to keep the insects away from the food, but there was no one to swish away the swamp fly that feasted on Qhuin's neck.

Qhuin saw the squire standing behind the prince. He gave Qhuin an affirming nod and the hint of a smile. The memory of an arrow piercing the rat's head was etched on the front of Qhuin's mind.

He looked to the end of the table. Kadesh-Cor was flanked by Chor and Sargon's empty chair. The prince looked confused. Chor leaned in and whispered to his father, who nodded slowly. He absently adjusted the bandage and looked coldly at Sargon.

Had the prince not known of his son's plan to execute me? The realization gave Qhuin a surge of hope.

Sargon stepped up to where Qhuin knelt. "Father," he began, "it pleases me greatly to see you so well. I did not expect that . . . I mean, we thought . . . while you were unconscious and thus unfit to rule . . ." He caught himself too late; his father was no fool. Sargon gathered his wits and lifted an arrogant chin. "While you suffered from your injuries, m'lord father, this bondsman was condemned to death for assault on a royal personage." Sargon looked down at Qhuin, then lifted his princeling chin even higher. "His intent was to kill a member of the royal household. His intent was to kill me!"

A ruckus of disparate reactions jolted though those gathered.

Hope collided with dread. Qhuin stared at the prince. Half an expression on half a face was impossible to read.

Sargon slid his fingers into Qhuin's hair, closed his fist, and cocked his head back. "The execution was to be at sunrise, Father. Chor stopped it when he informed me of your remarkable recovery. I was grateful to hear of it, of course, but I do hope that—"

"Hope what? Pray, tell me, boy, what did you hope?"

Sargon swallowed hard and stuttered. "That . . . that as my lord father you will punish this slave for attacking your son. That you . . . you will put his head on a spike."

"On a spike? By the gods, how is it possible you issued from the same loins as your brother? Is this not the reinsman who drove you to your first catch? Is this not the horseman who protected a wild tarpan from the whip of an abusive bungler? Is this not the bondsman who held the point of the sword at your throat, and then stepped away? I watched from the bluff. Are you really such a fool?"

Sargon let go of Qhuin's hair and staggered back as if struck. "But I thought—"

"Hold your tongue!" Kadesh-Cor inhaled to regain the dignity of his position, then turned to Algord, who stood with his hand on his sword. "Free him of the chains."

"No!" Sargon pulled his sword and hammered the pommel on the table. A loaf of bread bounced off a platter, and ripples of mead quivered in the quake. "He needs to be punished!"

"Is this not the horseman that kept the stallion from killing me?"

The princeling's lips quivered in search for words. None came. His shoulders curled onto his chest in humiliation.

"Do as the prince commands!" the captain of the kingsriders barked.

Algord glanced at Sargon, then dropped to one knee and removed the shackles from Qhuin's wrists and ankles. He stank of sweat, and the breath coming from his disfigured face was fouled by a rotted tooth. He locked eyes with Qhuin in a battle of wills.

Qhuin held the man's gaze, though he wasn't sure why. The rusted iron fell away. Qhuin gripped his bleeding wrist with his other hand to soothe the pain.

"His collar as well," Kadesh-Cor ordered.

A younger kingsrider hurried forward. The rusted iron of the collar scratched Qhuin's neck as it was pulled away, and he touched his bare skin with his fingers. The rush of freedom came again.

Qhuin eyed Sargon's sword as he climbed to his feet. He half expected the princeling to burst into a rage and hack him to death. Instead, the princeling backed away, glowering at Qhuin with a face that promised revenge. More than revenge—a long and painful death. Darkness swirled up to extinguish the glimmer of hope, but then Kadesh-Cor spoke.

"Set him a place at my table."

"What?" Sargon shouted.

"The man who saved my life will sit at my table," Kadesh-Cor said.

Sargon turned and, without returning his sword to its sheath, bounded down the short incline. He slipped on the mud and almost fell. Algord followed.

"Come and sit, reinsman," the prince said, gesturing to the bench at his left. "It seems my son has lost his appetite and left his seat for you."

In spite of his discomfort and the storm thundering in his head, Qhuin did not miss the curious look of satisfaction on Prince Kadesh-Cor's face.

Nimra stepped forward and spoke to the prince over his shoulder. "By your leave, m'lord, may I have him washed first, and his wounds tended?"

"Yes, of course."

— —

Qhuin followed the young squire to the tent. He wondered again why the prince would chose this boy, but the answer he gave himself made him smile: *Because the boy is an exceptional archer.* Qhuin's eyes fell on the bow slung over the squire's shoulder. The fletching of his arrows danced in the quiver in cadence with the hobbling gait.

Where had a common squire learned such extraordinary skill with the bow? Hitting the rat at that distance—even had it been standing still in daylight—was a good shot for a seasoned hunter. Putting an arrow through the brain of a head bobbing about in the shadows of moonlight took the skill of a champion. Qhuin wondered if Nimra might have competed in the king's tournament, but the greater mystery still puzzled him. Why had he appeared in the darkest hour of the night to save a slave condemned to death?

Nimra set a surprising pace for a boy with a crippled leg. Qhuin was slowed by tender feet, one of which was bare, while the other had only a filthy stocking stiff with crusted blood.

Qhuin wanted to express his gratitude to Nimra and ask him why he had come to his rescue, but even a squire in servitude was an "esteemed person" compared to a slave.

He knew he must only speak when spoken to.

A slave! The lowest of all creatures on earth save the ass with a burden on its back. He suffered the curse of silence inflicted on a slave. His mind was in iron shackles. He lived in a prison of ignorance without answers to questions he could never ask.

Qhuin prayed to the gods that Nimra would speak to him first. He was amused how often he called upon the gods since he had long since concluded there was no such thing.

They skidded down a muddy slope. The squire struggled to stay on his one good foot, but he looked back to make sure Qhuin was all right.

Qhuin opened his mouth as if he was about to speak, but changed his mind.

Nimra circled behind the royal tent. The banners emblazoned with the Blackthorn sigil furled in the gentle breeze. They passed a copse of aspen to where a tent was pitched at the edge of the encampment. It was smaller than Prince Kadesh-Cor's tent, though more elaborate in design and decoration. The fabric was crimson, and the sides were swept up from the ground and tied to a frame at the base of the roof, then draped in gentle swags to a trio of ridges.

There were no banner flags nor sigil, only yellow braids that glistened in the breeze and identified the abode of the courtesans.

Nimra reached the tent and swept the drapery aside. He gave Qhuin a curious look and gestured for him to enter.

Qhuin could remain silent no longer. As they came face-to-face, he bowed his head slightly and spoke. "Honorable squire, I owe you my life, and I have great need to speak of it. Forgive me for—"

"Forgive you?" He looked puzzled, then the epiphany came and a broad grin broke on his face, making him look even younger. "Oh no. No, no," he said. "It is you who must forgive me."

Qhuin was taken aback by the unexpected reaction to his show of deference and humility.

Nimra chuckled. "I never forget the rule 'When the blood is blue, speak when spoken to,' but I always forget that I must speak first when—"

"—talking to a slave, m'lord."

Nimra slapped Qhuin on the shoulder and laughed out loud. "We're all slaves in one way or another. I was waiting for you to speak, but you said nary a word. I worried you might be mute." He laughed again. "Or perhaps angry that I killed your furry pets."

Qhuin could not remember the last time he'd laughed with such honest abandon.

A young woman appeared at the edge of the tent. "This way, m'lords."

"Come," Nimra said. "We can talk while they make you presentable for the prince." He brushed a lump of dried mud from Qhuin's cheek, then put an arm around his shoulder and stepped into the crimson tent.

The brave man is not the man who does not feel fear but the man who conquers fear. It was odd place to remember one of Rusthammer's aphorisms, but Qhuin felt the truth of it. He had been bold enough to speak. It was like he had opened a window and a flock of meadowlarks had flown in. Singing.

Both courtesans awaited them. The older woman had red hair and a long face. Her cheeks were smudged with red powder and her eyes were outlined in black. Her cotton shift was adorned by ruffles and gathered to a thin brass collar around her neck that left her shoulders bare. The softness of her bosom swelled from the fabric where it swooped under her arms and fastened to the embroidered girdle around her waist.

The younger woman filled a porcelain basin with water that had been heated over a fire. He recognized her from the night before when they had been tending to the prince. Her hair was the color of aged honey, and it twisted in a thick tangle across her shoulders. Her eyes were large for her small round face, giving her the appearance of a doll. Her lips were full and sad and colored with pink stain.

Qhuin lowered his hands and wrists into the bowl as the girl finished pouring the water and moved away. He rarely washed in warm water, and it burned like hot ingots where it pressed against the wounds gnawed by the rats. After a few moments, the pain diminished, and he scrubbed away the crusted blood. He took a deep breath and closed his eyes.

He felt inclined to thank the gods for his good fortune, but he pushed the thought aside. He could not quell the hunger he felt for a power greater than himself, but it was not the gods who had saved him. It was a squire with a twisted foot and the skill of a champion.

"I am forever grateful to you, m'lord," he said again. "I don't know how I shall ever repay you, but I will find a way."

"Your honorable intent is repayment enough. I took great pleasure in destroying the beasts."

"How is it you happened into the woods and why?"

Nimra's eyes flitted to the girls and a finger rose to his lips.

Qhuin understood. A woman condemned to a life of pleasuring men could never be entrusted with knowledge of things that needed to remain secret.

"I am compelled to inquire after the fine results of your archery exhibition, m'lord." The twinkle in Qhuin's eye was reflected by a happy twitch at the corner of the squire's mouth.

"It began as a promise I made at a tender age." Nimra smiled. "I was seven years old before I understood who I was . . ." He barely stumbled over his words and continued quickly. "Before I accepted the truth that this lump at the end of my leg would never be gone." He thumped it on the floor, and Qhuin felt an urge to console him with a comforting hand.

"What I lacked in my legs, I would make up for in my arms. If I couldn't outrun the dragon, I had better be able to put an arrow in its heart."

The older of the two women reached into the water and took Qhuin's hands. Her touch startled him, and he pulled away.

"Does it hurt?" she asked.

"No, no, but I can wash myself."

"Of course, m'lord," she said, "but it pleases us to serve."

M'lord? Does she know what I am? A slave no better than she except that I . . . ? He fled the lurid thought.

The courtesan gently lifted Qhuin's hands from the basin and removed the leather yoke from his shoulders. She began to unbuckle the straps of his leather jerkin, and he stopped her.

"We need it off to clean the mud, m'lord," she said. She raised her eyebrows slightly and smiled. She held his gaze as she moved his hands away, then unbuckled the straps and removed his jerkin.

The younger woman returned with a bucket and knelt at his feet. The wool from his one stocking stuck to the crusted sores on his ankle. Both of his feet were splattered with dried mud. She lifted his feet and lowered them into the water. The water softened the scabs, and she rolled the woolen fabric away. She watched his face for the slightest wince of discomfort.

"Her name is Leandra." Nimra broke the uncomfortable silence.

Qhuin inhaled deeply and tried to relax, but his limbs trembled.

"You are kind to remember, m'lord," Leandra said. Leaning forward on her knees, the gossamer linen of her bodice hung open, exposing the soft whiteness beneath.

Qhuin knew he should look away but could not.

Leandra looked up and caught his eye but made no move to cover herself.

"Her sister's name is Effy," Nimra said as the other woman loosened the strings on the cotton undergarment and lifted it over Qhuin's head.

Effy reached for the belt about his waist. "And your breeches, m'lord?"

Qhuin pushed her hand away. "No!"

"Strip them away, lad, and they'll give you a thorough bath." Nimra laughed.

Qhuin's face flushed crimson, but his mind was riveted on the stone hidden in the inner pocket of his leathers. *Had they seen it?* Rusthammer's warning was in his head again. *'Tis a treasure you must never divulge and never be without.* Qhuin gripped the leather band about his waist and let his other hand fall across the hidden stone. "It is well enough as it is," he said.

Effy shrugged and returned his hands to the basin. She soaked a cotton cloth in the warm water and began to wash the mud from his face.

Being washed by another person was an experience Qhuin had never imagined. Sitting partially undressed with courtesans caressing his hands and feet and face was both discomforting and delightful in ways Qhuin had never imagined. The touch of the girls' soft hands stirred a flutter of fire moths in his belly.

Then, strange as it seemed, he saw the face of another girl, darkened by a blemish, but beautiful in the moonlight. The memory came with the feel of her lips on his cheek. *Meesha.*

CHAPTER 65

Drakkor climbed the crumbling stairway to the cluster of structures built beneath the overhanging cliff. The way was lit by burning pods of sheep's fat.

It was said that the ancient ruins of Hellosós, nestled in steep cliffs, were more than a thousand years old, the oldest evidence of humankind existing in the known world. When it was built, or by whom, or how such a feat was accomplished remained a perplexing mystery. The city and the high wall that surrounded it were built on the backs of monolithic stones the height of a man or more. No one knew where the great stones had come from or how they were moved.

The great earthquake of annum 1037 destroyed parts of the city, though the foundations remained. Some of the structures were reduced to piles of brick. Others remained and rose from the valley floor like a precarious stack of hollow blocks.

South of the city was a narrow and tortuous valley passageway. Once known as the Valley of Caves, it had been renamed Couloir of the Curse'ed more than a century ago when the city had become the place of exile for those infected with the plague of putrid flesh.

Since none dared risk the horrid contagion of oozing fluids and rotting flesh, the knowledge of the ancient ruins had passed away. The city was lost save for the legends and tall tales that traveled the King's Road.

Hellosós was now the dominion of Drakkor. His private chamber in the ancient ruins was an elaborate warren of cavities and connected rooms.

Many areas in the archaic labyrinth were open to the outside, covered only by a canopy of silk. The furniture was sparse, but the abundance of furs and fabrics on the floors and walls softened the starkness of the bricks and stone, creating a certain illusion of splendor.

Drakkor unbuckled his broad leather belt and set his sword and scabbard aside. He removed the sculpted chest piece of boiled leather. Sweat darkened his blouse, leaving a lingering shadow of the armor. He removed the black stone of fire from the pouch around his neck. Its cold heat both chilled and burned. The flicker of the candles was swallowed by the core of its dark translucence.

Anger gripped his chest, and his heart pounded faster as he stared at the mysterious stone. His failure to get the stones of fire from the temple of Oum'ilah screamed in his head.

He felt betrayed, but there was no one to blame. In all his preparation, the way had been opened to him. He had learned to use the magic of the stone he carried. He could feel its power growing within him, his understanding of its secrets becoming clearer. In besieging the Mountain of God, he'd been certain the whole of the prophecy would be fulfilled. He would gather the stones, learn to use their power, become king, and, by his brilliance, be crowned with endless life.

He had failed.

A hard knot tightened at core of his being. An old man, a witless giant, and a boy had defeated him. Worse, the boy had escaped with the stones. *His* stones! He wondered if his assassins had found them yet. Recovered his stones. Captured the boy. Killed the giant. Ravished the girl. It was only a matter of time.

Drakkor's men had seized the temple of Oum'ilah intending to make it a stronghold for the Blood of the Dragon. Drakkor would have allowed it had they not been thwarted by the curse. *What else could it be? Was the old man a sorcerer?* He shuddered as fragments of what had happened on the mountain returned to taunt him.

— —

The sanctum, the sanctuary, the chancery, and accessible chambers had been ransacked and searched for the legendary treasures of the temple. Every ornamentation of gold or silver or precious stones was pillaged from the shrines, the walls, and the hanging chandeliers.

As twilight crept toward night the day after the attack, Drakkor gathered the Blessed Sages and anyone else still alive.

"It is senseless for you to die," he said. "Your loyalty is misplaced. Your blessed Oracle has abandoned you. Your god of the mountain has gone missing and allowed your brothers to die."

The sages huddled like sheep caught in a winter storm.

"I regret the old man in whom you trusted has brought such misfortune upon you. My men will find a way to the summit. The Oracle will be thrown from the heights and the boy brought to me. We will stay until I get what I have come for."

The courage of the boy who dared to stand against him in the sanctum gave him pause. That brave but stupid boy. How he wished the postulant had followed him. Had spared him the setback and complications he now faced.

Blessed Sage Kurgaan stepped forward and wagged a crooked finger in Drakkor's face.

"The God of gods and Creator of All Things will not forbear His holy mountain to become the residence of evil." The Mankin's voice was strong and his warning spoken without fear. "The winged spirits of God will not allow your men to reach the hallowed fane." His head hardly reached the bandit's belly, but he sounded like a giant.

"In your murder of innocents and your desecration of this holy place, you have invoked the wrath of Oum'ilah."

Drakkor laughed. "And where exactly is this angry god of yours?"

"You and your minions of evil shall be cursed and grievous afflictions will drive you from this holy place."

Drakkor gripped the Mankin and lifted him by his neck until their faces were close. "You threaten me with a curse, old fool?"

"Evil begets evil," Kurgaan choked. "As I have spoken it, by the powers of the God of gods, it shall be done."

Drakkor was about to crush the Mankin's throat when a fierce wind howled across the court. Black clouds covered the mountain, and the sun disappeared. Drakkor's men had heard the sage's curse, and when the storm erupted, they feared the power of the Mankin's god.

"Leave them be, Lord Drakkor," the fearful among his men cried.

Drakkor released the Mankin but stood defiant in the pelting hail and mocked their fear.

The Mankin gathered the others and disappeared into the endless halls.

The darkness thickened and even fire would not burn. Drakkor's men claimed to see ghosts of the temple in the endless night—a giant shadow just before their fellow soldiers died.

Drakkor killed the first man who dared suggest they leave the mountain. No superstition was more powerful than the fear of death, and so the desecrators of the temple withstood the fearful night.

"There is no curse," Drakkor bellowed. "It is the darkness of the storm and shall pass." And so it did—the fierce winds ceased, the hail stopped, and the black clouds that covered the mountains blew away.

As dawn broke, the wounded kingsman from the south steps limped to Drakkor with the bad news.

"The boy who took the stones escaped with the giant, and took a girl with them."

Drakkor killed the messenger and then turned to Lliam Rejeff. Rejeff had been the first kingsrider to step forward and pledge his sword to Drakkor after Captain Borklore lost his head. The wound in his arm had healed, but his face remained scarred from the fire.

"Take twelve of your most trusted men. Go after the boy, the giant, and the girl. Kill the giant, but bring the boy—and the stones—to me.

Chase them to the end of the known world and beyond if you must, but do not fail me!"

Rejeff pounded a fist across his heart in the salute of loyalty. "And the girl?"

A scoff of a smile twitched at the corner of Drakkor's mouth. "As you will, loyal Rejeff."

Rejeff and his men had not been gone an hour before the scourge of death came.

Bees rose up from the cliffs in a billowing swarm of yellow and black. The stentorian hum of their wings was piercing. Their stings were deadly. The encampment of brigands and turncoat kingsriders erupted in chaos. The air was so thick with the winging, stinging insects the men could hardly gasp a breath without inhaling a bee into their mouths or lungs. The stingers went deep, the barbs held fast, and the toxic poison set fire to their skin. Their horses went wild.

Drakkor was left no choice. Whether from the curse of the Mankin, the displeasure of the god of the mountain, or extreme misfortune, he relented and retreated.

In the madness that followed, his men loaded their horses with plunder and rode from the mountain. Some of them dragged kidnapped victims across the rumps of their horses.

The last thing Drakkor had seen was the huddle of sages in a pocket of light, untouched by the swarm of bees. He could not scrub the image from his mind, which troubled him.

— —

Anger pulled him back from his vexation. He gripped the stone so tightly in his fist his knuckles turned white. He inhaled deeply to calm himself, then, glancing about the chamber to be certain he was alone, he returned the stone to the sack and put the sack in a small bronze vessel. He glanced about a second time, then moved the thick fur of an ice-bear pelt aside and pried up a slab of stone, perfectly cut and fitted into the floor.

The opening beneath was one end of a large chamber covered by a row of flat stones laid side by side. It was large enough to hide a man, but Drakkor had more important things to protect.

He lifted the shroud covering an iron box and placed the vessel with the stone inside. He remained crouched as his eyes wandered over his secret treasures.

Drakkor's raid on the temple of Oum'ilah had not yielded the stones of light as planned, but it had added treasures of inestimable value to his secret city. His men may revel in gold and precious stones. Not he.

Drakkor dragged his fingers across the large book next to the iron box. The leather cover was worn and tattered, but the touch of it soothed the fire still smoldering in the pit of his stomach. There was no other like it in the known world. It was a cubitum wide and a cubitum and a half long. The ancient pages of goatskin made it as thick as the span of a man's hand.

The archaic book had been brought to Drakkor during the raid of the temple. He had hardly cracked the thick, stiff leather of the binding before he felt its mystical power. He had heard of its existence but never imagined that he would find the grimoire of ancient mysteries. The lost book of secret spells and dark magic. The forbidden, covert oaths and secret combinations of the ancients from the time of the great tower.

The sight of the book unraveled the twist of anger in his stomach. He replaced the shroud, the slab of stone, and the ice-bear pelt. He left the room and passed beneath an arch that opened to a broad stone porch.

Looking down, his gaze swept over his new stronghold. He did not believe his misfortune on the Mountain of God was governed by the curse of an old dwarf. No mythical God of gods could thwart his destiny. *There is no power but my own, the magic of the stone of fire and bequest of she-dragon.*

Anger twisted again, but he pushed it away. What he had imagined to be a fracturing of destiny was in truth good fortune. The ancient ruin of Hellosós was a better location to establish a stronghold.

It was a hidden place protected by a valley of fear. With the number of men quartered here, repairing walls and building shelters, it was becoming a village. The thought pleased him.

The pounding of the blacksmith's hammer gave his secluded world the cadence of a beating heart as if the ancient ruin was a living thing. Sparks erupted with each clank of the hammer like a fleeing horde of lightning bugs. A kitchen had been built around an ancient kiln. Salvaged timbers had been fashioned into a long table where his men gathered to feast and drink and lie about their exploits when the sun was gone. Even the kingsriders, many of whom he did not yet fully trust, were allowed to join.

There was a growing number of women as well. Most were low-borns or prostitutes willing to trade themselves for what they imagined was a better life than the despair of their grim circumstance. Some of the women were captives, taken as slaves and servants to work in the kitchen and serve the needs of a permanent encampment.

Six temple virgins had been kidnapped during the raid. When Drakkor found out, he whipped the men who had brought them and ordered the girls returned to Village Candella.

Drakkor knew his men were puzzled by his contradictions. Some believed he'd taken them into his confidence, but there were none who really knew him. Who he was or where he came from. All that had happened in the years he'd wandered in the lands northward, beyond the River of Smoke. He spoke of his past only as "the years of cleansing." No one knew what that meant.

From where he stood on the open porch, the yellow flames of lanterns below was a tiny universe of glimmering stars. To the east, he could see the fires of the kingsriders who were quartered at the entrance of his secret city.

When they fled the mountain of the temple, many of the kingsriders conscripted from Borklore's command ran away. Some deserted from fear. Some had a change of heart and wanted to escape Drakkor's army. All but a few of them were gathered up and taken to Hellosós where they were separated from the core band of men he could trust and kept under guard.

Once a traitor, always a traitor. He knew the dictum, though he hoped some of the turncoats would prove themselves loyal. Some already had. Those who didn't would die in battle or would be killed by Drakkor's own sword.

As he thought of them, his mood turned foul. Some few of them had recently managed to escape the compound. He'd had to double the guards at the encampment.

The night fell silent except for the faint wailing of the wretched souls cursed with the plague.

The valley of the Curse'ed was another reason Drakkor had bivouacked the turncoat kingsriders at the entrance to the ruins of Hellosós. It was where the ancient wall closed off the canyon. Remnants of the magnificent gate that had once stood there could still be seen. The ornate arch had long since fallen and lay in massive chunks of broken stone carved with images and strange symbols.

On the other side of the wall, three leagues southeast, those stricken with the plague lived in caves and primitive dwellings. From time to time, a few desperate infected people tried to sneak into the ruins to steal a pig or dog or a flask of wine. Some came to the gate to beg. The kingsriders encampment was a human wall that isolated Drakkor and the men of the main garrison from the sickness.

There was a sudden noise and frantic movement in the village below. Men ran from the cobbled road leading to the gate and stumbled into the plaza. They were shouting. *A warning?* Drakkor strained to catch the words, but they were lost in a cacophony of commotion.

"Drakkor! Drakkor!" Other voices joined the choir screaming for the bandit king. He strode down the steps. By the time he reached the plaza, most of his men were there. They had run from their hovels, their horses, their chores, and their leisure. A few cowered behind broken walls and pillars, uncertain what had caused such tumult.

"The curse'ed have breached the gate," the runner gasped as

Drakkor approached. He pointed to the portal that spanned the entrance to the cobbled road.

"How many?" Drakkor demanded.

"I saw only two of them before I ran. They were hunched and dripping with pus and poison and—" Before the man could finish gasping out his words in short and frightened breaths, Drakkor crossed to the portal in long, swift strides.

Something moved in the shadow.

"Show yourself!" Drakkor demanded.

A terrified child, no more than six, stepped into the glow of the fire. He shuffled a few steps forward and stopped, his eyes downcast. A woman edged herself behind him. She was young, and her long black hair shimmered in the firelight. She might have been beautiful if her arms and legs had not been wrapped with gauze stained by pus and blood. She held a wrap of gauze across her face with a stump of a hand; her fingers had rotted away. Her dark eyes peered from sockets deepened by lumps of flesh like warts of a toad.

Drakkor was rarely without words, but he stared at the boy and his pitiful mother in silence.

"He is not infected, m'lord," the woman said. Her voice was muted by the soiled rag across her face. "Save him from me! I beg you. He was born before I was stricken, but they condemned him as a curse'ed one because I touched him—because I held him in my arms. Please, gracious lord! Take him from me and save him from the horror of my affliction." The woman fell on her knees and wept. "I beg you, save my child, mighty lord, and for your kindness the God of gods will bless you with the wishes of your heart."

The invocation was a familiar one among peasants and pilgrims, usually easy to disregard, but her weeping words caused a strange tingling to race up his spine.

An archer nocked an arrow and stepped beside Drakkor. "By your leave, m'lord. Shall I end their misery and put them to the fire?"

"No!"

The man choked back his fear. "But the air is poisoned by their breath. The men and I—"

"Stand down and cover your face with wet wool if you fear the poor woman." Drakkor opened his palm to the archer. "Your knife," he demanded.

The woman gasped. "No, no—have mercy, gracious lord."

Drakkor calmed her with a reassuring hand and squatted until his eyes were level with the boy. Moving the blade with caution, he cut away the child's ragged clothes. Drakkor twirled a finger, and the naked boy turned in a circle. His eyes were bright and clear, and, though his skin was dirty, there were no oozing pustules.

"Are you hungry?" When the boy nodded, Drakkor held out a hand and the nearest of his brigands handed him a piece of bread smeared with pig's fat, which he gave to the boy. The boy hardly moved until Drakkor nodded his head. The child took a hungry bite and then another.

Drakkor stood and looked at the women of the kitchen who were gathered in a cluster near the wall. He motioned for the youngest to come forward.

"What is your name?" Drakkor asked.

"Batyah, m'lord."

"This child is yours, Batyah." He ushered the boy toward her. "You are no longer required in the kitchen. Raise him as your own and treat him well."

The boy's mother watched with tears streaming down her face. "May the God of gods bless you forever," she wept.

"Fill two baskets with food," Drakkor said to the other kitchen women. "And follow this woman until she has passed the gates, then leave the baskets for her and also a flagon of wine."

They hurried to obey.

Drakkor looked after the mother as she walked away. She stopped at the portal for one last look at her son, then disappeared into the darkness. The mother's sacrifice for her child was an act of selflessness that Drakkor had never witnessed. An act of pure love he didn't understand. His thoughts were as tangled as a fistful of worms.

Compared to the mother's love for her child, the loyalty of his men was hollow. He was almost overwhelmed by a suffocating emptiness. He whirled and ascended the steps to the ruins of the ancient city.

CHAPTER 66

"I want the stallion!" Kadesh-Cor said. "Whether he is the Equus of legend or, as Horsemaster Raahud has supposed, an Equus given to me by the gods in my own time, it is the same."

The evening meal was finished. The prince stood at the end of the table and surveyed his invited guests.

"We have no fear of wild men nor monsters, m'lord." The captain's husky voice quavered. "We will ride into the fires of the infernal abyss if it pleases the king, but we are his, and without his command, we may not risk life and limb in search of a horse."

"Equus is more than a horse, good captain," Kadesh-Cor said.

"Yes, m'lord," the kingsrider replied with a slight tilt of his head. "Still."

Qhuin sat at the table. To his surprise, he had not been dismissed when the eating ended and talk of catching Equus consumed the conversation.

He sat in Sargon's place at the left hand of the prince. His wrists and ankles had been smeared with an elixir of oil, wine, and honey and then wrapped in silk. His clothes were damp from being washed, but his feet were dry. The courtesan had fitted him with stockings and somehow found and cleaned his boots. He remembered the girl's hands caressing his feet and quivered.

He was clean and fed and sitting in the company of nobles engaged in a conversation about horses. As a boy, he had often looked from his place in the stable to the lighted windows of the great house, wondering what it might be like to be included among men of high station. He had never imagined he would actually experience anything like this.

I am a slave. The thought shuddered through him.

He was uncomfortable sitting in Sargon's place. The princeling had not returned. Qhuin supposed he was licking the wounds of humiliation inflicted by his father. As long as he remained in the presence of Prince Kadesh-Cor, Qhuin knew he would be spared Sargon's wrath.

But he also knew the expedition would end. They would return to Blackthorn. The attention of the prince would be on other things besides the fate of a slave. Sargon's revenge had been temporarily thwarted, but his anger and humiliation still raged and retribution would surely come.

Qhuin felt a tingle and glanced over his shoulder to see Nimra watching him. Having the squire nearby gave him a strange sense of safety. He turned back as the prince spoke to the captain of the kings-riders.

"In the absence of my grandfather," the emphasis on his familial connection to the king was like the strike of a war hammer on an iron shield, "I am your sovereign lord and ruler, and thus my word to you, loyal captain, is the same as the king's command."

The kingsriders at the table stiffened. A few moved their hands to the pommel of their swords.

Even with only one good eye, the prince detected the ruffle of movement. The danger.

"Baron Magnus of Blackthorn," the captain said as he bowed low, "I acknowledge your eminence, but by the king's command, I am charged with your safekeeping and the return of the king's company to Kingsgate and of you and yours to Blackthorn."

A murmur of surprise and admiration scurried through the

company at the captain's bold defiance. Qhuin could see some of the gullies, cooks, and teamsters gathered about the elevated shelter, eavesdropping on the conversation that would determine their fate.

"You are a lion, m'lord, but you misjudge your strength," the captain said with delicate care. Two kingsriders rose from the bench. One stood with his thick arms folded across his breastplate. The other circled toward the Huszárs on the other side, who eyed him with misgiving.

Qhuin knew the kingsriders had not been invited by the prince, but were there by the king's command. "For the prince's protection," was the official explanation, but everyone knew about the king's paranoia. The kingsriders were there to protect the king from his fears of defection and disloyalty—a fear that included his own beloved grandson and heir.

Kadesh-Cor sat in silence and stared at his hands. A knot of muscle pulsed in his jaw. He rotated the tankard with the tips of his fingers and traced an emblem of a stag hammered in silver relief.

"Well enough, then. If it is I and the king's company that gives you cause to refuse, so be it. I will return with you. Others will remain and continue our expedition." The prince clapped a hand on his son's shoulder. "My oldest son and Horsemaster Raahud will lead a few men to the Oodanga Wilds to capture the stallion, and bring him to Blackthorn."

Horsemaster Raahud accepted his fate with a modest bow, but Chor's face turned ashen. He glanced around as all eyes turned to him, and he rubbed the back of his neck. He chewed his lower lip to stop the quiver.

The captain shook his head. "Horsemaster Raahud must go north with you and the company, m'lord. He is required to look after the stock and insure a safe return. Who else is qualified to bring the captured horses to the king's stable?"

Kadesh-Cor glanced at Qhuin.

Does he see me as a horseman? Qhuin felt a fleeting flush of pride.

"And my orders of safekeeping include the princelings. Your sons must return with us as well," the captain added.

Chor sighed in relief and turned toward his father. "And what of the king's council at First Landing?" he asked. "The season of Mis'il S'atti is soon upon us, and it is impossible to say how long it may take to find this horse, and I . . ." The tendons in Chor's neck tightened as he sucked in a rapid breath. "It is the express wish of your lord grandfather that I attend the council with you as firstborn heir. And with what has happened, with your wounds, I feel it necessary that I remain with you."

Kadesh-Cor hunched slightly and lowered his head. A bitter sigh slipped past a disappointed smile.

"Nothing would please me more than catching the horse for you," Chor said, the fingers of his hands trembling, "but there is no time and I fear that—"

Kadesh-Cor cut him off. "I know what you fear. To your shame! The king's gathering at First Landing is not until the Moon of Falling Leaves. There is time."

"Not for you and your sons," the captain said stubbornly.

Qhuin watched the games of the highborn with fascination.

Kadesh-Cor punished the captain with a cyclops eye until the kingsrider looked away.

The prince inhaled deeply and turned to the Huszárs. "It is left to you, then, noble friends. You came to hunt the wild horse. Who better than you—the fearless riders of the Huszárs! What better way to repay the endless favors I have showered upon you, my kinsmen, than for you to do for me what I cannot do for myself?"

The prince glared at the captain with a single defiant eye. Invited guests, whether kin of the royal household or not, were outside his responsibility. Dared the captain oppose the prince yet again?

The captain shrugged complacent approval.

The Huszárs shifted as if the wool against their skin was suddenly unbearable.

"Take whom you will and what you need," Kadesh-Cor said to

Huszár Elcun, the oldest among them. His beard was streaked with gray, and his weathered skin was the color of old leather. "The poets will write songs about the men who captured Equus." Lightning flashed in his eye at the thought of it. "The children of your children's children will know your names and sing your song, and you shall never be forgotten."

The Huszárs shuffled, ill at ease, trading expressions of trepidation and mumbling quietly among themselves. They arose from their stools and huddled a few paces away. They spoke too softly for Qhuin to hear, but he didn't need words to understand what they were saying. Their discomposure shouted their rejection of the prince's request. They were not going south. All but one.

"I'll go, m'lord!" It was Baaly. He broke from the huddle and limped forward. His right hand rose like he was a pupil waving for his tutor's attention. His bravado broke the cluster of Huszárs, who turned to face the prince.

"At least there is one of you who is not a cowering eunuch." The insult was more spit than spoken.

Huszár Elcun restrained the boy with a hand on his shoulder. "I'll not allow my nephew to chase after your mythical horse. None of us is willing to endure such risk, m'lord."

"Only cowards are afraid of fables and old wives' tales," Kadesh-Cor scoffed. "Have I not treated you as favored kin? What have I ever asked of you in return?"

Baaly resisted the grip on his shoulder, but his uncle held fast.

"You are always most gracious to those of us blessed to be your kith and kin, m'lord. We are not ungrateful, but the boy is injured, and as for the rest of us, well . . ."

"I am more than your kith and kin! I am your prince!" Kadesh-Cor thrust his chin at the older man. "My men from Blackthorn would face the fires of the underworld on my command and take the entire company with them at the point of their swords, if required." He glowered at the captain of the kingsriders and asked the question without words. *Will you support my desires by your arms?*

The captain adjusted his broad belt and looked away. "The Huszárs may stay or go as they wish, m'lord. We shall not draw our swords to compel them."

Kadesh-Cor pushed against the dressing on his face, then twisted and pushed again. Blood oozed from the edge of the silk and trickled to his chin in a jagged line of crimson. His fingers trembled. His exposed eye tightened to a bottomless black hole. The change in him was palpable. A shudder passed from the soles of his feet to the crown of his head like a wraith rising from the earth. Except for the crooked crack of red, his face was gray.

"I want the stallion," he growled beneath his breath. "By the gods, I swear that Equus will be mine!"

CHAPTER 67

"Take them alive!" Captain Machous's orders had scarce been spoken before his twenty-five kingsriders burst from the trees and rode hard for the small group of bandits by the river west of Loonish.

The bandits scrambled to mount their horses and plunged into the shallow river. They had hardly gotten wet before another score of kingsriders appeared from a copse of trees on the opposite bank and rode into the water toward them.

Machous had divided his force, sending half of his men to cross upstream and block an escape to the Plains of Loonish. By the time the bandits turned their mounts, they were trapped on all sides.

The bandits shouted to each other. Their horses thrashed the water into foam as their rumps slammed together in a defensive huddle. Three of the bandits were archers with arrows nocked and bows at full pull. The rest of them drew swords.

Captain Machous had seen the tactic before. *Are they kingsriders?* The thought bolted through him and collided with itself.

"Stand ready," Machous commanded, and his men held their position. A young officer handed him a torch. He walked his horse into the river and rode to where the bandits gripped their weapons in grim determination. As the light of the torch fell across the faces of the captives, he pulled up short. His fleeting suspicion was confirmed. "Akkad!" He remembered the archer with whom he had ridden as a fledgling kingsrider before Akkad was assigned to Captain Borklore's command.

"Captain Machous?" Akkad's face twisted in disbelief as he lowered his bow.

———

The horses were picketed and camp set. Machous's fifty filled their bellies with meat sliced from the wild boar turning over the fire. They shared a flask of wine and sipped sparingly.

Machous hunkered in a squat before Akkad. The turncoat kingsrider sat with his back against a rock. His hands were tied. He twisted his head in a vain effort to wipe his cheeks on the shoulder of his blouse. He gasped for breath in heaving sobs.

"You weep with fear when you should be bawling with shame." Machous looked at Akkad, but his words were meant for all of the traitors. "You swore an oath of allegiance to the king. You were honored by the sigil of a kingsrider. You know the punishment for treason." Machous tightened his jaw as the pain of personal loss of the slaughtered kingsriders transcended rank. "Borklore and I were friends as boys. Long before we aspired to the honor of kingsriders."

"Drakkor threatened to cut off our heads if . . ." Akkad gasped a sob to catch his breath. "He is a monster. I know it is hard for you to understand how we could possibly agree to join him, but—"

Machous cut him off. "You deceive yourself by looking for a reason. Whatever the cause you conjure to salve your disgrace, there is *nothing* to excuse it!"

"We were wrong. We are shamed, and we know that, but we risked our lives to escape and come back and make amends and—" His words gushed out in a flood of emotion.

"Come back? By disappearing into the Plains of Loonish?"

Akkad swallowed, the lie clear on his face.

Machous clenched his teeth to control his anger. He stood up. "Where is he now?"

"After we fled the Mountain of God, we camped in the ruins of Hellosós. He is building a stronghold there. We escaped six days ago, and so whether he is still there or not—"

"Hellosós is a legend," Machous snapped. "There is no such place."

"We did not believe it either until we went there. It lies beyond the valley of the curse'ed ones. None but the infected has been there in over a hundred years for fear of contagion. That is why he went there. He hardly needs an army to protect him when he hides behind a wall of fear and superstition."

"How do he and his men go in and out?"

"We wrapped our faces with wet wool. It is said the air is poisoned by the breath of the infected. When we must cross the valley, the infected ones are driven into the caves by some of their own—scullions that Drakkor rewards with cannabis. The rest of them do as they are told for a crust of bread and sip of wine."

"And none of his army are infected?"

"A few have been. They were killed and their bodies burned. One man woke with a pustule on his neck. He was dead and burned before the sun set."

"Drakkor shows no fear of the infection?"

Akkad shook his head. "He passes through the couloir without the wool and comes close to his scullions. He laughs at our fear. One rumor among the men is that the lord prince is protected by a magic stone he keeps in his possession, though—"

Machous cut him off. "Lord prince?"

Akkad shuddered at the slip of his tongue. "No, no! Forgive me, honorable captain." He sucked in his breath as if he could retrieve the misspoken words. "He is no lord nor prince. He is a demon. He demands obeisance. If we forget, we are put to the whip." He twisted, and Macheous saw the telltale wound of a lash on Akkad's back. "When we came down from the Mountain of God, some of us attempted to escape. We failed. After that, he treated us like prisoners, not soldiers. He kept us separate and under guard."

"Fools! What did you expect? That he would honor and trust a gang of traitors?"

Akkad shook his head in shame and slumped forward. "We are worse than fools," he mumbled. "We are lost men and forever doomed. Our days are ended. To stay was to live as low castes in the clutches of Drakkor's claws or die from the plague of putrid flesh. In running, we live in fear of Drakkor's assassins and being discovered by the king." He shrugged, defeated. "Even if we had returned to Kingsgate, we would've been put to the ax."

Machous tightened his jaw again and narrowed his eyes. The thought came slowly but with clarity. "Who is the ranking kingsrider among the betrayers yet alive and loyal to Drakkor?"

Akkad's face lifted, his expression uncertain but hopeful. "Meshum Tirbodh, commander of the archers."

"And the first to kill one of our own!" a voice called from the darkness.

Machous swung the torch toward the sound of it. The man was twisted on his side, his hands tied behind him. The guards let him squirm like a turtle on its back. "Shot him in the back as he rode for help!" the fallen man said. "The man he killed was my brother!"

"By the gods, Captain Machous," Akkad pleaded with a sudden gush of emotion. Half-light flickered on his face, one side glowing orange and the other fused with the shadows of night. "We know we are worthy of death, but we plead for your mercy. Grant us a chance to make amends for our disgrace. Let us renew our oath and, if we are to die, let it be in the service of our king."

"Can you take me to Tirbodh?"

Akkad nodded. "He is likely still camped at Hellosós."

"Is it possible to approach in darkness?"

"Yes, but . . ." He swallowed hard. "We must pass through the valley of the curse'ed. It is the only way."

"I understand. You said a wrap of wet wool around our faces?"

"Yes, but we passed only in daylight. By night, it is too dangerous. Some of the creatures have gone mad, their brains rotted away. Like animals, they prey upon anything that moves in the darkness. If one of the unclean touches you or you breathe the rotten air they exhale . . ." Akkad licked his dry lips, obviously terrified of returning to the colony of the living dead.

"You're a dead man either way," Machous said. "You say you wish for redemption and to die with honor. This is the way."

Akkad nodded. Machous offered him a drink from a goatskin flask. Akkad gulped water, then choked when it came too fast.

"We will never reach Hellosós with so many soldiers. Drakkor's scullions will send word the moment we enter the valley." He coughed again. "We will be caught," he shuddered, "and Drakkor will not kill us quickly."

Machous stepped to a rock and held the torch high. By the length of his shadow he might have been a giant. "I seek the bandit Drakkor by command of His Greatness, Orsis-Kublan, Omnipotent Sovereign and King. I stand before you as if I were he, and it is his voice you hear in your ears." The words hung in darkness before being swallowed by the surrounding darkness.

"You are traitors to the Peacock Throne and are hereby sentenced to death!" He raised his hand, and half a dozen kingsriders stepped from the gloom into the glow of the torch. Each gripped a two-handed broadsword. Hardly an executioner's ax, but if swung by a man of might, the same in the end. A tremor of fear rocked through the men until the ground fairly trembled.

"But I am a merciful man," Machous said after the condemned had time to contemplate the end of their lives. "You need not die this night—if you swear allegiance to the king anew and go with me to Hellosós and put an end to Drakkor."

The sound of oaths and promises filled the night like a croaking choir sung to a melody of weeping. The kingsriders returned their broadswords to their scabbards with a swish and clank. The bonds were cut, and the traitors were set free.

Machous turned to Akkad. "Take me to Commander Tirbodh."

———

Machous and his fifty returned to the main encampment near Village Mordan with Akkad and his eight men to plan for their attack.

A crust of bread and a sip of wine. That was all that Akkad said it took for Drakkor to buy the loyalty of the curse'ed. So that is what Machous would use to buy it for himself.

Under the cover of darkness on the night before Machous's planned incursion into Hellosós, five carts would be driven into the Couloir of the Curse'ed and left with the oxen in yoke.

The carts would be laden with fresh fruits, barley bread, and wheels of cheese. One would be filled with kegs of ale and flagons of good wine. He would also include fresh cottons and even linen. The curse'ed would be drawn to the carts and, while they were distracted, Akkad and another archer from Tirbodh's command would lead Machous and seven of his best men through the valley, past the ancient gates of Hellosós, and into the encampment of turncoat kingsriders.

It was a simple plan—dangerous—but one that could prove highly effective.

Before the procession of carts left Village Mordan, Machous added five sheep, seven goats, and a gaggle of geese. As his offering grew from a single cart with a few essentials to five carts spilling over with food and raiment and relief, Machous felt a curious emotion. Unfamiliar as it was, it satisfied him in a way he could not explain.

Before the sun rose over the eastern wall, the news had scurried into every hovel, shelter, and shanty. A caravan of food and wine and raiment had come in the night. Every one of the condemned still able to walk or crawl gathered at the laden carts like a swarm of ants to a bird fallen dead.

Some pressed their faces into the dirt, believing it was Mother

Earth that offered her gifts in sorrow for their pitiful misfortune. Pilgrims thanked the God of gods and Creator of All Things for His kindness. The wisest among them read the parchment that bore the sigil of the king and told the truth of it.

> *Drakkor is an outlaw and enemy of the Peacock Throne. These gifts are from your king, who cares for you. He honors you for your loyalty to him. Take no action to thwart the workings of the king.*

Akkad, Machous, and his men wrapped their faces and hands in wet cloth and passed through the dreaded valley on the far side.

When they reached the south end of the ruins of Hellosós, they hid themselves behind the ancient towers that stood beyond the gate. One lay in ruins. The other was half standing and offered good shelter and a place to hide until dark.

On the wall of the ruined tower, Akkad drew a diagram with a chalk stone, marking the positions of the night watch on either side. Akkad and the archer led the chosen men to the outposts one by one. It was too easy. All but one of the night watch sat by fires against the chill of the night. Glowing targets in a gallery of blackness.

The deaths of Drakkor's watchmen were silent and swift.

CHAPTER 68

Tirbodh's snoring stopped with a coughing snort, and his head jerked forward. He froze when the point of a dagger touched his throat.

"Make no sound," Machous whispered as Tirbodh awakened to his senses. His blade was pressed into the softness beneath the man's chin. "If I wished you dead, you would be."

"Captain Machous?"

"Commander Tirbodh. Or should I say *traitor*?"

Machous lifted his blade, forcing Tirbodh to rise slowly on its point. Tirbodh squinted at the dark shapes of the men standing at the opening of the shelter, which was built into an alcove of an ancient wall. Akkad and the second archer stood with arrows nocked and bows half drawn.

Tirbodh's shoulders sagged, and Machous could see the man understood what had happened and why they were here.

Machous punished the disgraced commander with his eyes. Tirbodh glared back with unblinking defiance in spite of the dagger at his throat.

"Will you kill me before I stand before my king to plead my case?"

"You are unworthy to lie on your face before the king."

"It is a right granted by the king himself."

Machous laughed. "If you faint from blood in battle or strike your commander or come to your duty drunk, perhaps you have right to plead before the king, but treason?"

"Have you never doubted the judgments of the sovereign?"

"Never!"

"Then you are either a fool—or the greatest champion of the king who ever lived." Tirbodh spoke smoothly, but his tone was uncertain.

Does he mock me at the point of my blade? Machous stiffened at the thought.

Tirbodh flinched as Machous increased the pressure on the dagger at his neck. "How is it possible that you and your tiny force have breached Drakkor's defenses, crossed the couloir without raising a warning, and passed the ancient gates unseen?

"Shall I discuss tactics with a commander in disgrace?"

"Has a single choice erased a lifetime of deeds? Since you refuse my right to stand before the king, perhaps you will honor my last request before you take my life."

Machous tightened his jaw. He was about to refuse when he realized patronizing the prisoner might serve his ultimate purpose. He pushed his pride aside. He kept the telling short but spared no detail as he talked the former commander of archers through the events of the previous days.

After Machous finished, the men sat in silence.

"What happens now?" Tirbodh asked.

"I will find Drakkor, kill him, and carry his head to the king as I have sworn."

"As one who has disgraced the emblems I once bore, I almost regret saying that you are destined to fail."

Machous could feel Tirbodh's eyes searching him. He could feel the pulse of his heart through the handle of his weapon. The bond between kingsriders was something understood but never voiced. Deeply rooted. Preternatural. *Unbreakable?* He held Tirbodh's eyes and slowly lowered the blade.

"You mock me with your flattery," he said. "I am hardly the greatest champion of the king who ever lived. There are few more renowned in the leagues of the kingsriders than you, Meshum Tirbodh, commander of archers." He spoke Tirbodh's title with honor and respect.

Tirbodh's tongue slipped across his dry lips in suspicion. He wiped the trickle of blood from his neck.

Machous motioned for Akkad and the archer to lower their weapons, then slipped the dagger into his belt. "I said I have never doubted the wisdom of His Greatness, Orsis-Kublan, Omnipotent Sovereign and King." He raised his chin, a wry smile tugging at his lower lip. "I lied. The truth is, I have, many times. My father was among the rebels who rode with Orsis-Kublan in the overthrow of the Romagónian kings, and to the day he died he also doubted. What I learned from my father has sustained me in the life I have chosen, the loyalties I have pledged."

Machous inhaled deeply. "He used to say that no man is perfectly right or completely wrong. We live our lives in shades of gray, in shadows. Sometimes in the dark and sometimes at the edge of light. The Book of Wisdom says we must always choose between good and evil. But sometimes we must also choose between good and good—or evil and evil. The apothegm is written: 'Seek the better of the one and the lesser of the other.'"

"Whatever you choose, you can never succeed," Tirbodh said, his voice contrite.

Machous offered his hand. Tirbodh took it and was lifted to his feet by the captain's strong arm. "Not without your help," he said. "You are destined to die—whether today by my hand, or at Kingsgate beneath the punisher's ax, or by this evil prince in whom you have misplaced your trust.

"You betrayed your king because you deemed him unworthy of your trust. There are times it is so. Even many times, perhaps, but neither is this sorcerer worthy of your trust. Has he not betrayed his promises already? I am told that, since coming from the Mountain of God, you are treated like men of low caste, not officers of a king."

Machous looked to Akkad, and Tirbodh followed his eyes.

"Whatever the failings of the king are, and however unworthy of your trust he may be, you must not tarnish yourself because of his shortcomings. You are a man of courage and honor and nobility. Drakkor is not worthy of a man as irreproachable as you. He is a rogue and a villain and the enemy of all good. He does not deserve a man of principle to stand at his side."

Tirbodh held the captain's eyes a long time, then slowly bowed his head. His hubris, anger, and resentment melted away in the heat of his rising remorse.

"We are not men who will be remembered in songs, my old friend," Machous said, "but we are good men who have lived with honor. On the day we die, our only hope should be that some we have known will say of us, 'They did the best they could.' In this moment, we are trapped by our destiny. By the whims of fate, we stand in a crucible of evil. It is only for us to choose the lesser."

At last Tirbodh raised his eyes. "What would you have me do?"

CHAPTER 69

"Equus will be mine! The gods decree it!"

Qhuin felt the weight of the prince's hand on his shoulder as he pushed to his feet and circled to the opposite end of the table.

Kadesh-Cor slapped his hands on the shoulders of the kingsrider captain. The man stiffened. Boiled leather creaked and iron clunked on iron. The captain's courage eroded in the acid drip of intimidation.

"Your men sit with their hands on their swords. It would seem the spirit of rebellion rises in proportion to the distance from king and castle. Or is it simply fear and foolhardiness?" He leaned close and croaked in a hoarse whisper, "The wrath of the king will surely come. Not here. Not today, but it will come."

He straightened as he continued his walk around the table. His fingers dragged across the tops of the men's shoulders. He stroked their helms and hoary heads with a condescending hand.

"Why do you choose to ignore the whisperings of the truth? Do you walk in willing blindness to push troubles from your minds? 'The man who does not see, always falls into the pit,'" he recited from the Book of Wisdom.

Qhuin winced at the dire warning of the prince.

"My lord grandfather, the king, is very old. The days of his greatness are shortened . . . to a very few." The tone was sympathetic, but his eyes confessed the pleasure of it. "His hours are spent in weariness and slumber. Carefully crafted royal lies protect his dignity, but death stalks the halls of Kingsgate."

The passing of a king was a calamitous event. As bad as things might be during the reign of a disfavored king, the one who takes his place could be even worse. The thought of a dead king and what might become of them in the inevitable wake that followed the transition of power settled over the company in a thick cloud of worry.

"Wipe the mud from your eyes. The king is dying, and when he journeys to the underworld, I will be king." Kadesh-Cor's bold words were more prophecy than prediction. A sorcerer more than a prince.

"Tolak may be firstborn, but he shall never sit upon the Peacock Throne. He is hated by the king. They have quarreled all their days. I honor the man who gave me life, but he is a fool. There is a wedge between us over the deference shown me by my grandfather and my claim to the castle at Blackthorn. Like the head of an ax left to rust in the crotch of an oak, our family is forever split, and the heaviest of the limbs is about to fall."

Qhuin could whisper to horses, but he could also discern the hearts and minds of men. He tried to envision the dominions of Kandelaar under the rule of Prince Kadesh-Cor. What would he choose to call himself? What honorific rose higher than "His Greatness, Omnipotent Soverign and King"? "His Divine Excellence"? The thought amused him.

Kadesh-Cor incarnated himself as omnipotent ruler and king for the men about the table. He thrust his chin and wagged a finger at his noble friends. There was blood from his face on his hand.

"It will be *my* feet you will wish to kiss when the day of your reckoning comes. It will be for *my* mercy that you will beg. It will be *my* wrath rained down for your rebellion, your mutiny, and your disloyalty in the Tallgrass Prairie."

He circled behind his kinsmen and scourged them with a lashing tongue. "The poets will write of you indeed. A song your children will sing to their children and their children to the tenth generation. A silly song of weaklings and milksops sung by jesters, clowns, and fools. A song of merriment and laughter. A song of cowardice to shame those whose blood you are. They will forget you, and you will disappear like the stench of hog rot blown by the wind."

The prince let the words hang in the air, and Qhuin could not take his eyes from the wounded face. He could feel the rising tension and prickling sense of looming dread.

A leather pouch hit the table with a dull, metallic thud and sagged to the shape of a fat, bruised pear. The jangling suggested coins. The weight promised gold.

Kadesh-Cor spoke first to the captain and his kingsriders. "If you refuse to obey the command of your future king"—and then to the Huszárs—"or repay the debt of kind tolerance, perhaps I can entice you with this." Kadesh-Cor gestured to the purse in the center of the table. "Everything has a price."

What sovereignty could not command, gold could buy. There was nothing in the prince's cloistered existence that cast doubt on the truth of that dictum. It did not come from the Book of Wisdom. It came from experience.

But he had misjudged the men around the table.

The captain stood, resentful and indignant. "By your leave, m'lord, we shall prepare for the return." Without waiting for dismissal, he left the table and pushed his way through the gathered company. The kingsriders followed, though not all of them with equal resolve. Three glanced back at the fat sack of coin that could change the destiny of their lives.

Prince Kadesh-Cor reacted to the kingsriders' exit by drawing his sword. It was a single-handed rapier with a long blade. A cut-and-thrust weapon. No one dared breathe. He laid the point of it against the leather pouch and slid it slowly from the center of the table to the nearest kinsman.

The man had been hunched forward with his arms crossed on the table, but now he sat up straight and swift at the offer. His face reflected fear, not fortune. His head moved side to side as he stood and backed away as if touching the pouch would bring instant death. He muttered an apology. "Not I, m'lord prince. I am a merchant. A man of goods. Not a hunter. Not a horseman."

Qhuin watched with fascination, surprised by the cowardice of these men whom he had admired.

The prince skidded the treasure to the next Huszár, closer until it pressed against the man's fat hand on the table. The Huszár picked it up. An audible gasp swept over the company like the sound of a rushing wind. He hefted the weight of the sack. "You are generous, m'lord prince, but . . ." He shook his head and plopped the pouch in front of the Huszár to his right.

Baaly's face brightened when the man had lifted the pouch, then faded as it thumped on the table again. The Huszár left his stool and moved away from the table. Others shrugged to their feet and followed as if the pouch of gold was a coiled viper.

Qhuin watched as the Huszárs shuffled away and milled about in discomfort. Only Baaly remained at the table. *The foolishness of youth. Naiveté or genuine courage?* Qhuin wondered.

"It is a day of disgust and disappointment." The prince broke the silence with surprising calm. "A day of regrets that will yet express themselves." He touched the bandage and worked his jaw against the pain he inflicted upon himself. The silk was outlined by dried blood.

"Lest it become a day of shame, you must never speak of what you have seen." He paused, inhaled deeply, and tilted his head, narrowing his exposed eye. "You must never whisper that Equus, the mythical immortal sire of all horseflesh created by the gods, is real. A magnificent stallion that you failed to capture. A horse whose blood we might have bred into our stocky horses of the north and spawned a generation of great warhorses like the world has never known. If I were you, I would not confess I had fainted from such a duty."

Kadesh-Cor thrust the point of his blade into the ground. "We can never tell our king that the stallion of the gods was in our hands and we let it slip away."

Qhuin felt his pulse quicken as a wave of unexpected feelings washed over him. "*. . . In our hands and we let it slip away."* The words were a luminous text against the darkness of his mind.

The prince steadied himself with one hand on the grip and the other on the pommel. "Whatever may come of your disobedience today, you have forfeited both honor and riches. And one thing more." His smile was a crooked line of satisfaction. "You condemn yourselves to the misery of wondering—What if? From this moment, you will never take a breath without the question. With your final thought, you will wonder what might have been."

The pounding of Qhuin's heart rose with the cadence of the prince's prophecy. Kadesh-Cor was addressing the noble and mighty who gathered beneath the canopy, but his words pierced the heart of a slave.

"What might have been?" Qhuin held his breath, and without conscious thought, his fingers tightened around the treasure in his secret bag. *Clutch freedom in my hand.* He could feel the cold heat of the stone through the leather. A sensation of power quivered up his arm and filled him with a sense of well-being. A calming sense of courage. The breeze had stopped. The only sound was the raspy *weeta-weeta-weet-tee-yo* from the tree above. The warbler had returned.

"I'll go!" Qhuin stood. "I will bring you the horse, m'lord prince."

Kadesh-Cor turned. His mouth moved in surprise. "You? You are nothing but a—"

A strong voice stopped him. "The finest horseman in your stable, m'lord." Horsemaster Raahud stepped forward. "If there is anyone present who can catch Equus, it is this man."

"You'll go?" the prince asked with rising curiosity and an edge of enthusiasm. "Alone?"

"I'll take Master Baaly, if allowed, m'lord."

Baaly pushed back from the table and picked up the heavy bag of gold.

Qhuin turned to the company. "And any other man here who is willing."

Baaly carried the bag to Qhuin and placed it on the table in front of him with the same display of bravado that almost got him killed. He looked to his uncle, thrust out his chin, and folded his arms across his swelling chest. It was settled.

In less time than it took for the warbler to whistle another refrain, the mood changed. A stir rippled through the company, but no one stepped forward.

"Half for each of you, then." The prince smiled. "You bring me the horse, and you will both be well rewarded."

"Master Baaly may do as he wishes, m'lord, but for my part, I do not wish for gold."

The prince beamed with pride. He shook his finger at his kinsmen. "You see? Here is true devotion. True fealty. The kind of loyalty I expected from you, who have a better cause to please me." Then, turning to Qhuin, he asked, "What is your name, bondsman?"

"Qhuin, m'lord. A'quilum Ereon Qhuin."

"The man my foolish son would have executed!" He shook his head. "If you succeed, if you bring me my horse, you shall have your share, lest any judge me unjust."

"I will not do it for your gold, m'lord," Qhuin repeated.

"What, then? You want my royal ring?" The prince barked a laugh and glanced about for a reaction, but his tone was condescending and the laughter sparse.

"I want my freedom," Qhuin said. The absence of the royal title was as loud as thunder across the Tallgrass Prairie. "I wish an oath sworn in the presence of all gathered that from the hour I put the horse into your hand, I am a free man to the end of my days."

"And if you fail?"

"Then I am dead in the Oodanga Wilds and will have a different kind of freedom. Nothing but death itself will stop me if you give me your oath."

The prince stared at Qhuin until the silence grew uncomfortable.

Qhuin feared he'd been too bold.

Kadesh-Cor lifted his sword from the ground and cleaned the tip on the cloth that covered the table. He held the weapon before his face and turned the blade slowly as if the answer he sought was hidden in his reflection in the polished steel. Sunlight struck the blade. Light danced across his wounded face. He turned suddenly and placed the point of the sword over Qhuin's heart.

"Get to your knees!" he commanded.

An audible gasp swept over the company.

Qhuin knelt slowly. He did not bow his head or lower his eyes. The muscles at the corners of his face quivered as he tightened his jaw.

"By what oath do you swear to accomplish this deed? What assurance of trust can I be given that you will not flee the instant you are beyond my sight?"

"I will swear any oath you wish, m'lord."

"By the gods?"

"I give no credence to the gods."

"Neither old or new?"

"No, m'lord."

"By what can you swear fidelity?"

"By my life and my honor."

A twittering of astonished murmurs rippled through the company.

"Your life belongs to me, and a slave is without honor."

"Then I swear by my life as the free man you will make of me and by the honor the great horse Equus shall bring to you."

Qhuin's blue eyes held the prince's unblinking gaze.

"I shall hold him to his oath, m'lord!" Baaly stepped forward and spoke in a husky bass with as much manliness as he could conjure.

"Our noble boy with the courage of a man. Well enough, then!" Kadesh-Cor lifted the sword from Qhuin's chest and held it aloft. "Hear your prince!"

A heavy silence fell over the gathering, a sense of reverence hovering in the warm morning air. Some people held their breath. Even the warbler was still.

"On this twenty-third day of Aru, Red Grass Appearing Moon, in season Res S'atti, of annum 1088, age of Kandelaar, I, Kadesh-Cor, Baron Magnus of Blackthorn and prince of the North, of the Royal House Kublan, do swear an oath and covenant with the slave and bondsman, A'quilum Ereon Qhuin, to wit—when he brings me the stallion, called by us, Equus, I will grant him his freedom from that very hour to the last breath of his mortal life."

A spontaneous cheer erupted from the congregation. In that moment, the dream of one man became the hope of all. The welling in the hearts of the men there that day would not be forgotten. Nor would any of them forget the courage of Qhuin, the man of unknown blood, the slave who would be free.

The cold heat of the stone coruscated from its secret place, sending a shimmer of warmth through Qhuin's entire being. It was the strongest surge of power he had ever felt, and he could no longer deny that some mystical force was working in his life. A power beyond himself, compelling him toward an unknown destiny.

The stone sent a second tremor of burning cold through his body. The pain of his wounds rushed before it like a wren before a raging wind.

"Stand," the prince said, and Qhuin rose to his feet.

A voice came from behind Kadesh-Cor. "If you'll have me, and if by the prince's good grace he should agree, I shall go with you."

The prince turned, but Qhuin knew the voice even before the squire hobbled into view.

"A slave is unlikely to need a squire to button his britches, Nimmer," Chor quipped, using the nickname with unusual familiarity.

"I'd be honored to have any help you could offer," Qhuin said and gave the squire a modest bow.

Qhuin did not miss the silent conversation between Kadesh-Cor, his oldest son, and the crippled squire.

"His ruined leg will slow you down." Kadesh-Cor frowned.

"We'll be on horseback, not walking," Qhuin said.

"Let him go." Chor leaned close to his father's ear so the rest of his murmuring was lost. It was the continuation of a private conversation. Prince and princeling. Father and favored son.

The prince turned slowly to look at Qhuin. "Are you certain he'll not be a hindrance?"

Qhuin remembered the sound the arrow made when it had sliced through the rat's head, a wet slurping thud like a fist pulled from a slurry of mud. He smiled. "He'll not be a hindrance at all, m'lord."

CHAPTER 70

"Who among you calls himself Blood of the Dragon?"

One by one, the men surrounding the fire looked up in surprise but not alarm. The stranger who spoke wore boiled leather and iron. The helm of a kingsriders' captain covered his head. He appeared to be alone.

A tall man with lanky arms and hair to his shoulders drew his sword and swaggered toward the interloper in open challenge. "If you gotta ask, I'd say you ain't here 'cause ya been invited." A guttural chuckling rumbled among the men at the fire. Some of them laughed out loud.

"Stop where you are or you die!" Machous said.

The man with lanky arms guffawed and pointed his sword at Machous's throat. The captain didn't flinch.

An arrow flew in from the darkness and slammed into the man's chest, puncturing leather, flesh, and bone, and stopping his heart. The bandit's eyes froze open in disbelief. He gripped the shaft, sagged to his knees, and toppled to the ground. The men at the fire froze and stared into the darkness.

"Is your fraudulent prince no more than a mouse who runs to his hole when the hawk is near?" Machous raised his voice to reach into the darkness at the edge of the plaza. He spit the mocking challenge like something bitter from his tongue and scanned the faces flickering in the yellow light.

A zealous brigand who'd been hunched by the fire leaped up with an unbuckled scabbard in one fist and the hilt of his sword in the other. He bounded toward the captain, but an arrow slammed into his stomach before his blade cleared the leather. He fell to his knees in a rush of anguish, gutshot but painfully alive. He howled in agony through lips already red with blood.

"Show yourself, Drakkor," Machous demanded. "Step forward and answer to your king. Or are you the coward the harlots mock in the brothels of the King's Road?" Captain Machous tightened his body, increasingly alert. His eyes darted in all directions, looking for any sign of aggression. *Which, if any of them, is the man I seek?* "Step forward lest I be obliged to kill every man here and return to my king with a wagonload of heads instead of one!"

The fire crackled, and a sputter of yellow sparks whirled into the blackness of the sky above the canyon.

A third man burst from the circle in an obvious dash for help. Arrows from the archers hidden by the night pounded into him before he could escape with his cry of warning.

"Pray, hold your archers, worthy captain. Lord Drakkor is not here." The bandit who spoke hovered over the man with an arrow in his belly.

Machous continued his inventory of the force, the risk, and the men present. Some looked familiar. *Kingsriders who had earned Drakkor's trust?* The thought was knocked aside by a voice from the darkness. It was deep and full, and Machous felt a tremor in his chest when the sound reached his ears.

"Is it only my head your king wants of me?" Drakkor stepped into the circle of firelight and strode forward until he was face-to-face with Captain Machous. His sword was in his hand, held ready at his side.

He wore no helm nor armor. "What of his once-loyal kingsriders? Does he not wish them back?"

"Your head on a spike will suit him well enough."

A mocking smile twitched at the corner of Drakkor's mouth. "Do you wonder why your kingsriders prefer this to the tyranny of your king?" He spread his arms. A murmur of amusement rippled through his men.

"I have come to avenge the death of Captain Borklore and—"

Drakkor cut him off. "Or perhaps you have come to surrender your paltry force or else die like a fool as he did." Drakkor squinted into the darkness. "There cannot be many of you, or else you could not have survived the curse'ed ones nor passed unnoticed through the gate. How many? Five? Ten, perhaps? Pretending to be an army?" He laughed again but there was no lightness in it. The brightness of the flame reflected in his eyes. "I am insulted you think me fool enough to fall for such chicanery."

"Surrender yourself to me and I will spare the lives of your men. I have no wish to slaughter them. Even the misery of the prison at Stókenhold will be more pleasant than death."

"Who is the brave but foolish captain the king has sent to die?" His tone was mocking, and his men sniggered.

"I am Ilióss Machous, High Commander of Kingsriders." Machous spoke with such confidence the brigands fell quiet.

A ripple of wary discomfort passed over Drakkor's face.

"Surrender your sword in the name of the king!" Machous demanded.

Drakkor's face turned sour. His eyes were black holes, darker than the night. "Are all of the king's commanders so clumsy in their bluff?" He scoffed with disdain. "Have you really come here with a half dozen archers expecting to take me captive and force my army to surrender?"

"Yes."

"Then you are more than a fool, Ilióss Machous," Drakkor snarled. "The finest of the king's archers are mine!" He turned to a man near the portal. "Fetch my commander of archers. I want him here immediately and my kingsriders with him!"

"I am already here, Drakkor." Meshum Tirbodh stepped from the darkness into the light.

Drakkor's face twisted in confusion. His mouth moved, but the words were slow in coming. "How did you . . . ? Where are your men?"

"All here, m'lord," Tirbodh said and raised his arm.

The silence was shattered by the shuffling of feet and the rattling of arms. Kingsriders stepped from the darkness on every side and into the firelight. Some wore armor. Others had dressed with haste and stood unclad. All held weapons at the ready—bows, swords, lances, and axes. Akkad and his men were among them.

"Stand steady," Machous commanded, and the kingsriders stopped. They stood shoulder to shoulder in a circle that surrounded Drakkor and his men at the fire. A heavy silence settled on the company.

Drakkor pivoted in a slow circle. His face pinched into a scowl of rage as he realized what had happened. The men surrounding them were not the kingsriders of Captain Machous. They were his men—or had been when the sun had set. Some of them were the traitors who had attempted to flee during the retreat from the Mountain of God.

He lifted his sword and swept it across the faces of the men in the circle. "You swore an oath by my blood. The taste of it is still on your tongue!" His gaze returned to Tirbodh. "Turn them back to me." His eyes glared with hate, and his words rasped up from the gravel of his throat. "Have you forgotten the tyranny of your king? What has this lying puppet of the king promised you? Clemency? Forgiveness? Mercy?" He scoffed.

Tirbodh tightened his jaw and the grip on his bow already at half pull. His eyes flitted to Machous, who affirmed the promises made with steady eyes and a nod.

"Has your king ever kept a promise?" Drakkor howled. "Have I ever broken mine? Do not be deceived. If you do not die here today, your head will adorn the road to Kingsgate."

Murmurs rippled around the circle along with a shuffling of feet and weapons. Machous's men glanced around warily. Men capable of treachery once might turn on them again.

"The king will keep the promises I have made," Machous shouted to the men, though his tone left an edge of doubt. "*I* will keep them! Stand ready. Today you redeem your honor."

Drakkor glowered in a final, desperate appeal to the turncoat kingsriders. "Kill these intruders quickly and be done with this, or else you are all dead men. If not by the hand of these whom you know to be merciless—" He waved a hand toward the brigands who moved toward their weapons. "Then by the bloody blade of the king's ax!"

"Surrender!" Machous shouted.

Drakkor's laugh was the growl of a wild beast. He turned as if swept up in a whirlwind and lunged at Machous with a slashing blow of his sword.

Instinct born of battle saved Machous. He parried the thrust of Drakkor's blade. Steel collided with steel in a clanking explosion of sparks that resounded against the crumbling walls.

Machous had hoped to force a surrender without the brutality of battle or spilling much blood, but he knew it was in vain. He dropped to one knee and lunged at Drakkor with fierce abandon.

Drakkor knocked the blade aside and danced away. But not fast enough. The point of Machous's sword opened a gash in the thickest part of his thigh. Blood stained Drakkor's leggings red.

Machous flourished his blade and pressed his advantage with a slashing blow to Drakkor's side below his leather chest piece. Drakkor faltered and lost his footing.

Machous swung his blade for the killing blow, but Drakkor blocked it, regained his feet, and staggered backward to the edge of the light. He pressed a hand to the wound in his side and looked at the blood on his fingers. A disdainful snarl twisted his lips.

Drakkor's brigands surged forward with a piercing call to battle as if they were a single creature with a hundred heads.

Tirbodh, Akkad, and the other archers stood their ground and let their arrows fly. The kingsriders tightened their circle in a rush of

blades and spikes and whirling bludgeons. The sound of steel striking steel and the thud of clubs breaking bones was swallowed in a cacophony of voices shouting in anger, bawling in pain, and shrieking in
death. The bravado was short-lived, however, and the bandits retreated
to a defensive huddle, back to back, to defend themselves.

And then—

"Enough!" A bloodied brigand threw his weapon to the ground
and thrust his arms into the air in surrender.

Drakkor's men were huddled like rabbits in a killing field. Most
followed the lead of the bloodied brigand and threw their weapons at
their feet. Those who refused to relent were quickly killed.

Machous's eyes flitted from Drakkor to the unexpected shift in the
battle raging behind him. His glance was hardly more than five heart-
beats, but when he turned back, Drakkor was gone. The bandit king
had disappeared into the darkness.

"Bind them hand and foot," Machous shouted to his men as he
pushed past them to where he had last seen Drakkor. He was about to
pass through the gate when he saw movement on the crumbling stone
steps that rose to the ruins.

Drakkor was halfway to the top, climbing awkwardly on his
wounded leg.

Machous gripped his sword with renewed determination and
ran for the stairway. A single thought hammered in cadence with the
pounding of his heart: *Bring me his head!*

CHAPTER 71

Dawn came early. Sunlight broke over the horizon and struck the highest banner of the royal tent, though it had yet to kiss the grass when Qhuin and his companions rode from the hunting encampment.

They were mounted on the finest and fastest of the Huszárs' horses. The animals had been taken from his faithless kinsmen the previous night by Kadesh-Cor and given to Qhuin and the two men who would ride with him to an unknown fate.

"The only brave among you," Kadesh-Cor had chided the Huszárs.

Baaly was given his Uncle Elcun's horse, to the older man's shame and humiliation. Elcun protested loudly but was chastised by the prince for his cowardice.

By the time Qhuin, Nimra, and Baaly had gathered provisions for their journey, Kadesh-Cor had managed to punish or worry each man who had refused his request to go after Equus.

Qhuin and his companions were fitted with breastplates of boiled leather, bucklers, swords, and short blades. Nimra carried two bows and extra arrows. Elcun insisted Baaly carry a long-pole weapon, though the lad had no training in its use.

The prince ordered that his Alaunts be sent with Qhuin to give the trio an advantage during the hunt.

The largest of the milk-whites was fitted with a double pack for provisions: tack and tackle for the horses and for catching the wild stallion, equipment for the camp, extra raiment, and food that wouldn't spoil. Fresh meat would be taken as needed. If the folktales were true, there was no end of wild beasts to slay for food on the far side of the swamp.

The prince ordered twelve wineskins filled for the expedition.

"For nourishment and courage," the cook said as he strapped the swollen leather flasks on the frame of the pack.

The hunters prepared to leave while most of the camp was still asleep. The kingsriders at guard, the gillies, and the camp cook arose before dawn to finish their tasks. Horsemaster Raahud was up as well to make certain the packs, tack, and saddles were properly placed and sufficient for the demands of the journey.

Raahud pulled Qhuin aside before the sun had fully risen. "You can do this, Qhuin," he said. "You are perhaps the only man on earth who can. You're the finest horseman I have ever known."

Raahud had never called him by his name before. Despite the chasm of inequality between them, Raahud gave Qhuin the kind of robust hug a man might give his brother in a reunion at the tavern.

"Find him, Qhuin. Bring him back," Raahud said, and then a laugh laden with angst rumbled up from his barrel chest as he added, "For all our sakes as well as yours."

Qhuin nodded.

Hearing Horsemaster Raahud speak his name. The level talk. The praise. So much had changed, but Raahud's embrace spoke to Qhuin in a way words never could. Qhuin understood that only when royal eyes were shut in slumber was it safe for a man like Raahud to embrace a slave.

But even at that hour not every royal eye was closed.

— -

Sargon peered through the crack of the flap of his tent. His eyes were a web of red from lack of sleep and blurred by a night of spiced ale. He blinked to bat away the pain in his head and see through the fog of drunkenness.

The princeling kicked the bare foot of the hulk of a man snoring on the animal skin behind him. Kingsrider Algord was up on one knee with his short sword raised before he was fully awake.

"You must go now," Sargon said, nudging the man again with his foot. "They are prepared to leave much sooner than I thought." The princeling peered through the opening again, taking care not to move the fabric. "Move quickly. The ride will sober you soon enough. I will tell the captain you are taken sick on spoiled meat and are convalescing in my tent."

"The captain will not trouble himself, m'lord. I am the least of the company, but what of your father?"

"My father cares less for your life than your captain does. He is vexed by the imposition of kingsriders on this expedition all together." Sargon helped the large man to his feet with a grunt and no little effort. "Be swift about it," he said and turned back to the open slit in the tent. He watched as Qhuin fastened the last of the packs to the cradle on the milk-white.

Sargon squinted at the slave, his eyes intense and full of hate. His rancorous mood came out in silent mutterings. *My father is a fool— worse than a fool! Can he not see the slave's intent to flee? And he would send that poor bastard Nimra to his death—not that it matters. The slave will surely murder the boys and be forever gone.*

Algord finished dressing. He wore a leather breastplate instead of his iron armor. Sargon fetched the man's baldric, scabbard, and broadsword.

Algord stared at the princeling for a long moment. "You are certain the prince shall never know of this?"

"He suffers from wounds in his head. He may not even live. It shall be as I promise."

"Swear it."

519

"You challenge my honor?"

"Swear it." Algord showed no fear or respect for the princeling.

"By the gods, I swear I shall bring you from Kingsgate to Black-thorn, where you shall be a captain and given all that I have promised—including the courtesan Leandra."

Algord flushed with humiliation, having confided his affections to the princeling while drunk on ale. "Swear by your blood."

"Do not test me, Algord, son of Gorshon."

The man pursed his lips and tugged on the lump of flesh that had once been an ear.

Sargon swallowed his anger and pulled a dagger from his belt. He drew blood from his palm and gripped the thick hand of the kings-rider. The wound was deep, and a dark drop of blood stained the toe of Sargon's boot.

"By my blood!" He squeezed hard, then wiped his bloody hand on the ragged flesh of Algord's scarred face. "But should you fail me, it shall be the blood of your throat that stains my boots."

— —

Qhuin swung into the saddle and led his companions toward the west side of the camp. He rode a short-legged stallion the color of old bones with a spattering of charcoal on his face and neck. The hunting dogs followed.

He harbored hope that the prince might rise to bid them farewell. Or was it a desire for Kadesh-Cor to reaffirm his promise of freedom? Qhuin found it startling to think he was on an errand for a highborn of royal blood, but until he delivered Equus to Kadesh-Cor, he remained a slave.

No, I am a man bound by honor who shall never be a slave again. I shall be free. He quivered as the joyous thought washed over him. *I shall be free, or I shall be dead.*

A black wheatear joined the warbler in a dawn chorus of birds that added a timbre of optimism to the bright morning.

He and his companions rode from the camp and followed the track through the copse of aspen where the courtesans' crimson tent was pitched. The yellow tassels shimmered in the morning light as if braided with threads of gold. Qhuin caught the movement of the flap as they approached the entrance, and his thoughts returned to the previous night.

———

A little after midnight, Nimra had escorted the courtesan Leandra to the royal tent where Qhuin had been given quarters.

"She is a gift from the prince," Nimra said.

Leandra had stepped forward and let her silk wrap fall away. Her white skin glowed in the flickering light of the single lamp.

"Knowing you may be killed in the wilds," Nimra explained, "our good prince sent his . . . He asked Leandra to attend you tonight."

Qhuin's heart had pounded at the sight of the woman standing naked before him, her beauty scorching a memory that would never fade.

The surge of heat that robbed his head of reason was doused by the cold-water voice of Rusthammer. *The code of chivalry is almost lost. Respect for women suffocates in the liberties assumed by the very men who once defended such ideals.*

Rusthammer had learned the code of chivalry from the warriors whose armor he had fashioned. He embraced the highest code of gallantry as his own and offered it to Qhuin: To protect the weak, to refrain from wanton offense, to speak the truth, to respect the honor of women.

Qhuin had been eight years old when Rusthammer sat him down for a man-to-man talk about why there were so many rabbits in the world. When the boy was older, the blacksmith talked to him about the different relationships between men and woman. He told Qhuin about his wife, about honor and abiding love.

Qhuin never forgot Rusthammer's face when he told him about her death. When she was killed, he swore a vow of chastity. "I will be with her again in the clouds of blessings," he had whispered, "and she will know of my fidelity or failings."

Rusthammer was ever present in Qhuin's life, but more than a notion of chivalry, Qhuin felt a sense of fidelity for the girl whose kiss could still be felt. A curious sense that she trusted him. *Meesha*.

Qhuin turned his eyes away from Leandra. "I mean no offense, m'lady—and I am grateful for your kindness—but you are free to go." He wanted to explain but words failed him.

Leandra flushed, confused by the rejection. She lifted the silk from the floor and clutched it to cover herself. She hurried from the tent but stopped at the open flap to look back.

"I shall be punished." Leandra's face was fearful and cold in the blue light of the moon.

"He shall not know of it," Qhuin said.

The smile on her stained red lips was bewildered but, in a strange way, hopeful. She floated to one knee in a swirl of silk and bowed her head in deep respect before slipping into the night.

"Please express my gratitude to the prince," Qhuin said to Nimra.

"I will, m'lord."

"No cause to mention I chose not to accept his offering."

"Of course," Nimra said, his gaze filled with curiosity and respect.

— ‑ —

The memory of the night faded in the bright light of morning. Qhuin's horse was eager to run. It snorted with impatience. He was about to give the animal its head when Leandra stepped from the tent into a misty beam of sunlight. The glow ignited her hair and kissed her shoulders with a rim of white. She was disheveled by slumber but modestly adorned and scrubbed clean of rouge. With the softness of her gray eyes no longer rimmed in black, she looked younger somehow. No longer the courtesan of the night.

Her smile was also no longer the beguiling temptation of a courtesan but the warm affection of a woman with genuine feelings, albeit confused and unexpected. She walked forward to the path as the riders approached.

Qhuin reined to a stop. Their eyes connected, and he felt his face redden. The rush of desire he'd felt for her last night came again, but the blush came more from what hadn't happened.

Qhuin never considered he might experience love the way Rust-hammer had explained it. Slaves were bred like cattle for strong blood-lines. In spite of his physical prowess, Qhuin was never coupled. Was it because of his dark skin? The superstitions against those of indigenous blood? He never knew, but he was grateful for the exclusion.

Now he nurtured the possible hope that honorable love and even marriage might yet be his as a free man. His dreams of freedom were always the strongest on the nights when he held the stone as he slept. He could feel it even now, pressed against his leg as if it was a part of him. The secret to his past. The promise of freedom in his hand. A tremor of hope shivered through him.

Leandra lifted her hand and offered him a handkerchief. "I am no lady, m'lord, but I pray you will carry my token on your quest."

Qhuin knew the tradition. When a warrior rode into battle facing the possibility he would be killed, his lady offered a personal token in exchange for his promise to return it to her when the fighting was done. The obligation to return a lady's cherished possession was supposed to bestow courage and extra strength in order to return alive and return the precious item.

"I am no warrior, m'lady, but you honor me." Qhuin lifted the token from her fingers. The handkerchief was woven of silk and fine linen and embroidered with tiny symbols in a swirl of graceful lines. He folded it and slipped it beneath his leather breastplate, over his heart.

"And will you bring it again to me, m'lord?"

"Destiny willing." He smiled.

"May the gods go with you." She backed away with a flutter of fingers, then raised a single finger and, touching her lips, floated a kiss his way.

Qhuin touched the flank of his horse with his iron spurs. The powerful animal bolted forward, and Qhuin rode with his companions from the camp toward his destiny. He did not look back.

CHAPTER 72

The breath of the dragon was fire and the dragon was Maharí and her flesh stretched over jutting bones and a black star splayed from the hole in her naked belly and she writhed to archaic rhythms and rose from crashing waves on the wings of a great bird and glistened in the sunlight and her laughter was a whirling wind and the Lord of Vengeance ascended in the storm and pushed the king from the bridge and he fell and was falling falling falling and the pounding of the waves was the pounding of his heart and it pounded pounded pounded—

Kublan jerked upright in his bed of furs, quivering as he escaped a dreaming death. He gasped for breath in cadence with the pounding that filled his sleeping chamber.

The king's bedroom was dark except for the glow of embers in the fireplace. The air was acrid with the smell of smoke. Kublan rubbed his eyes with the heels of his hands, pushing away the cobwebs of the night.

Who dares come to my private chambers in the middle of the night? Where are my watchmen?

He looked at the door. It was closed and locked from the inside by

524

an iron bar that had been set into a cradle. Talons gripped his bowels like a raptor crushing a rabbit. He had not set the bar in place.

The pounding came again, and his grand bed shook. When he turned and saw the cause of it, he fell back with a gasp of terror.

An enormous shape of a man loomed at the bottom of the bed. The figure hammered the pommel of his sword against the thick wood of the bedpost. In his other hand he held a heavy sack.

Kublan stopped breathing.

"You sleep soundly, Orsis," the dark figure said, his voice the sound of boots walking on crushed rock.

"Watchmen!" the king yelled.

"Your men are gone for the night. Sleeping by command of the king." A mocking laugh sounded in the darkness.

"Watchmen!" Kublan yelled again, but his voice was weak. A spike of terror in his throat prevented him from swallowing. He narrowed his eyes to penetrate the darkness. "Who are you? What trouble cannot wait until morning? By the gods, you shall wish that—"

The intruder interrupted with another throaty laugh. "Ah, but you will forgive me, m'lord, when you see the prize I have brought." He sheathed his sword and walked to the fireplace. He dropped the heavy sack. It struck the hearthstones with a thud.

"You'll want better light to see by, m'lord." He squatted and poked the embers with an iron rod and then put another log on the fire. Hot coals ignited dry wood.

The man rose from his stoop, laid the poker aside, and faced the king. The firelight painted his face with an orange glow. He wore the boiled leather and iron of a kingsrider, but no helm. His skin was dark, and his hair and beard were the color of river mud. His nose was large and broken.

"By the gods, Captain Machous!" Kublan's laugh held a note of scolding. It was not like the captain to ignore propriety, and the king was unnerved that the man had entered his sleeping chamber uncontested, but the rush of warm relief he felt pushed his annoyance aside.

His favored captain would be forgiven. "You frightened me nearly to death. I trust you have good news to report."

"Indeed." Machous's smile was strangely cold and arrogant.

The captain's omission of the royal title did not go unnoticed, but Kublan was eager for news. "So the rumors are true? You found the bandit's stronghold and cannot wait to boast of your triumph." He slapped his thigh and laughed.

Machous extended his chin with the slightest of nods. The arrogant smile remained.

"Tell me." Kublan crawled to the bottom of his bed on his knees in spite of the pain in his bones. "Did you find Drakkor?" His eyes flitted to the sack, and when he spoke again, his voice was pitched higher. "Did you kill that fiendish dog who calls himself Blood of the Dragon?"

Machous lifted the sack. Something heavy bulged at the bottom where the coarsely woven fabric was colored by a dark stain and stiffened by a blackened crust.

Kublan stared at the sack and then jerked upright at the sudden dawning. "You brought me his head!" He exhaled a wheezing gasp at the image flooding into consciousness—himself standing at the council of First Landing before all the rulers, nobles, and firstborn heirs, holding Drakkor's severed head in his hand.

The vision was so clear. So exhilarating. So destined. "For your great triumph, Machous," he said, "I will make you commander over *all* the armies of Kandelaar!"

Machous walked from the fireplace to the carved footboard. "You are generous, gracious lord." A fleeting smile confessed a private thought. "I shall take great pleasure in commanding the armies of Kandelaar."

Machous opened the sack and reached inside.

The king raised up on his aching knees for a better view.

Machous lifted a decapitated head by its tangled hair and held it up for the king to see. Backlit by the fire, the face was in shadow.

"You are the greatest of champions," Kublan exclaimed and clapped his hands together.

The captain stepped forward, and the flickering light fell across the dead man's face. A lumpy scar ran from the bridge of the broken nose to the jaw; the skin was raw where it passed through the beard. The eyes were dark, open and empty.

Kublan felt as if an iron fist with knuckles of barbed steel slammed into his chest. His ecstasy turned to horror.

It was the head of Captain Machous.

Impossible!

"Ahh!" Kublan scrambled backward in dread and slammed into the headboard. The bold relief of gargoyles carved into the thick wood dug into his spine. A beast with the wings of a dragon, the claws of a bear, and the head of a cat. The ancient gods of the tower chiseled in black wood.

He couldn't breathe. He gasped and clutched his chest as a bolt of pain shot through his body and down his arm. His heart pummeled out of control.

The man who looked like Machous threw the dead captain's head onto the furs where it tumbled forward until it bumped against the cowering king.

"He was a fierce warrior, your Captain Machous," the intruder said.

Kublan retched, but there was nothing but bitter bile. The unblinking eyes of his dead captain stared at him. He covered the ghastly object with the bedcover, his limbs shaking.

I have gone mad! The thought trembled through him, and he curled up like a child and abandoned himself to destruction.

In that moment, a burst of strange light filled the room. It was palpable, bright and blinding, but at the same time dark.

Kublan covered his eyes. When he dared look again, the shafts of light were converging on a glowing stone in the palm of the intruder's hand as if caught in the vortex of a whirling wind.

The man before him no longer wore the armor of a kingsrider. He no longer looked like Captain Machous. His hair was dark, his face was clean-shaven but scarred by an ugly pockmark, and his skin was the color of rusted iron. His mouth twitched in a baleful smile.

Some primitive instinct of survival filled Kublan, and he lunged for the silken sash hanging beside the bed. The strange man tried to stop him, but the king grasped the sash with both hands and clung with all his might as he tumbled from the bed.

A clamoring of bells rang out in distant chambers and echoed through the halls. The cacophony was followed by the sound of voices and hurried footfalls of boots and bare feet on stone floors.

———

The Raven to the King bounded down the spiral stairway three steps at a time. Built for defense, the column was narrow, steep, and twisted tightly downward. The Raven slid his shoulder against the wall to keep from falling.

He had been preparing for bed when the king's alarm sounded. He was still mostly dressed, and since his quarters were directly above the king's, he was the first to arrive. The heavy oak door strapped with iron was closed. He hesitated out of habit, then grasped the ornate ring and pulled. It hardly moved, and he knew the interior iron bar had been slid into place, locking it from within.

"Your greatness?" The Raven knocked three times then slapped the door with an open hand. "Your greatness?"

Three watchmen and a pair of night maids arrived and formed a loose semicircle behind the Raven. Two of the men carried poleaxes, while the other carried a short sword.

"Gracious king!" The Raven raised his voice and pounded on the door again, this time with a fist. "Are you all right?" He tried to peer through a tiny crack in the door without success. He put his ear to the wood and pounded again. "Can you hear me?"

The grating sound of iron sliding on iron was unmistakable. Someone was pulling the iron bar aside and opening the door from the inside.

"Stand ready," the Raven whispered, and the watchmen took a battle stance and prepared to use their weapons.

The dull clank of iron was followed by the rasping protest of hinges as the door opened partway. Light from the sconce on the opposite wall fell on Orsis-Kublan's face as he leaned into the narrow opening.

"Are you all right, m'lord?" Relief rushed through the Raven upon seeing the king.

"I am," the king answered. "I was caught in a dream. I am embarrassed to have troubled you with such disturbance."

One of the night maids stepped forward. "Shall we come in, m'lord, and attend you? Or perhaps fetch wine from the kitchen to help you sleep?"

"No, no," Kublan said in a surprisingly strong voice. "I must get back to bed. Go now. All of you."

"I will help you back into bed, m'lord," the Raven said, worried by the king's behavior, and started through the door.

"I can do it myself," the king said and started to close the door.

The Raven stopped it with his hand. "Let me sit with you a while, then. I am worried that—"

His words were cut off as the king—with surprising strength—yanked the door shut with a thud.

━ ━

Inside the king's sleeping chamber, Drakkor slid the iron bar back into place and lowered the latch. He returned his stone to its secret place and trembled through the wave of pain that always came.

He crossed to where he had blocked the garderobe door with a heavy chest. He pushed it aside and opened the door. Huddled on the floor, eyes closed in fear, His Greatness Orsis-Kublan looked anything but omnipotent. It was evident the once infamous king had never experienced such humiliation and shame. He was nothing but a pathetic old man afraid for his life.

Drakkor dragged him back into the chamber and propped him up against the footboard.

"Who are you?" the king demanded in a trembling voice. "By what evil power have you—"

Drakkor waited silently, until he saw the realization in the old man's eyes.

The king drew in a sharp breath. "You are Drakkor, the Blood of the Dragon!"

Drakkor squatted before the king. His eyes were cold, but a laugh rumbled in his throat like distant thunder. Scornful. Mocking. "What I was, I am no more. From this hour, I am the Prince of Dragonfell, and the bandit Drakkor, whom your mighty kingsriders could not kill, shall be my enemy as well as yours, and I shall be your chosen champion and savior."

Kublan's face wrinkled in confusion. "But why do you not kill me now? If it's a slow death you intend, you shall be denied," he wheezed. "I am old, and my body is weak and—"

"Because the death of a king brings chaos, and the age of chaos is not yet. Also because only a king has the power to forge an alliance with the Prince of Dragonfell and secure a confederacy with the dominions of Dragonfell."

"I would never—" The king twisted his head toward the door and yelled out, "Watchman! Help!"

Drakkor gripped his throat with his fist and cut off his words and his breath.

"There is none who can save you but me. You have seen the power of the dragon's blood. Even a king who claims the favor of the gods can die—a snake in his bed, or poison in his cup, or by the dagger of a kingsrider whose face you have mistaken." Drakkor relaxed his grip on Kublan's throat.

"No," the king choked, but there was no energy in it.

"Tomorrow, I will stand at your side and you"—he lifted the king's chin—"will do all that I require of 'His Greatness Orsis-Kublan, Omnipotent Sovereign and King.'"

"No! I would rather die!"

"Oh, *you* will not die. If you disappoint me, it is not you, but the one most precious to your heart who will suffer a drawn-out death."

Terror filled the old king's face and a great sob of despair escaped his throat. One word quivered from his lips. "Meesha."

— — —

Tonguelessone stared at the king with unblinking eyes as the hulk of darkness hovered over him. She'd been awake in the bedroom adjacent to the king's when she saw the ribbon flutter by the door. It was attached to the cord that hung by the king's bed and, when he pulled it, it alerted her that he needed her help. By his command, she was never more than a breath away. She had hurried to the door and peeked through the crack in the door. What she saw filled her with disbelieving dread.

The nursewoman had seen the magic of the king's cult of mystics and the mysterious workings of their dark arts. She had beheld strange rituals performed by the high pontiff. She had seen many frightening things. But nothing she had seen or imagined compared to what she witnessed in the flickering light of the king's private chamber.

Fear for her own life was swallowed by a greater fear for the king whose life was hers to keep. She knew she should run for help, but who would believe the demonic sorcery she had witnessed? How could she ever describe the image now etched into the darkness behind her eyes?

She held her breath and screamed a silent prayer to her secret God of gods.

EPILOGUE

The pelting rain slowed to a drizzle, but by then the bottoms of the cages were a foul pudding of mud. The creatures' coarse hair was soaked, and the stench saturated the damp air—rotted fish mingled with an odious trace of sulfur. The smell of the creatures was noxious to most men, but not to Jákkol. It was the fragrant miasma of vengeance.

Jákkol was the son of Ormmen of House Romagónian, and but for a single act of violence, his father would be king and he the crown prince destined to sit the Peacock Throne. But it was not to be. His grandfather had been dragged from the throne by the rebel, Orsis-Kublan, and murdered in the public square.

Jákkol fought to keep the dark dreams that haunted him by day at bay but "What might have been" was never more than a whisper away.

The inner rage came again. *Contain it. Control it. Save it. The day of vengeance is coming.*

He narrowed his thoughts as he always did to escape the foul mood that came when he allowed himself to dwell on the way fate had cheated him. He replaced it with his expectations of the future. It helped to clear his head .

What might have been may yet still be, and vengeance will be mine. The mantra echoed in his head like an incantation. It brought him back to the moment.

Jákkol breathed deeply of the acrid scent that hung in the air. His vision of vengeance was bright as the morning sun.

In the warren of cages below, a bald brute of a man scrunched his nose in a useless complaint. He was called Beastman, his real name having been long forgotten. In handling Jákkol's creatures for so many years, he'd become something of a feral beast himself.

The creature at the end of the pole he held wanted to rip him apart and devour his flesh. The hardwood shaft was fastened to a serrated iron collar around the creature's neck. The noose could be tightened, loosened, or released by a leather thong that ran to the end of the handle.

The beast growled at its captor, teeth bared. A thick squamous skin the color of dead moss stretched over the creature's skull. The forehead between the bulbous eyes was a flat horn of armor. Patches of bare hide showed were no hair grew or where it had been chafed away by the rusted iron bars of the cages.

Ugly lumps of vestigial flesh and bone protruded from the shoulders, a remnant of something horrid and unimaginable. The beast's shoulders quivered as if the grotesque knobs had once been wings and the creature was trying to fly.

Jákkol looked down at his creature and his Beastman matching their strength and fieriness against each other. In some strange way his affection for them was the same.

Beastman used the pole to force the creature through a chute of iron rails lashed to saplings. The channel sloped downward from a warren of iron cages hidden among the boulders at the end of a narrow gorge. Fractured walls rose from the floor of the ravine.

The beast's back stood as high as the Beastman's chest. It twisted its massive head and attempted to bite the bald man's throat despite the spiked collar around its neck. A wreath of crusted blood marked its neck beneath the iron collar. In the rain, old scabs melted and ran in rivulets of dirty red.

The creature's eyes rolled back in mindless rage. The sockets were a wrap of slime and wrinkled flesh below a flange of bone and heavy brow. The eyes were black and fractured yellow. A transparent membrane flicked across the black-and-yellow orbs—the eyes of a reptile. They dilated and diminished to the cadence of the creature's angry snarls.

Jákkol owned hundreds of such creatures. The alpha males were isolated in an alcove on the north side of the ravine, confined by an iron fence that spanned the narrow opening between the walls. The he-dogs were separated from the she-wolvves, which were caged with their pups. Many cages held frolicking young whelps, weened from their mamas and fighting over the daily ration of venison or fowl thrown into the cages.

Mating pairs and birthing bitches were loosed in the natural enclosure that opened to the meadow at the far end of the gorge. There were natural dens there, among the caves and fallen trees.

"He-dogs," "she-wolvves," "pups," and "whelps" were convenient words to distinguish age and gender, but they were not a wholly accurate description of what the creatures actually were.

How these monsters had remained undiscovered for so long was a mystery. That Jákkol found them in a place that most believed only existed in legend was cause enough to recognize the gods. He didn't. He had no use for the gods, old or new.

The only cause that mattered to Jákkol was his crusade of vengeance.

His Greatness, Orsis-Kublan, Omnipotent Sovereign and King, will meet my creatures soon enough.

The rage of the primitive creature swirled up in a piercing howl.

How soon will my father and the old warrior arrive? And what of Maharí? Why has she gone silent?

The howl came again. Jákkol smiled as the sound rippled through him in a wave of warm affection. His savage predators would soon do his bidding with mindless obedience. His ferocious horde of dragon-wolvves was nearly ready. His long-awaited war of vengeance against the Peacock Throne was about to begin.

ACKNOWLEDGMENTS

Thanks to Chris Schoebinger, who put the core idea into my head and whose persistent encouragement helped me find my way to the Kingdom of Kandelaar where I met some remarkable people.

Thanks to the team at Shadow Mountain whose support makes it possible: Heidi, Lisa, Richard, Malina, Derk, Karen, John, Ilise, Sarah, Madeline, and Isaac. Thanks to Jay Ward for the cover art.

And as always thanks to the smartest woman I know, Sheri Dew, who persuaded me to turn my screenplays into books and make some movies of the mind.

And finally to Jack Stone. Thanks again for your patience. I will get to your incredible adventures as soon as I can. What happened to you in the Amazon is beyond belief!